Praise for *A Cold Season*

'An itchy tension-cranker of parental paranoia'   *SFX*

'A strong debut novel . . . unfussy and clear . . . images from the book soon turned up in my nightmares' *Black Static*

'This is a very spooky story. You'll love it if you're into tales of the occult, or a fan of film classic *The Wicker Man* . . . disturbing, in a devilish *Midsomer Murders* kind of way'
Judy Finnigan, *The Daily Express*

'A scary read that will chill you to the bone . . . Beware if fact and fiction suddenly start to blur' *crimesquad.com*

'A terrifically chilling tale. A sterling debut which bodes unspeakably well for its author and beyond'
scotspec.blogspot.com

'An assured and finely-crafted piece of work, probably the best horror debut since Joe Hill's 2007 novel, *Heart-Shaped Box* . . . you need to read *A Cold Season*. Just make sure you know where the light switches are' *readerdad.co.uk*

'Alison Littlewood's *A Cold Season* has taken the horror world by storm' *thisishorror.co.uk*

'*A Cold Season* is an intelligent, sensitive book. Its chills are delivered with precision . . . Littlewood excels at driving home a feeling of discomfort' *spooky-reads.com*

Alison Littlewood's first novel, inspired by her winter commute to snowy Saddleworth, was *A Cold Season*. Her short stories have been selected for the anthologies *The Best Horror of the Year*, *The Mammoth Book of Best British Crime*, *Best British Fantasy* and *The Mammoth Book of Best New Horror*, as well as featuring in genre magazines *Black Static*, *Crimewave* and *Dark Horizons*. Other publication credits include the anthologies *Magic: an Anthology of the Esoteric and Arcane*, *Resurrection Engines* and *The Mammoth Book of Ghost Stories by Women*. She lives in Wakefield, West Yorkshire, with her partner Fergus.

You can visit her at www.alisonlittlewood.co.uk.

PATH OF NEEDLES

ALISON LITTLEWOOD

Jo Fletcher
BOOKS

First published in Great Britain in 2013 by

Jo Fletcher Books
an imprint of Quercus
55 Baker Street
7th Floor, South Block
London
W1U 8EW

A CIP catalogue record for this book is available
from the British Library

ISBN 978 1 78087 146 2 (PB)
ISBN 978 1 78087 147 9 (EBOOK)

10 9 8 7 6 5 4 3 2 1

Typeset by Ellipsis Digital Limited, Glasgow

Printed and bound in Great Britain by
Clays Ltd, St Ives plc

For those we lost: Marjorie and Miriam, Nev and Mark

PROLOGUE

When Alice Hyland woke, she knew that a new year had begun. No matter that it was April instead of January; to her mind a new year meant new life, and she knew that daffodils would be pushing green shoots up through the cold dark earth and the sun would be shining over the top of Newmillerdam Wood. She knew this because her bedroom was full of birdsong, so clear and insistent she couldn't bring herself to resent the fact that it had awakened her. She stretched as she crossed the room, her footsteps silent on the soft grey carpet, and pulled back the curtains, revealing bright morning light.

Alice closed her eyes and pictured the bird, singing so hard its heart might burst. She smiled at herself and opened her eyes again, and as she did, her smile widened: she had expected something nondescript, a grey-brown little thing, feathers fluffed against the early-morning cold. Instead, the bird sitting on a branch of the just-budding apple tree in the centre of Alice's garden was so bright as to be almost iridescent, its head pale turquoise, its body darkening to the colour of the sky in summertime Greece.

It was impossible.

Its beak was open and the notes came tumbling through the air towards Alice, a song of joy and life and irrepressible *there*ness.

She blinked. It didn't look like a budgerigar escaped from some cage, or a blue jay or anything else she'd ever heard of. She'd seen a kingfisher once, remembered the brilliant blue flash as it half flew, half fell towards the water – Alice had thought it *was* falling, but the bird had brushed the surface of the river and fluttered upwards onto a branch, revealing its rust-orange breast. This bird had no such colouring; it was much smaller than a jay, even smaller than a kingfisher, and it was blue from head to foot: stridently, undeniably blue.

The Blue Bird. It was like something brought to life from a fairy tale singing out its heart in her garden, like a good omen. She'd not covered 'L'Oiseau Bleu' in her lectures for some time, had been concentrating on the basics: 'Snow White', 'Cinderella', 'Little Red', stories her students were familiar with. Maybe it should be back on the syllabus. As Alice pushed open the window she saw the bird was truly beautiful. Cool air came in and Alice thought she smelled springtime in it.

'L'Oiseau Bleu' was a fairy tale from the turn of the seventeenth century, and the bird was Prince Charming in disguise. 'Sing on, sweet prince,' she whispered under her breath, and wondered what her students would think if they could see her now, just roused from sleep, leaning out of a window and talking to a bird, her pale hair tangled about her face. She should go inside ... and yet the blue bird was looking at her, its tiny water-bright eyes fixed and staring. She almost didn't like it. Birds didn't stare like that, did they? A bird of prey perhaps, spying its next meal, not this small, timid thing.

Chrr-chrr-chrr. The shrill rhythm repeated over and over, evolving as Alice listened; now sounding almost like words, then whistles that rose to an unpleasant squeak, and then a series of pulses like an insect might make: *ch-ch-chrr-chrr*.

Alice broke her gaze and caught hold of the window catch. She should take a shower, get dressed, start all the normal, everyday things. Maybe she'd rummage through her source texts, find the tale about the blue bird who transforms into a man. And she looked up to see the bird coming at her in a flurry of feathers and beak and claws—

She gasped, started back and slammed the window closed in time to see the bird pull up short on the other side. For a moment she saw each individual wing-feather spread wide, the finer, darker feathers delineated on its breast, and she braced herself for the dull sound of fragile bones breaking against glass.

It did not come; there was only silence, the room strangely empty without that high, relentless birdsong.

Alice straightened, brushing strands of hair from her

face, peering through the window. She couldn't see the bird anywhere. As she bent closer the top of her head met the glass and the sound, though small, made her jump. There was nothing in the tree, nothing on the ground, and now the bird had gone it felt like it could not have been, that she had never seen it at all. Then she saw it had left something for her, a little piece of blue, lying on the windowsill.

She opened the window again and looked about in case the bird should return, but this time there was no movement, only the soft sough of the wind playing through the branches in the woodland beyond. The breeze didn't penetrate her garden; the leaves of the apple tree did not stir. Alice reached out and picked up the feather. It was small but fully and beautifully formed, and the blue was a little paler, from somewhere high on the bird's body. Holding it carefully by the quill, she examined it. It felt like a gift, a benediction, a glimpse of something at once impossible and undeniably real, and as blue as the sky in springtime.

CHAPTER ONE

Angie Farrell knew the photograph was hidden beneath her handbag, the black clutch with the silver studs which was still sitting where she had abandoned it the night before, on the table. She set down her bowl of cereal next to it, slopping a little skimmed milk over the side, and started spooning cornflakes into her mouth. The crispness was too loud, hard against her teeth, jarring in her skull. She'd had a drink when she got in, and then another – she hadn't meant to, but she'd been torn between going straight to bed or waiting up for Chrissie, and instead she'd found herself standing alone in the lounge, staring at her reflection in the mirror. The house had been silent, and cold: the heating had long since clicked off and winter hadn't quite given up its grip.

Angie hadn't switched on the lamp, but the sidelong glare of the fluorescent light in the kitchen had illuminated the lines settling deeper across her forehead and around her lips. She hadn't moved, and she hadn't looked at the photograph again. She had seen it already; she didn't need to look at it twice. She had checked the clock, though, and seen that the dance was over, and that was when she had decided to open a bottle of wine, no matter that it was just her. Maurice left years ago, bought a cheap bar on one of the more unfashionable stretches of Spanish coastline with his bit of fluff. He'd not even lingered long enough to ask for a divorce; it was Angie who'd had to do that, Angie who'd had to organise everything, as if Maurice was suddenly the younger one, his new woman's youth rubbing off on him. It was Angie who'd had to tell Chrissie she was now a child of a broken home, and she'd tried not to relish those words, even though she was fizzing and spitting with spite. It was Angie who had to drink alone.

She stirred, leaned across the table and dragged the bag towards her, bringing the photograph with it. She pulled it from underneath the bag and turned it over and for a moment she was dazzled by her daughter's smile.

No, not dazzled: she winced.

Chrissie was framed by a chain of giant daffodils and daisies, their stalks spun of green twine, the white petals narrow strips of paper, the yellow ones fragile tissue, almost transparent where spotlights shone through them. The lights cast a warm glow across her daughter's skin and picked out bright points on the crown she wore – just a cheap plastic thing covered in glue-spotted sequins, but in that moment her daughter had made it look like something magnificent. It was in her eyes too, the knowledge of her own blithe beauty. The photograph had been taken at the spring dance. Chrissie was surrounded by her class-mates, though she wasn't looking at any of them; it was they who looked at her; that was their job. She was Christina, crowned before them all, queen of the dance, queen of the springtime in her coral dress and her cheap crown. Everyone else smiled up at Chrissie, her adoring courtiers.

Angie was in the picture too. Angie hadn't been smiling.

She dropped her head as her eyes filled with tears. She ran a finger over the picture but found no smooth skin or satin dress, only a cold surface she couldn't penetrate. She was full of the things she wanted to say, but didn't know what they were; she only knew she was so proud of Chrissie, her beautiful little girl – and at the same time she wanted to tear the picture in two with her teeth.

It had started with Mr Cosgrove. There weren't many teachers at the dance; the parent-helpers covered it, mums like Angie, those who weren't forbidden to be there by their kids for fear of embarrassment. But Mr Cosgrove had been there, and he looked like one of the cool teachers, the kind who tell their pupils to call them by their first name. Angie didn't know his first name but she had crossed the dance floor and sidled up to him as he ladled fruit punch into a paper cup. He grinned and passed it to her. The DJ was playing some throbbing beat.

'Good tune,' he said. He pronounced it 'choon', and

that was when Angie knew he was one of the cool teachers. She didn't know the name of the band, but she recognised the sound from the CDs Chrissie liked to blast from her room and she nodded along to the rhythm. She took a sip of the punch and pulled a face.

'I know,' said Mr Cosgrove, 'it could use something.'

She turned and gave him her smile, the full beam, and nodded. She was still moving to the music. She had a good body for dancing, worked out at the gym four times a week, five when she could manage it. Her hair swung around her face, a shade darker than Chrissie's pale blonde. Mr Cosgrove was probably in his late thirties. He was regular of feature and untidy of hair, unshaven. Angie liked untidy hair in a man, imagined for a moment what her daughter would say if she put out a hand and ran her fingers through it, right there in front of everybody; she smiled, imagining the scandalised shrieks. Chrissie was somewhere behind her, no doubt at the centre of a huddle of her friends. They'd all be covering their mouths with their hands while yelling their gossip over the music. No doubt they were wondering why no one had yet sneaked vodka into the punch. Angie was beginning to wonder too.

'You must be Chrissie's mum,' Mr Cosgrove was saying. He put out a hand and she shook it, catching it only by the fingers. She could feel the bones beneath the skin.

'Angie,' she said. 'My name's Angie.'

'Nice to meet you, Angie. I'm Matt.'

Angie felt the muscles in her face relax and she took a

deep breath. 'It is a good tune,' she said, and he held up his paper cup and touched it to hers before taking a deep draught. An impulse took her and she opened her mouth and started to form the words that would take the two of them somewhere else, put a real drink in their hands, if only for a little while, then he was speaking and the impulse curled and died. She could taste it, already a stale, dead thing.

'Here we go,' he said, rolling his eyes. 'The big moment.'

The music died away and Angie could feel her heartbeat again rather than the steady *duh-duh-duh* of the music. She was vaguely disappointed; she wondered if she would ever again feel the fluttering inside that meant a new man, wondered if her husband still got that with his bit of fluff. She scowled as an older teacher stepped onto the stage and up to the microphone.

He cleared his throat and the room hushed. He had a bald patch that shone damply under the spotlights and he touched his hand to it before bringing it to the microphone. Angie wrinkled her nose, thinking of someone else coming along and taking hold of the damp, cold metal.

Two smiling girls in low-cut dresses stepped onto the stage and flanked the teacher. Their waists were tiny, tight, never stretched by fat before being punished by hours in the gym. They were smiling. One of them held an envelope and the other held a velvet cushion that appeared deeply purple in the dim light. On the cushion was a crown.

Angie already knew what was going to happen; it was potent in the air, latent in Chrissie's clenched hands. Her daughter stood at the front of the crowd, her posture loose and effortless, smiling a casual smile that belied the tension in her fists.

The teacher flicked the microphone, ignoring the dead sound that echoed around the room, and cleared his throat again. He muttered something, how *delightful* it was they could all be there, how *beautiful* everyone looked, but how there could be *only one queen* of the spring dance.

One smiling girl passed him the envelope. The other glanced at the crown.

He opened the envelope, the paper sticking to his clammy hands, and gave another *cough-cough* of embarrassment. 'A popular choice,' he said, looking around. 'Our new queen is Chrissie Farrell.'

Applause erupted, and there were shouts, the occasional low jeer drowned out by the rest. Angie smiled, or thought she did, but there was sorrow in it too: *so long ago*. She felt a hand on her arm: the teacher, and he was smiling at her. She couldn't remember his name.

He nodded up towards the stage and his eyes remained there as he spoke. 'Isn't that your daughter? Come on, you can go closer.'

And of course that was what Angie wanted; what mother would not? She looked up and saw that Chrissie was beautiful, and pride came at last. Her eyes stung. Was she crying? She allowed herself to be led to the edge of the stage and stood there clapping as Chrissie received her crown, displaying her even white teeth. Her skin was smooth as buttercream.

'She's a lovely girl,' the teacher said, clapping, still at Angie's shoulder, easy in his louche posture and his untidy hair.

Angie frowned, and that was when everything turned to white. She winced, then the dark rushed back. She looked at Chrissie and saw yellow afterimages dancing about her daughter's face and when they cleared she saw Chrissie hadn't flinched at all, had taken the camera flash as her due. Mr— What was his name? He was still clapping, and as he did, his eyes flicked up and down her daughter's body.

Later, when the photographs were printed and Chrissie thrust the picture into her hands, Angie saw what it had caught: the crease between her eyes accentuated by her expression, the dry-looking skin, her narrowed eyes appearing almost sly. All she could think was: *I thought I had been smiling.* In the picture she wasn't smiling, wasn't the image of the proud, happy parent that she should have been. She looked envious; she looked unhappy. She looked old.

Angie turned to the teacher, meaning to ask him for that drink after all – not for tonight, Chrissie might want her around, but another time maybe – and found an empty space at her side. The teacher was standing by a group of girls, bending so that one of them could whisper in his ear. He was smiling.

'Mum.'

It was Chrissie. Her daughter looked shorter than she had on the stage, and not merely because of the platform: she seemed somehow diminished, just Chrissie, her daughter, once more, the crown on her head a cheap plastic thing. Angie smiled back – a real smile – and reached out to put her arms around her.

Chrissie took a step away, wobbling on her heels, and held something up to ward off her mother: the photograph. 'There's a bunch of people going to Kirsty's after,' she said. 'I might be late.'

'Chrissie, we spoke about this.'

'Mum, don't *start*.'

Angie shut her mouth so abruptly she heard her lips snap together, and the smile turned to a scowl. 'Chrissie, I came here tonight because of you – and now you want to go off and—'

Chrissie rolled her eyes and pushed the photograph at Angie; she had to take it or let it fall to the floor.

'I *have* to, Mum. *Everyone* is. Stop treating me like a kid, okay? Take the picture home, will you?' Chrissie leaned forward, kissed her mother lightly on the cheek and was gone, with only a flash of vibrant coral dress as she vanished among the others.

Angie held the photograph tight against her breasts. It was a long time before she held it out and looked at it properly, and she didn't like what she saw, not at all. She glanced around her. The DJ was playing another tune she didn't know and the dance floor was becoming crowded. A couple filed past her, so close the girl's dress swept Angie's legs. The teacher with the untidy hair seemed to have gone.

She wound her way back to the refreshments table, the picture tucked under her arm, and poured another cup of punch. She couldn't see her daughter but the photographer was still there, in one corner, and girls were lining up for him, giggling. She could hear a printer whirring beneath the interminable thud of the music. Angie headed over there. There would be other pictures of Chrissie among the rest – *and of you*, a voice whispered in her mind; another picture to show she wasn't the way she appeared in the image she held.

It's a photograph. It only shows the truth.

She shook her head to clear her mind and went up to the table, spread with images of young girls: girls in red dresses, black dresses, pink dresses, their hair worn high or spilling around their shoulders. Their smiles were all the same.

'Can I take that?'

A picture was pulled from Angie's hand. She was in the way, as ever, cramping their style. She recognised the self-pity in her thoughts, decided she didn't care. Then she heard something that made her stop and listen:

'Cosgrove, yeah, you're not kidding!'

'Fit as anything. You seen his hair?' A squeal of laughter.

Cosgrove. That was him, the cool teacher.

'Single an' all.'

'That's not what I heard.'

There was a break in the words – they had moved on or lowered their voices – then:

'Shagging Whatshername in Beaver's group.' There was a high giggle that made Angie think of glass. *Beaver*: didn't Chrissie call her form tutor Beaver? Mrs Beavers, her name was.

Shagging Whatshername in Beaver's group.

'Dirty bastard.' This time both voices joined in the loud, shrill laughter that went on for a long time until suddenly the camera flashed, turning everything white once more, making colours garish and faces pale: bringing everything into the light, if only for a moment.

Shagging whatshername in Beaver's group.

No, Angie thought, *it didn't have to be Chrissie, of course, it didn't.* There were other girls in the class, and other groups; there was always other gossip. It didn't even have to be true. The man might not be sleeping with anybody, much less a pupil. He surely wouldn't risk so much for so stupid, so flighty a thing. And then she remembered the way the teacher had looked at her daughter, his eyes flicking up and down her body, the way he'd moved away from Angie without a word. The way he had bent so that a girl could whisper in his ear, so close he must surely have felt her warm breath on his neck.

No.

If she didn't trust a man such as Cosgrove, she had to

trust Chrissie. The girl wouldn't be so stupid, wouldn't waste herself that way. Of course it wasn't Chrissie they'd been talking about; she should think better of her daughter. Chrissie could walk into a room and own it with her million-watt smile. *Her daughter.*

'Do you want your picture taking?'

Angie looked up, startled, and shook her head. No, she didn't want her picture taking; she didn't even want to be here any longer. She stepped back and allowed someone to take her place. She glanced around the room again. It was all going off exactly the way it should. There was no need for her to be here, not now. There were more than enough adults, and it wasn't as if Chrissie would notice. Angie was already taking out her mobile phone to call a taxi as she slipped out of the door.

If only she hadn't started to drink after the dance, she would have called Chrissie last night. It wouldn't have helped, of course – the girl would have recognised the number and ignored the call – but it would have made Angie feel better. Of course, she had realised before too long that her daughter wasn't coming home. She should be angry, she supposed, but it was difficult to feel anything except lethargy. She could call her now, but she wasn't ready, couldn't bring herself to face Chrissie's antagonism. Chrissie had been with her friend Kirsty, she'd said. She never listened to her mother when she was with her friends.

Angie sighed. At least it was her day off; she could

always go back to bed. She'd hear the door bang when Chrissie walked in – she always slammed it – so she could wait until then to rouse the energy for the argument that was no doubt their due.

Angie pushed away the half-eaten cereal. She had a sudden, vivid image of the teacher, Mr Cosgrove: a close-up of his face, the features pleasantly grizzled like some fast-living rock star, and that made her think of the giggling girls. She pushed the thought away. Chrissie would never get mixed up with someone like that; why the hell should it have been her they were talking about? Not everything had to revolve around her daughter, like – like a crowd around a stage.

She heard a sound at the door and waited for the metallic skitter of Chrissie's key in the lock. Instead she heard the slap of the letterbox, and a moment later the dull thud of something hitting the carpet.

At first Angie didn't move; she just stared down into the mush that had been her breakfast, then she pushed herself up from her stool and went to see what it was.

A brown-paper parcel was sitting on the carpet. It rested at a thirty-degree angle to the door, facing away from her, and there was something wrong with it. *It should be fastened with string*, Angie thought. It was that kind of parcel, care-fully wrapped, carefully folded. She didn't know what it was about it that was off, somehow – and then she walked closer, and she did: her name and address were printed neatly in black marker, but there were no stamps. It could be from one of her neighbours, perhaps – but then why write her address? Angie shook her head. She was being silly, the result of her hangover; she was looking a gift horse in the mouth.

She picked up the parcel, feeling the dry, clean paper. How long was it since she'd had a parcel wrapped in brown paper? It was nice, a pleasantly old-fashioned thing to do. She shook it and heard something shift inside, kept looking at it as she turned and walked back into the kitchen. She collected the scissors and snipped along a fold, opening the new edges and the slit tape, smoothing out the paper. There was a light grain in it, a diagonal pattern which felt nice under her fingers. She opened the scissors, slipped the blade under the top of the wrapping and slid it down the length of the parcel.

There was a box inside, new and unmarked, not yet reused the way Angie recycled old packaging, taping new addresses on top of the old. The box was pale tan with black elasticised strips around it. As Angie slipped off the bands she thought she caught a faint smell, as if the wrapping had been stored somewhere musty.

She lifted the shallow lid, revealing a spill of white tissue paper, and smiled in spite of everything, the evening she'd had, the headache, the queasiness that lingered in her stomach. *Good things come in small packages*, she thought, *and even better ones in tissue paper*, wrapped in layers and layers of it, crinkly like—

—like the lines around your eyes.

Angie pulled a face.

There was a smooth object inside the box, her fingers had touched it: glass. She pulled out sheets of tissue paper and laid them carefully on the breakfast table. She could see the glass now, and it was crimson, the stuff inside it at any rate. She saw it had leaked a little in transit, a dark, almost brown splodge clinging to the last of the tissue, sticking layers of it together. Angie pulled it free with a hiss of frustration and saw what was in the box.

It was a bottle, old and heavily ridged: *Ridged for poison*, Angie thought. Whatever it was filled with was dark, clotting, the same stuff that had leaked on to the paper. She saw there was some of it on her fingers too, and she pulled her hand away. There was a smell, and she couldn't think how she hadn't noticed it before because it was *strong*, this scent, cloying and tainted and *strong*. She wanted it away from her nostrils, out of her house, and she moved to push the box away and her eyes flicked upwards and she saw why the bottle had leaked; she saw the thing that had been used to stopper it, and she opened her mouth and froze. She *heard* the scream, though, she was sure of it; she heard it inside her head, and it went on and on, over and over. She knew it would never stop, that scream; *had* never stopped—

There was no sound, none at all. Everything was silent, except in Angie's mind, as she stared at the thing and heard the silence and felt everything going on around her, the leaves outside continuing to grow, flowers pushing their heads up from the earth, and she wanted it all to stop; because this couldn't be happening. This wasn't possible, not possible at all.

There was a toe stoppering the bottle, pushed hard into the narrow neck so that the skin had folded back and wrinkled. It wasn't a big toe, that wouldn't have fitted, Angie thought, and she didn't know why she thought that, why it even mattered. She knew whose toe it was; she recognised the pale orange of the nail polish, so carefully chosen, so carefully applied. It was too bright now, a ridiculous colour against the greyish, dying skin – *dead*, Angie told herself, the skin was *dead*, and the word wouldn't register, wouldn't connect with anything in her mind. She knew this was because she didn't want it to, not yet: not ever.

It had been the cause of one of their little arguments, that colour. They had been in Leeds – they had travelled up there especially to buy the dress and the make-up (to save Chrissie stealing Angie's – not that that had ever worked), and they'd stood for hours in the shop, trying this shade and that, and it took so long to choose and it was still orange. Angie had told Chrissie so, said it was hideous, but Chrissie insisted that it wasn't orange at all, it was coral, and it matched her dress.

It doesn't match your dead skin, Angie thought, and laughter rose in a fat bubble. Her hand shot to her mouth and she actually got hold of her lips, twisted them to keep that laugh inside.

The nail was almost crushed at one side. It looked as if it had been pinched in something: pliers, maybe.

Angie turned her head away. She felt tears on her cheeks, though she hadn't felt them coming to her eyes.

She looked back at the thing on the table, the tissue paper scattered around it like handfuls of snow, the smooth sides of the box. *It was new*, she thought. *No traces*. And she wanted to laugh again. Suddenly her legs gave way and she found herself on the floor, clinging to the edge of the table. Then she *did* laugh but it came out in a weird sound, *hunh-hunh-hunh*, and Angie started to cry.

It's not her, she thought.

Someone only hurt *her. It's only a toe.* Anger rose, a sudden cold fury that someone would hurt her daughter, take thick metal snippers to her daughter's soft skin. She was chilled right through. Her shoulders shook with it, a sudden cold that gripped tight and wouldn't let her go. She was alone. She hoped for some kind of anger at that, the old, comfortable bitterness that might drive all of this away into some other place.

But she was *gone*. Chrissie was gone, and Angie didn't know where, because she had left the dance, she had allowed her daughter to go off alone just as though she wasn't Angie's little girl, Angie's *baby*. A pain shot right through her, ripping open the middle of her chest, and she leaned forward, wrapping her arms tight around her body. She rocked herself and a moaning sound escaped her lips. *How odd*, she thought, *how odd to make such a noise, out loud, when I'm here on my own.* She knew the box was still above her, on the table. It couldn't be real, and she didn't want to look and *make* it real once more. Somewhere she could hear a bird singing and she half raised her head. Her eyes were blurry. She thought she might be sick, surely she had to be sick, but no, her stomach had settled. It was traitorously stable, when the rest of her was this empty, reeling thing.

She had to call the police.

She gripped the tabletop, making sure she didn't touch the box – never again – and pulled herself up. It was her legs that were unsteady now, not her stomach. She crossed the room to the telephone, feeling like when Chrissie had persuaded her to go roller-skating, back when her daughter was small. It had been all right when they were out there, gliding around the rink with all the rest; it was when she'd taken off the skates that she'd started to wobble, as if the world had become an untrustworthy thing on which to put her weight.

She didn't know what she said to them. She remembered having to repeat it three times, and wanting to scream when she was asked to say it again. '*Her toe*,' she kept saying, '*it's her toe*.' She only thought about the blood when she came to explain; she hadn't consciously recognised, before then, what was in the bottle. '*It's blood*,' she said, and that was when she started to cry, hard and out of control. *Ugly crying*, she had always thought of it, but now she didn't care. She could be ugly for ever if only Chrissie would come back, healthful and whole and smelling of peaches.

Angie found herself sitting by the telephone and shaking with sobs, the handset back on its rest, and she didn't know whether she'd finished talking to them or simply hung up. She tried to remember giving her address and found she couldn't. She *felt* like they were coming, though; they had to be, because if they didn't she was just going to sit here until somebody did. She hoped – *hoped* – that person would be Chrissie.

The thought of her daughter made her stop shaking. She couldn't sit here, she had to be strong, she had to find her little girl and bring her home, safe and sound as she had always been. Then she remembered Chrissie's mobile and picked up the phone once more, hitting 1: the speed-dial number that would connect her to her only child, of course it would. She would be there, her tone casual and dismissive as ever, and this time Angie wouldn't mind, not at all. If she didn't answer – it would just be Chrissie ignoring her, probably pulling a face at her mobile and laughing with her friends as she let her voicemail pick it up, because she didn't need her mother, she was with her friends, still having a good time. Still healthy; still *whole*.

It didn't ring.

Angie sat with the phone in her hand and looked back

at the table. The box was still there, the clouds of tissue paper around it like a bad spell. She turned instead towards the window and was surprised to see everything was the same as always. Her neighbour's hedge needed trimming. The shrubbery was hazed with pale green buds and the sky was a faint blue; it would be a clear day. Somewhere, a bird was still singing. She became aware of it slowly, heard it grow more forceful before dying away and starting up once more in a shrill chorus. The Fullers' door needed painting; it was peeling right down to the wood and Angie had always wondered why they didn't do something about it. Her own driveway was looking messy, the flagstones uneven. She traced the lines with her eyes, the places where the ground was pushing up from beneath. She tried not to think about anything, tried to remember to blink, to breathe.

Finally she heard a vehicle coming up the hill. It was still out of sight but she knew the car would be white, and that it would have neon stripes along its side. She watched the turning of the lane but it wasn't a car she saw coming around the corner, not at first: it was the postman, his bag loose at his side, a clutch of letters in his hand. He turned in at the Sandersons' gate. His lips were pursed, as if he was whistling, and Angie knew it was because he was mentally singing along to the tune playing on his iPod – he always did that. *He hadn't even been*, she thought. The postman hadn't delivered the package. Someone else had done that – someone she might have seen, if she had only looked out, if she hadn't been sitting at the table, hungover and feeling sorry for herself while her daughter suffered.

Hopefully, she thought, and tried to block out the alternative.

The car rounded the corner and she saw it *was* white, that it did have a neon strip along its side. It had blue lights, too, and they were whirling, momentarily painting the Fullers' door and the Sandersons' gate, dappling her own chipped drive.

There were no sirens. *Too late*, she thought, and forced herself to move towards the door.

CHAPTER TWO

Sandal Magna was an odd place, PC Cate Corbin had reflected as she'd headed down the road towards it. They would go 'into Sandal', or 'down Sandal', never into 'the town' or 'the village'. She knew this was because the place didn't have a centre: there was no village green or high street or parade of shops or even a church to form a bull's-eye on the target. It was prime commuter land, a place where people rested their heads between trips into Wakefield or Leeds or Sheffield or even, on the East Coast main line, as far as London.

Sandal was a few twining streets that slotted between a series of fields and landmarks, and it struck Cate that maybe it *did* have focal places, after all; it was just that they had been there for centuries, had lost the power and meaning they'd once had. Sandal Castle came up now, a snag-toothed ruin that always looked at its finest just after dawn, when the pink-and-blue sky was reflected in the boating lake at the foot of the hill. At the other end of this stretch of road, if she took a right, was Newmillerdam, the country park that drew day-trippers from across the district. Hundreds of years ago it would have been used by huntsmen. Now most visitors simply skirted the lake, 'doing the flat path' as Cate thought of it, before heading to a choice of pubs for a reward in a pint glass. Few ventured into the dark green woodland beyond.

It was a quiet place, an easy patrol, the through-routes and housing clusters divided by long swathes of green. There would be the occasional opportunist burglary or vehicle break-in; car thieves would sometimes come and nick black Audis or BMWs off convenient driveways. Cate glanced at the traffic heading off in the other direction, towards the motorway; people heading to other places, bigger places, where things *happened*. In a couple of years that would be her, moving out of the small flat she'd rented on the edge of Wakefield, going to Manchester perhaps, or London. For now, it would have to do. It was the place she'd been raised, though since her parents had left, retiring somewhere greener still, she could feel how the ties keeping her here were thinning. Once she'd put in her time building a solid foundation in policing, she could think of moving on for good.

She was still thinking this shift wasn't going to be any different when the radio burst into life. She acknowledged, flicked the blues on and pulled out to overtake.

Cate took a deep breath as she pulled up next to the house. She had driven quickly but forced herself to concentrate through the twists and turns coming onto the estate, glancing at road signs as she took each turn. It was a carefully cultivated habit. *Always know where you are*, her tutor constable, PC Len Stockdale, had said to her, and it still didn't seem that long ago. He had sometimes tested her on it, stopping mid-conversation to ask the name of the street they were on. It was his way of teaching her, and it had stuck; if she ever needed to call for help, she would know exactly where she was. This time it wasn't strictly necessary, since she knew back-up was already being despatched.

The house was set into a row of others towards the top of a hill. The whole place was lined with wooden gates and gardens that would be described as pleasant, the houses self-contained, neat, separate. Number 17 seemed as quiet as the rest. Cate glanced towards it; in the largest window, between wide-slatted blinds, a face looked back.

She paused to radio in her time of arrival before stepping out and reaching for the doorbell, wondering briefly if it would be better, after all, that she had got there first. PC Stockdale was an old hand, but his 'don't mess' demeanour – possibly also carefully cultivated, more likely the product of his experience – was better suited to handling Saturday-night drunks than a woman in distress. She could already imagine the way he would look at her when she opened the door; no, the face she had seen at the window didn't need Stocky, not just now. Cate, on the other hand ... she took another deep breath as the door opened.

The woman was older than Cate had first thought. Her skin was pale, even against her harshly bleached hair, and her hands claw-like as she grasped at the dressing gown she wore, a shining silk thing printed with brilliant purple bougainvillaea. She smelled of coffee, old perfume and perhaps, beneath, the taint of stale wine. Cate identified herself and the woman nodded, though she didn't appear to understand the words. She stepped back and Cate followed her into the house.

The woman led the way into a spacious kitchen and indicated the table. There was a box on it. It was surrounded by the litter of white tissue paper, the remains of breakfast, and an empty wine glass. Cate looked at it, automatically noting the ring of lipstick around the rim. She wasn't sure why she did this, only that she wanted to miss nothing.

'There.' The woman was crying, silently and without fuss, tears oozing from her eyes as if crying was something she always did.

Cate pulled a pen from her pocket. She reached out to use it to pull the box towards her, realised even that might disturb any evidence and instead leaned over the table, peering to see into it. Her eyes widened. She could smell it, a kitchen smell that made her think of knives. She could see the glass nestling inside the box, the light catching the ridges on its surface. It floated across her mind that its texture would probably capture only fragmentary fingerprints on its surface; then she focused on what it held. She could see the toe. There had been trial cuts, she saw that at once; the skin was severed in a couple of places, crushed where the blade had pressed down. Either that or someone had failed to cut all the way through and started again. She looked away from it, moved her gaze to the crumpled paper scattered across the table.

'You touched it?' It was a needless question but she asked anyway. She had to keep calm, allow herself time to think. There was only silence, and she turned to Mrs Farrell to see the woman's eyes fixed and staring, her pupils a pale, fragile blue. She was terrified. Of course, she was terrified, and Cate knew she wanted nothing but reassurance: *It's all right, ma'am, we see this sort of thing all the time. It's just someone having a laugh; that's not really a toe in there. You didn't really think—*

'And your daughter didn't come home?' Cate prompted again, and the woman shook her head, though there was still no sign of understanding in her eyes, only that blank fear. 'Is there someone who can be with you? A husband or a friend – someone I can call for you?'

Mrs Farrell didn't answer. Cate reached out, touched her arm, and she jumped. Cate's mind was racing. She had to get CID in here, crime-scene tech, make sure supervision was on its way. They'd need the area securing – the kitchen, the hallway, anywhere the parcel might have been.

They needed to get a description of the child circulated, a family liaison officer contacted for the mother. And Mrs Farrell – she would need checking herself, her fingerprints taken to eliminate any traces she'd left on the things she'd touched. The thoughts came in a rush. Cate could feel fine prickling all over her skin, like a faint breath of static.

They'd also need to check the house, as discreetly as possible. If there was any sign of struggle . . . Most murders were committed in the home, and most murderers were family members. She looked again into Mrs Farrell's blank eyes. The woman was traumatised – but how badly, and from what? Was it only the thought of what had happened to her child, or something else? It didn't seem likely.

She thought of the skin around the severed toe, the way it had been crushed and cut, and she shuddered. It might have been better, after all, if Stocky was here: he wouldn't have had to think about what to do or what to say.

'Come through,' she said, taking Mrs Farrell's arm. She steered her towards an open door which led into a darkened lounge. The room was a little musty, the curtains still drawn. A pair of shoes, black and strappy and with glitter on the toes, had been kicked off and left in the middle of the floor. She led her to the sofa and the woman sat like an obedient child, not saying anything, just staying where she was put.

Cate slipped back into the kitchen and spoke into her radio. The house seemed quieter than ever, her voice too loud, but when she returned to the lounge Mrs Farrell showed no sign of having heard. She didn't seem capable of taking in anything at all. Cate took another glance around the room and saw a photograph in a silver frame standing by the television.

The picture showed Mrs Farrell in better days, her hair freshly feathered, smiling a red-lipstick smile. Her cheeks glowed with blusher and her eyelashes were painted with the kind of electric-blue mascara that had been in fashion once. Next to her was a young girl, blonde, pretty, effortless in her wide white grin. Cate stared at it. The thing she noted, more than the similarity in the shape of the women's faces, their noses, their lips, was the fact that they were wearing the same dress. The daughter's was yellow and the mother's was white, but they were still the same. *Oh dear*, Cate thought, then pushed it from her mind; she picked up the frame and turned to Mrs Farrell.

'Is this your daughter?' she asked, her voice gentle. She held the picture in front of the woman. 'How old is she now?'

Mrs Farrell turned her head at last, not looking at the photograph. She nodded.

'Can I take the picture?'

The woman didn't answer, just started to cry again, soundlessly, and for a moment Cate let her. 'Mrs Farrell?'

'That's Chrissie,' the woman said at last. 'She's fifteen.'

A sound blared out as someone rapped at the door, and they both jumped. Cate hurried to answer, relieved that someone more senior had arrived. Some day, she would handle cases like this. She would be the one who stepped in, gave orders, made everything happen the way it should. For now, she was ready to hand over this scene – and Mrs Farrell – to someone else.

It wasn't until much later that the second call came in. Cate was in the car once more, her hands tightly gripping the wheel as if she could regain some grasp on the regular routine, on the ordinary houses and streets and places she had known that morning. It was as if everything since then had passed in a daze; the things she had seen, the arrival of more senior officers, Cate following their instructions with a quiet calm that didn't quite reach her insides.

Now she was headed back out. Instead of taking the route she'd planned, though, she pulled up short of the junction she'd been approaching and listened. At first, she wasn't sure what she'd heard.

This time, when Cate responded, a frisson of excitement mingled with her nerves, like a cold line down her back.

CHAPTER THREE

Cate took the corners fast, blue lights flaring on the low stone walls as she headed away to the south, towards Ryhill village. This time she didn't look around for road signs; she was going way too quickly, and anyway, this was an area where signs were few. There was nothing around but wide green fields, nothing to say where each turning led. She whipped around another ninety-degree turn, swinging wide and jouncing across the potholes. It wasn't a well-kept road – it wasn't well-used. She thought she could hear another siren under the sound of her own and as she pulled onto a straight stretch she saw she was right: there was another police car vanishing around the next bend.

Ahead of her, she glimpsed a row of red-brick houses that marked the very edge of Ryhill. This was ex-mining territory, where once-thriving pit villages now slept amid the greenery. Open-cast land had been reclaimed, turned into Anglers' Country Park; reservoirs that had once fed a coal-bearing canal now provided ideal nature reserves. Not far away was the Heronry, a lakeside trail with hides for birdwatchers and its own visitors' centre. She had gone there as a child to feed the ducks; she still remembered their squabble and squawk, the snapping beaks.

She turned in the direction of the Heronry now, away from the houses and the village, swinging around a left-hand bend and entering the wood. The road immediately dipped and she fell under shadow, but she could see where the other car had pulled up; its siren had been silenced but its lights still sporadically lit the underside of the leaves and branches.

Two men stood next to the car. One was maybe in his fifties, one younger, callow; both wore oilskins and clutched fishing rods. A black and white sheepdog lay next to them, its head on its paws, one twitching ear betraying its wakefulness. The elder man lifted a hand, raised his index finger in what Cate thought of as a Yorkshire wave, then pointed towards the trees. There was a small clearing where patches of earth lay dust-bare between the trunks. It was a problem area: people came here to dump old fridges and mattresses under cover of the trees. There was a heap of rubbish there now, a pile of plastic bags, the naked spirals of bedsprings rising from the shapeless, wilting forms.

Cate turned her head and was startled to see the fisherman up close, leaning across the bonnet, each vein on his nose and cheeks clearly visible. He was still expressionless; she found herself wondering when he'd forgotten how to smile. He pointed, sticking his arm straight out towards the trees, and she opened the door to hear a single word: 'There.' He pronounced it with two syllables. *Thee-er*.

She followed his gesture, and this time she saw a figure standing under the lacework of shadows. She recognised her old tutor constable, Len Stockdale, at once; but she didn't recognise the shine in his eyes. As she approached she could feel him simmering, a glow rising from him she could almost see. Then he said, as if they'd won something: 'Here first.'

She peered past him. She saw flashes of colour, the dirty white and garish blue of plastic bags, and something else, a clean, shining coral. There was a smell too, both sweet and bitter beneath the tang of rotting garbage, and the faint whiff of chemicals. Stockdale shook his head. 'It's a girl, a teenager. I checked for vital signs, just in case – no go. There's no point in you seeing it too, love.' He reached for his radio, started to call it in.

She stepped to one side so she could see better. The clean coral shade she had glimpsed was a girl's dress. It was long and flowing and spread over and around a shape that was lying on the ground. The fabric was thin and shining, satin or silk maybe, too fine to afford any warmth. It stood out clear against the dull greys and browns of the tree trunks and bare ground and the mulch of trodden-down rubbish. There was a pile of oily rags nearby, an apple that was half eaten and browned.

Cate couldn't yet see her face, but she remembered a photograph of a carefree young girl in a yellow dress, her features so much like her mother's. She remembered too Mrs Farrell, tears leaking from her eyes, her expression one of blank, empty shock; the woman who needed to know what had happened to her daughter.

She glanced at Len Stockdale and went closer.

She had seen death before. It was a part of her work, a regular event, and often it was rough, messy death, bodies broken by a spill from a motorbike or ruined by decay before being found in some quiet flat. Now she couldn't understand her own reluctance as she leaned in and looked at the girl's face.

Her skin was pale, dead white against bright red lipstick. The first thing Cate noticed though was her hair, which also heightened the paleness of her skin, because her hair was black: *black*. Cate felt a flood of relief as she took in the brutally cropped fringe. Chrissie Farrell, as she had seen her in the photograph, had had rich blonde waves spilling over her shoulders.

But of course, this girl was still someone's daughter.

Cate's eyes narrowed. The hair hadn't just been cut, it had been hacked. It was jagged around her face, and so dark it was almost bluish. It was not a natural colour. It wouldn't have been styled that way. She sniffed the air, trying to identify that chemical smell, thinking of hair colourant; she thought she had it, then it was lost beneath the tang of bleach. She felt sure, all the same, that the girl's hair had been dyed.

She peered more closely at her face. The skin was so pale, faded like other dead bodies she had seen, and yet unlike them too. She thought she recognised its shape, though, the line of the girl's nose, her cheeks, her lips. She thought of Mrs Farrell once more, the picture of herself and her daughter wearing the same dresses, their faces pressed close together, and she grimaced.

She drew a deep breath, forced herself to take in the rest of the scene. The body – *Chrissie* – had one hand resting on her chest, the fingers curled around an object she held. It looked like a hand mirror. It lay face downwards so that she couldn't be sure, but Cate thought that was what it was, an old-fashioned mirror, its carved handle widening to a wooden oval. It didn't seem like anything the girl would own.

Her eyes flicked back to that black hair. She had thought there was something clinging there, that some rubbish was entangled in it, but she saw she was wrong: it wasn't rubbish but a plastic crown, fake jewels jutting out, sequins that appeared merely dull in the filtered light.

And the girl's lips. The bright lipstick painted over them was clumsy, cheap-looking. Cate thought again of the girl in the photograph – that girl surely wouldn't have painted her lips in such a way. Perhaps after all she was wrong, this might not be Chrissie Farrell; it might be the start of someone else's nightmare.

An image rose before her eyes of the tissue-lined box on Angie Farrell's kitchen table. She remembered the stopper in the glass bottle and glanced towards the girl's feet. They were covered by the fall of her dress and she couldn't see them, but she remembered the colour of the nail polish she'd seen on that single severed toe, and she knew it almost matched the shade of the bright coral fabric.

She took a step closer, tried to see, instead, the girl's fingers: perhaps her nails would be painted with that same shade of polish. One hand was curled around the mirror, hiding the nails. The other lay at her side, and Cate looked at it – and she caught her breath.

'Not what we're used to seeing, is it, love?' Len's voice came from behind her and she jumped. Slowly, she shook her head.

'Back-up's on the way. CID are coming.' His voice was a tone lower than usual and Cate remembered that he had two children, a boy and a girl, both teenagers. He'd complained about them endlessly on their early patrols, saying they lived to vex him; mostly, Cate had thought they actually confused him. It was odd how people could live in the same house and not understand each other at all. That made her think of Mrs Farrell again. No doubt she'd give anything, now, to be vexed by Chrissie.

'We need to get a cordon set up. You better go and talk to them. Get their details for the scene log. Keep them back.' He gestured towards the fishermen and Cate nodded.

She took one last look at Chrissie Farrell, her ragged hair, her ruined hand. The girl's eyes were open, staring up at the trees looming over her, and something about them stopped Cate. She had seen the twisting overhanging branches reflected in her sclera, but now she saw it wasn't a reflection after all: the marks were *in* her eyes. The shadows were the leak and stain of burst blood vessels, rising from beneath: petechial haemorrhages, a sign of suffocation. However, when Cate's gaze went to the girl's neck, the skin there seemed unmarked, as pale as her face.

The fishermen were father and son, though they didn't even look at each other as Cate spoke to them. They only occasionally met her eye, preferring to stare down at the ground or away, along the road, as if wishing they were somewhere else. Even the dog stood a distance apart, staring into space, its tongue lolling in an unknowing grin. The boy kept glancing at it, as if trying to work out what it was doing there. His knuckles, still gripping his fishing rod, were the colour of bone.

The elder's face was immobile as he spoke. Their name was Dereham, and they came out here a lot to fish, but this time their trip had been cut short. They had been walking from the village – the man nodded towards the line of houses that marked the edge of Ryhill, and Cate caught a glimpse of red brick through the trees – when the dog had headed into the woods.

'He dun't normally run off,' he said. 'An' 'e wouldn't come back. We 'ad to follow 'im.' Cate saw sorrow in his eyes. 'It was me lad here who called the police. I dun't hold truck with them mobile phones, me. I spoke to 'em, though. It were me as told you about it.'

His son nodded, looked away, as if embarrassed.

'An' then we waited. That was all.'

Cate asked a couple more questions, found that was pretty much it. The Derehams had seen a couple of cars go past – families, passing through on their way somewhere else, or heading for the visitor centre away down the road perhaps – but no one had stopped or even seemed to look into the woods, until the police had arrived.

She could hear more sirens now, in the distance. She knew they wouldn't be long, and sure enough another police car rounded the bend and pulled up behind her own. There was another car behind that, unmarked: the cavalry. It was all too late for Chrissie Farrell. Soon the place would be crowded with CID, scene-of-crime officers, photographers, the coroner; and after that nothing, only an empty space where Chrissie had been, a small spot where the garbage was pressed a little flatter than the rest.

Car doors opened and people stepped out. Some she recognised, most she didn't. They were plain-clothes, CID. They would take over, she and Len would assist them, complete their statements, and that would be it. She had known, since she first arrived at the scene, she wouldn't be on the case for long.

She wondered who would break the news to Mrs Farrell, whether the woman would have to identify her child. Whether her blank eyes would fill with relief when she first saw that stark black hair.

Len Stockdale was already at the police station when Cate got back, just ahead of her once again. As she expected, CID had stepped in and taken over; now there were only their statements to complete. She was still relieved, although now she was away from everything she couldn't help feeling something else she couldn't quite identify, unless it was a trace of disappointment. So early in her career, and she'd just had a brush with what must be a major case. The way the body had been left – it wasn't a straightforward death. Why do that to her hair, to her lips, her hands?

Her hands.

The girl's hand had been lying at her side, curled in on itself, but Cate had still been able to see her fingers. It looked as if the nails had been ripped from them; they were caked in dried blood. She clenched her own hands into fists, a gesture less aggressive than protective.

And of course it wasn't only Chrissie's hands – and she *was* thinking of the body as Chrissie, was more sure than ever that it had been the girl in the photograph, in spite of the hair – it was her feet as well. Someone had pulled out her nails, cut off her toe, done that to her hair and her lips, then put that crown on her head, perhaps in mockery.

Cate closed her eyes. When she did, a quite different image of Chrissie came into her mind, one she hadn't known was there. She pictured her as a young child with golden curls, home and safe, being cradled by her mother, who was reading to her from a book. Just a little girl, being read her bedtime story.

She shook her head. She didn't know why she'd thought of it, but it seemed important somehow.

Of course it is, she thought. *Chrissie is someone's daughter. And her mother should never have to see what's happened to her child.*

'It's about vanity,' came a voice at her shoulder.

For the second time that day she jumped; it was Len. 'What?' she said.

'It fits. The mirror, the crown, the hair dye. Pulling out her fingernails. It's all about vanity, having a go at her for dressing herself up like that. Putting her out with the trash.'

Cate frowned.

'And the bottle. Sending back a perfume bottle to her mother, as if to say that's all there was to her.'

She turned and looked at him. 'Vanity,' she repeated.

'It's probably someone who's been watching her, or

maybe even a random thing – someone who hates young girls dressing up like that, thought he'd teach her a lesson. The way it's posed – it's a weird one. Not just someone who lost their temper and grabbed her throat; someone's thought about this. Definitely premeditated. Probably an older bloke who can't be doing with the way they do their hair and paint themselves and chatter, totter around in their high heels. Giggling.' He paused. 'Being *social*. Maybe this guy's not social. He could be a loner, so he hates other folk who fit in, who're—'

'*Alive*,' she breathed.

'That's it. And so he does this.'

He didn't say *kills* her, and Cate noted the way he avoided the word, liked him for it. She remembered the photograph she'd seen of Chrissie, the girl wearing the yellow dress, her mother the white. She couldn't seem to separate it from the thing the smiling girl had been turned into: the staring eyes, the bloody hands. 'The bastard tortured her,' she said.

'Doesn't like them, does he? Prancing around in their fancy dresses and their make-up. That'll be the way he sees it, I reckon.'

There was something in Stocky's voice, and she remembered his own daughter: she wondered if he was thinking of her now, imagined he probably was. *Prancing around in their fancy dresses and their make-up.* She could imagine him saying that about his own child, but she knew his voice would be resigned at worst – laced with bemusement, maybe, but there would be a hint of something else too: pride. The thought of anyone putting their hands on his child, punishing her for developing and growing into a woman, would light him up with rage; destroy him with grief.

She wondered if anyone had spoken to Mrs Farrell yet about the body in the woods. She found herself hoping, for a moment, that they had not: *Give her a little longer*, she thought. *Give her that, at least.*

Still, something was bothering her about what Stocky had said, something that wasn't right, that didn't ring true. She couldn't think what it was. Cate closed her eyes and at once that image of Chrissie was waiting there, a little girl leaning over a book, her mother smiling. Mrs Farrell's lips were moving over the words.

Suddenly Cate knew why she had that image in her mind of a child and her bedtime story. She opened her mouth to tell Stocky and closed it again. It was ridiculous, nothing but her emotions getting in the way: he'd think she was a fool, and he'd be right. The crown, the hair, the mirror – Len had seen it at once, this *was* all about vanity, and if Cate had been thinking straight she'd have seen it for herself.

Except the bottle that had been delivered to Mrs Farrell hadn't really looked like a perfume bottle, had it? It must have been cheap perfume to come in such a large bottle. And the glass had been old, of such poor quality she had seen tiny bubbles caught within it, and those deep ridges, the contents barely showing through the thicker bands – it looked like something that might be found in an antiques shop. Glass with ridges like that – hadn't it once denoted that the bottle held poison?

CHAPTER FOUR

The detective superintendent from CID was dark, middle-height, middle-aged, and self-contained as a bullet. His natural expression seemed to be one of distrust or disdain, Cate wasn't yet sure which. He wasn't local, had been brought in from a neighbouring serious crime squad, and had brought a small army of detectives with him.

She remembered Len's words: *It's a weird one. Not just someone who lost their temper and grabbed her throat; someone's thought about this. Definitely premeditated.*

CID were clearly taking a similar view to have brought so many and so fast. She imagined these briefings would be a regular occurrence until the culprit was caught. Around thirty were now seated in the incident room or standing at the back; Cate and Len, called in to this morning's briefing to present their evidence, were standing.

The detective superintendent stood and rapped the front desk – *hard knuckles*, Cate thought – and the room fell silent. He introduced himself as Heath, the senior investigating officer. He pointed out some of the team he'd brought with him and she caught DI Grainger, several detective sergeants, DCs Thacker, Laughlin, Paulson, Westerton, Judd; then she lost track of the unfamiliar faces. The whiteboard at Heath's back was already marked with names, times, dates. Angie Farrell was on there, and the daughter, Chrissie Farrell.

Any doubt was gone: the dead girl had been identified as Chrissie. Her mother had made a positive identification, and Cate winced at the thought; she could all too clearly imagine her catching a first glimpse of that black hair, assuring anyone within reach that no, that wasn't her daughter, not her Chrissie: she didn't have black hair, didn't they *know*? Only to begin to see the girl as she had, recognising the shape of her face, her eyes, seeing her own features written upon it. And then what?

Cate shook the thought away. The SIO was outlining what had happened when the 999 call had come in from Mrs Farrell, about her macabre gift. The body left at the fly-tipping site, as could have been expected, had been found to be missing the toe that had been wrapped and hand-delivered to her mother's house.

'Nice,' he said. 'And it wasn't even Christmas.' He waited for the muted laughter to subside before holding up a photograph. Cate recognised it as the one she'd obtained from Mrs Farrell's house, but there was nothing odd about it now; there was only the girl in the yellow dress, her mother cut out of it. Frozen in time, Chrissie grinned out at them, showing her shining eyes, her white teeth.

'She was fifteen years old,' Heath said. He glared out across the room, and his gaze met Cate's, just for a moment. 'So she's young, she's pretty. She went missing following a school dance, at which she had been crowned the beauty queen. She expressed wishes to stay at a friend's house' – he consulted his notes – 'Kirsty Gill. Early indications suggest that Chrissie never got there. There was an argument and Chrissie left the dance alone. Sometime after midnight she was abducted, tortured and dumped near Ferry Top Lane at a known fly-tipping location. She was discovered by passers-by shortly after her mother, Angela – Angie Farrell – had the box hand-delivered to her home, containing a bottle of blood, most likely her daughter's, with the severed toe used as a stopper.'

He paused and scanned the room. His eyes were oddly pale for one so dark, and Cate wondered how far the piercing glare they gave him had helped with his career.

'We're about to release some of this information to the press. But hear this: the detail about the girl's toe is being withheld. So it doesn't leave this room, understand? It's important; it could help us nail the bastard.' He glared once more until he appeared satisfied he had impressed this detail on everyone. Then he picked up some papers, ran through some details about how the girl had been found. He showed crime-scene photographs and pointed out the things that had been found with her: the crown, the mirror. It seemed Cate and PC Stockdale would be left with little further information to offer. When he got to the girl's hands, though, he paused.

'Her fingernails weren't only torn out,' he said, 'there were traces of bleach on her hands, and some of it on her face. It could be that was done before he started on her nails, though it's more likely it was done afterwards to cover up trace. If it was *just* afterwards – I don't need to tell you what that would have felt like. Likely we've got a sadist on our hands as well as a weirdo.'

Cate stared up at another of those crime-scene pictures. Hadn't she noticed something about the texture of the girl's skin? And it had been so pale.

She would have screamed, she thought. *If she was still alive, she would have screamed while he did it. Or at least as long as she could.*

Of course, the forensic pathologist should be able to ascertain whether the girl had been alive or dead when it happened. She found herself hoping she had already gone, that she hadn't known anything about the things that had been done to her.

Heath continued. He pointed out that the location of Chrissie Farrell's death had yet to be identified. All they had was a dump site.

A dump site, she thought. What had Stocky said? *Putting her out with the trash.* The murderer had had his fun somewhere else. Her face felt tight, the muscles tensing of their own accord, and she realised Heath was watching her. She let out her breath, forced herself to relax her expression. He looked away. Had he really been focused on her at all?

'A partial fingerprint has been recovered from the mirror,' he continued, 'but it's only a smear – unlikely to be good enough to match. The crown has the opposite problem, since it's covered with them, one overlaid by the next. She probably passed it around for her friends to see it.' And then he paused, and this time he *did* look at Cate, then at PC Stockdale. 'We have no way of recovering tyre tracks from the mud at the side of the road because of the subsequent arrival of police vehicles. There is an additional possibility of interference with any footprints between the body and the road.'

Cate's breath froze. She did not dare look at Len. How could they have been so stupid? They had secured the immediate area, but not the route in or out. They had been too busy rushing in, seeing for themselves what had happened, trying to be first on the scene. *Here first*, Stocky had said, except they hadn't been, had they? It was the killer who'd been there before them, perhaps leaving traces of his passing in the dirt, only for them to be trampled over by Stocky and her. Unless the killer had carried the body in through the trees, they might have destroyed all trace of him. She hadn't even thought of it, had rushed in herself, wanting – no, needing – to see if it was Mrs Farrell's child under the trees, abandoned there with her eyes wide open. Len had been blinded by his enthusiasm, she by her emotion. And she remembered something else he had said:

Not what we're used to seeing, is it, love?

No. No, it wasn't.

Heath had already moved on, wasn't looking at Cate any longer. He was outlining who would be questioned, which lines of enquiry followed up. They were beginning with the people who would have been last to see Mrs Farrell's child, her friends from the dance, a boyfriend, maybe, anyone who might potentially have witnessed her abduction.

'Assuming she was abducted,' said Heath. 'She may just have gone off with someone she knew, possibly another of her friends; but it's also quite possible she was selected at random. The parcel was delivered to her mother's house, it's true, but whoever did this might have got the address out of the girl.'

Cate tried to imagine a schoolchild doing this to Chrissie, taking pliers and pinching them around the girl's fingernails, stretching them around her toe. She found she could not.

'PC Corbin.'

She looked up, startled. The SIO's voice was suddenly loud; people were shifting in their chairs to look at her. She thought again of the way they'd rushed into the scene, found herself reddening. 'PC Stockdale and – Corbin, I believe. Please be so good as to let us know if you have anything to add; any observations about your attendance at Angela Farrell's property and indeed, at the dump site.'

A few of the ranked detectives exchanged glances – and smirks – as the latter was mentioned. She swallowed. There *was* something she wanted to say, she just wasn't sure she was capable, at this moment, of saying it. Then Stocky shifted at her side and cleared his throat, and the group's eyes passed from her, and Cate took a deep breath.

'PC Stockdale, sir,' he said, needlessly. 'Nothing to add about the scene: you've covered everything. But I have a theory about the case.' He paused, coughed. Then he proceeded to outline what he'd said to Cate after they'd left the site, about the hair, the crown, the nails, the feet. That it was all about vanity: the mirror, the dye, the bottle. 'It all fits, sir,' he concluded, and there was silence as the room's attention passed to Heath.

The SIO stared at Stockdale as the silence stretched out, then gave a terse nod. 'As I stated previously,' he said, 'we're not ruling out the possibility that we've got a weirdo on our hands. If I find it necessary, we'll have a professional profiler review the case.' He placed the emphasis on the word 'professional'. 'Until then, we're looking at the most obvious lines of enquiry.'

He started to turn away, twisted his head back again, slowly, when Cate raised her hand.

'Yes.' Heath started straightening the notes on the table in front of him.

'PC Corbin, sir.' Cate hesitated, forced herself to speak louder. 'Sir, the scene in the wood reminded me of something. It was the way Chrissie – the victim – had been posed. The way her hair had been cut, the crown and the mirror.'

Heath was staring down at the desk, but Cate could feel Stocky's gaze on her. She knew it wasn't an encouraging look, could see from the corner of her eye that he did not seem pleased. 'I know it may sound odd, but anything we think of at this stage—'

'Do continue,' said Heath.

'It reminds me of a fairy tale.' Cate paused as a ripple passed around the room. Stupid: of course she had been stupid, should never have spoken out, should have listened to her own instincts. Stocky must have been right, it *was* about vanity, of course it was. Everything fitted. With her idea, so many things didn't: the severed toe, the finger-nails. Still, it was too late, she had no other choice than to press on. 'Her hair was dyed black,' she said, 'and the mirror – it was old-fashioned, an old looking-glass. And the way she was left in the woods. It made me think of Snow White.'

As soon as she said the words that image rose before her again, the way she'd been seeing Chrissie Farrell in her mind, a young child, her hair falling over her face as she smiled over a bedtime story. There *had* been a reason for it. She knew exactly which story Chrissie's mother would have been reading to her child, if only she could hear them as well as see them. Suddenly she was sure it *did* fit. She didn't understand how, but it felt right.

Heath was already turning away. 'Noted,' he said. He swept up his notes without further comment and was gone, walking from the room without looking back.

Cate turned to Stocky and found he was still staring at her. She could see the trace of disappointment in his eyes, and perhaps something else. 'Fairy tales, Cate?'

She gave a wry smile, shrugged. 'It seemed a good idea at the time.' She was relieved when his mouth twitched. 'Okay, so we're looking for a gang. Seven height-challenged fellows, one with a constant cold, another a little stupid, one decidedly miserable. Should be easy enough to spot.'

Cate laughed, raised her hands and let them fall, and he subsided; or she thought he had. Instead, as they made to leave, he started up a low whistle, the chirpy refrain from the 'Heigh-ho' song. Cate tried to smile once more, hoping no one would hear him, that it wouldn't catch on. Thankfully, he satisfied himself with chuckling as they left. And Cate told herself that he had been right, it *was* funny; but she could still see the contempt on Heath's face as he stared at her across the room; feel the sting in his final dismissal.

CHAPTER FIVE

The blue feather was sitting neatly in the palm of Alice Hyland's hand. It was smooth and slightly curled and she held it up and peered at it, saw the perfection of each individual barb, the way they came together to form a smooth curve at its tip.

She shifted her gaze from the feather to her laptop screen, which displayed a news report: TWITCHERS IN A TWITCH, it said. The journalist had been enjoying the puns the story afforded. *Birdwatchers flock to West Yorkshire after rare bluebird sighting.*

They weren't sure what kind of blue bird it was, and Alice wondered, if they could see the feather that rested so lightly on the palm of her hand, whether they could work it out. There was a picture of a pair of birdwatchers – twitchers – a man and a woman. The man wore large round glasses that looked in themselves a little like binoculars and they had identical smiles. There was a picture of a bird too, and it was small, like the one she'd seen, but not so brilliant; not nearly.

Alice bit her lip as she read on, remembering the way she'd slammed the window on the small, fragile creature. She might have killed it. She wondered what the twitchers would have said to that – she imagined being caught in a flare of flashbulbs while carrying the poor thing to her wheelie bin, the man with the jam-jar glasses and his frizz-haired wife wearing identical expressions of horror.

She went to her window. Her first impression had been correct: a bird such as the one she'd seen had no place in England. Bluebirds were from North America, where the Navajo had considered them sacred, associating them with the rising sun. There were other myths too, ones that associated it with happiness, prosperity, good health – and the birth of springtime. That brought a smile to her face. She looked up into the branches of the apple tree, the blossom just coming in, tight parcels tinged with pink and tipped with the promise of white flowers.

The news report said the circumstances of the bird coming to England were a mystery, that it could have escaped from some private aviary. Alice looked through the apple tree's branches, seeing the darker treetops beyond her garden. Newmillerdam. The bird might be out there now, hungry and cold. Or maybe nothing remained but feathers like the one she held in her hand, discarded and scattered where some fox had seized it. She should have let it in. The poor creature had only been seeking a little warmth, and she had slammed the window closed.

L'oiseau bleu. A symbol of hope, of life: of springtime. A prince in disguise. A lost creature that had stepped out of the pages of a fairy tale and come looking for a home, fixing her still with the thought of its bright black eyes.

CHAPTER SIX

Cate hadn't expected she would see Mrs Farrell again, and judging from the expression on the accompanying detective's face, he didn't think she was needed either. Apparently though, despite her distress, Angela Farrell had remembered Cate, and had asked if she was going to be there. It was out of respect for Mrs Farrell's state that Detective Superintendent Heath had agreed – no, insisted – on her attendance.

Mrs Farrell's face was raw, her eyes watery and somehow exposed-looking, her puffy skin accentuating the shadows under her eyes. She had applied make-up anyway, black lines that wavered above her eyelids and smeared almost to nothing beneath them. She was sitting in the lounge, in the same place Cate had last seen her. She was clutching a damp tissue, her nails bitten ragged, and Cate thought she had aged overnight.

Detective Constable Dan Thacker stood in the middle of the room, where Mrs Farrell had once cast aside her party shoes. He wasn't looking at Cate, had barely acknowledged her presence; his eyes were fixed on Mrs Farrell. He was tall, stooping a little so that she could see the raw skin where the back of his neck had been shaved. His jaw was set.

Cate glanced around the room. Little had changed, the curtains were still drawn, and she wondered if Mrs Farrell had opened them since the day her daughter did not come home. Her eyes flicked to the mirror that hung over the fireplace. The words 'Mirror, mirror,' ran through her thoughts and were gone.

She still hadn't been able to put Heath's contemptuous look out of her mind.

'So you left the dance,' Thacker said in a low, smooth voice. 'Can you remember what time that was?'

Mrs Farrell glanced up at him, then away, as if she'd barely understood the words, was merely acknowledging the sound of them. She mouthed something Cate couldn't catch.

'Mrs Farrell? It might help, if you can remember.'

Her hands fidgeted in her lap. 'I don't know. I don't know.'

When he spoke again, Dan's voice was softer. 'Did you see her again before you left?'

She shook her head and he sighed.

Cate left her seat, knelt by Mrs Farrell and took her hand. 'I'm sorry we have to go over these things,' she said. 'Really, if we didn't think it might help, we wouldn't ask you. What happened when you last saw Chrissie? Do you remember what she said to you?'

The woman glanced up at her. 'She – she told me to stop treating her like a kid.' She paused, bit her lip. 'She was with her friends. She's always like that with–' She broke off.

'It's all right. Take all the time you need. You know we're going to do everything we can.' She felt a pang when she said that: *They*, she thought. They'll do everything *they* can.

Mrs Farrell put a hand to her face. 'She kissed me,' she said. 'She kissed me on the cheek.' Her fingers were kneading the place, as if she could bring the touch of her daughter back.

'And who was she with?'

'No one, not then. She didn't want her friends to see her talking to me. You know what they're like at that–'

At that age, Cate finished silently. That was what the woman had been about to say, and then she had realised that her daughter was never going to grow up, would never be any older.

Dan cut in. 'We understand, Mrs Farrell. So she said she was going to spend the night with Kirsty Gill. We've spoken to Miss Gill, and it seems she had a disagreement with your daughter. She seems to have felt, at the time, that your daughter had been made queen of the dance unfairly.'

Mrs Farrell met his eye, as if he had reached her at last, drawn her out of wherever she had been hiding. 'She *was* the queen of the dance,' she said. 'Chrissie was beautiful. Of course she won. She was always going to win.'

'And there appears to be some jealousy. Not unusual at that age, but do you know whether Chrissie had any particular enemies at school? Anyone who would want to hurt her?'

Mrs Farrell's face crumpled. She started to speak, compressed her lips. Slowly, she nodded; then she shook her head.

'Mrs Farrell?'

'There was always jealousy.' She gulped at the stale air. 'There were a few girls who didn't like her. She talked about someone called Sarah. Deborah Wainwright. Tanya Smith. A few of them, it changed all the time. Chrissie was so pretty – of course, they were jealous. Anyone would have been.'

'And Kirsty Gill?'

Slowly, she shook her head.

'So Chrissie's argument with her friend must have been sudden. Something that could have blown up out of nowhere.'

Tears welled in Mrs Farrell's eyes. She glanced at DC Thacker, then at Cate. It was as if she was trying to read them both, and finding she could not. Her eyes narrowed. 'You're saying—'

'I'm not saying anything, Mrs Farrell,' Dan said. 'I'm just trying to find out what might have happened to her.' He changed tack. 'So, when she didn't come home—'

Mrs Farrell put her hands to her face, pressing the damp tissue against her skin. She kept them there, shook her head. 'I thought she was safe, with the others. I never thought – I thought she'd gone with Kirsty. It's what she said. I should have stayed. I know I should have stayed.' She looked up, grasped Cate's arm, turned to her. 'I'm sorry,' she said, gasping out the words, as if they were something she had to say, as if they would bring her daughter back. 'I'm *sorry*.'

Cate waited until she had gathered herself. After a while the woman slumped in her seat and threw the tissue aside, instead mopping at her eyes with her fingers.

'Is there anyone else who harboured any ill will towards her?' Cate asked. 'And what about the girl's father – where is he?'

She shook her head. 'He's been in Spain for years. Chrissie went out to stay with him a few times. Not for a while, though. He's coming back now, for the—' Her eyes went distant.

'What about anyone you thought might have been watching her, or following her? Were there any online acquaintances she'd spoken about?' Dan said.

'I don't know. Chrissie thought making friends online was lame.' Mrs Farrell let out a spurt of breath, the nearest she could come to a laugh.

'All right,' he said, 'we'll follow it up anyway, Mrs Farrell, just in case. We'll need her computer, with your permission.'

Dumbly, she nodded.

'And you're quite sure she wasn't seeing anybody?'

'There were a few boys, no one special. She never seemed that interested. She finished with the last one months ago. It wasn't anything serious. Chrissie wasn't—' She glanced up, a sharp movement this time, and looked away.

'Mrs Farrell?'

'Oh God,' she said. The colour drained from her face. 'There was someone at the dance – I'd forgotten.'

'What is it?' Dan prompted.

'Jesus.' She looked around, her eyes wild, as if looking for the answers. 'Him,' she said. 'Oh God, him.'

'Who, Mrs Farrell?'

Her mouth worked. 'Cosgrove,' she said, a note of triumph in her voice. 'That's it. He said his name was Matt Cosgrove.'

'Who is he?' Dan said.

'Her teacher.' Angie Farrell's eyes had an unhealthy gleam. 'I heard someone talking at the dance about him, some girls. I thought it was just gossip, you know.'

'And they said?'

'He was seeing someone in her class. That he was sleeping with someone.' Mrs Farrell put her hand to her mouth. 'But not Chrissie. Not my girl. She wouldn't have done that. She was better than that, valued herself. She was going places, my Chrissie. She would have said no. She wouldn't have let him—' Her voice ended in a wail. 'Oh, God. He must have made her. And when she said no, he – he did that to her–' Her voice rose, and she scrambled to her feet.

'That bastard,' she said, turning to Cate. 'I thought he liked me, but he didn't, I saw him watching her, and I *knew*, I *should* have known. That bastard.' Her voice broke and she started to cry, jagged, ugly crying, and the tears spilled down her face and she let them fall.

CHAPTER SEVEN

Cate headed back towards the police station. It had been a ball-breaker of a day, as Stocky would have put it. A number of uniforms, Cate among them, had been sent out on grunt work. Even a newcomer like her knew that the first forty-eight hours in a murder case were the most important, and CID had mobilised to gather information; they were using uniform to fill in the gaps, talk to the less promising witnesses and report back to log the information. She knew it was on the periphery of the investigation but even so she couldn't help feeling energised by the process, to still have some small link to the case.

She hadn't been able to put the image of Chrissie Farrell out of her mind, a young girl laid out in a thin dress, helpless, exposed to the cold and the insects and the birds. It felt good to be doing something to help. Although . . . for now, CID needed to know as much as possible as soon as possible; as soon as that phase was over, Cate would be back on the beat. She'd be dealing with neighbours' disputes or bag snatches or stolen cars. And that was fine, she couldn't expect anything else at her level, and yet—

Chrissie Farrell's eyes had been open. She had been looking up at the empty sky, waiting for the rain to fall into them; for the crows to come.

Cate shook her head, trying to dispel the image. The things she'd seen didn't normally get to her, not like this, but then it was obvious that there was nothing normal about this case. And yet CID already had a suspect, had pounced on what the mother had said about Mr Cosgrove. According to the rumour mill at the station they thought they'd got him signed, sealed and delivered, neat as a parcel pushed through a letterbox, wrapped in a brown-paper parcel and layers of white tissue.

She wondered if someone like Heath was really the type to jump to a rapid conclusion about anything, then remembered the way he'd looked at her in the briefing; pushed the thought away. She still couldn't imagine him as someone who'd be easily led down one path or another. Those eyes of his; they made it seem he was seeing through everything.

Over the last few hours, Cate had gained the distinct impression that the school had a rumour mill of its own. CID had been there earlier, talking informally to Cosgrove and some of the other teachers who'd been at the dance, along with Kirsty Gill and Chrissie's closer friends. But from what she'd gathered, it was Cosgrove's interview that seemed to have stuck in everyone's minds.

Cate had been questioning some of the kids who had been there on the night of the girl's disappearance, along with some of the bemused parents, and it seemed every one of them had their own question to ask: the same one, in the main. They'd all had the same shine in their eyes when they asked it, too – a shine that came from excitement, not from sorrow. They'd all wanted to know the story Cate couldn't tell:

'What's with Mr Cosgrove?'

'Is he a paedo?'

'Was he doing her?'

It seemed – unless it was just another rumour – Matt Cosgrove had taken exception to the same question being asked by CID at the school, resulting in raised voices and his storming out of the room they were using. Unfortunately for him, that hadn't gone unnoticed.

Cate wondered if CID were having more success than her. The sense of rumours circulating and growing made her uneasy – at some juncture they would have to locate the source, unpick it, find what kernel of truth lay at its centre. Certainly the girls she'd questioned hadn't been aware of Chrissie seeing anybody, hadn't noticed her with anyone out of hours other than her friends. The only thing she knew of that had lent the story wings was Cosgrove's apparent indignation upon being asked the same question – which wasn't necessarily surprising. Now the witnesses seemed to expect the police to answer the question: no one had any answers of their own.

It might not be what CID wanted to hear, but Cate was beginning to think the rumour was being carried only on its own breath. She wondered what they were making of it now; found herself imagining what it would be like to really work a case like this one. She felt a shiver of excitement in spite of herself. For now, she *was* working the case, if only in a small way. Mentally she ran through the people she'd been speaking to about what had happened on the evening of the dance.

The closest she'd come to getting anything on the teacher was with the last girl she'd seen – Sarah Brailsford, her name was. At first, she had seemed different; she had actually noticed the teacher watching Chrissie Farrell during the dance. What was it she'd so eloquently said? 'He was, y' know, eyeing her up.' On pressing, though, the girl had added: 'I thought he liked me too,' and she'd looked away, as if she could mask the sudden jealousy in her eyes.

That chimed with something and Cate let her thoughts drift, trying to make a connection. What came into her mind was Mrs Farrell.

I thought he liked me, but he didn't, I saw him watching her. She frowned.

Cate hadn't spoken to him, but now she found herself wondering about Mr Cosgrove. Was he really so attractive? What impression would she have gained from him? If he'd done this, cut and broken and destroyed the girl, would Cate know? Would she be able to *feel* it somehow?

She shook her head. If that was how it worked, they wouldn't need the investigative team. One look at Heath's pale eyes and the murderer would fall into their lap. All it suggested in reality was that Matt Cosgrove was a popular teacher, someone that schoolgirls liked to gossip about and flirt with. But sleeping with one of them? There was nothing to prove it. Any vague intimation had dissolved into nothing as soon as Cate tried to pin it down. And when it came to the facts, it seemed the girls' favourite teacher had hung around to the end of the night to see everyone away safely – doing his job, his duty, while Chrissie had gone off on her own.

Of course, Cosgrove might have spotted her later, when he was driving home in his car. Would the girl have refused a lift from her teacher? Cate doubted it. He was in a position of trust, and it was a long way home, especially in Chrissie's heels. She wondered what kind of state the victim's feet were in. If she'd set off to walk, it was unlikely she'd have escaped the odd chafe or blister, something to show for it on her feet.

Like a missing toe.

Cate shook her head to clear it. How *had* Chrissie been planning on getting home? Had her friends even thought twice about where she might have gone? It was nothing but a blank; although that wasn't to say Cate hadn't discovered anything at all. Sarah Brailsford had seen Chrissie flounce off, 'worse for wear'. Her nose had wrinkled as she'd said it, and then she'd straightened her expression;

as if she hadn't liked Chrissie, had felt a moment of scorn, only to remember that the girl was dead.

There was always jealousy, Angie Farrell had said. Then she'd named names, the girls who didn't like her daughter: *someone called Sarah*. There had been no surname. Had she meant *this* Sarah? It was certainly possible, but as the sobbing woman had said, school was like that; it changed all the time. Now, though, it might help them: Sarah had still been keeping an eye on Chrissie and her clique when they'd headed off into a quiet corner and Kirsty Gill had pulled a small bottle of something – Sarah thought it was tequila – from her bag and passed it around.

'Kirsty had some,' she said, 'and then Chrissie. And then they all did, and they were laughing. And I went up, because – well, I thought they might give me a swig, if I'm honest; if I told them I'd seen. But when I got there they'd started to go on about the crown, so I didn't ask, I just listened.' Her expression changed. 'Probably a good job. My dad waited up. He went ballistic about the time as it was. If he'd smelled it on me . . .'

'What did you hear?' Cate had prompted.

'Chrissie was pissed, I reckon. She can't have been used to it. She was slurring a bit. Showing off that stupid crown. Then Kirsty said something about how she thought *she* might have won, and Chrissie burst out laughing, and Kirsty just looked at her. She said something back, but I couldn't hear that. It was too loud in there.'

'And what then?'

The girl's lip twisted into a sneer, and that too faded, as if she had to keep reminding herself that her schoolmate wasn't coming back. 'She said something about them never standing a chance,' she said. 'And Kirsty said thank you very much, and the others said something too, but I can't remember what. They just – argued, you know. I do know what Chrissie said, though, before she went off.'

'And what was that?'

The girl sighed, looked away. 'She said they were a bunch of jealous bitches who couldn't win a beauty contest if they were shagging the judge.'

And that, it seemed, was all: Chrissie had flounced out, and the girl hadn't seen her again, didn't know if Chrissie had called for a taxi or tried to hike home in her stilettos.

Couldn't win a beauty contest if they were shagging the judge. Interesting choice of words.

Still, the girl was only fifteen. *Fifteen.* And no one had seen her home.

Cate sighed as she approached the station. The only other thing she could think of – that she couldn't get out of her mind – was the bird.

Another girl had mentioned it, and once she did, she hadn't seemed able to stop. Hayley Moorhouse wasn't a particular friend of Chrissie's but she had been at the dance, and had stayed around until the end along with her boyfriend Mike. In fact, both had left the dance late. Mike had been in the toilets; he wasn't well, she said, and all her friends were gone; her dad had been parked outside waiting for them, and it was near midnight. When they went out Hayley could tell he was mad, even through the car window. 'He were there ages,' she had said, glancing at her brooding parent. He had been present at the interview but hadn't looked at his daughter, had stared instead at his hands, picking at his fingernails with ferocious impatience. It had been easy for Cate to imagine how angry he would have been.

'We rushed off,' the girl said. 'We was giving Mike a lift. There was just Mr Cosgrove left, an' he was getting his keys out and locking up. He shouted bye. There wasn't anybody else. Only us and me dad.'

Cate nodded, smiled.

'That was it,' said Hayley. 'Except – it was weird.'

Cate looked at her, encouraging her to continue.

'It's just – it's daft, I shouldn't mention it really, only there was this bird. It was sitting on the wall, an' it were bright blue, like someone's budgie or somethin'.' Her eyes went far away. 'It weren't singing or owt. It were just sitting there, looking about. Pretty, though. It was really pretty.' Her eyes snapped back to Cate. 'I liked it. Only, I didn't see anything else.' She had glanced towards the window as if she could see the bird still sitting there; she pressed her lips together.

Cate looked upwards now to see that the sky was a clear pale blue. *A budgie.* She could imagine the expression on Heath's face if she mentioned that. His mouth would purse up as if his cup were filled with battery acid instead of coffee.

As if in answer to her thoughts, Cate saw the SIO as she pulled in at the station. He was standing at the edge of the parking area, pacing up and down, pressing a cigarette to his lips. It was an odd kind of smoking, sharp and quick, as if he'd almost forgotten how, or was feeling guilty and going through the motions as quickly as possible.

He watched her as she stepped out of the car and approached, and she nodded, greeted him. 'Any joy?' he asked.

She was surprised he'd spoken to her – he'd been so dismissive at the briefing, had seemed to include her in Mrs Farrell's interview on sufferance. She recounted the main points of what she'd found out and took a deep breath. 'There was nothing concrete on Cosgrove sleeping with the victim, sir, only rumours. There might be more to it, but I didn't find more than schoolgirl stories today. Not with the people I spoke to, anyway.'

Heath paused with the cigarette raised halfway to his lips. He looked at it as if he'd only just realised what it was and flicked it to the ground in disdain. Cate decided it would be a bad time to remind him of the litter laws.

'Schoolgirl stories,' he said, and sucked in air between his teeth. 'Funny, that's pretty much what the man himself called it.' He glared at Cate.

'Perhaps one of the other witnesses—?'

'I doubt it.' He jerked his head. 'Slippery bastard.

Anyway, he's got an alibi, of sorts. Drove straight home after the dance, woke up his wife when he got in. 'Course, that's only his wife, but we've got nothing on him. Now he'll probably get a brief, just in case we come sniffing.' Heath stared into space as he said this last; it was almost as if he'd forgotten Cate was there.

She murmured something about getting on with her report, and he didn't look at her as she went inside. It occurred to her that if Cosgrove had got wind of the rumours that had started buzzing around the school, not to mention the mothers' grapevine, they couldn't really blame him for getting a solicitor.

Is he a paedo?

Of course, the pressure of knowing they were onto him might also make him slip. And if he *was* their man, it couldn't hurt to have people wary of him.

Underneath, though, the case felt as insubstantial as the rumours about Matt Cosgrove's sex life. As far as she'd seen they had nothing to go on, no other suspects and no meaningful evidence. She remembered the way Chrissie's mother had said Cosgrove's name, seizing upon it as if it could bring her daughter back: her desperation. It was that thought that made up her mind for her; that, and the niggling feeling she still had low in her stomach, curled there like a worm in the bud.

CHAPTER EIGHT

It was early and Alice threw open the bedroom window. There was a nip in the air, but she wanted to breathe in something of the outside, to look out and see nothing but trees. Her room had the most beautiful view in the house, and the early morning was the time to see it.

This morning there was no blue bird perched in the apple tree. She was half glad – she still hadn't shaken off her guilt – but half disappointed too. The thought of twitchers scouring the woods for the rare sight she had seen so easily from her window lent it an exoticism that before she had only sensed.

She shook her hair back. The sky was a pale but perfect blue; it would be sunny yet cold, like yesterday. Beyond was the woodland, the heart of it still dark, almost black, fading to an almost colourless grey in the distance. Somewhere, a bird cried. It wasn't the varied chatter she had heard before but the strident scrape of a crow, a harsh and isolated sound that made Alice think of lonely places, abandoned places. That in turn made her think of the body that had been found only a few miles away to the south. She had heard about it on the news. If she headed to Newmillerdam, around the lake and through the woods, then crossed the open fields, she wouldn't be far from where it had happened. The report had been vague, saying only that the death was suspicious, and Alice wondered what had happened to the victim; what had been *done* to her.

She grimaced, turned away and headed for the shower. The hot steam in the tiny bathroom was welcome, but it soothed rather than invigorated, inviting her back into sleep. She ran through the work she needed to do that day. She had essays to mark, and she looked forward to seeing her students' thoughts and ideas about the fairy tales they had been reading. That was always the beauty of it for Alice, the way each story changed with the teller, the way each listener could interpret it a little differently. Still, this was her third year running the course and the novelty was beginning to wane. There was a tendency to find the same ideas and interpretations threading through the essays she was handed each week, something she would have to try to shake up.

She pulled on jeans and a checked shirt, tied her hair into a pony tail. She could get the marking done first – over breakfast, probably – and then go for a walk. She thought she might head around the lake today rather than through the woods: she would stick to the path.

Then she paused as she heard the sound of wood scraping stone.

It was a gate opening, the gate at the front of the house. Alice padded downstairs, went into the lounge and looked out into the narrow lane; she found herself involuntarily drawing back so she was hidden by the curtains. Odd: there was a policewoman walking towards the door. A second later there came a sharp tap.

It was probably a mistake; the police had the wrong address, or were maybe looking for someone else. A sour taste flooded her mouth. *Bad news*. She thought of her mother, a single intimate moment that pierced her; bending to kiss the old woman's forehead, seeing her white scalp through the thinning hair, a reversal of the way her mother had once kissed Alice. She hadn't been able to take care of her, had had to put her in a home. But wouldn't the staff simply have called her, if there was something wrong?

She wouldn't find out what had happened by standing here, unmoving in the early-morning chill. She pulled open the door and saw the policewoman was probably not much older than her, maybe even a little younger. She looked up now, as if surprised to see Alice standing there: definitely the wrong house.

'Alice Hyland?' she asked.

Alice frowned. All right, the correct house, but there had to be some other mistake. 'Is something wrong?' she blurted.

The policewoman started to shake her head, then she asked, 'Could I come inside?' and Alice's stomach turned to water. The policewoman must have seen something in her face because she tried a smile. 'It's all right,' she said, 'I just wanted to ask you a few questions. I'm hoping you might be able to help me.' She held a folder in her hands and now her fingers tapped against it.

Alice led the way through to the kitchen at the back of the cottage. The policewoman followed, gave her name as PC Cate Corbin and said that yes, she would like tea. Alice switched on the kettle, got mugs out of the cupboard, heard the hiss as the water began to boil. She still wanted – no, needed – to know that the news wasn't bad, maybe wasn't even meant for her at all, although the everyday act of making tea was comforting; surely someone with bad news to impart wouldn't allow it to be delayed in such a fashion.

'Nice view,' a voice said at her shoulder, and Alice let out a hiss of her own. She hadn't realised the girl had followed her, and hadn't heard her approach over the sound of the kettle. Is that what they did – tried to unsettle people? But she hadn't done anything wrong.

'Sorry,' the policewoman said, 'I didn't mean to make you jump.'

When Alice turned, the girl tried a smile. She didn't appear to be trying to tell Alice anything, wasn't bursting with questions; still, her eyes were serious and there was a directness to her gaze; Alice didn't doubt she could be pushy if she wanted to be.

'Was there something you wanted?' The words came out more bluntly than Alice had intended, and she softened it with a smile. She picked up the mugs, handed one over.

'There's nothing to be concerned about,' said the policewoman. 'I'm here because I think you may be able to help me with some information – in a professional capacity, that is.'

Alice frowned. 'I'm a university lecturer,' she said, 'up in Leeds. I – I get the train.' After a pause she added, 'I study literature.'

'I know. Could we sit down, Miss Hyland? It's a rather sensitive matter. It's nothing you need worry about, not personally, though it is rather serious.'

Alice gestured towards her pine table and the policewoman set down her mug, slipped into a chair and placed the folder in front of her. She drew the mug closer but she didn't drink from it. She sat there as if she were strangely reluctant to continue. 'I'll be honest with you, Miss Hyland,' she began.

'Alice.'

'Thank you. Call me Cate.'

It felt odd, being on first-name terms with this stranger in uniform, but Alice nodded.

'I'm here because I have an idea about a case I'm working on and I thought you might be able to clarify matters. Really, you could say I'm here on a hunch. I'm looking for information in connection with a murder investigation.'

Alice started, but Cate held up a hand, as if to settle her. 'I was hoping you could help me. The victim was found in a very particular – pose, let's say. Certain items were placed around her. I'm not at liberty to tell you what all of those were, but maybe some of them might mean something to you.'

'To me? Why would they?' Alice blinked. She had seen the news about the body found in the woods – was that what the policewoman was talking about? She'd been shocked by it, and that was where, for her, it ended. She had never met the girl who'd been found; she didn't know anything about her.

But the policewoman was moving on, already describing the scene: a young girl, little more than a child, dumped at the edge of the woods. A mirror had been placed in her hand and her hair dyed black. She had been a beauty queen – the crown was still on her head. Her fingernails had been pulled out and a part of her – Cate didn't elaborate – was sent back to her mother.

'I'm sorry,' said Alice, raising her hands and letting them fall again, 'but I don't know why you're telling me any of this.'

Cate stared at her a moment, as if making an assessment. 'I didn't altogether want to show you this, but I did get clearance, and – to be honest, you'll probably only see what I'm getting at if you look at a picture.' She began to open the folder she'd brought.

Alice started quickly shaking her head. 'Wait a minute

– are you saying there's a picture of a dead body in there? I don't want to see it.'

Cate paused. 'I realise this is all rather untoward, but you really may be able to help us. Cases like this – they can be open to many interpretations, and those interpretations will influence the lines of enquiry that are taken. This is – well, let's say it's a different interpretation. I think it's worth looking into, even if it comes to nothing.'

Alice frowned. She had no idea what the girl was talking about. Interpretation of a murder? What did that even mean? She shook her head, but somehow she didn't stop the policewoman when she slipped a single picture from the file and laid it on the table. She kept the rest covered.

Alice didn't want to look at it, but it was impossible not to let her gaze creep over the picture. She could see a pale, hazy figure, a splash of colour surely too bright to be blood. She was seeing it in fragments, individual details, small things her mind could take in, nothing more. Then her eyes went to the girl's face and she swallowed. The girl looked pitiful. Her skin was stark against the bright red lips and black hair – *ebony* was the word that came to mind, and that did make her think of something.

'What part?' she asked. It came out more sharply than she'd meant; she supposed it was shock, from looking at the photograph. Death – at least this kind of death – was something she saw on TV or read about in books; it wasn't something that intruded into her life. Now she was seeing for herself that it could be brutal and merciless, torturing and maiming before it ended.

'What do you mean?' Cate sounded puzzled, and yet a little hopeful too.

'You said something was sent to her mother. What was it?'

Cate paused before she answered. 'A bottle,' she said. 'A bottle of her blood.'

Alice frowned. 'Strange,' she said then, 'No. No, it's stupid. It looks – it can't be.' She pushed the picture back across the table, covering it with her hand. She had looked at it – been *exposed* to it – for nothing. 'It's almost like something out of a fairy tale,' she said, 'but the blood – no, it doesn't really fit. And the dress isn't really the right colour. The hands – no.'

'It reminded you of something.'

'Only for a moment. The way she looks, her hair black, and all—' *Ebony*, she thought. 'It looks a little like Snow White, when she was sent out into the forest with the huntsman, but it isn't quite right – it doesn't quite fit. And – for a start, if that was how it was meant to be, the bottle of blood would have been stoppered with her toe.'

The sight of the policewoman's face froze her. After a moment she said, 'There *was* a stopper.'

'I can't say, Miss Hyland.' Cate's reply was quick, but her tone told Alice everything.

'There was, wasn't there? Only you didn't expect me to know.' Alice crossed the room and picked up a satchel by the door. She opened it and leafed through the papers inside. 'Where is it? "Cinderella" – "Hansel and Gretel" – no.' She pulled out a sheaf of notes, riffled through them and sighed in exasperation. 'It doesn't matter. I know the variant. It's Italian, I think. The queen orders Snow White to be taken out and killed by a huntsman because she's jealous. She's no longer the fairest of them all, and we all know how she hated that. And she orders that part of the girl is brought back, to prove she's dead. Of course, the mirror was really the stepmother's, but—'

Cate broke in, 'She ordered the huntsman to bring her a bottle of blood?'

Alice nodded. 'Stoppered with the girl's toe, yes. In Italy, anyway. That's where that variant came from, I think.'

'Variant?'

'That's right. Fairy tales date back centuries. They're from the folk tradition; they were never really meant to be written down. They were passed from mouth to mouth, usually by women – there was a whole tradition of oral storytelling. It's wonderful, really – each teller would add their own detail, put their own experiences into the tales they told, and each listener – well, they could hear something different in it each time too, according to their own background and experiences. It's fascinating. And yet the stories have something that remains essentially *theirs*, you know? They're powerful. Some say it's because they're archetypal, that—'

'So a variant is . . . ?'

Alice smiled. 'Sorry. I get carried away on the subject. It's my specialism. My – enthusiasm, I suppose. Whenever the tale is told, it's a little different, you see, and each different telling is called a variant.' She paused. 'So in this particular version, the huntsman had to send back a bottle of blood. In other variants he had to send back different things. It gets pretty gruesome' – her eyes flicked to the table – 'in other versions, the stepmother demands the lungs and liver, and she has them boiled in salt water and eats them. In another she wants the heart – always popular, the heart – and in another, I believe it's her intestines and a blood-soaked shirt. You have to remember, some of these stories came from brutal times. Life and death – they were close, you know? They weren't hidden away from us by undertakers and hospitals or—' Alice glanced at the picture and looked away. 'Sorry.'

'It's all right.' Cate was staring at her. 'So you think there's actually something in this? That the body was posed to resemble a children's story?'

'Oh, they weren't for children,' said Alice, 'not originally. It was only afterwards that they were gathered together by people like the Grimms, and even they put a warning on the original book to say that they weren't really suited to children. It's just that people wanted to read them in that way, and market pressures dictated— Sorry, I'm going on again. What I'm saying is, the tales changed over time; they became neutered. But this . . .' She frowned. 'It's going back to the dark side of folk tales, isn't it? Not some safe, anodyne telling – it's real.' She paused. 'They were red in tooth and claw.'

'What?'

'Fairy tales.' Alice spoke more slowly, her voice sober. 'The real fairy tales, red in tooth and claw, that's how I think of them.'

Cate was staring into space. After a moment she realised Alice was watching her and she tried to smile; she failed. 'I need to go into this in more depth,' she said, 'go through each aspect of the MO and work out how it relates to the stories. I'll need to get something together I can take to the team. MO means *modus operandi*.'

'I know what it means,' said Alice. 'I watch TV.' She nodded towards the table. 'Do you want another cup of tea?'

Alice went through each item in turn, responding to prompts from Cate. After a time the policewoman removed her hat, revealing straight brown hair, cut short and aggressively pinned down with clips. She made notes as they went. They started with the obvious: Snow White was a king's daughter, hence the crown. Of course, that could also have been a coincidence, a remnant of the dance the girl had been to the night before, but they went with it. The black hair – Snow White's mother had wished for a child with hair as black as ebony, lips as red as blood and skin as white as snow. Alice glanced back at the photograph as she said this and Cate repositioned it in front of them. This time Alice found it easier, and she looked at it for a while, noting the viciously black hair – it seemed obvious now that the colour was from a bottle. The lipstick too looked as if it was from another era – a harsh red the colour of pillar boxes. She squinted. Hadn't the colour bled a little onto the girl's face? There was no way the girl would have applied it like that. Of course, it had probably been smeared afterwards. She frowned. She didn't want to think about how that might have happened. The face in the photograph was pale, death bringing a pallor that had faded her cheeks and paled even her eyes, which were wide open and staring.

Cate explained the traces of bleach that had been found on her skin.

Alice reached for the picture as if to pick it up, then drew her hand back.

'Not easy to look at,' Cate said.

'No,' she said. 'No, it's not.'

They were silent for a while. Then Alice asked, 'Do you think that's why he did it?'

'What?'

'To make a story of her. Like he distanced himself from this somehow, from the reality of what he was doing.'

'Possibly,' Cate said. Then, in a noncommittal voice, 'Are you all right to continue?'

Alice drew a deep breath. She thought, running through the story in her mind. 'All right,' she said. 'So Snow White's real mother dies, and the king marries again. The stepmother is vain – very vain – and she possesses a magic mirror. It tells her she's the most beautiful woman in the land.' She gestured towards the picture. 'I'm assuming that's a looking-glass in Snow— I mean, in that girl's hand.'

Cate nodded.

'So it fits, although really it should be the stepmother's. Okay. Gradually, Snow White grows more beautiful, and the stepmother becomes more and more jealous. Eventually the child overtakes the mother in looks and the queen orders her killed.

'The huntsman takes her into the woods. Now, the most common variant of "Snow White" is the German, because of the way the Grimms collected it and wrote it down. In that, she demands he brings back the lungs and liver. But Snow White is so beautiful the huntsman can't kill her – lucky for her, he lets her go, and he brings back the lungs and liver of a boar instead. Here though we have the Italian variant – the bottle and her toe. Again, so far, it fits.'

'All right.'

'So Snow White wanders through the forest, lost and scared, until she finds the cottage where the dwarves live. Again, the dwarves are really famous because of the German version – "Snow White and the Seven Dwarves". They let her stay, and she takes care of the house for them. But the witch – the queen – still has her mirror, and it tells her that Snow White's alive, and she can't bear the thought that somewhere, someone is alive who is more beautiful than she.'

'Vanity,' murmured Cate.

'Vanity. Exactly. And so she disguises herself as a pedlar and goes off to kill her. First she gives her some stay-laces, and draws them so tight the girl faints, but she doesn't die. Failure to kill her number one. Then she tries a poisoned comb.' She peered into the picture. 'Did you find a comb anywhere?'

Cate frowned. 'I don't think so.' She reached into the folder and examined more photographs without Alice seeing them. 'I don't see one.'

'Well, after that, in this variant anyway, she gets Snow White to eat a poisoned apple. In the Italian, I think it's a poisoned cake. Whichever it is, this time she's done it: a piece lodges in the girl's throat and she falls down as if she's dead. That's where this story appears to end. In the fairy tale, of course, there's the handsome prince, the apple is jolted from her throat and she's revived and they live happily ever after.'

Cate laid a photograph down on the table. In it was the girl's hand, the fingers curled inwards around their bloody tips. A little distance away, amid the grey mulch of other people's rubbish, was a half-eaten apple.

'There we have it,' Alice said, and frowned. She pulled the photograph towards her. 'I don't get it,' she said. 'Her hands – why did he do that to her hands?'

'I was hoping you might be able to tell me.'

Alice shook her head.

'I suppose it's only a story,' said the policewoman.

'Whoever did this might have had reasons of their own that had nothing to do with it.'

'No,' said Alice slowly. 'There's something.' She stayed that way for a while, running her finger across the table, close to the picture, but without touching it. Then she snapped her fingers. 'She did housework for them,' she said. 'She looked after the dwarves. She scrubbed the floors and cleaned their clothes.' Her voice faltered. 'He could be saying she worked her fingers to the bone. All the same, as a comparison, it's too much. What was done to her . . .'

'I agree,' said Cate, 'but this girl – her mother said she'd painted her nails before the dance. They'd argued over the colour of the nail polish. Maybe this is because nails like hers wouldn't have fitted the story, they wouldn't have been suitable for that work, not practical, and not appropriate for the role at that point. A vanity.' Her voice went quiet.

It was Alice who continued. 'That could be it. Or he could just have been cruel.'

Cate shook her head as if rousing herself. 'I could smell bleach,' she said. 'It was on her hands, too. Of course, I didn't know that at the time.'

'You smelled it? You mean – you *saw* her like this, for real? You were there?'

Cate sighed. 'I was one of the first on the scene.'

Alice thought she was going to say more, but she did not. She shifted her gaze past the policewoman to the window, where she could see into her back garden. 'Was the apple poisoned?' she asked.

Cate frowned. 'We don't know yet.' She followed Alice's gaze, then turned to her. 'Wait – there was a poison bottle.' She explained the ridges on the bottle that had been sent to the girl's mother.

Alice nodded. 'The mother,' she said, 'is she really her mother, I wonder? Or could she have been a stepchild? Only, in the story – at least, in most versions of it – it's Snow White's stepmother who's the cause of everything. She's the one who's jealous, who tries to do away with her stepdaughter.'

'I'll check,' Cate said. 'It's an interesting thought.'

'Of course, in the original versions of fairy stories, it was often the real mother who was the villain. People like the Grimm brothers softened that, though. It was part of making the tales safer, less frightening, more suitable for children. They often turned the mother into a stepmother, distancing her, and those versions are much better known.' She paused. 'Of course, if it turns out the girl was adopted or from a previous marriage, you've got something more complex on your hands. It means this girl wasn't picked at random. Whoever did this might have been watching her, finding out about her.'

Cate nodded, but she was miles away, lost in concentration. 'I'll look into it.'

Alice subsided. She glanced back at the window, suddenly remembering the blue bird, and it struck her afresh how odd it had been. She was used to burying herself in fairy tales; now it seemed they were stepping out of the woods, walking in through the door and into her life.

She shifted her thoughts back to the story the photographs had told, the story of the beautiful girl who finds her prince. And her mouth fell open.

'What?' asked Cate. 'What is it?'

'It's just – the girl was at a dance, wasn't she, the night it happened? I saw it on the news. She was made the springtime queen or something. They made a big thing of it, how tragic it was.'

'Yes,' said Cate, 'I saw – and yes, she was. She was wearing the crown when we found her.'

Alice slapped her hand down on the table. 'Why didn't I think of it before?' she said. 'I'm such an idiot—'

'What have you seen?'

'It's the crown,' Alice said. 'It wasn't just because Snow White was the daughter of a king, it's more than that. She went to the dance and she won the contest; she was made a beauty queen.'

'And?'

Alice let out a short laugh. 'She was *crowned*,' she said, 'the fairest – don't you see? Chrissie Farrell was chosen because she was the fairest of them all.'

CHAPTER NINE

Cate headed towards the police station, walking quickly across the parking area towards the personnel entrance at the side of the building. The folder was clasped under her arm and she felt conscious of its weight. The words written there were running through her mind, almost as if they were whispering to her. She glanced down and saw the scattering of cigarette butts at the foot of the steps, pictured Heath scowling as he paced back and forth. Would he really listen to a story like this? She wasn't sure. She'd had to get permission to show the crime-scene photograph to Alice, but it was DI Grainger she'd obtained it from, not the SIO. Perhaps that had been a mistake. Would Heath think she'd deliberately avoided him? But then, perhaps she had. She'd never seen the man without that harsh look, his mouth pulled down at the corners even when his expression was neutral. And there was no way he'd have forgotten the way she and Stocky had charged in at the fly-tipping site, possibly trampling crucial evidence underfoot.

But surely he would have to listen now? Her information threw a completely new light on the case. Chrissie had been made part of a story, its threads deliberately laid, and that could change their whole approach to the investigation. If what Alice had suggested was true, it could even implicate new suspects – as she had said, the mother was often the villain when it came to fairy tales. They were full of family relationships that had gone wrong, become twisted. Wasn't that how many of them began? A wicked stepmother, jealous of her daughter's beauty – when Cate thought of that she couldn't help thinking of the photograph that had been cut in two, the one with Mrs Farrell wearing that ridiculous dress, white to her daughter's yellow, but like her daughter's, all the same. Just what had the woman been trying to prove?

Another image of Angie Farrell rose before her. Cate half closed her eyes, saw the woman's fixed stare, her confusion; her pain. Could she really imagine she had been involved, other than through leaving her daughter alone that night? Surely the girl's mother was too ruined to have done such a thing?

But the fact remained that someone had singled Chrissie out, and perhaps that someone had known she was going to be crowned that night.

The fairest of them all.

Cate clutched the folder closer to her chest as someone

emerged from the main entrance, the one used by the public, and almost collided with her as the woman rushed down the steps. Cate felt the petite young woman's lank, unwashed hair against her hand, caught a glimpse of hooded eyes, a sallow complexion. She thought for a moment of creatures confined to dark spaces, scurrying out into daylight, an act of inordinate courage. *Someone's in trouble*, she thought, as she went around to the side door, tapped in the keycode, pushed it open and stepped into the lift. She shifted her feet impatiently as it began to rise.

As she headed towards the incident room, she saw PC Stockdale at his desk, and he was watching her. She went up to him and started, 'Len, you won't believe what I found out. I went to speak to—'

He opened his mouth, but Cate didn't give him a chance to cut in. 'I was right,' she said, 'it *was* staged, just as I thought. I went to see a lecturer from the university and she knew all about it. We went through everything—' She indicated the folder she held.

He didn't even glance at it. 'Easy, tiger. Don't tell me you're still chasing fairy tales.'

'But it fits, Len: the crown, the hair, the nails . . .'

He let out a spurt of air. 'The magic godmother, the dwarves – you been off with the fairies, Cate? Hope you haven't been imbibing fairy dust – there are laws about that sort of thing, you know.'

Cate waved his comments away. 'But this is it, Len, I'm telling you. She even knew about the toe.'

'Whoa – wait a minute.' His expression changed. 'You *told* someone about the toe? That's confidential information, Cate, you heard the SIO. That information was to be withheld, from the press, witnesses, from everybody.'

'That's just it: I *didn't* tell her about it; it *she* told *me*. It *is* the old fairy story, or a version of it, anyway. She knew exactly what we should be looking for. The stepmother in the tale tells a huntsman to go out and kill her daughter, right? And he's to send back a bottle of blood stoppered with her toe as proof she's dead.'

He frowned. 'Okay, I admit that's weird. I'd be careful how you tell Heath, though. He'll rip you a new one if he thinks you've been blabbing about the toe. And I'd give him half an hour, if I were you.' His thin-lipped expression gave way to a slow smile. 'Looks like they've got the bastard.'

'What?' Cate was startled. She had the evidence they needed to break this case. It was neat: it *worked*. It could be a real opening in her career – and it would give Chrissie Farrell the justice she deserved.

'It's Cosgrove,' Stocky said, settling back in his chair. 'He only lied about his alibi, didn't he? His wife's been in: seems he didn't go straight home that night – he didn't get back until the early hours. She couldn't give him away quick enough. Hell hath no fury like a woman scorned, and all that.' He relished this last, rolling the words around in his mouth.

Cate looked at him blankly. *Hell hath no fury* – yes, she

could understand that, but with Mrs Farrell in mind, not this Mrs Cosgrove. She remembered the woman who had brushed by her as she approached the station, her downcast eyes and sallow skin. Had that been the teacher's wife? She didn't look full of sound and fury – if anything, she had looked defeated.

'What do you mean, *a woman scorned*? Why'd she change her mind – has he admitted to seeing Chrissie?'

Stocky shrugged. 'Not yet,' he said, 'but the wife's certainly heard the rumours.'

Cate felt misgivings at that. As far as she knew, no one had managed to trace that particular story to its roots; even if it looked the most likely option, she didn't quite trust it. She looked at Stocky now, the satisfaction in his face, and wondered how far it was prompted by thoughts of his own children, the things he'd do to anyone who harmed them. But perhaps her own scepticism was just rooted in her desire to be the one whose instincts were right. *Vanity*. She sighed. Neither she nor Len Stockdale were important here, she had to remember that; the important thing was Chrissie Farrell. She drew a breath. 'So what now, Len? Are they bringing him in?'

'Oh, yes. Ostensibly it's to help with enquiries, but I'll wager he'll be feeling exceptionally helpful, if only to get round his wife.' He chuckled.

Cate glanced at the clock. She guessed they'd wait until Cosgrove was home before speaking to him. Plucking him out of a classroom wouldn't just be part of their investigation, it would be making a statement, and one that would probably land them with a harassment suit. Still, if anyone saw him getting into a police car it would probably be enough to finish his career for good. And if it *was* him—

I hope you're watching this now, Chrissie, wherever you are: watching with your eyes wide open.

The door to the incident room opened and Heath appeared. Cate caught his attention and he scowled, glanced at his watch. 'Five minutes,' he said, and retreated.

'Wish me luck.' Cate clutched the folder tightly and turned to follow the senior officer.

Heath glared down at Cate. He'd led her into his office, pointed her towards a chair, then remained standing while she recounted her findings so that she was forced to look up at him. She decided he'd probably done it on purpose. It didn't strike her that someone like Heath would do anything that wasn't deliberate.

He still didn't speak, and she wondered if he was waiting for her to say something else; but there was nothing else. She pressed her lips together and caught her hands between her knees to keep from fidgeting.

'Good investigating, PC Corbin,' the senior investigating officer said, slowly. He sighed. 'Kids' stories. Very good.'

Cate paused. 'The stories weren't really meant for kids. They're folk tales, really, some of the oldest stories known—'

He cut her off with a look. 'It *is* of interest,' he said, 'particularly the part about the toe.' He fell silent, and Cate realised it wasn't deliberate this time; he was thinking. 'You've heard we're watching Cosgrove?'

'Yes, sir.'

'But this could be important, possibly even the reason the killer singled her out: as you say, they could have known she was the one who was going to be the school beauty queen. Cosgrove might have had that information. It's more likely a simple case of sleeping with her and her threatening to tell, of course, but we need to follow up every lead. And he teaches English, I believe. So he might have had the knowledge.' He paused and looked at her, musing. 'Good work. Look, I'll be cutting back on uniforms before long – we won't need the numbers. But you should stay on this. I want you on attachment to CID. I'm going to request that you join the investigating team, at least for now.'

Cate stared at him. But he hated her, didn't he? She'd trampled all over the body dump site. The import of what he'd said struck her and she took a deep breath. It was a real case, real police work; she hadn't envisaged being involved with anything like it for years yet. She had a sudden image of herself locking up her flat for the last time and moving on to something new.

'Thank you, sir.' She tried to keep from smiling. Then she remembered Len Stockdale sitting outside, his gruff cynicism when he talked of CID, the barely concealed excitement when he'd seen Chrissie Farrell's body. *Here first.* There had been that note of triumph in his voice. And there was his certainty when he spoke of *vanity*, of some loner who couldn't bear to see a young girl in her heels and make-up. Now she would be on the case, following up her ideas, while he continued with the same old routine.

But Heath hadn't finished. 'I want you to suggest some lines of questioning – to me this time, please, not DI Grainger.' He let that sink in. 'I've got someone picking up Cosgrove, but at least for the time being he's "helping with enquiries" – he misled us on an alibi, that's all, and there are a dozen reasons he might have done that. We need more before we can make a collar. Unless he cracks under the pressure and 'fesses up, of course.' The corner of his mouth twitched.

Cate nodded. Maybe he would crack under the pressure, not just from the police, but from his wife: *Hell hath no fury*.

The door opened and a voice spoke directly behind her. 'Sir, there's been another one.'

'Another what?'

'A body, sir, dumped in the woods. Another girl. It's a different location, but it sounds like it could be connected.'

'Shit.' Heath let out his breath in a long hiss.

Cate got to her feet. It was one of Heath's detective constables standing there – she thought his name was Paulson. He glanced at her, looked away again.

'Same place? Same MO?'

'Not quite, sir, but it sounds like it's another weird one – she may have been posed, like the other girl. This one's deeper in the woods – a place called Newmillerdam. It's a few miles from the first.'

'You know the place?' Heath asked Cate.

She nodded. 'I just came from there. It's—'

'Then you're with me.'

'Boss?' Paulson's tone was incredulous.

Heath silenced him with a look. 'And hurry up. We want to get there before the press start trampling all over it, not to mention the bloody ramblers.'

He paused and Cate thought at once of her own trampling over the first site. She expected him to make some sarcastic comment, but he didn't.

'Well, Cate? This is your chance. You in or not?'

But she didn't move. 'It's not that, sir – what about Cosgrove?'

'All in hand. Paulson, you're staying. Cosgrove will be in before long – DI Grainger leads, understand? I want you to get into his ribs, concentrate on the evening of the dance, where he went, what he did, when he did it – and what the hell he was doing when he said he was back home with the wife. And take your time. Got that?'

Paulson nodded, but he didn't speak. His skin looked a shade paler. Cate felt his gaze on her back as she followed the SIO from the room, walking past the desk where Len

Stockdale was still sitting. She gave him a brief nod. His eyes were narrowed, and he showed no sign of acknowledging her at all.

CHAPTER TEN

Newmillerdam was directly between the estate where Angie Farrell lived and the road to the Heronry where her daughter had been found. The name applied alike to a small village and the lake by which it stood. Unlike the spot on the road where the Farrell girl had been found, the route through Newmillerdam was relatively busy: the A61 cut between the waterside and the village, giving drivers a view of the lake surrounded by trees. Nestled at the waterside was a small, decorative boathouse, built in the nineteenth century so the upper classes could enjoy the view while hunting and fishing. There was a pub at each end of the lakeside stretch of road, and at one side there was a large car park. At weekends it would be thronged; now it was about a third full, and Cate recognised a few of the vehicles huddled together close to the trees. Beyond them, the car park led directly onto the path that wound around the lake. That was the route most visitors took: a wide, even footway ideally suited to mothers with prams or pensioners out for a gentle stroll.

Heath swept into a parking space and yanked on the handbrake, ignoring the pained squeal of cabling. He got out without a word, already focused on the harassed-looking PC standing at the edge of the trees. 'That way?' He jabbed an outstretched finger towards a narrow, over-grown path that Cate had barely noticed. The PC nodded and stepped aside and he stalked past, hissing over his shoulder, 'Ask for ID next time.'

Cate followed him, and immediately brambles clawed at her ankles. This path was nothing but a dirt line between swathes of livid undergrowth encroaching upon the little piece of ground between them. She could hear traffic on the road quite clearly still, and yet the tall, stately trees rising all around her held a sense of presence that made it seem distant. Cate almost felt, if she listened hard enough, she would be able to hear them breathe.

Then she heard another sound, not one she would have expected in this quiet place: someone up ahead barking, 'Clear the area, please.' An elderly couple came into view, darting looks back over their shoulders. Heath stood aside to let them go, and they stared at him before continuing towards the car park.

'There are other pathways coming into this area,' said Cate. 'You can head into the woods from pretty much anywhere around the lake. You wouldn't need to take a path, not if you knew where you were going. It'll be a nightmare to secure.'

Heath didn't answer. Between the trees, white shapes were moving: scene-of-crime officers, 'SOCOs', wearing protective overalls to avoid contamination. Heath registered their presence at the site and checked on progress. The doctor had already left, having certified death, and the photographers were just finishing, releasing the scene to the SOCOs. He grabbed a couple of the white suits and threw one to Cate. As she pulled it on he jerked his head: *Hurry up.*

Heath strode on ahead, up a wooded slope, and they emerged into a large, flat clearing where the trees, a mix of native oak, ash and birch, had recently been felled. The ground was littered with a mass of tangled branches and broken twigs merging with long-dead bracken. Here and there stood young trees, each surrounded by a little fence with a sign at its foot: HOLM OAK, GOLDEN HOLLY, SNAKE-BARK MAPLE. On the very edge of the clearing was a bench ornately carved with the word ARBORETUM. It was a collection of trees amid the trees, an open air museum for unusual specimens to be cultivated. Cate had heard about this new arboretum; somewhere close by was an older one that had gradually been subsumed by the main woodland. She noticed some of the local tree wardens were standing around the edge. From the look on their faces, she guessed they had found the body.

The SOCOs were in the middle of the arboretum, up to

their knees in old wood. They were trying to erect a tent around the place, but were being hampered by the little fallen branches, and it wasn't yet covered. Heath got as close as he could, and Cate followed in his wake. There was a flash of red on the ground: *blood?* Another step and she could smell something sweetish and unpleasant. The brief buzz of a fly was lost beneath Heath's low whistle and she went to his side.

At first she couldn't make sense of it. For a moment she thought there was blood everywhere, then she realised it wasn't blood at all: it was a red cape, half covering a young girl who was lying on her side, her face turned towards the ground. Her hair was hidden under a hood drawn up over her head. This time the similarity to a fairy tale was inescapable: it was Little Red Riding Hood lying amid the fallen trees, her eyes turned away from whatever she had found there.

Cate's gaze went to the girl's arms. Where they emerged from the cape there was something bright, an unnatural sheen, and she caught her breath. The skin below the elbow had been ravaged; there were specks of blood, and everywhere, what looked like metal pins had been pushed into the flesh.

'Jesus.' Heath bent down, peering at the body, and Cate took a deep breath and forced herself to concentrate. The resemblance to a fairy-tale character was obvious, reinforced by the old-fashioned wicker basket that lay just beyond the reach of the girl's hand. She was Little Red, taking gifts to Grandmother; the basket's contents were covered with a red-and-white checked cloth; a half-crumbled loaf of bread jutted from it along with the neck of a bottle. For a moment Cate wondered if it too was filled with blood, but it was larger than the one that had been sent to Chrissie's mother. Then she saw it was a wine bottle, and the foil seal was intact. Next to the girl's body, these things looked incongruously domestic. Breadcrumbs were scattered around the basket and she wondered if birds had been drawn to the feast. She hoped they hadn't started on the girl's body.

She leaned in and looked at Little Red's face. This girl didn't look anything like Chrissie Farrell. Even under the pall of death, Cate could see that she was gaunt, with the fine lines around her lips that betrayed a habitual smoker. Her face was bruised, unless it was some sort of discoloration. And unlike Chrissie's, her eyes were closed. There was something else that struck Cate as being different, too: she knew she had seen something without really taking it in. She looked back at the girl's arms, studying them more closely this time, and she saw it: beneath the crusted blood from the pins were marks that were older still. Then it was obvious: she had the track marks of a drug user. And her thinness – no, this was no Chrissie Farrell. Chrissie had been healthful, beautiful, cared for. This girl was not.

Heath's voice broke into her thoughts. 'Christ,' he said, 'talk about fairy tales, Cate. So what killed her, do you think? Is there a big bad wolf around here somewhere, or did story time at the library just get seriously out of hand?'

Cate never got the chance to answer; one of the SOCOs stepped forward and took hold of the edge of the girl's cape. He raised it, and Cate saw there was blood after all, getting tacky where it had been exposed to the light. A fly crawled from beneath the fabric and lifted itself into the air as the SOCO turned the cloak back further.

Cate took a deep breath and instantly regretted it. The smell was stronger now, pervading everything, embedding itself deep in her throat.

The girl's belly had been torn open – that was why it smelled so strongly. The stomach contents had spilled amid the entrails, and there was more blood, gelatinous and bright, and the pale gleam of fat. Amongst everything were yellow-white blowfly larvae, clustered like balls of sticky rice.

The SOCO let the cloak fall back again.

Cate looked up to find Heath's eyes fixed on her. 'Feel all right, Corbin?'

She was surprised he'd asked; she nodded. Yes, she was all right: it was bad, but on the face of it, she had seen worse. It was what lay beneath this scene that was disturbing, like something stirring the surface of dark water.

'I think you'd better get your expert down here.' Heath's voice was unexpectedly quiet. 'We're going to need her to take a look. ASAP.'

Cate stared at him. She remembered the way Alice Hyland had reached for the photograph of Chrissie Farrell's body, obviously not liking to touch it; her reluctance, as if the paper itself was tainted.

'No time to be squeamish, Cate,' he said, as though reading her mind. 'It's no good waiting for reports or photographs. If she can help, she needs to do so fast.' He nodded towards the path. 'Go and find a uniform, get them to fetch her.' He met her eye. 'I'm going to want you to stay on-site.'

CHAPTER ELEVEN

Alice was staring into her mirror when she heard someone banging on the door. She jumped, startled. She had been whispering something under her breath, barely conscious of what it was. Now she realised: *Mirror, mirror*, she had been saying. She hadn't been able to get Chrissie Farrell out of her mind since she'd seen the policewoman's photograph: the fairest of them all, with her wan skin and pale eyes, staring up at nothing. She shuddered, suddenly reluctant to answer the door. Inside, her fairy tales stayed where they belonged, close and yet distant: *safe*. In order to reach their magic Alice had only to open a book. The things that Cate Corbin had shown her . . . She frowned. She knew the tales had their own power, but to see them intrude on reality in that way . . . she didn't want to think about it. She didn't want to know who was knocking at her door. She stood there, staring into the mirror, brushing back her pale blonde hair.

Then the banging came again, *blam-blam-blam*, and she

knew she couldn't ignore it. If she had ever had a choice about becoming involved, it had vanished when Cate put the dead girl's picture into her hand.

It wasn't Cate at the door. This time it was a policeman standing there, glancing over his shoulder as if impatient to be gone. Alice's eyes narrowed. 'What is it?' Her voice came out harshly, making her think for a moment of the rooks that lived in the woods at the back of the house.

He frowned. The skin around his eyes was raw-looking, as if he hadn't slept in a long time. He introduced himself as PC Nicholls. 'Ms Hyland, we need your help, if you're willing,' he said. 'There's something we need you to look at.'

Alice was silent as the policeman eased the car down the lane and turned onto the main road. She couldn't take in what it was he wanted. The silence was awkward, and she felt he was waiting for her questions: where were they going, exactly? What was it he wanted her to see? She didn't ask anything. After Cate's earlier visit, she didn't want to know. She stared out of the window, only half conscious of their whereabouts as they headed past Newmillerdam Lake. A stab of sunshine found its way through the clouds and reflected back from the water. The day which had begun so clear had changed, and paleness closed over the blue like scar tissue. She looked at the wing-mirror on her side of the car and saw the faint outline of her face layered beneath another reflection, of the clouds overhead. It made her feel like a ghost. The fissure where the sun shone through blanked out half of her forehead and her left eye, and she shuddered.

The car slowed and the policeman flicked on the indicator. They hadn't even left the lakeside; she had thought they would be going further, the Heronry perhaps, somewhere else not so close to home.

Everything happened quickly then: he pulled in near an unmarked van. The rear doors were open and someone was sitting on the baseboard, easing white overalls up their legs. A uniformed policewoman was standing at the edge of the woods, watching their arrival.

Alice just sat there while PC Nicholls got out. Her limbs felt heavy, almost as if she were being pushed down into her seat. She glanced at her reflection again: *Mirror, mirror*. Then her door opened and the officer was there, waiting for her to step out, and after a moment, Alice did. She suddenly wanted to ask all the questions he'd no doubt been expecting earlier and she opened her mouth, but he was already turning towards the trees. Alice looked up and saw their dark crowns, heard their soughing as a breeze caught the topmost branches. It occurred to her that she could have refused to come – they surely couldn't have made her – but now it was too late. She followed him, passing into the cool shadow of the trees.

Everything felt dreamlike, as if she had stepped into the pages of some story, and not one of her choosing. The policeman gave her white overalls to put on and took her name and details and added them to a register. Seeing it being written down made it worse somehow, as if this must really be happening.

She took the unfamiliar clothing in her arms and the strange fabric rustled and slid under her fingers. The policeman gestured impatiently and she started to pull it on over her clothes. She found two smaller pieces among the material; she didn't know what to do with them until she saw the policeman pulling similar items over his shoes. She did the same, relieved she didn't have to ask.

She heard voices and looked up to see two people in identical white suits coming towards them through the trees. Oddly, being dressed the same way made her feel more out of place. The newcomers stopped to exchange a few words with the policeman she was with and ignored Alice. She caught the words 'something in her mouth'.

PC Nicholls shot a glance towards her. 'Now, please,' he said, his voice pinched, and led her uphill. Alice looked at her feet, saw the clinical white overalls brushing past bursts of red campion and clusters of woodruff. She thought back to the morning she'd opened her eyes to the sound of birdsong; the way she had known, deep inside, that springtime had come. Then the wood opened out into an odd place, where the trees grew behind fences and the ground was scattered with old wood.

The policeman led the way towards a group of people in the centre of the clearing. There was a bad smell, nothing she could identify; her mind didn't want to register what might be the cause. The officer stood back to let her see.

There was a body lying on the ground. It was at once real and unreal, a figure she knew as well as her own face: a girl in a blood-red cape lying next to the basket she was carrying to her grandmother.

Alice closed her eyes and shook the image away. Instead, she caught another glimpse of that springtime morning when she'd awakened and known that something new was about to begin; the blue bird flying at her with its wings outstretched.

She blinked. One of the white figures stepped towards her and with a start, Alice recognised Cate. She didn't say anything, and when Alice glanced about, she noticed the other people dotted around the figure on the ground were all watching her, waiting for a reaction, for her to do or say something that would make everything begin again. But how could she make sense of something that didn't make any sense?

Alice didn't want to see their eyes on her any longer, so she looked back at the girl on the ground. The cloak was so bright it was violent against the dull greens and browns of the earth, like an illustration from a book, everything a little too clear, too vivid. And it was all a little *too* right. Even the basket by the girl's side was exactly as it should be, the arch of the handle, the checked cloth covering the contents. Now Alice had begun to notice the detail, she couldn't take her eyes from it. She edged closer; the smell grew worse and she made a choking sound in the back of her throat and stepped away again.

'Take your time,' said Cate.

Alice just stood there, her hand over her mouth. Nobody moved and nobody spoke; there was silence, save for the silvery sound of foliage stirring in the breeze.

Surely Alice had nothing to give; this scene must be obvious to anyone. There didn't appear to be any hidden signs, nothing obscure like in the photographs of Snow White. No one could possibly mistake it for anything else. *Red in tooth and claw*, she thought. She had said it before, many times, but had she really believed it? She forced herself to look at the body again, suddenly glad she couldn't see the dead girl's eyes. She could see her arms, though, and when she looked at them, really *looked* at them, it sent a shock through her.

'They're pins,' Cate said, and Alice realised she was standing at her shoulder.

'No,' Alice said slowly, 'I don't think they are.' Despite her reluctance she leaned closer, wanting to be sure. 'No, they're not pins. They're needles.' Each silver point was tipped by a narrow eye.

'She chose a path,' said Alice, backing away, 'in the story. Little Red was sent into the woods by her mother, taking some food – it varies from version to version, sometimes it's a pot of butter or bread and milk, in others cake and wine. Instead, she encounters the wolf. He asks which way she's going to the grandmother's house and he makes sure he gets there first. Little Red has to choose from the path of pins or the path of needles.'

Her eyes narrowed. The girl looked so thin – it made her look so vulnerable. She was glad the cloak was covering much of her body, keeping her face half hidden. But her arms – the needles had caught her attention first, masking what lay beneath. Was the skin there bruised from what had been done to her, or was it more than that?

She took a breath and held it, moved closer to the girl and bent down so she could see her face. She told herself it wasn't so bad, but she had to steal a small breath, and that *was* bad.

The girl's skin had paled in death – at least, she *thought* it was that – but wasn't there a faint bruise underlying the shadow of her cheekbone? This girl didn't look like some fairy-tale princess, she wasn't like the first: someone's daughter or granddaughter who had been cherished. She hadn't been crowned, hadn't been honoured, she wasn't the queen of anything.

She glanced back at the track marks on her arms before stepping away. It looked as if this girl had chosen the path of needles long ago.

Cate stood at her side and prompted Alice with questions as they stood at the edge of the clearing. Alice kept her eyes fixed on the trees; she didn't want to see that body any more, or watch what they did to her, what indignities she still had to suffer. She tried to tell herself that it wasn't real, any of it, but Cate's questions intruded, making her realise that it was. Her sense of dislocation remained.

She wanted to go home, to turn her back on this and pretend she'd never seen it.

'The way she's been left looks more obvious this time,' Cate said. 'No one would take it for anything else. Anyone can see it's a fairy tale.'

Alice drew a deep breath. 'You know, you're right. I'm really not sure you need me any more.'

'There must be things he's done that could give us some indication of what he's thinking – don't forget, we don't know these stories like you do. We might miss even obvious things that you would see at once. And this has all been done deliberately, the placing of each little thing. That took forethought, planning.'

Alice remained silent.

'The thing about the pins – what did you say it meant?'

'They aren't pins,' said Alice. Her voice was faint. 'They're needles.'

It was Cate's turn to be silent. Someone standing nearby shuffled their feet and Alice realised a man was watching them. She felt Cate's hand on her arm and she took a deep breath. The air was mercifully clean.

'The path of needles and the path of pins,' she started. 'When Little Red Riding Hood meets the wolf – or the *bzou*, the werewolf – he wants to race her to the grandmother's house. She can choose which path to take. There's a lot of disagreement about what the path of needles or the path of pins signifies, or even if it means anything at all.' She paused. 'There is one interesting interpretation, though.'

'Which is?'

'Some people think it can be seen as a choice between sexual maturity and innocence.' Alice took another deep breath. 'The story was shaped by retellings throughout rural France before Perrault wrote it down in the late seventeenth century. Oral storytelling was a female tradition, and female work – sewing, spinning, weaving – often cropped up in the imagery.

'Back then, girls who reached puberty were often sent to spend a winter with the seamstress, though not just to learn sewing skills; it was about learning refinement, kind of a finishing school. They called this "gathering pins". When they had finished, they could accept a sweetheart, who would often give pins as gifts.

'On the other hand, threading the eye of a needle was seen as a sexual symbol. In some regions, prostitutes even wore needles on their sleeves as a way of advertising themselves.'

Cate shifted her feet. 'So this girl—?'

'She could be a prostitute. I suppose that part's up to you. Of course, the red of the cloak can be seen as a symbol of sin or sexuality. Little Red is an innocent who chooses the wrong path, or leaves it altogether.'

Both of them fell silent.

'He didn't kill her with the needles.' The voice was loud, intruding on Alice's thoughts, and she turned to see the man who'd been watching them earlier.

'This is the senior investigating officer,' said Cate, 'Detective Superintendent Heath.'

He nodded at Alice. 'So what did she die of, in these stories of yours?'

'It varies. In some versions, particularly the earliest, she doesn't die at all but uses her own wiles to escape. In the better-known ones, though, she gets to the grandmother's house and the wolf is waiting for her. He's eaten the old woman and now he wants to eat the girl. He gets her to take off her clothes and burn them in the fire, since she won't be needing them again.'

'And then he eats her,' said Cate.

Alice sighed. 'Mostly, yes, the wolf gets her in the end.'

'He certainly got her this time,' said Heath, and then added, more quietly, 'There's no need for you to see that.'

Alice grimaced. 'You know, some would suggest that her death is her punishment for leaving the path, for being disobedient.' She frowned. 'Some of the stories stressed that as their moral. I wonder why she was left out here, though? Little Red has to go through the forest, the deep dark of the trees. It's odd that she wasn't left further in the woods. But then, I suppose it makes a certain amount of sense – the fallen woman among the fallen trees.'

Heath let out a breath. 'On the other hand, it may just have been because he wanted the body to be found. This place is a work in progress – there must be wardens about most days, although they didn't spot her until now.' He gestured around the clearing. 'That could mean he has local knowledge. The first dump site – that might have been someone driving around, trying to find somewhere quiet. This time he's thought about it, been more organised.' He paused. 'Thank you, Ms Hyland. Cate, if there's nothing else, we need to get this screened off properly before the press descend. And we need to organise a search of the rest of the clearing.'

Alice didn't move. 'Didn't someone say there was something in her mouth?'

'Where did you hear that?' Heath snapped. He glared at Cate, and Alice realised someone had spoken out of turn: like the bottle stoppered with a girl's toe, it was another of those details meant to be withheld. She opened her mouth to say it hadn't been Cate who'd told her; closed it again when she saw his expression. There was something in his eyes that didn't brook being questioned.

'If your theories hold true,' Heath said, 'perhaps you could tell us what it was.' He shot a glance at Cate. 'If no one's told you already.'

Alice noticed that Cate too opened her mouth to speak, but she didn't say anything either.

'I don't know what it could be,' she said. 'There's nothing left in her mouth in the story. She's the one who's eaten, in fact, by the wolf. She does sometimes eat what the wolf leaves for her, though, when she arrives at her grandmother's.' She paused to collect her thoughts.

'All right: first of all, the wolf beats Little Red to the cottage. He eats the grandmother, but he doesn't eat all of her; he saves a little of her flesh and puts it in the pantry, and he drains some of her blood into a bottle—'

She broke off and they stared at each other.

'When he's done that and the girl arrives, the wolf tells her to eat, so she finds the things he's left for her, and eats part of her grandmother – a cannibalistic meal. In some variants he fries the grandmother's ears and pretends they're fritters. That's the Italian version again, I think. Always interesting, the Italian versions.'

Heath gestured for her to continue.

'The other thing she's given in that version is the grandmother's teeth. He boils them in a pot and pretends they're beans. I never really understood that – it'd be pretty hard to fool anyone beyond the first mouthful.' She saw the expression on Heath's face. 'Ah. Well, that's odd. I wonder where he got the teeth from?'

'Never mind about that,' said Heath.

Alice knew he wasn't dismissing her words; this man took in everything, even when giving the impression it was beneath his notice.

Cate was focused on Heath, her look purposeful. He motioned her aside and started to talk in low tones, words Alice couldn't catch. They moved further away; they appeared to have forgotten her. She kept looking into the trees. She didn't want to turn and walk across the clearing again, to see the body that was lying there. If she did, would the policeman who'd brought her here even still be around, let alone be prepared to drive her home again?

She looked about, keeping her gaze away from the patch of red. Other officers were closing in and she watched as they resumed their work. One of them looked up and narrowed his eyes, staring at her as if wondering why she was still there. Alice looked away.

It looked as if Cate and Heath had come to some kind of decision; they headed off towards the far side of the clearing, leaving Alice alone. The trees weren't far away; there was a narrow path leading roughly towards the lake. It wasn't the way she'd come, but at least it would take her away from here, and from the things she'd seen – the things she'd *smelled*. It would take her home. She longed suddenly for her cottage, its safety, its warmth. If she was there, she could forget; everything would be all right.

In the next moment she was walking away and into the trees, entering their shade. She felt better at once. She did not look back, nor did she wait for anyone to notice that she was leaving.

When Alice was halfway down the hill, her legs began to shake. She stopped walking and leaned against a tree, then stood there, staring at her arm. She was still wearing the white overalls the policeman had given her. She didn't know why it had come as a shock to realise it now; she only knew that even though she'd been able to see it all the time, had heard the rustle of it, she somehow hadn't taken it in. She started to peel the stuff off, pulling free of it, until she was just Alice once more. When she saw it lying bright and artificial against the green she realised she couldn't just leave it there. If the police found it, it could lead to all kinds of mistaken suspicions, couldn't it? She should give it back, to Cate maybe, not one of those others who had stared at her. She gathered it up, wadding it into a tight ball, carrying it with her.

She caught a glimpse of water somewhere below, the light striking silver from the flat grey surface. She was completely alone now, and for the first time she realised she might be out in the woods with a killer: someone who knew this place, who had walked the same paths she had. Strangely, though, she didn't feel afraid. It was all so unreal. She felt like a character from one of her books, straying from the path, but safe in the knowledge that all of this was nothing but a story. The real Alice was no doubt far away, wrapped in a blanket in her favourite chair, drinking something warming, enclosed within the walls of her own home. She couldn't possibly be here, having walked away from the police like that. She couldn't possibly have seen the things she'd seen.

Alice closed her eyes. Was that how someone had done this to that girl in the clearing? – by not seeing her as real, only a character, to be torn and broken? That must be how they had taken her, pushed needles into her skin. And then what? She didn't want to think of it any more. It made her wonder how the girl had died, and how badly.

He didn't kill her with the needles.

Alice shivered and went on. She was almost at the

lakeside path – she could see the sandy gravel through the trees – when she saw the bird.

Once she had seen it, she wondered how she had failed to notice it before. It was the only bright thing amid the trees. It sat on a low branch, and it was looking at her. She recognised its small shining eyes, the brilliant blue feathers. It did not take fright and fly away, or even move; it simply sat and watched her, as though waiting for something. Alice wasn't sure she liked it – but of course it would see her as a threat; it was only natural that it should stare at her like that.

The bird rose from its perch, spread its bright wings and flew. It landed a short distance away and began to sing.

Alice didn't even think about what she was doing: she followed.

The trees closed in around her. Tall beech had given way to silver birch, the spindly trunks scabbed and surrounded by whip-like branches. Somewhere the breeze sighed, causing the trees' limbs to tremble. Alice kept her eyes on the bird, which fluttered onwards, always keeping a little way ahead. It was heading around the hillside, not down towards the lake or up towards the clearing. It was becoming harder to push through the branches now, and the bird was getting away from her. Alice could see it only in brief splashes of colour, but its intense, pure song drew her on. The wood was quiet and dark and Alice was alone, and it was strangely peaceful, being away from everything and everyone. This place was unreal, a place where no one could hurt her or force her to see things she didn't want to look at. It felt as if the wood belonged to her and her alone.

Belying her reverie, a dog's loud bark cut into the day. Alice jumped and put a hand to her chest; told herself it was only a dog, nothing out of the ordinary. The harsh bark came again and Alice realised that it was somewhere close, and that its body must be big, to make such a sound. Then she saw it pushing through the undergrowth, a solid black creature, its tongue lolling from its jaws. A voice followed it through the trees, an ordinary man's voice, calling, 'Here, boy!'

Alice remained motionless. The dog had stopped too, its legs braced, its small eyes fixed on her. After a moment it rustled away.

Alice looked around for the bird, but it had already gone, and her sense of calm had gone with it. She didn't feel safe any more. She didn't want to see the man with the dog, and she didn't want him to see her. She edged away, not liking to turn her back, then, as soon as she had gained some distance, she turned downhill once more. It wasn't long before she reached the lakeside path and stepped from the soft earth onto a level surface.

A family was walking towards her, a mother and father and a little girl waving a stick. They looked happy, and Alice guessed they were just ending their walk; they probably hadn't even heard about what had been found such a short distance away. They had a dog, too, but it wasn't the one she had seen; it was small and white and wagging its plume of a tail as it rooted out new smells. The child gave an excited cry as a mallard splashed down into the water, and the father pulled a bag from his pocket and handed her a slice of bread.

Alice turned in the other direction. A man was standing on the path, looking at her. He was about her height, and hunched solidly in a warm coat. He was wearing binoculars around his neck. 'Excuse me, miss,' he said, 'sorry to trouble you.' His voice was thin and dry, like the physics teacher Alice had had when she was in school. She didn't approach him. It was odd, but now she was standing on an open path, in clear view of anyone walking around the lake, she was wary. As if he sensed her unease, he didn't approach either.

'I'm looking for a bird,' he said, touching one hand to his binoculars. 'It's a very special bird. I'm sorry to disturb your walk, but I saw you come out of the woods and I wondered if you'd seen it.' He pushed his glasses further up his nose. 'It's very rare, you see. I was hoping to catch a glimpse.'

Alice opened her mouth to ask a question, though she already knew the answer. She asked it anyway, because she wanted time to think: 'What does it look like?'

'Oh – forgive me. I get so tied up in – it's blue, you see. Very unusual. You'd know it at once if you saw it.' He licked his thin lips, lifted his glasses away from his watery brown eyes.

She hesitated. The blue bird had come to *her*, she was sure of it. It had *revealed* itself to her. She found herself shaking her head.

'Oh, what a shame. My colleagues were so sure— Well, never mind. They just thought— Well. You never know when, do you? You can't name the hour. Perhaps I'll see it tomorrow.'

Alice nodded, *yes, of course he might see it*; but she somehow didn't think he would. It was a secret thing, *her* bird, a sight meant for her and her alone. As the man waved and headed towards the car park, she wondered if it would come back later; whether it would sit in her apple tree, looking at her as she watched it from her window, singing in her garden.

It wasn't until she started to follow the birdwatcher, matching her pace to his, that she saw the police cordon at the end of the path. There was an officer there wearing a bright tabard, and he was questioning a man who held a large black dog on a tight leash.

'Of course I'm fine,' Alice said. Her nerves had failed her when she'd seen the officer was the same young policeman who'd brought her to Newmillerdam, what felt like hours ago. He was questioning anyone emerging from the path, taking their details and writing them in yet another register. 'I thought they'd finished, and the person I was with – Cate Corbin – she went off with that other man.

Her boss.' Alice held out the overalls she carried, and the policeman stared down at them.

There were other walkers behind her now, shuffling their feet with impatience as they waited for their turn to leave. The twitcher who'd spoken to her earlier was among them. She wasn't quite sure how she'd passed him. He must have stopped, watching the ducks maybe, or sitting on a bench while she'd gone past in a daze. As soon as she'd seen the policeman everything came back: the girl lying in the wood with no life in her, no way to go home again. Alice glanced across the lake and up the hill. Behind those trees, her own home awaited. Its rooms were warm, its walls comforting.

The policeman asked her to stand aside while the others went through. They each had to give their name, and she saw the birdwatcher waving his binoculars at the end of their strap. 'Oh yes,' he was saying, 'considerable excitement.' Alice presumed he was talking of the blue bird rather than the murder, although when she looked across the car park she saw people gathering there, milling at the edge of the road, whispering to each other. Considerable excitement, indeed. The dead girl in the woods would be the talk of the area for years. If people knew Alice had seen the body they would probably camp out on her doorstep to hear her story. And all the girl would be known as would be Red Riding Hood or Little Red, her own name forgotten; unwittingly and unwillingly she would be placed at the heart of stories of her own, new stories, mutating and growing each time they were told, just as the folk tales originally had.

At least the birdwatcher didn't appear to care, and nor did the man with the dog, or anyone else; they were already leaving, heading away towards the car park or along the road. The policeman turned back to her and offered to get someone to take her home, and she muttered that it didn't matter; she would make her own way back. A wave of exhaustion washed over her. At least for now, she was finished: no more police dragging her into things that didn't concern her, showing her things she didn't want to see. She put her head down and walked away, following the road, just another walker heading towards home.

CHAPTER TWELVE

Alice woke early. For a while she lay there and stared at the ceiling, but that wasn't what she was seeing. It was as if her mind hadn't yet adjusted from the sights and impressions of the day before; images rose before her eyes, faded and were replaced with others, none of them pleasant. She got up and put her hand to her head. A thought occurred to her and she caught her breath, rushed downstairs in her bare feet, checked the front door and then the back. She stayed there leaning against the cold, hard wood, and shook her head. Of course she'd locked it, she probably didn't even have any need to lock it. The things she'd seen . . . they didn't happen, not really, hardly ever. Not outside stories.

She looked around the familiar kitchen. The walls were pale yellow and sunshine slid down them in buttery streaks. It was all right. Her things were exactly where she had left them, the world was behaving itself again, everything in its place. Everything was still out of kilter, though; her home was still here, but it felt as if she herself had changed. She still had that sense of dislocation she'd felt in the woods.

When she turned to the window, she saw the sky had broken. The grey sheet that had stretched over the woods the day before was shattered, slashed with light; the tops of the trees were in constant movement, sending back golden glimmers. It was right that it had changed, right that the woods should echo her mood when her own sweet cottage did not.

Alice sighed. She flicked the switch on the kettle, heard the hiss and crackle of the element doing its work, though she already knew she'd never be able to sit and relax over a cup of tea. She saw her satchel in its usual place in the corner, a foreign object. It was fat with assignments from her latest class. She had several days before she had to hand them back, but she could at least make a start, let the day pass in familiar and comforting activity.

Alice quickly showered and dressed before sitting down at the kitchen table with a mug of camomile at her side. She picked up the papers and leafed through them. The assignment had been on gender in fairy tales, the roles women take for themselves or are given: the wicked stepmother; the innocent, usually dead, real mother; the youngest daughter, beautiful and destined to have everything. The ugly sister, who was not. Alice grimaced, wondering whether Chrissie Farrell would be dead now if she had been born ugly. She pushed the thought away. Fairy tales were hers: *hers*. She couldn't let the things she had seen ruin them for her. She had loved them since she was a little girl, listening to the stories at her mother's knee. Her mother, who couldn't always remember what Alice looked like when she came to visit now. She sighed. She often wondered who her mother thought she was, what impressions she formed of her, when each time she saw her was like the first.

Now it was Alice who told her mother stories; they were all she could offer, recounted incidents from the years they'd spent together, the funny and the dramatic and the inconsequential and the sad all mixed up together, hoping they would connect with something in her mind and make her *remember*, because her mother's memories were gone, and with them part of her life. The reality of their days had been turned into nothing but words, and she never knew if her mother really understood or believed them.

It was something else she didn't want to think about. She took one of the papers from the pile. Ironically, it was Larissa Horbury's, a girl destined to have everything if ever there was one: she was blonde, pretty, confident, and she knew the world belonged to her. Her work was entirely unoriginal. Alice pushed her essay aside and found another, this one printed on mauve paper, the student's name hand-written with fanciful circles dotting every 'i'. Alice found herself staring at the wall. Had it become so routine so quickly, this class? And yet, shouldn't that be a comfort to her now?

She forced herself to read a couple of lines. Fairy tales stripped, wrapped, assigned a time and a place, analysed and finally put away in a box, transformed into a number, 57 per cent perhaps, or 65.

The second dead girl's face flashed into Alice's mind and she shook her head. Death wasn't like that in fairy tales, not really. Heads were chopped off clean. There was no blood spatter, no DNA. And it was never difficult to find the killer; everyone knew who was the witch, who the princess – they showed it on their faces, the evil displayed in ugliness or disfigurement, the maidens always beautiful and good, retaining their looks even when they were dead.

Alice frowned. That had made her think of Snow White. Perhaps she was turning into a detective after all, making connections she hadn't consciously thought of? She closed her eyes and thought of Chrissie Farrell, her beautiful face. In the story, Snow White had been so beautiful the huntsman had decided not to kill her, but it hadn't been that way for the girl. The real Chrissie was frozen now, alive only in photographs – *Who is the fairest of them all?* – and cameras, like mirrors, tell only the truth. Chrissie, youthful and lovely, had been crowned at the dance. She would stay beautiful for ever now, never grow old like her mother or her friends, never lose her looks: a life caught behind a glass picture frame instead of a glass coffin.

The immortal beauty: a heavenly ideal for any prince. Love was never in the offing for Snow White, not really, at least until everyone believed her to be dead. Lovely to look upon and never answering back. Alice wrinkled her nose. What she saw in her mind's eye, though, was another girl, clothed in the red of spilled blood, lying helpless and lifeless amid the fallen trees: the girl given over to the way of needles, who had wandered so far from the path she never would find her way back. But what was she trying to tell her? What had the killer meant to say? Alice thought back to the crime-scene photographs that had been spread on this very table when this all began. The beauty queen – Chrissie – had had her eyes wide open, staring up as if to meet someone's gaze, her dead beauty left to be seen and admired. Perhaps the killer too had wanted admiration: *Look. This is what I can do.* Little Red had been different, her face downturned as if in shame, a bad girl to the end.

The beauty queen and the whore. Had the roles been forced upon them?

How many variants of these tales had there been since the beginning of the world? And now these girls – displayed for others to find them and draw their own conclusions – they were variants too, intended for their stories to be deduced, puzzled over, teased from them.

She pushed the papers aside. This wasn't helping. In the past she'd loved to unearth the early tales, the ones steeped in violence and intensity; she'd always discerned a certain wild magic in their rawness. Now she had a pang of nostalgia for the clean, sanitised versions, the pastel-painted fables that said girls who don't stray from the path won't get eaten. Chrissie Farrell didn't appear to have done anything to deserve her fate other than to be beautiful. Little Red—

Little Red. Had the second victim really been a prostitute? It didn't fit the image of the kind of fairy tale most people would know. Alice closed her eyes and thought of her own image of the character: not so much beautiful as cheekily pretty, black curls framing apple cheeks and shining eyes. And her mother, standing in a doorway, bending to kiss her daughter's face and straighten her hood. Little Red skipping towards the deep black forest, where danger lurked and wolves walked as men. A *red* hood.

It struck Alice now that she'd at least have dressed her child in something that might pass beneath notice. Instead she'd been sent into the forest in a red cloak that would mark her out like a spotlight: the wood that was full of beasts and huntsmen and madness and things hidden in the dark, waiting for innocent flesh, ready to feast on blood and kisses alike. Or perhaps she wouldn't have sent her at all. Why send her daughter to such a place? She could have gone herself, sent her father or a woodsman, anyone except Little Red.

No, it was the mother who had sent her child away, with only a few words to protect her: *Don't leave the path*.

But surely she had already known what Little Red was going to do: she had known it as soon as she called out those words and planted the idea in her mind.

CHAPTER THIRTEEN

The incident room was full for the early briefing. Heath didn't acknowledge anyone or catch their eye as he walked in; he simply began, updating, outlining progress and listing actions to be taken. The atmosphere was quiet, tense. Cate had seen Len Stockdale on her way in, though he wasn't here now; he was probably already heading out on the beat. He hadn't greeted her, had just nodded from across the room, his expression one of quiet interest.

He would have been especially interested now, as the SIO turned to the subject of Matt Cosgrove.

'DI Grainger spoke to Cosgrove about the night of the dance, when the first victim went missing. He claims not to have been anywhere afterwards except home; says he was merely confused about what time he got in. He says he stayed until the end of the night – we do have corroboration for that – but then he had trouble setting the alarm. It kept going off and he had to unset it and start over; ended up checking the building a couple of times to make sure nothing was amiss. We've no corroboration for that part, no call-out registered at the alarm company, no reports made of any problems, but if Cosgrove just unset the thing and started over, there's nothing amiss in that.

'However, since we questioned him the first time, Cosgrove's barely been out of the house – and we know this, since we've had him under surveillance. There's no way he managed to get out, kidnap this new victim and dump her.'

The SIO looked up, scanned the room. His expression was sombre, but his eyes were bright.

'We have to find out who she is. You all know what you're doing – Dan, Missing Persons. Laughlin, chase Forensics. The scene's remaining cordoned until further notice. Start questioning anyone who's been around in the woods. Question anyone you can find, in fact. If there's any CCTV at the car parks, I want DS Searl in Intel checking it till his eyes bleed. Got that?'

Everyone nodded.

'Well, what the fuck are you waiting for? There's a killer out there. And I'm not getting any younger, that's for fucking sure.'

They rose to escape, then Heath said, 'A quick word, PC Corbin.'

She followed him towards his office, ignoring the curious looks cast in her direction. He didn't speak until they were inside, the door closed.

'You're doing some good work, Corbin, but I want you to be careful.'

'Sir?'

'This expert of yours. Where'd you find her again?'

'Through the university. She runs a course in—'

'Folklore, right. So she knows all about this stuff. Yet she wandered off into the woods, straight after looking at a dead body: went for a walk. A *walk*. Don't you find that strange? A killer dumps a body in the woods and she gets one sniff of the scene and charges off into the trees.'

'I think she was probably confused, sir. It takes people in different ways.'

'What does?'

'Their first body.'

Heath drew himself up, a clear signal for her to leave. 'Well, let's hope this isn't her *first* body, Corbin. Let's hope it's her *only* body, hmm?'

CHAPTER FOURTEEN

Dan Thacker presented Cate with a stack of paperwork. He saw the look on her face and gave a mock-smile. 'This stuff accumulates pretty fast,' he said. 'I want you to go through it, make sure you're up to speed on everything. Then you might see some actual action.'

She took it from him.

'You're going to need our details too – mobile numbers and such. And we'll need yours. We don't tend to use radio – we don't go through the Comms suite. We talk too much.' He smiled, and this time she smiled back.

'I think that's about it, apart from remembering names. Oh, and don't let Paulson push you around. Don't let him tell you his name's Richard, either – we all just call him Paulo.'

'And Heath?'

Dan gave a wry shrug. 'Heath is "sir",' he said, and he left her to get started on the pile.

She couldn't help being disappointed; she could feel

the buzz running around the incident room and here she was catching up on old news. At the top of the stack was the forensic pathology report for Chrissie Farrell. Cate shook her head to clear it. Dan was right, she needed to be up on whatever the team knew, and they still needed to find out what had happened to Chrissie. They *had* to find out.

She forced herself to think back to the first scene. Chrissie Farrell, in comparison with Red, had had a relatively clean death, apart from the removal of her toe. She tried to summon an image of who might have done that to her, but could see only a shadow. Was the killer calm while cutting through the flesh? Did they feel anything for her as the blood vessels burst in her eyes?

The cause of death was, as she had suspected, smothering; The build-up of carbon dioxide in her blood was confirmed in the report. She had been right in thinking she couldn't see any bruising to the girl's neck. Instead, Chrissie had been choked by something blocking her throat; they'd found abrasions in her windpipe, although the object itself had been removed. So that too was reminiscent of the fairy tale, like Snow White being choked by a poisoned apple, appearing dead until the offending object was jolted loose. If only life could have been restored so easily to Chrissie Farrell.

The fairest of them all, Cate thought. She'd read some texts on forensic psychology and remembered that this particular cause of death – smothering – was usually a spur-of-the-moment act, born of rage, often carried out by someone who knew the victim. The way this had been done was different: it smacked of premeditation. It had remained true to what happened in the fairy tale, but also to the image of Snow White, killing her without destroying her beauty.

There were other injuries besides the ones she was already aware of. There were several small cuts on the inside of her arm, which could not have been seen from the way the body had been laid out. What had that meant? There were ligature marks on her wrists, too: she had been tied up while this had been done to her – but *where*? There would have been blood; the girl would have screamed. It had to be somewhere she wouldn't have been heard.

Cate drew in a deep breath and read on. She almost didn't want to know what must surely come next, but then she found it, and breathed out in relief. Chrissie Farrell's toe had been cut off *post mortem*. She wouldn't have felt the pain, wouldn't have known anything about it. That would be one small consolation for her mother, at least. She scanned down the page, and the next item made her wince. The toe had been done *post mortem*, but her fingernails had not. The blood in and around the wounds showed the girl had been alive. Cate closed her eyes against the thought. Why would anyone do that? Had the killer actually enjoyed torturing her?

She picked up the photograph of the girl lying in the clearing, her dead eyes staring up into the sky. She remembered Chrissie as she had been in another photo-graph, in another time: her direct gaze, her smile. She breathed in deep, forced herself to *think*. Snow White was supposed to be murdered in the wood before the huntsman brought a piece of her back, wasn't she? Maybe that was the reason the toe was done later. But in order to take care of the dwarves' house, she'd have to be alive – hence what had been done to her hands. Maybe someone hadn't done this for their sick pleasure; maybe they were sticking to the story after all.

The story seemed to underpin everything now – or maybe Heath was right, she was getting too close to it; she had paid too much attention to Alice's way of seeing things. The fairy tale didn't belong with the dry words of the report, analysing and cataloguing the girl's death.

Off with the fairies, Stocky had said. And Heath: *There a big bad wolf around here somewhere?*

Exept there was, wasn't there? There *was*.

She knew the SIO's humour was just a necessary part of his role – if the police didn't have that as a defence mechanism to shield them from the sick things people could do to each other, they wouldn't be able to cope for long. She remembered Alice's calm seriousness when she had looked at the body. Alice had never had to develop that kind of shield in her job. Perhaps it would have been easier on her now if she had.

Maybe she needed to work on that too.

She examined the picture of Chrissie once more. If she

didn't look at her face, she could almost – not quite – imagine the girl was sleeping there, dreaming, perhaps, of some story she'd become a part of. Her dress shone out against the earth, a clean sharp colour. Cate frowned. That wasn't right, surely? Little Red's clothes, hidden by the cloak, had been spattered and stained. Had someone undressed Chrissie and then dressed her again for her final display? They hadn't found any buttons fastened wrongly or anything of that kind, but that didn't mean it hadn't happened; whoever it was could have taken their time. Something must have been done about the blood.

The blood. Cate flicked back through the report. The toe had been cut off *post mortem*, after her heart stopped beating. There wouldn't have been much blood. How had he filled the bottle to send back to her mother? Of course – that must have been the reason for those cuts on her arm, that's how he'd collected her blood. She'd been alive then, maybe watching her killer as he'd caught it in that old glass bottle. It would have been neater, surely, more true to the story, if he'd cut off her toe when she was alive and taken her blood that way, rather than leaving more marks on the body. Maybe he'd had difficulty doing this, after all. But Little Red – her stomach had been ripped open. The blood: the smell of it . . . Had he found it easier the second time? Was the killer starting to relish the things he did, push himself to go further?

She realised she couldn't help thinking of the killer as 'he'. It would have taken strength to move the body, even more so in Little Red's case, and that suggested a man. Now she wished she'd been able to see Cosgrove herself, to look into his eyes. Would she have thought him a man capable of doing this?

She went back to the report. Whatever else she'd had to endure, there was nothing to suggest the girl had been raped. Cate frowned. There were no conclusions she could draw from that; it didn't mean the attacker had been a woman. If it was a man, he might have been incapable, or had so far objectified the girl he didn't see her in a sexual fashion – that could rule out Stocky's theory about this being an attack on her vanity.

That didn't seem like Cosgrove, though, or at least what she knew of him. *I thought he liked me*, Angie Farrell had said. *I thought he liked me, but he didn't, I saw him watching her.*

Or perhaps the killer hadn't touched the girl because that wasn't part of the story he was trying to tell.

There wasn't much else relating to the body. They'd found some trace evidence on the dress, fibres clinging to the back of it, most likely picked up from car upholstery. That might have happened when the body was dumped, but it was telling that the fibres were found on her back – she might have been seated. Had she got into a car of her own free will? Possibly – so that could mean it was someone she knew, or someone who could lure her into their vehicle. A taxi driver, maybe?

Cate sighed and looked back over the report. She had

wondered if Chrissie had set off to walk home, but aside from the severed toe there were no signs of injury to her feet – only a small blister which could have been caused by nothing more than wearing towering heels to a school dance. There was no reason to think she had set out to walk, but it couldn't be ruled out either. And the girl had been drunk, that was confirmed by the alcohol levels in her blood. She could have been confused, possibly incapable of fighting someone off, or maybe she'd been happy to accept a lift from anyone if it meant getting away from the friends she'd quarrelled with.

That made her think of the girl's mother, that photograph with their faces close together, wearing the same dress. How close had they really been? Angie Farrell had left her daughter at the dance, after all. And Alice Hyland had pointed out that it was often the stepmother who was the villain. Cate had looked into that, but as she'd expected, she'd found that Mrs Farrell was Chrissie's real mother; she'd thought as much from their resemblance. But then, hadn't Alice said that in the *original* tales – the older versions – it was the true mother who did such terrible things?

That could be Angie Farrell as she had seen her in the photograph. In real life . . . she remembered the woman's terror, her bewilderment. She'd given the impression of being vain, yes, but it ended there: Cate didn't believe she could have done these things to her daughter. Maybe Heath was right – she *was* getting too caught up in the stories, at the expense of the evidence before her eyes.

She went back to the file and scanned down the last items, leafed through the details of the rubbish that had been found alongside the body. There had been an apple, half eaten and discarded, she had seen it. At the time she had considered it as something that might yield DNA evidence but was probably unrelated, just another piece of human detritus – until she had spoken to Alice, when she had asked Heath for some further tests to be done.

She found that report and read it with increasing puzzlement. The apple hadn't yielded any human DNA evidence, which was odd; there were traces of insects and birds, nothing more. She had thought it might have been used to choke the girl – it would have fitted the story. How had the bite-marks been made, if not with a human mouth? Were they carved into it deliberately, or was it nothing to do with the scene at all?

Cate's heartbeat quickened as she flicked through to the results of the tests she'd suggested. And then she found it: significant quantities of a toxic pesticide. The apple found at Snow White's side had not been eaten, but it had been poisoned.

As Cate finished scanning the files, Len Stockdale appeared at her shoulder. He slid into the seat opposite, looking her up and down as he did so. She felt suddenly conscious of being in plain clothes while he was in uniform.

'Going well, then?'

'Not so you'd notice.' She tried a smile, but he didn't return it. Instead he handed across a crumpled piece of paper, presenting it with a flourish, playing secretary.

'Message,' he said. 'You looked busy.'

She wasn't sure if he was really being helpful or if there was a trace of sarcasm in his words. He was no doubt wondering why they hadn't already collared the teacher. *Vanity*, he'd said, and he'd be sticking to it. Stocky liked to get things done; paperwork irritated him. Taking telephone messages would no doubt irritate him too, unless he'd done it to make a point.

Cate kept her expression neutral and glanced at the note. Alice's name was written across the top; she hid her reaction to that too. Stocky would have known who she was: her expert on fairy tales, part of her theory on the case. But with Little Red her theory had been vindicated, hadn't it? But she couldn't help thinking of what Heath had said about her contact. It *was* a little strange: Alice had only just seen a body mutilated and dumped in the woods, and off she went, all alone, into the trees. And yet the lecturer was her lead, her insight into what might be going on here. She might even be her passport to keeping her place on the team.

'Problem?'

'No, it's fine. How are things with you?'

He grunted. 'A lot to be getting on with.'

'I'm sorry if I left you in the lurch, Len. I didn't know

this chance was going to come along – it's a good opportunity for me to learn.' She sighed. 'I'm sorry, but I have to do this. It would be good if we—' Her voice tailed away.

'If we . . . ?' Len's face was without expression.

'Never mind.' She looked at him. *Here first*, he'd said at the body dump, and now he looked almost sulky. Was he wishing he was on the case himself, thinking about how he'd be doing it differently? It occurred to her to wonder if he'd ever thought of applying to CID. Maybe he'd even done it; maybe his application had failed. She bit her lip. No, he could surely have made different choices if he'd wanted to. And it couldn't be helped now, she was on this case; it was too big for her to turn her back on it.

Here first. She sighed. Was she so very different, after all? It *was* a great chance for her, and she couldn't deny she found the investigation exciting. And if she decided to specialise in future, to join CID for good, her experience in this investigation would surely be a boost to her career.

She thought of the dead girl she'd so recently seen, her face pressed into the fallen branches, and she grimaced. No, Stocky was probably just thinking of his own kids, wanting to see justice done to whoever had hurt Angie Farrell's. She looked up, meaning to ask after them, his family; but Stocky was already pushing himself from his seat. He walked away without looking at her again.

*

At first Cate didn't think anyone was going to answer the telephone, and she started to wonder what Alice might be doing. She had an image of the girl walking through the woods, ducking under low-growing branches; she knew what Heath would say to that and tried to push the idea out of her mind. It just seemed fitting to think of her that way – and why not? Alice loved nature, that was obvious from the place she'd chosen to live. She belonged there, and Cate could envy that, in a way. She thought of her own small flat, its walls freshly plastered and painted when she moved in, and compared it unfavourably with Alice's untidy kitchen. She hadn't had time to accumulate any mess; she wasn't planning on staying long enough. She'd needed somewhere, and the flat had been convenient. It suited her that it didn't feel like home – that might even have been part of the reason she'd chosen it. This was not her destination, not somewhere to put down roots, get into a relationship, settle down; it was a stopover. For Alice, though – she belonged at the edge of the woods, her head full of fairy tales; a half-wild, storybook place.

The phone was picked up with a breathy, 'Hello? Sorry. I was outside, picking some flowers.'

Cate's mouth twitched. She greeted her contact.

'Ah – yes, I'd been thinking about things and I wanted to talk to you. It's a woman, do you see that? From the stories. It must be; it was always a woman.'

'Pardon me?'

Alice drew a deep breath. 'Sorry; it's my fault, I'm not

explaining myself very well. It's just, in the stories, it's the stepmother who tries to kill Snow White, we know that much. The wolf in "Little Red" – well, I think that's misleading, because it's the mother who sends her into the forest, isn't it? All alone, where the big bad wolf lives? And telling her not to leave the path – isn't that asking for trouble, really, putting the idea into her head?'

Cate caught her breath. 'That's just the story,' she said. 'The reality could have been different. Anyway, are you saying they were *both* killed by their mothers, and left that way coincidentally?'

'No – I'm saying everything's been done to fit the stories, and it would fit them too if the killer was female.'

Cate paused. 'All right,' she said. 'It's a theory. I won't rule it out, but we have to take into account that someone overpowered these girls, and that probably required strength; someone certainly had to move them. We can't rule out the idea that it could be a man.'

But Alice hadn't finished. 'A woman could have lured the girls to go with them somehow. It's obvious, really, isn't it? They might have trusted a woman, gone with her for some reason. And it's not just about the characters in the stories, the evil stepmother or the faulty mother – women tend to know more about fairy tales than men. I've never had more than 5 or 10 per cent of males on my course. Someone knew a fair amount in order to set this up.'

Cate narrowed her eyes. Yes, they did: the killer was

someone who was knowledgeable, who knew the area. And she remembered Heath's words: *went for a walk. A walk. Don't you find that strange?*

She said goodbye, hung up. They had to focus on the facts, not Alice's fictions, and that came back to the victim; it was the girl they had to think about now. They had to find out who had killed her and how they'd done it, and to do that, they also needed to know who she was. Cate was obviously going to be busy, assuming Heath kept her on the team. Stocky might not like it, but she couldn't help that. She looked around the desks, couldn't see him now – perhaps he was getting on with some of that work he'd mentioned, no doubt wishing he could pass the filing on to her. Would she always be around to do it for him? Stocky seemed happy where he was, despite his odd demeanour earlier. But did he think she would stay here for ever? Unlike him she had no family here, only a half-empty flat and her own ambition, pulling her in different directions.

'We have an estimated time for the body dump.' She jumped as the voice came from behind her. It was Dan Thacker. 'It was in the early hours. We're double-checking Cosgrove's movements now, but Heath's right, it doesn't look like it could have been him.'

'Okay. Thanks for letting me know.'

'We also have a possible lead on a mis-per.' He paused, grinned. 'Come on. Looks like you're with me.'

CHAPTER FIFTEEN

The girl's figure was little removed from a lithe young boy's, and her hair was white – it could be a wig or possibly it was so tormented by bleach that it had turned to straw. Her eyes were close-set and looked shrunken behind harsh black eyeliner. Her thin lips were also rimmed with a dark line of some plum-coloured make-up, which was bleeding into a smoker's puckered skin. She looked about seventeen, and as if she hadn't slept in three days. She had given her name as Kiara, something that sounded so unlikely Cate found herself wondering if it was actually true.

They sat on either side of a chipped Formica table in a greasy spoon on the outskirts of Leeds. It was raining outside, a warm spring shower, and the café was overheated. The greasy glass was steamed up and running with moisture; there was no way Dan could keep an eye on them as he had promised.

The girl was on edge, paranoia making her skittish,

which was why Dan had opted to stay outside and let Cate talk to her alone. Kiara's black-lined eyes kept darting towards the door, as if she was expecting a pimp to burst in on her at any second, or maybe other toms, ready to rip her to shreds for talking to the police.

'It's all right,' Cate said, 'you're not in any trouble, like we told you. It's just, we heard you'd spoken to someone on the beat, that's all – you said your friend was missing, and we want to help, if we can. We want to try and find her.'

The girl threw herself back in her seat, sighing noisily. 'Weren't none of you bothered when I said. How come you've turned up now?'

Cate glanced at the opaque window once more and answered. 'Your friend's disappearance might be related to a case we're working on. I can't tell you any more than that now, I'm afraid. Do you want a drink, Kiara? Water? Coke?'

She rolled her eyes. 'I'm not your friend,' she said, 'so don't try and act like it.'

'All right, then let's get to it. You told a police officer your friend was missing. You said she got into a car – you didn't know what make or colour – and she never came back. You didn't see the driver either. Right so far?'

Kiara was staring at the table. She sniffed, and her face relaxed for a brief moment, making her look much younger. Cate spoke more softly: 'And you didn't see anything else? – you didn't get a look at the registration plate?'

'Look,' the girl said, 'I was busy, a'right? I just wanted 'em to listen to me. We watched out for each other, 'er and me – we always did. Only that night it was really clear, like, and there was this bird singing, and all I could think was . . .' She paused.

'Was?'

'About 'ow it used to be when I was a kid.' She almost smiled. 'I hadn't thought of that in a long time – being a kid, I mean.'

Cate sighed. 'Help me find out what happened to her, Kiara, please.'

Kiara flashed her a glance. 'I didn't see it,' she said, so low Cate almost couldn't hear. 'I didn't see a car, like, didn't see if she got in, a'right? But I 'eard one, so she must've done. What else could it've been?'

'You didn't see her get into a vehicle?'

'No. Like I said, I 'eard one. It was speeding up, like it was driving away. And when I went back round the corner, she weren't there no more.'

Cate drew a deep breath. 'You gave her name as Candy. We both know that's not her real name. You said she was eighteen. I'm not sure that's her real age, either.' She found herself looking down at Kiara's skinny arms, the pale skin, mottled with the same track marks the victim had. What had Alice called it – *the path of needles*? She wondered how long it was since this girl had made her choice; whether she'd ever really had a choice to make.

Kiara sat up straighter and put her hands on the table,

ready to push herself up. 'You found 'er,' she said. 'She's dead, in't she? That's what this is, in't it?'

'I can't say, Kiara. You understand, we haven't made any definite connection between this other case and your friend. We need a name – then we'll see what we can do for her.'

'For my friend, or some other lass you've found? You said you dun't even know it's 'er.'

'No, we don't, I'm not going to lie to you. But if we have her real name, we may be able to track down a relative, or someone else who can help.'

Kiara sniffed, wiped her nose on the back of her hand. 'She talked about 'er gran once.'

Cate stared before she spoke. 'All right. Maybe she can help us work out what happened to her. That's all we want, Kiara. We're not looking to cause trouble for you or your friend.'

The girl scowled. 'I think she 'ad a flat in south Leeds, a'right? 'er name's Treesa.'

'Treesa – Teresa? Teresa who, Kiara?'

'King. It weren't 'er dad's name. She called 'erself that for 'er gran. She never 'ad no dad, not really.' Kiara's face reddened, then she pinched her lip between her fingers. It made her look more than ever like a child, and Cate found herself wondering how she had passed from those days to this, how anybody did. Without the harsh eyeliner, her dry skin, the pallor of tiredness, given a good night's sleep instead of plying her trade in some stinking alley, and the girl might have been pretty.

She muttered something.

'What was that?'

Kiara pushed herself to her feet, her chair scraping across the cheap lino. 'I said you'd better find her.' She turned, strode across the café and yanked open the door. She looked back once, a brief, angry glare, before heading outside and into the rain.

CHAPTER SIXTEEN

The old woman lived on the edge of an industrial wilderness, a labyrinth of crumbling concrete, twisted metal and discarded things. It was grey even in the height of springtime, but she rarely looked out of the window: the view was masked by yellowing net curtains that gave the light inside an odd tone, as though from an enraged storm.

Her house was at the centre of a row of red-brick terraces, and each room was long and thin. Sometimes she could hear her neighbours moving around, their footsteps banging on the stairs, doors slamming. She rarely heard their voices, but when she did they were raised and yet muffled too, as if they could only shout in vowel sounds. She didn't try to make out the words and she didn't interfere when the accompanying banging sounds became softer, as though fists were falling on flesh rather than a door or table. It was none of her business. She didn't trouble her neighbours and they didn't trouble her. Sometimes they would play loud music into the night and she would lie awake in the dark, listening to it, trying to work out what it was about the muffled cadences she liked.

She never troubled to play music herself. When her granddaughter had been young, all breathless excitement at every little thing, she had watched her jigging along to music on the television, songs to which the child had inexplicably known the words, and felt like she was speaking some language she'd never learned. She remembered wishing she could ask someone about it, but her daughter – the child's mother – was long gone by then, and the father had disappeared long before that. Anyway, she wouldn't have been sure how to frame the question. At those times, the child had been her joy. Sometimes she had looked at her and wondered where on earth she had come from: surely not her own daughter.

The child had filled these rooms with laughter, seeing delight where the woman saw only walls. Now she was gone too, and only the walls remained. Her grandchild had discovered new things as she had grown: learning what boys were, what life was. They had not been good things for her to learn.

She pushed herself up from the sofa – it never used to sag that way, and she couldn't remember when it began to be such an effort – and shuffled into the kitchen. It was small, and she could put her hand on everything she needed just by turning around, but it was hers, and it was a comfort that her things stayed where she had put them now. Perhaps it had been a good thing the girl had gone after all. She could even leave her purse on the sideboard, open to view, and it would not be touched.

And yet – there were no sounds now except her own, no *thrub-thrub-thrub* of the music Teresa had liked, music without words.

She turned on the tap hard, so that the water gushed loudly against the sink. She glanced up at the window and saw shadows moving against the dim yellow light. She blinked. Her eyes were slow to focus and watered continually, as her own mother's had before she died. She sloshed the water in the bowl, ready for the washing-up. That was what she would do, plain, ordinary things, the kind of things on which her life was built. The shapes outside were coming closer. It could be the council again, going to see the family next door, or the police; she wasn't sure which and didn't really care. It was always one or the other, knocking and knocking and trying to get in.

She jumped as a sharp rap rang out against her own door. She turned and faced the sound as if it was something she could see.

They would go away soon and leave her alone. She leaned over and turned off the tap, and silence flooded back.

The knock came again, tight, hard knuckles, and this time she forced herself to move. From the hallway she could see two shapes through the glass panel in the door; it made her think of an occasion – what, twelve, thirteen years ago? – when the bailiffs had come. She had stood against the wall, just like this, keeping quite still so they wouldn't see her move. Teresa had clung to her legs then and she'd put one hand on her head to steady the child, the other over her sweet little mouth. Teresa hadn't needed it, she had remained quite still, not saying a word. It was as if she had known.

The letterbox opened with a clatter and a voice called through it, 'Mrs King? We need to speak to you.'

It wasn't a debt collector's voice.

'Mrs King?' The voice was a young woman's.

For a moment her heart jumped, dully painful, as she thought, *Has she come home?* But no, it hadn't been Teresa's voice. She didn't want to let the woman in, all the same. She wanted nothing more than her own quiet rooms, the familiar things; and then she walked to the door and turned the key because she knew that when the world came knocking, it wouldn't leave without taking what it demanded: your money, your television, your sewing machine; your self-respect. Your life.

When she saw the young girl standing on her doorstep, a young man at her side, she knew; she could sense it. They weren't in uniform, but they were police. She could smell it on them. Their eyes were already full of sympathy and she could already hear the empty phrases running through their minds. *The child*, she thought.

She looked at the policewoman and the policeman standing next to her, threw the door open wider so that it rattled against the wall and motioned them both inside.

CHAPTER SEVENTEEN

Alice slipped out of her back door without troubling to lock it behind her and walked through the garden, ducking under the apple tree's lowest branches. The wood was there, waiting, and she let herself out of the gate and stepped into it. It was late evening, but under the trees it was already dark, rich in shadows. Everything was silent except her footsteps against the grey, hard-packed ground. Outside her gate the beech trees stood like stone pillars, and there was no undergrowth; the path was knuckled with tree roots and stones, everything as grey as the rest in the half-light.

There was a glimmer of red somewhere up ahead of her, a bright blood colour, and when she saw it Alice knew that she was dreaming. It was the dead girl. She was in the woods now, at one with the trees and the insects and the birds. The path of needles and the path of pins were behind her; she would not find them again. She had no choice left but to wander the lost places.

Somewhere above, a large bird stirred and a branch wavered. There was the burbling roll of a wood pigeon's call, the answering cry of something she didn't recognise.

There was a reason she had to speak to the girl, she knew that, but she couldn't think what it was. She started to head after her anyway, then broke into a run. Hard ground gave way to softer earth thick with undergrowth, everything a new, soft green. The trees were thinner, their trunks silver and pale. Ahead of her was another glimpse of red.

Alice tried to call out for the girl to wait and found she couldn't speak; there was only a bird's cry, high and snipping like silver scissors, somewhere on the edge of hearing. She ran faster, through a deep drift of bluebells that looked almost purple in the dim light. A drop of rain fell onto her face and she realised she could smell it in the air, sense it in the gathering blackness: a storm was coming.

Then she saw that the girl had stopped after all; she was watching her, peering from behind a tree trunk, her face a pale oval. Her lips were pressed into a flat blank line, but Alice had the impression of sharp teeth hidden behind them. Suddenly she wasn't sure if it was Little Red leading her onwards or the wolf. The girl looked hungry. She pulled the red cape back from one arm. There was a strap wrapped around it and she pulled it tight. In her other hand she held a needle. It was long and sharp and held promise in the droplet that clung to its tip. The girl thrust the needle into her flesh, keeping her eyes on Alice as she depressed the plunger. Her eyes, which had been nothing more than dark smudges, suddenly shone.

Then Little Red was running again, ducking into the trees while Alice stared at the place she had been. She shook herself, tried to follow, but the trees resisted her, blocking her with their branches, fighting her. She couldn't see the girl any more. The ground was covered in fallen branches and dead bracken and smothered by a mulch of long-dead leaves. Alice stood still and listened; everything was quiet as a held breath and she felt alone. She couldn't go back – she hadn't found what she was meant to see. She started walking again, steadily this time, looking about her. To each side were only the scabbed trunks of birch and ash, but ahead was something different, a sprinkling of white flowers on the ground.

Alice emerged into a clearing that was coated in fresh soft grass. It was no lighter here and she looked up to see the sky was smudged with cloud and scattered with the first stars.

When her gaze fell to the clearing once more, she noticed something else. Opposite her, under the edge of the trees, was a wooden hut. It wasn't some rough-made thing but neat and sturdy, its freshly sawn edges a pale gold against the bark-covered walls. It had no door; instead, there was a simple opening, curtained by dripping rain which had started to fall more heavily, making a hissing sound all around her; it almost sounded like there were words in it. Alice ran, drops falling on her clothes and hair, soaking her, but she still paused at the entrance, before peering in. It was dark inside, but the hut appeared to be empty. As she ducked under the roof, the rain transformed into a solid heavy drumming.

There was a wooden table inside the hut, with two chairs drawn up to it. The furniture was crudely made and much too big, as if intended for a giant. At first Alice thought that was all, there was nothing else, then she saw something on the table. She heaved herself up onto one of the chairs and leaned over it.

The thing was a book. Like the table and chairs it was too large, and like them it was made of wood. At first she thought it was only a carving, a solid thing, not something with pages that could be opened, but when she put out a hand and lifted the cover it moved easily. As she turned to the first page, somewhere out in the woods a bird began to sing.

CHAPTER EIGHTEEN

Cate took a seat in Heath's office. She'd been summoned as soon as she got to the station, ahead of the morning briefing, but Heath wasn't there; when the door opened it was Dan who walked in. He nodded at her and moved to the other side of the room, where he remained standing. It made her feel out of place, despite the almost-smile he cast in her direction.

As she waited, Cate found herself thinking of that very first briefing when she'd put her hand in the air and mentioned fairy tales, the way Stocky had whistled the 'Heigh Ho' song afterwards, and laughed at her. It seemed a long time ago.

The door slammed back and Heath entered, walking rapidly, as if he didn't have time for this; he was frowning, but then, Cate couldn't remember a time when he didn't look annoyed. 'Let's get to it,' he said, and jabbed a finger towards the whiteboard. 'All right, so our second victim's

Teresa King. And you've informed the parents?' He jerked his head towards Cate.

She stood, went closer. 'We haven't found a mother, sir. She abandoned the girl some time ago, apparently. There's just a grandmother, and yes, she's been told. She was quiet about it, didn't seem too shocked, but I get the impression she never would show her emotions, if you know what I mean. She hasn't had anything delivered to her, no bottle of blood or anything like that.'

He didn't respond. 'The girl was dumped in the woods near Newmillerdam Lake, only a few miles from the first scene. No convictions, which comes as a surprise, judging by the company she kept. A charming young lady by all accounts, not much in common with the first aside from age and sex.'

'Not as such,' said Cate.

'Corbin?'

'I just mean they could be compared not in their similarities to each other but their similarities to the characters they were chosen to represent. Little Red – I mean, Teresa King – was found in the guise of a girl who'd left the path, who'd chosen the way of needles. The only relative we could find was a grandmother, not a mother or father. And Chrissie Farrell, as we know, was the beauty queen, the fairest of them all ...' Her voice tailed away when she saw Heath's expression.

'Make sure you don't get carried away, Corbin. We have to treat this as we would any other murder case, by examining the evidence, following the leads we have. Until your friend's theory gives us a suspect it's not a hell of a lot of use to us. Yes?'

Cate subsided, then changed her mind. 'It does fit, sir – and I know Alice Hyland has this idea it's a female killer, but Cosgrove does teach literature, so he might have the knowledge. We could check out the specific subjects he's been covering, maybe try to get a look at his bookshelves. Anything on folklore might show—'

'Cosgrove has an alibi,' snapped Heath. 'Signed, sealed and delivered this time. The guy's barely been out of the house since the first case except to go to the school and back. We've been keeping an eye on him. He might as well have been in fucking prison.'

'It's a big school. He might have—'

'There are no unauthorised absences. We've had him under surveillance, plus the school has staff on the gate during breaks to stop the kids sneaking off to the chippy. No sightings of Cosgrove on either count. Now *your* contact, on the other hand . . .'

She looked up again, startled.

'You have to admit it's odd. She knows all about these fairy tales. She knows the area. She shows up conveniently in time to cast her eyes over the latest girl's body.'

'We *asked* her to—'

Heath held up a hand. 'Devil's advocate, Corbin. I'm just pointing out that you can see suspects everywhere. She even knows the other location we have so far – she lectures in Leeds, doesn't she?' He paused, allowed that to sink in. 'And she insists it's a female killer. Isn't that what you said?'

Cate nodded.

'What you need is *evidence*. But for now, make sure you keep your distance – and watch her, that's all I'm saying.'

Cate was silent, though she felt her cheeks reddening, as much with guilt as chagrin at Heath's words. If she hadn't brought Alice Hyland into this, the most the woman would have known about it would be what she saw on the evening news.

Or outside her window.

She had a sudden image of Alice as she'd seen her, breaking off from looking at the crime-scene photographs and turning to the window as if taking mental refuge in the apple tree that grew in her garden.

The *apple* tree. And a poisoned apple had been found next to Chrissie Farrell's body. But no: Alice's tree was still in blossom; it wouldn't fruit until later, in the autumn. She forced herself to concentrate on what Heath was saying.

'The interviews are under way,' he said. 'Passers-by are being contacted, anyone who was walking in the wood at the time the body was discovered – anyone we know about, anyway. There are entrances to those woods at any one of a dozen places, and that's if no one climbs over a wall or a fence. It stretches right along the A61, and there are routes heading away through farmland; there's one path that follows an old railway line for miles. Obviously whoever dumped the body couldn't have got that far carrying it, but there could have been any number of people wandering about in the woods.

'The estimate is that Teresa King was dumped some ten or eleven hours before being discovered. That means a lot of potential witnesses could have just walked away. We're keeping a cordon around the woods for now; if people go walking there they might do so regularly, and we might still get a chance to talk to them. They might come back.' He looked at Cate. 'Maybe the killer will.'

CHAPTER NINETEEN

Alice looked out of the window. The sky was a pale grey-blue, gently misted over with fine cloud. It might burn off as the day warmed, but for now, everything was lit in soft, muted tones. The trees blurred and shifted in the breeze. It made her think of a watercolour painted wet on wet, the colours bleeding into each other. The air would be cool and tempting. She glanced towards her bag, thrown down in the corner. She still had marking to do, but she knew if she sat and put the essays in front of her she could never fix her mind on the words. It was as if she'd become attuned to this new mystery she had been presented with; she couldn't leave it alone.

She grabbed her jacket and headed out, taking the gate that led from her back garden into the woods. After a while she slipped off the jacket and felt the cool air on her skin. The trees were alive with birdsong, though when Alice looked up she could see nothing, not a single bird.

She found herself heading in the same direction she

had taken in her dream. At first the path was grey and ridged with roots, just as she had seen it then. She felt quite sure of the way. It took her along the hillside, roughly parallel with the lake and out of sight of the shoreline path. After that she kept moving, not really paying attention to where she was going, so that for a while the landscape she'd seen in her dream felt more present than the real.

Soon the ground softened and Alice found herself walking through drifts of bluebells, their perfume wafting in the morning air. She was heading towards the deepest part of the woods, where tracks and pathways criss-crossed each other at every step, making it easy to become lost. She didn't try to follow the route she'd seen in her dream any longer – she didn't think she could if she tried; it probably wasn't even real.

The path narrowed and Alice picked her way around fallen branches and the twining roots of trees. The ground was spongy underfoot, almost unpleasantly so, and it was quiet; Alice stopped to listen.

The birdsong had ceased. The only sound was that of branches stirring, the soft touch of leaf against leaf, small noises she wouldn't ordinarily have noticed.

Ahead of her, between the trees, white wood anemones were scattered across the ground.

She swallowed. The woods didn't feel so friendly any more, didn't feel like *hers*. She couldn't remember this place from any of her previous walks. She tipped her head back, seeing trunks and branches receding away from her towards the sky. It wasn't brightening but growing duller, a flat, even grey. She went on and reached a clearing, smaller than the one she'd dreamed about but still *there*. It was peaceful and quiet, and Alice smiled; she'd found herself looking for the hut as if it had been a real place that she could revisit. Of course there were only the trees, but then she stared, because there *was* something nestled beneath them after all. She hadn't noticed it at first, not because she hadn't seen it exactly, but because the colour blended so well with its surroundings. She only saw it now because the thin slit across the canvas had stood out as she scanned everything else, a dark slot hanging in the air. She took a step back, her chest tight, as if she couldn't get her breath.

The thing was a canvas tent, not brightly coloured like ordinary tents but mottled with the greens and browns of camouflage. As she watched, it rippled, then fell still, and a man's head appeared through a gap in the fabric.

Oddly, Alice recognised him.

He smiled and gave her a little wave. He grabbed the binoculars that hung around his neck and waved them too. 'It's my little home from home,' he called out.

She thought for a moment of turning and walking away – running, even – and then he spoke again.

'I'm still looking,' he said. His voice was faint, hardly any force behind it, and Alice leaned forward to hear him better. He smiled again. His expression was guileless and a little downcast.

Slowly she crossed the clearing. 'The blue bird? Haven't you seen it?'

'Not yet, but I'm quite determined, you see. Quite the little mouse.'

It occurred to Alice that she hadn't once thought of the blue bird all the time that she had been walking. 'I'm sorry. I've probably spoiled it for you,' she said, glancing around as if even now it would be flitting away from the noise she'd made. She looked back at his hide. It was just fabric stretched over a simple frame, probably not much to carry; the sort of thing a child might play in. And here he was, a grown man, alone in it – for how long?

Now she was alone with him.

He smiled, a disingenuous smile, nothing calculated in it; he was just a birdwatcher, disturbed in his hobby. He touched a hand to his binoculars again as if they were a talisman to keep the world at bay. 'No matter,' he said. 'It hasn't been this way, and I dare say it won't. My luck isn't in, it seems.' He suddenly thrust out a hand, stepping towards her. 'Bernard Levitt. B, E, R . . .' and he spelled it out for her, his whole name, as if she were going to be tested on it later.

She tried not to smile.

'Oh, it's quite a serious business,' he said. 'I've noted several species. *Phylloscopus sibilatrix. Pyrrhula pyrrhula.* Even a rather fine *Muscicapa striata*, which came and sang to me for a time.'

She nodded politely, though she had no idea what he was talking about.

'Listen,' he said, and pointed one finger up at the sky.

At first she didn't know what he meant; then she realised she could hear birds again. Somewhere distant, almost beyond hearing, was a high *snip-snip-snip*, and she pictured something tiny hiding amid the leaves. Over that were laid musical notes, running up and down the scales with joyful abandon. Beneath that was the rasping croak of something black and ragged.

'Beautiful, isn't it?' he said, and he started to name them for her, Latin names that Alice could connect with nothing: *Streptopelia decaocto* and *Fringilla coelebs*, *Corvus corone* and *Phylloscopus collybita*, one after the next so that, without thinking about it, she took a half-step back.

'It's my hobby, you see,' he said. 'I know I take it rather seriously.'

He looked quite crestfallen, and she almost wanted to apologise. Instead she asked, 'Aren't you worried, being out here alone?'

'Oh, you mean—? No, not me. And it's so quiet here. Really, quite a long way from where it happened. Terrible thing, though. Terrible. Um . . .'

Alice knew then he was going to ask about *her*, about whether she was afraid, and she found she didn't want to think about it. It had felt all right when she was alone – better than being here with a stranger. When it was just

Alice and the trees it was comfortable, like being at home; as if it *was* her home.

Levitt still hadn't got the words out, so she asked, 'What about the blue bird? Do you think it'll come here?'

A shadow crossed his face. 'I don't know. There are no rules when it comes to the blue bird.' He sounded almost bitter. 'It isn't from these parts; it could be anywhere. But I'm hoping it will come to me eventually.' He scanned the treetops, light pooling on the lenses of his glasses.

'Well, I hope so,' said Alice, thinking of the way it had come to her, and not once but twice. It didn't seem fair now; he had tried so hard, while she had done nothing to earn the sight of it.

'Do you, dear?' He smiled at her.

She glanced at him, looked away. It occurred to her that he was younger than he looked; it was his odd ways that made him seem prematurely old. He stirred, waving his binoculars in jerky movements. She wasn't surprised he needed a hide if that was how he moved; birds would never come anywhere near him.

She realised that both of them were just standing there in silence. 'I should go,' she said, and he smiled and said goodbye. Alice backtracked across the clearing. She glanced around only once, didn't really take in the hide at all this time; perhaps she wouldn't have seen it in the first place if she hadn't looked at that very spot. The thought was disconcerting. Perhaps she had been reckless after all, walking in the woods the way she had.

But Levitt was right, it was a long way to the place the girl had been found; that was on the other side of the lake. It was a long way too from where she had seen the blue bird, and she wondered if she should have told him. On reflection, she was glad she hadn't. She remembered his brown eyes fixed on her as he recited his dull lists of species. She didn't want the bird to be reduced to that, categorised and labelled with some Latin name she couldn't understand. Anyway, she didn't like him.

Besides, what could he do if she had told him? She'd last seen the bird near where the girl had been found and he couldn't go looking for it there. The police would be all over it, watching for anything unusual. She wondered what they'd make of Bernard Levitt – but then, they knew of him already; they had taken his details at the lakeside path. And he hadn't done anything, he was only doing the same as Alice – enjoying the wood as it should be enjoyed, carrying on with life. She looked around and saw that the hide was already lost, blending perfectly with the woodland at her back.

CHAPTER TWENTY

The trouble with witnesses, Cate reflected, was that they remembered the aftermath rather than the event itself. She had spent the morning following up on some of the details they'd taken in the woods, accompanied by a rather quiet DC Thacker, and all they'd managed to ascertain was that yes, there had been a disturbance, and that the police had been everywhere, disrupting everything. No one recalled seeing anything strange in the hours before the girl had been found.

Cate hadn't seen much of Len Stockdale, though she'd heard what he was doing now, and as they drove along the A61 she suggested they call by at Newmillerdam. Dan nodded his assent, indicated and turned in. He was lost in his own thoughts.

The young policeman on the entrance was someone Cate vaguely knew; he waved them through. The sky had brightened since the early morning, but even so it began to spit with rain as Dan pulled into a space. The car park, usually busy, was a bare lake of asphalt with a few police vehicles at one end and a couple of cars and a solitary van at the other. The police presence at the main entrances must be keeping the walkers away.

She looked towards the gap that led from the car park to the lakeside path and there was Stocky, leaning against a gatepost, his notebook in his hand. He was idly flipping the cover back and forth and scowling; he was facing out across the water and didn't appear to have seen them yet.

'I'll just be a minute, Dan,' Cate said, but when she stepped out of the car and headed towards her old tutor, the detective followed.

At the sound of their footsteps Stocky turned. He'd put on his friendly face, the one he used for dealing with the public – people he didn't intend to lock away – but as he recognised Cate his expression changed into something else.

'Hi, Len,' Cate called out. She was conscious of Dan close at her heels and felt a momentary irritation – had he been told to watch her, as she had been ordered to keep an eye on Alice?

Stocky adjusted his expression, putting on a wry smile; making an effort, maybe.

'We've been interviewing all morning,' Cate said. 'Any joy here?'

He shrugged. 'None. Freezing my arse off.'

Cate looked around. The lakeside path was almost

abandoned. She could just make out a family on the opposite bank, a woman hastily throwing whole slices of bread
to the ducks, as if trying to get it over with, while her
children watched.

'At least you have a nice view.' She tried a smile.

'I'd swap it for a comfy police car.'

She didn't know what to say. She almost wanted to
apologise that she wasn't the one standing there in the
cold, but she swallowed it back. Then she remembered
the van at the other end of the car park. 'Whose is that?'

'Dog walker – Gary Wilson. He said he'd be half an hour
and stick to the path. He can't get up to the arboretum,
we've got it marked off.' He snapped out the words.

'Okay.'

'That's about it, apart from the twitchers, chasing some
bloody birdie around the woods.' Stockdale's tone softened. Now there was nothing for them to do but leave
him to it, he was becoming talkative. He gestured towards
the slope where Little Red had been found – no, Cate
reminded herself, *Teresa*. Teresa King. 'There are still a
couple of SOCOs up there.'

'Is Heath around?'

He snorted. 'Haven't seen him – tucked away in his nice
warm office, probably.' He glanced towards Dan and his
eyes slid away. 'If he's got any sense, I mean.'

Dan straightened, raising himself to his full height.
'We'll go and check on the SOCOs, Cate,' he said softly.

Stockdale shrugged and looked away, but as they walked

towards the woodland, Cate could feel his gaze on her back.

They headed into the woods, up the slope towards the arboretum. The rain turned into a feather-light mist that dampened their faces and whispered against the leaves. When they emerged into the clearing they found the SOCOs packing up their things and disassembling the tent they'd eventually managed to place around the scene. Soon there would be nothing left but pathways that were a little more deeply trodden than before and a faint imprint among the fallen branches that would soon be covered by new growth. The taint of morbid excitement would linger a while yet. Cate wondered how long it would be before some walker claimed to have seen a ghost, eager to turn the girl's story into their own. After a time, that would be all that remained: the stories.

Dan greeted the SOCOs. It sounded like things had gone badly for them: they'd found a few footprints near the body and had taken mouldings of them, and found a scrap of fabric that could have been there for years. A wider fingertip-search of the arboretum had turned up more items, discarded sweet wrappers, lollipop sticks, cigarette butts; nothing they wouldn't have expected in a place like this. It looked like the best chance of finding any real evidence lay with the body itself.

The body itself, thought Cate: *Teresa King*. Of course, people were impersonalised after death, it was a necessary part of the job, but she couldn't quite get used to it. It was for the police to sort out the aftermath; they had to leave it to the families to grieve. And yet there was a sense of sadness hanging over this place.

'Shall we head down?' Dan asked. Cate turned and he pointed, not the way they had come but towards a narrow path that led towards the lake. It looked steep, and was shrouded in trees. 'Short-cut.'

She grinned and followed as he pushed his way between low, wiry branches. Everything was damp; everything dripped. She pictured Stocky, standing out in the open in the rain, the expression that would be on his face. At least it might make him feel better when he saw the state of the two of them. Dan let a branch swing back now and shining droplets flew from it, soaking into her clothes. She could see the lake ahead, glimpses of grey; the slope was beginning to level out. Then she grabbed Dan's arm.

There was someone below them, walking along the path; she could hear their footsteps. She wasn't sure why she'd stopped; she had done it without thinking.

'What's—?' Dan started, and she shook her head. She had no explanation to offer; after all, they had let walkers resume using the lakeside paths, wanting the local community to get back to normal as soon as it could.

But the sound of footsteps had stopped too. She peered down through the trees. The lake was like a misted mirror, hazed with light rain. In front of that she could see a patch of the red-brown path, and as she watched, someone stepped into it. Cate recognised them at once.

She started down, strode over a boggy strip separating the wood from the path and landed in front of the walker.

Alice jumped back; her eyes widened, then she visibly relaxed. 'Cate.'

Cate noted the woman's surprise and felt unaccountably irritated. Didn't Alice realise she was playing into Heath's hands? What had he said – something about her showing up conveniently, in time to see the body? But of course it hadn't been like that, it was she who'd gone to Alice, wanting to use her expertise. But she couldn't shift Heath's words – and the way he'd said them – from her mind.

When she spoke, her voice was abrupt: 'What are you doing here?'

Alice frowned. 'I live here.'

Cate looked at the rain-misted lake and the trees; then she glanced up the opposite slope. She couldn't see Alice's house, but she knew it was there, just beyond the woods. Of course it was.

'I always come walking here,' Alice said, 'when I want to think.' She sounded a little hurt.

'Okay,' Cate said in a softer tone, 'but please, be careful, that's all.' *Watch her*, Heath had said. *Watch her*.

'I will – although I don't feel like they're here any more, do you?' Alice looked around, her eyes unfocused.

'They?'

'Whoever did this – oh, I don't know. It just feels like

they've moved on, doesn't it? I'm probably being stupid. It's just that I *always* walk in these woods. I don't feel like I should let something like this drive me away. What would I do? I'd sit inside and stare at the walls.'

Cate sighed, but it was Dan who spoke: 'That might be best, at least until this is over. You never know who might be around.'

Alice met his eyes and opened her mouth as if she was about to say something, then she closed it again and looked away. 'I'm sure you're right.'

Once again Cate felt an irritation she couldn't explain. 'You're getting soaked,' she said. 'Maybe you *should* head home for now.'

Alice shook herself, took hold of the jacket that was wrapped around her shoulders and pulled it on. She smiled at Cate. 'Okay. Well, I'll see you again.' She turned and walked away while Cate and Dan remained where they were.

'She's an odd one,' he said.

Cate watched Alice until she reached a turn in the path and was lost to view. She realised the girl would now be within sight of Stocky, that she would have to explain her presence all over again. He would probably be even more blunt than she had been, and she felt a stab of guilt as she remembered Alice's hurt look. The girl was right: she should be able to walk in the woods that spread from her own back door without having to justify it. She pictured

Heath's face, sneering. She knew exactly what he'd say if he found out that Alice had been walking in this stretch of the woods: *They like to come back*, he'd say. *They like nothing better than to revisit the scene of the crime.*

CHAPTER TWENTY-ONE

When Cate and Dan got back to the station they found everything in a stir. The autopsy results were in and the forensic pathologist was being ushered into the briefing room. After a quick glance at each other, they slipped inside and the doors closed behind them.

The pathologist was an older gentleman, with clouds of white hair clinging above his ears, his scalp shining under the strip-lights. He shuffled papers in his hands, cleared his throat and looked out at them over his half-moon glasses. Cate imagined him peering over the girl like that, her body opened out like a book for him to read; Alice's way of seeing things rubbing off on her, perhaps.

'The time of death is estimated at between 2 a.m. and 3 a.m.,' he began. 'From the lividity on the victim's body we can ascertain she was moved after death and before being found. So she could have been transported in a car, or some other method of conveyance.'

Cate found herself turning to exchange a glance with

Len, but of course he wasn't there; there was only Dan, who looked back at her, half puzzled, half appraising. Cate faced front again. She knew why he had looked at her that way; it was the same expression he'd worn earlier when she'd asked him to wait while she hurried back down the lakeside path after Alice, ready to intercede between her contact and Len Stockdale, before he could start to question Alice, or note down her name in his book.

Dan hadn't asked why she'd headed off so quickly; hopefully he had thought she just needed a quick word with a fellow officer, but she wondered now if there was some suspicion in his mind. She hoped he wouldn't notice a small omission in the record; thanks to her intervention, Alice's presence near the crime scene had not been noted. She wasn't sure why she had done it, not really. It had been stupid, but it couldn't make any difference.

Heath was standing at the front of the room, glowering at the gathered officers while the pathologist spoke, and she felt a mingling of guilt and relief. If he'd found out about Alice's presence at the lake he'd never have let it go; it would have been time and attention that wasn't focused on finding the killer. But she knew she had created a problem with Stocky too. He'd done what she'd asked, but she knew he hadn't liked it. He had only agreed because she was so insistent it couldn't matter. When Cate finished speaking to him at the lakeside, there had been a new look in his eyes, and it wasn't one she liked. She'd already annoyed him by being singled out as part of this investigation, but until now she'd never given him cause to doubt her abilities, or her judgement.

She forced herself to focus on the pathologist's words.

'The teeth placed in the victim's mouth were those of a child,' he said. 'They're milk teeth, and they appear to have fallen out naturally rather than having been drawn. Judging from their condition, that could have been quite some years ago.'

The room had fallen silent. Cate's heart began to beat faster and she wondered if everyone was thinking the same thing: that this could be the breakthrough they needed. If the teeth were years old, kept since someone was a child – they could even be the killer's own teeth. She stuck her hand in the air and called out, 'Is there any way of telling if they're male or female?'

'Not yet, I'm afraid, not so far. There are differences in male and female teeth – the canines are bigger in males, and there are differences in crown dimension, for example – but we haven't found anything conclusive in the examples we have. We are making attempts to extract DNA from the pulp, in which case we will be able to ascertain sex, but my feeling is that the teeth are too old and it is likely to be too degraded. It's a slim chance.'

Cate's mind was racing. If they could extract DNA, they could test it against Cosgrove's. And if it wasn't him, they could at least test Alice's theories and confirm once and for all if the killer was a man or a woman. Or was she getting too close to Alice's ideas? She took a calming breath.

They didn't even know if the teeth had once been the killer's; they might be anyone's. He could have dug them up, for all they knew. What was wrong with her? She had to do as Heath said, slow down, try to be methodical.

An image of Len Stockdale flashed into her mind; he had that same look in his eye. *Are you really sure you know what you're doing, Cate?*

Someone else asked, 'Do you think the teeth could be the victim's kid? Maybe she had a child somewhere.'

Cate started. She hadn't thought of that.

The pathologist shook his head. 'There are signs that Teresa King had had an abortion in the past. It wasn't in her medical records, so she might have gone under a different name, or had it done somewhere – unofficial, let's say. I don't believe she's ever given birth. From the scarring I'd say it was unlikely she'd ever have been able to have children, had she lived.'

Cate winced. The girl's options for a family had been taken from her when she was little more than a child herself: the path of needles, indeed. She pictured Teresa standing hollow-eyed on some street corner, waiting for someone, anyone, who might come along and decide they wanted her, for a time.

The pathologist cleared his throat and looked around the room to make sure he had everyone's attention. 'The cause of death was as expected,' he said. 'There was massive blood loss from the girl's abdominal wound. The odd thing, however, is the cause of the wound. It was strikingly obvious that the flesh had been torn as well as cut. Furthermore, there were distinct signs of claw-marks to be found within it.'

Cate felt the buzz that jumped from person to person and sat up a little straighter herself.

The pathologist took off his glasses. 'It looks as if she was attacked by an animal, clawed, possibly bitten, but the only traces of animal activity have come from the insects and birds that interfered with the body at the scene. In wounds like this we would expect to find dog DNA – hair, saliva; or perhaps signs of foxes biting at the corpse. However, we found nothing of the kind. The body was remarkably clean.'

He held up a hand, holding back any questions, and the room fell silent. 'From superficial appearances I would say she was the victim of not only a human but also an animal attack, possibly by a large dog. The girl had liga-ture marks on her wrists and bruising to her face: she was certainly overpowered and restrained. It's quite possible she was conscious while the wounds were inflicted and unable to do anything to prevent it. I saw something similar once where an attack dog was effectively – very effectively – used as a murder weapon. But as I say, the wounds in this case are too clean, and the lack of further evidence of the animal is highly unusual, if not remark-able.'

The questions began: 'Could you have missed some-thing?'

The pathologist half turned away. 'Highly unlikely, although we *are* carrying out further tests.'

'What if the killer had prepared the animal – washed it?'

'What if he'd cleaned the wound?'

'We would still expect to find some sort of transfer – epithelial cells from its skin, hair . . . no, it isn't likely.'

'So it might not have been an animal at all?'

'The pattern of the wounds suggests it was, but we can only state what the evidence tells us.' The pathologist straightened. 'It's up to others to do the guesswork.'

'Could it have been a wolf?'

Cate couldn't see who'd asked the question, but she saw its effect. Everyone was quiet, waiting for the answer.

The pathologist paused. 'As I said, it might fit the pattern of the wounds, but the lack of trace evidence would make it somewhat remarkable. As would the appearance of wolves in Wakefield.' He raised his eyebrows, peering over his glasses until the sniggers faded from the room, and then he turned away. The briefing was over.

Everyone started talking, each turning to their neighbour to make comment, and Cate several times caught the word 'wolf'. Suddenly she knew, with a tight feeling in her stomach, that's what they would call him; she could already see it in tomorrow's papers. THE WOLF STRIKES. THE WOLF STALKS. THE WOLF IN THE WOODS. This was exactly what the investigation didn't need, a serial killer invested with a name like that; something that set him – or her – apart, making them just a little less than human, so that if a member of the public should happen to meet them, pass them in the street or in a shop, they would never recognise them for what they were.

And she realised something else. *Massive blood loss*, he'd said – that was what had killed the girl. In other words, she had been alive when he'd done that to her. Her heart must still have been beating. *Had* she been conscious? Little Red meeting the wolf at last, at least in some guise – not safely within the covers of a book but someplace real that was full of blood and pain and death, and someone looking on, with – what? – on their face. Pleasure? Satisfaction? Joy?

She clenched her fists.

'You okay?'

She looked around and was surprised to find it was Dan who'd asked. She was about to answer, but then Heath was at the front of the room, stepping forward for a few last words, and the moment had gone.

He told them that they would be kept informed about any further DNA results, that they were bringing in a profiler to give further insight. They *were* treating the murderer as a serial killer, then, Cate thought. They must feel, as she did, that this wasn't over.

She wondered what a profiler would make of Alice's ideas. Of course, they'd probably assume the killer was a man; they usually were. She found she wanted to talk over the latest findings with Alice – or perhaps it was the reality of the girl's death that had made Cate think of her, the lecturer whose world seemed half composed of fantasy. She tried not to think of the victim, her body exhausted by drugs and bad living, tied down while some animal attacked her. Sometimes there could be too much reality; it would be comforting, after all, if it were nothing but a tale to frighten children.

CHAPTER TWENTY-TWO

Cate parked at the head of the narrow lane by the wood and walked towards Alice's cottage. As she let herself in at the little green gate, she saw Alice sitting in one of the windows, her blonde hair falling over her eyes as she bent over a book. She stood there for a moment, feeling like an intruder, and Heath's words echoed in her mind: *watch her*. But she hadn't expected to see her like that – she hadn't meant to sneak up on her. She'd only parked at the end of the lane because it was narrow, and it was pleasant for walking; the evening had turned brighter than the day and the air was now clear and warm.

Watch her. Heath's voice had become insidious; that man trusted no one. Cate felt guilty whenever she thought about it, the way her contact had been interrogated over her lakeside walk. And yet here she was standing motionless, watching Alice after all. She roused herself, went up to the door and knocked. After a moment it opened and Alice stood blinking on the threshold as if her eyes hadn't yet adjusted from whatever she'd been reading.

Cate realised she didn't have a clue what she was going to say, but Alice saved her the trouble by smiling a welcome and stepping back. Cate followed her inside and watched the girl busying herself about the kitchen, pouring floral-smelling tea from a china pot. Late sunshine slanted through the windows, warming everything.

'I've been thinking about this case,' said Alice, as though it was she who had asked Cate to come. 'I can't get it out of my mind.'

Cate smiled. 'Maybe you should have been a detective.'

Alice let out a spurt of laughter. 'That's funny. The other day, I actually thought you should have studied literature. The way you saw a fairy tale in that first girl's death – it wasn't obvious. Not everyone would have thought of it.'

'Not me, I belong in the real world.' Cate paused. 'Sorry. I didn't mean it to sound like that. It's just – I always wanted to join the police, to get out there on the street, do my bit. Studying stories, over and over – it leads only to itself, doesn't it?'

Alice raised her eyebrows. 'Well, not this time, obviously.'

'But don't you ever—?'

'What – want to escape my ivory tower? Like Rapunzel, let down my hair?' Alice tilted her head, half smiling, half mocking. 'Not me. I always – I don't know. I grew up on these stories, I suppose. I always felt there was a little bit of magic in them, somewhere, if I could only find it. My mother used to call me Alice in Wonderland.' She leaned back on the counter and her eyes went distant.

'Used to?'

Alice sighed. 'She still would if she could recognise me, I suppose. My mother isn't well – she doesn't remember much. She's in a home now.' She hesitated. 'I couldn't really cope with her on my own. I sometimes wish I could go back, you know – to those times.' She set down her mug with a bang. 'It's stupid: I'm like an overgrown kid, still looking for the bloody wonderland.' She caught Cate's eye. 'Of course, there isn't one – there certainly isn't a handsome prince. Typical,' she spat, and Cate found herself laughing.

After a moment, Alice laughed too. Then she grew serious. 'I'll tell you why the old stories are important,' she said. 'They're all about how one day you might grow up to have a good heart, or slay the dragon, or overcome problems, to value love instead of possessions. Now all the stories we tell our kids are about how you might grow up to be on TV, get rich or marry a footballer, because we started to tell stories about real things, to model ourselves on real people. And this is what you get.' She paused. 'I always loved fairy tales. I always thought I'd *like* anyone who loved them too. Now all this is happening and the death is real and I don't know any more. It's as if the things I love have turned into horrors.'

Cate nodded. 'I kind of know what you mean. It *is* too

real.' She explained the pathologist's findings, the claw-marks that had been found on Teresa King's body.

'Red in tooth and claw,' Alice said, and Cate remembered it wasn't the first time she'd used those words.

'Of course,' Alice said, 'some see Little Red as a replay of older stories still, of ancient myth – the way people used to try and understand the world. Little Red is supposed to be about the death of the evening sun and the coming of the dawn. It's quite an optimistic interpretation, actually.' Her eyes went to the window, the sunshine streaming in, and Cate followed her gaze. The apple tree was now a mass of white blossom; it made everything look so peaceful.

For a while Alice seemed to forget that Cate was there, and then she explained: 'Little Red is the evening sun, shining on Grandmother Earth; the wolf is the night which swallowed her, which desired to keep the earth in darkness; and dawn comes in the guise of a hunter, slaying the night and freeing the sun from its belly, bringing life to the world once more.

'Some say it grew out of ancient Hindu stories,' she added, 'that it's really about Indra, the sun god, trying to save everyone from a dragon that's trying to devour the sun.'

'You didn't mention that before.'

'Mention what?'

'That version of the story. You talked about an Italian one, said it explained the teeth being there.'

'There are lots of variants – or versions – hundreds of them, from all over the world. I didn't think it was relevant.'

'But maybe it is. Maybe we need to look at *all* of the versions, see what was missing as well as what was present.'

'Maybe.' Alice sighed. 'Of course, in that particular story, Little Red and the grandmother come back to life. I suppose *that's* what's really missing.'

CHAPTER TWENTY-THREE

Alice stood in the doorway, watching the policewoman walk down the lane, listening as her footsteps faded. She remained standing there, and after a while she realised she was listening to another sound, higher and sharper; somewhere, a distance away, a bird was singing.

She went through the house, made her way to the back door and opened it onto the garden. Daffodils gleamed in the soft light. Everywhere new flowers were opening, bright splashes of colour. Then another shade caught her eye, a flash of brilliant blue flitting from branch to branch of the apple tree: the blue bird had come back to her. Alice stared, feeling strangely satisfied, and something else: proprietorial.

She smiled at herself. She should do something practical for the creature, set out food for it, instead of just standing here watching; but it was singing now with great gusto, thrusting out its chest and chirruping. It didn't need Alice, it was something healthy and free that had bestowed its presence willingly, like a gift.

Alice shook her head. She wasn't Alice in Wonderland, wasn't in some fairy tale; she was only Alice, and she belonged in the real world. She had chores to do, marking and reading and washing-up.

She went inside, closed the door and found that she hadn't managed to shut out the blue bird's song after all; it had followed her, shrill and insistent, into the house. Unconsciously, her hand went to her pocket. She found something that was at once smooth as glass and rough as a cat's tongue, depending on the way she touched it: the blue feather the bird had given her. It had been with her, all through the woods and the things she had seen, placed in the pocket of whatever she chose to wear, something magical yet close. When she peered out of the window again, though, the bird itself was already flying away.

CHAPTER TWENTY-FOUR

Ellen Robertson opened her eyes and saw the pale butterscotch of the ceiling. She smiled. In some ways the house still didn't feel like hers, but in other ways it did. This room was one of the things that did; she loved the way the sun slanted through the window in the early mornings, turning everything to warmth. She never felt alone here, despite the fact that her husband had already left for the day; he liked to catch the early train and make a good impression. She hadn't yet found a job, although if things went to plan, that might not be necessary. One never knew how quickly these things could happen – or, indeed, how long it could take.

The smile faded and she smoothed the sheets down over her body, allowing herself to drift a little longer. After a while a sound intruded, pulling her back to the present. A bird was singing, not some delicate tune but a shrill admonishment that went on and on. Perhaps it was more than one bird; they could be sitting in the eaves, squabbling together. It might even be a nest, lined with down and full of hungry beaks.

She didn't know if she liked that thought or not, but she slid out from beneath the sheets and went to the window. The view was of hills and fields, stretching on for miles. Traffic was already whining down the distant motorway, the sound travelling clear across the flat spaces. Then a blue shape flashed past, startling her.

She stepped back. She hadn't expected to actually see a bird, let alone one of such a strident colour, but perhaps it hadn't been a bird at all. It could have been a rag flying on the wind, or a discarded sweet wrapper.

She leaned closer and looked down into the garden, and saw it sitting on the wall. It *was* a bird, it was still singing, and it was still undeniably blue. Her eyes widened. Hadn't there been something on the news about this? It was rare and beautiful and strange, and here it was, outside her window. If she was quick she could take a picture. Maybe she could send it to the newspaper. She hurried towards the study, ducking automatically under the low doorframe; it was something else she had rapidly got used to, that made the house feel like her own.

She had just worked the camera out of its case when she heard the banging on the door. It was loud and as insistent as the blue bird's song and she jumped, her heart thudding. For a moment she was frozen, staring towards the stairs, wondering if there could have been some mistake. She wasn't expecting anybody. No: the banging came again, hard and rapid.

She glanced towards the bedroom. If she went to the door she might miss her opportunity to photograph the bird, but she couldn't ignore knocking like that; it must mean something. Anyway, the blue bird would probably have heard it too and been frightened away.

She had already started for the stairs when the knocking came again. She couldn't stop herself jumping as she ran under the door and as she hurried to answer she banged her head against the frame.

CHAPTER TWENTY-FIVE

Len Stockdale looked up as Cate sat down at her desk. She tried to gauge his expression, but it didn't spark any warning lights; he looked a little guarded, perhaps even subdued, although his tone was friendly enough.

'Any developments?' he asked.

She pulled a face. 'Not really.'

He opened his mouth, looked as if he was going to make some sarcastic comment – 'Nothing you can tell me about,' perhaps – but he resisted the urge and closed it again. Then he said, 'I hear they couldn't get anything from the teeth.'

She sighed. 'The sample was too degraded – too old.'

'I hear they definitely haven't found any animal DNA in the wound, either. They've packed in trying.'

'Really?' She'd known they were doing further tests but she hadn't heard the results, and she didn't know they'd given up.

'Nothing, not even around the claw-marks. Though that

pathologist couldn't find his arse with both hands. That poor kid. She—'

'They really found nothing, not even skin cells? If a dog had—'

'They don't think it was a dog, Cate.'

She took a deep breath. She had known that news of the investigation would spread through the station, but wasn't sure how she'd come to be briefed by PC Stockdale, when she was on the case and he was not.

He smiled, though there was no humour in it. 'Don't worry, Cate. I'm only in it for the donkey work, remember? I have a wood to stand guard over.' He met her eye and this time there was something in his expression; Cate remembered the way she'd asked him to ignore Alice's presence by the lake and she changed the subject.

'So if the wound was clean . . . How do they think that was possible? If it was a wolf—'

'A wolf?' Len let out a sharp laugh. 'It's not a wolf, Cate. They're only calling him that.'

'I know, but the killer is doing this to fit the story, and the story had a wolf in it, so—'

'So.' He took a deep breath and shifted in his chair. 'You don't want to get drawn in too deep, Cate. Keep your head, or you might be blind to it when anything happens that's outside your way of thinking: when he slips.'

She paused, feeling the weight of experience behind his words. Then she couldn't stop herself: 'It *fits*,' she said, 'all except for the lack of skin cells or hair from the animal.'

'Maybe he didn't use an animal. Maybe he made the marks in the wound another way. He might have wanted it to look like that, but did it in some way that he could keep sterile.'

Cate stared at him and he looked back at her, not speaking. It flashed into Cate's mind again that Len must surely, at some time, have thought of moving to CID. *Of course* that must be how it had been done. Why hadn't she seen that for herself? She should have thought of it. As the silence stretched out, it occurred to her that maybe he was right about other things too. Maybe she *wasn't* seeing things clearly. In another way, though, didn't it also mean she was right? The killer had wanted to follow the fairy tale, and so he – or she – had created claw-marks without claws.

She tried to cover her confusion. 'Was there any other trace?'

'Not that I heard. Oh, but they did find something in the bread. Pesticide, I believe, like at the first scene.'

'Poisoned bread – for Grandmother?' Cate didn't try to hide her incredulity this time, ignoring Len's expression. She couldn't help it: unlike the claw-marks, this didn't fit at all. Little Red Riding Hood was taking food to *help* Grandmother, not to kill her. So what was that supposed to mean? Or perhaps it was a mistake, the poison had been used to subdue her, and the bread had merely been contaminated ... except in that case, they would have found traces of it in the body.

She stared helplessly at Len. What had he just said – that she should stand back from this, take a longer view? *Or you might be blind to it, when anything happens that's outside your way of thinking: when he slips.*

'I have to go,' she said, casting a glance at her watch. She was about to go off shift, and she needed to speak to Alice Hyland. She didn't tell Stocky, though, and she tried not to see the expression on his face as she hurried away.

Cate knocked on the door and waited. When Alice opened it and stepped back in surprise, she shrugged helplessly. 'Sorry to bother you again,' she said, 'but something came up. May I?'

Alice gestured her inside and she followed her into the kitchen. 'There's been some new information released. They found poison in the bread that was taken from the basket at the Little Red Riding Hood scene – can you tell me about it? Do you know what variation of the fairy tale it's from?'

'Variant,' Alice corrected, speaking automatically; her expression was distant. Then she stirred. 'It's not from a variant. The bread's meant for the grandmother. It isn't from any version of the story I know.' She frowned. 'Are you sure? It doesn't make sense. Little Red takes food to the grandmother because she's ill, or old, or frail. The grandmother is torn apart by the wolf, then so is Little Red. The huntsman—' Suddenly she yawned widely, showing the pink inside of her mouth. 'You know the rest. We went through all this. There's no poison.'

'What about the other one you told me about – where Little Red is the dawn or something like that? Isn't the earth being poisoned? And the earth is the grandmother.'

'It's being enveloped in darkness,' said Alice, 'not poisoned exactly, not in the sense you mean. I'm not sure what that would mean, really: the bread just shouldn't be poisoned. It's an exception, I'd say. Maybe your killer got it wrong.'

'You really think so?' Cate couldn't keep the tone of excitement out of her voice.

Alice shrugged. 'They must have. Unless they needed the poison for something else. It's not in the story, anyway.' She sagged, leaning against the kitchen table, and Cate noticed how tired she looked. Was that what she had done to her with her questions?

'It all comes back to the stories,' she prompted. 'Can you think how it might fit?'

Alice shook her head. 'Not that part.'

'It must mean something.' She clenched her fist, stopped short of battering it against Alice's table. 'Why all the stupid stories anyway? This is driving me mad.'

Alice took an audible breath and began to pace up and down. She didn't look at Cate; her expression was calm, as if not conscious of being watched at all. 'All right,' she said, 'so these girls – the murdered girls – have been pictured like characters in fairy tales. This much we know.

But it's more than that, it's like they *are* the stories, or someone's own variant of them, anyway: a new way of telling them.' She paused. 'You know, I keep thinking about that girl, the one I *saw*. The one in the photographs – that wasn't the same, was it? Not like seeing her in the flesh.' Her voice cracked. 'I couldn't help thinking – all those police, the cars, the effort. It wouldn't have happened if it wasn't for the stories, would it? Without that – the red cape, the basket, all of it – she'd be nothing but a dead girl dumped in the woods – no, worse than that: a dead *whore*. At least this way someone cares.' She turned her eyes on Cate. 'So the tales count for something. At least being part of a story means she *matters*.'

Cate opened her eyes wide in surprise. 'Of course she matters.'

'Does she? She's not just another dead junkie, a hooker off the streets? Junkies die all the time, don't they?'

Cate took half a step back. She hadn't expected such vehemence from Alice, not about something happening in the real world: Alice only seemed to half live in the real world, come to that. This is what she, Cate, had done, dragging her into it, firmly and irreversibly. 'I'm sorry,' she said, 'but of course I care.' As she said the words she found herself wondering how much: would she have wanted to be on this case so badly if it was as ordinary, as sordid, as another dead junkie?

Alice was staring into space, her mouth hanging open. 'What is it?'

'Christ,' Alice said. Her eyes focused on Cate. 'Do you think—?'

'What?' asked Cate. 'Alice, are you all right?'

'They die *all the time*,' she said. 'What was it about these cases that was different?'

'The way she was posed. You know that. I saw it and it made me think of—'

'Exactly. It made *you* think.'

'I don't know what you're getting at.'

Alice raised a hand, snapped her fingers in the air. 'How do you know there haven't been others?'

'Oh—' said Cate.

'Exactly,' said Alice. 'I know the Farrell girl was different, but maybe there have been others, ones like the prostitute. There might have been others where nobody bothered to think, or nobody saw it the way you did. You need to look at old cases – older, anyway. See if any of the bodies looked posed, if anything was found with them. The first girl, in the photographs – it wasn't that obvious it was supposed to be a fairy tale. This might have been happening for years.'

Cate didn't answer. Instead she took a long, deep breath. She was already running through everything she would need to do: she must speak to Heath again and make sure they'd accessed all the old case files – unsolved murders with sus circs, particularly involving young women, look at missing persons. It was likely they'd done it already, but maybe they could turn up something new. It could give them the breakthrough they needed, give the profilers more to work with, find DNA or other evidence they could use to piece together a real suspect list.

Stocky couldn't doubt her any longer after that; with a breakthrough in the case that had come from Alice, Cate would be vindicated. And she would need Alice more than ever. If she looked through the old cases she might not see the things Alice saw. As unpleasant as it was – as undesirable, to have a civilian dragged into this – if she saw anything that felt likely, she would have to ask Alice to review the cases too.

She was trying to work out how she would explain that to Heath – and to Stocky – when her mobile rang.

'I know you're off duty,' the voice said; it was Dan, 'but there's been another one. It's at Sandal Castle. I suggest you get over there now.'

'Is it the same? Posed, like the others?'

'No,' he said, 'not the same at all.'

'Then why—?'

'She's still alive,' he said, 'that's why not. The ambulance is on its way. As am I.'

The phone went dead.

Cate and Alice stared at each other. Then Cate got moving, headed for the door. She turned and looked back. Alice was still watching her, and she had a question in her eyes. After a moment, Cate said, 'Come on.' The girl – if it was a girl – who'd been found at the castle would be rushed into hospital. If there was anything to be gleaned from seeing the place where she'd been found, the *way* she'd been found, it would be best if Alice was there to see it too.

CHAPTER TWENTY-SIX

The old grey stone of the castle was darkening to black in the fading day as Cate pulled into the parking area. The cracked asphalt was pulsing with blue flashing lights and when she opened the door she heard voices, low and urgent. The sound was inimical to the peaceful, silent sky, the ancient presence of the place. The castle walls were a jagged line topped by the reaching fingers of its ruined towers. The air was cool but unexpectedly humid, as if the spring dusk would at any moment turn to rain.

Cate glanced back at the access road. The other side of Manygates Lane was lined with houses that faced the castle grounds; most of the windows were dark and it was impossible to see who might be watching. Near to where she stood, a neat path led away towards the visitors' centre.

Cate strode up the short bank that divided the car park from the castle grounds and Alice followed. Figures milled about, busy sectioning off the site, and she recognised

Dan, who nodded in greeting before he saw Alice and frowned. He looked at Cate.

She asked: 'What's happening?'

He pointed into the site. 'She's there,' he said. 'She's gone. Dead when we got here.'

'What? You said she was all right.'

'No, I said she was *alive*, that's what we were told when this was called in, but when we got here, she'd already gone. The doctor's called it.' His voice dropped an octave. 'Looks like the people who found her made a mistake. She *looked* alive, though. I doubt she'd been dead long.'

'Jesus.' Cate stared towards the castle.

'Heath won't like it,' Dan said in a low voice, looking at Alice. 'Didn't he say—?'

'I know what he said.' Cate swallowed. 'It's my responsibility. I thought—'

'Corbin.' The hoarse, tired-sounding voice cut her off. Heath was striding towards them. 'Dan – make sure this place is shut down before the fucking circus arrives.' He looked towards the visitors' centre, then finally back at Cate. He turned without saying anything else, then, over his shoulder: 'Hang around. You too, if you will, Ms Hyland.'

Cate stood with Alice as the evening grew darker and a yellow moon rose over the castle walls, and then out of their grasp. Alice didn't speak, just watched everything, and Cate wondered how she could be so calm – but perhaps she was like Cate herself: outwardly quiet while inside, the questions burned. They faced the shattered remnants of the curtain wall, those eroded towers outlining the scene. Before them the ground undulated over long-buried structures. She knew that it dipped steeply into a dry moat nearer the castle. Now she could only make it out by the shine of spotlights. In contrast to the sudden brightness, the short-cropped grass around the place looked almost black. SOCOs came and went, their hooded figures turned to ghosts against the shadows.

There was another light too, somewhere higher up and further away. It streaked the sky, almost as if it were floating; Cate knew it must be from the wooden platform built across what would once have been the highest point of the castle.

She had visited this place with her parents when she was young, and occasionally she still came walking here when the mood took her. Though little remained of the original castle keep, it was set atop a huge mound – the motte – probably created with earth excavated from the moat. In recent years that wooden platform had been built over it so that tourists could walk up there and enjoy the view without clambering over rough stones, destroying the history under their feet.

Battles had been fought and lost in the fields around this site. Somewhere was a commemorative stone that marked the death of Richard Plantagenet at the Battle of Wakefield – she'd never forgotten that old mnemonic for remembering the colours of the rainbow: *Richard of York gave battle in vain*. Now there was nothing to see but a field.

Someone strode towards them, his feet silent on the grass, but his presence commanded attention all the same. 'Ms Hyland,' Heath said. 'Come with me.'

He headed away with Alice at his side and Cate followed, keeping close so that she would hear anything that was said; but he didn't speak, didn't give anything away at all. They paused only to pull on protective clothing before he led them towards the moat. Cate began to make out details: a short distance away was one of the newer wooden structures, a bridge that crossed the ancient defences – but they stopped before they reached it, near the glow she'd seen which resolved itself into individual points of light. Figures were moving down there, passing in and out of the shadows.

Heath took one step onto the banking. 'A moment,' he said, addressing Alice again; he still hadn't said a word to Cate. He half stepped, half slithered away from them, disappearing into the ditch with a muffled curse. Alice glanced at Cate, then followed, taking Heath's hand when he backtracked to help her down. Cate scrambled after them; Heath was already heading further along the moat, taking Alice with him.

The girl lay a short distance away, surrounded by more lights and the pale overalls of scene-of-crime officers, who stood back when Heath approached. Both of them stopped and looked on, not speaking. Cate peered between them and saw the body.

She was facing upwards, her blank eyes staring into the blank sky. She had been covered with a large coat, but her dress spread beneath it, the white fabric of the full skirts shining in the spotlights. She looked a little older than Chrissie Farrell and Teresa King; her face was pale, calm, almost serene. Cate thought at first that her dark blonde hair was patched with colourant, then realised it was streaked with mud.

Heath said something in a low voice and a SOCO stepped forward and lifted the coat away, revealing that the girl's dress was muddied too, as if she had been rolled down the slope. Perhaps whoever placed her here had struggled to move her. Cate looked at the bank next to the body and noted that the area had been kept clear; probably the reason they'd climbed down further along the moat, so as not to trample over any footprints the killer may have left behind.

There was something else too. The way the girl was lying – it wasn't quite right, not *organised* enough. One arm was splayed at her side, the other trapped beneath her. For a moment Cate wondered if this was linked to the other cases at all, or was something else: then she saw what had been revealed beneath the coat. A single white rose had been placed on the girl's body, and an image flashed into Cate's mind of the girl's hands resting on it, holding it in death. Was that how she'd been left? She had been discovered by someone who'd assumed she was alive; perhaps they had done this, disturbed the positioning of the body when they tried to revive her.

Cate squinted and saw a narrow band wrapped around the girl's dress, drawing it in close to her body. She thought at first it was a belt, but it was too thin, like twine; then she saw it was green, a wiry stem, and there were thorns jutting from it.

There was something lying next to her head, too. Cate shuffled further around; no, it wasn't *next* to her head, it was fastened to it, a small hat such as a child might make out of paper. She almost hadn't seen it in the shadows because it was completely black.

Heath stirred, squinting around at Cate as if he'd just noticed her. 'PC Corbin,' he said, 'you'll do. I want you back up top. The people who found her are waiting up there – accompany them out of here, would you?'

Cate murmured her assent. She felt the night's cold cut through her as she turned her back on the scene – and on Alice. Why keep her contact here and send Cate away? But there was work to do, and she was needed to do it; she couldn't think about that now. She concentrated on retracing her steps and climbing the steep side of the moat in the dark.

The couple who'd found the body were middle-aged, their faces pale, and they didn't ask questions, didn't say anything at all; they just waited for instructions. The woman drew her coat tightly around her and looked at Cate with a plea in her eyes. *We don't belong here*, that look said.

For a moment Cate felt lost, as helpless as the girl who had been left in the ditch; then she led them away back to the edge of the car park by the visitors' centre. Dan was still there and he caught her eye and came over.

'If you wouldn't mind coming with me,' he said to the man, and led him a short distance away from his wife.

Cate looked after them and realised he'd done the right thing in separating the couple. It meant they could each take an initial account of what they'd witnessed before the pair could discuss what had happened, possibly influencing each other's formal statements. All the same, she wished she could hear what they were saying.

She turned to the woman, who watched as Cate took out her notepad and flipped it open. Cate spoke gently, taking down her details for the record and so that any background checks Heath felt to be necessary could be carried out; though her instincts told her that the couple were just as they appeared, innocent passers-by who'd encountered more than they had ever wished to see on their evening walk.

They were married, the woman – Sandra – told her, and out for a stroll, like they often did at this time of day. They'd parked at the boating lake at the foot of the hill and walked up to enjoy the view from the top. She cast a concerned glance in the direction of the lake when she said that and Cate knew she was thinking that the gates would have been closed down there, locking their car in.

Cate remembered what she had seen in the moat and mentally shrugged; there were worse things.

'So you were the ones who called the police?'

'And the ambulance, love. I mean, we've 'eard the stories. I asked for the police first, but Gerry said we'd better check, and I said, no, it's like the others, the ones in the paper. He checked anyway – he was brave, braver than me – and it was like we said, she was still alive.'

Cate looked over at Gerry, who was talking to Dan without looking at him; his eyes were fixed on the ground. He wore only a thin shirt and now he wrapped his arms around himself. Cate realised where the coat had come from that was covering the girl.

'How did you ascertain that she was alive? Was she conscious – did she say anything?'

Sandra grimaced. 'She didn't look like she was dead, that's all. Gerry tried her wrist, and he thought he felt a pulse, only she didn't seem to be breathing. I – he wasn't sure.' Her voice broke.

'So he touched her hands. Did he move—?'

'He tried to do the kiss o' life, love,' Sandra broke in, 'but after that he tried her wrist again and he didn't feel a pulse at all.' She looked at her husband, a wild look in her eyes.

'And then what happened?'

'Nothing, love. We called an ambulance. It was me did that. Only it came and went, and *that* one' – she pointed towards the motte – 'he said she were dead after all, that it wasn't any use. Gerry didn't think so, though. She had a pulse. He *thought* she had a pulse. That's what he said.' She shuddered. 'I couldn't have touched her, not me, but he did, my Gerry. So brave, he was. An' he left her his coat.' She met Cate's eye. 'I don't suppose he'll want it back, now. And it wasn't any use anyhow, was it?'

No, thought Cate, it wasn't any use. They were too late, always too late. Maybe if someone had seen the girl earlier – she remembered the abandoned form lying on the ground, her pale dress, its delicate material too diaphanous to protect anyone against the dark hillside on this cold night.

When the witnesses had left, Cate found Dan again. He was still at the edge of the site, making sure no one unauthorised crossed the line. 'Your friend gone?' he asked.

Cate shook her head. 'Alice is still going over the scene with Heath.'

'Ah – is she? Which one?'

'Which what?'

He pointed ahead of them and a little to the right, upwards to where the other light still shone. Cate had put it out of her mind; she had been too preoccupied, though now she thought of it, she'd heard footsteps up there too, hadn't she? The hard echoing of footsteps on a wooden platform, way above the moat.

'They found something else up there. I'm not sure what.'

'Another victim?'

He shook his head.

Cate took a deep breath. 'All right. I won't be long.'

She felt Dan's eyes on her back, but he didn't say anything as she headed into the dark once more. Heath hadn't ordered her away from the scene, had he, not specifically? He'd told her to look after the witnesses and she'd done that; she had listened to the woman's story and taken her details. Now she was simply seeing what else she could do.

Once she'd passed the light coming from the first scene, it was easier to see the second. Cate felt exposed as she crossed the ditch via the wooden bridge, her footsteps rapping loud on its surface. She caught a brief glimpse of light and shadows in the moat below, and then she turned away and faced the steps that would take her up the side of the motte. They were steep, looming above her in the dark. At the top were more lights, and voices; she couldn't see their source from here, or make out the words.

The sound of her footsteps announced her approach long before she reached the summit.

The platform was wide and flat and cold and larger than she remembered. A sharp breeze swept over the top, bringing with it a strange taint, and for a moment she thought not of death but of a childhood memory: the van that used to come round the houses when she was young, selling its wares to all the mothers along the street. Then the thought was gone.

A huddle of SOCOs were grouped around something on

the floor. One of them was kneeling on the wooden panels as they bent over a small object that glittered in their lights. It was gold, bright gold; Cate stepped forward and saw it was a dish, and she breathed in and caught a mouthful of that stench, an acrid tang that caught the back of her throat. There was something inside it that she couldn't make out. A part of a body, maybe? She could see only that it was dark, some stinking, viscous substance with small objects floating in it. That was all; there was nothing else to show who the girl had been or who she was supposed to be, what story she had become.

She looked out across the landscape, the roads mapped out by orange pinprick lights, houses by their yellow windows, the fields nothing but darkness. She could see for miles and it struck her that anyone up here would be exposed too; anyone could be out there now, looking up at them. Even the killer might be there, watching. She shivered before taking her leave of the SOCOs and letting them get on with their work; the girl and the things left with her passing on to others, her story becoming part of someone else's, at least for a time.

Dan was still there when Cate returned, but Alice had not come back. She squinted across the scene and thought she caught sight of her contact with a taller figure, Heath, emerging from the moat and heading for the bridge. She might have met them there if she'd been a little longer; now she wasn't sure if that would have been a good thing.

She listened for their footsteps on the wooden stair, but wasn't sure if she could make them out.

She frowned. If Alice and Heath were looking at the same thing she'd seen, would they view it the same way? It was like Alice had said, everything was a variant, different things noticed or interpreted differently. Why on earth had the dish been placed there, and why hadn't it been with the girl?

What came into her mind though was not a golden bowl but an image on a page, an illustration from a storybook she'd had when she was young. On it was a beautiful girl with golden hair, and she was clutching a rose to her breast. It was 'Beauty and the Beast', wasn't it? There had been a merchant, and his daughter – the youngest, it was always the youngest – had asked him to bring back a rose from his travels, just a single rose, while her sisters demanded rich dresses and jewels. Unfortunately for the merchant, when he saw such a flower it had been in the Beast's garden, and plucking it had landed him in deeper trouble than her sisters' demands ever had.

This girl had a rose, and its thorns, wrapped around her body.

She tried to remember the rest of the story: Beauty had gone to live with the monster, had feasted in his splendid castle. Was that feast served in golden bowls? Possibly – probably. But then why the stinking mess left in the bowl here, tonight? Was the killer saying the feasting had turned foul? Why?

She shifted her feet, impatient for them to return. Why had Heath kept Alice with him and not her? She wished she could hear what they were saying. Perhaps he was angry that she had brought her contact here – and she could understand that. He'd obviously recognised the need for Alice's input, but that didn't change matters: he'd told Cate to watch her. Perhaps now he wanted to observe Alice's behaviour without her being there to interfere, to spoil it somehow. She frowned and wrapped her jacket around herself more tightly. Whatever the reason, it felt like Heath didn't entirely trust either of them. And why should he? He hadn't wanted Alice at any more crime scenes, and she had known that, and yet she had brought her along without so much as checking with him first.

She looked up to see two shapes heading towards her: Alice and Heath, almost as if they'd materialised from the dark.

Heath didn't acknowledge Cate's presence; instead he said, low and quiet, to Alice, 'Thank you, Ms Hyland.' He held out his hand and she shook it. Then he walked back the way he'd come.

Cate found herself reluctant to speak.

'It's another classic one,' said Alice. Her voice was sombre but calm.

'Beauty and the Beast?'

'No,' Alice sounded surprised, 'not that. It's "Sleeping Beauty". It's obvious really, when you know the story. She's surrounded by thorns – and the cap, the dish; she's even got a rose. In some variants that was her name, Briar Rose.'

This girl had a name, Cate thought. *They all had names.* She pushed the thought away. When the police *knew* her name, they could call her something else; until then, Briar Rose would be the way they referred to her, like Snow White and Little Red, their lives reduced to nothing but characters. It wasn't Alice's fault.

'He wants a full briefing in the morning,' Alice continued. 'I'm to come down to the station. I'll cancel my morning lecture.'

Cate swallowed down her questions and her pride. 'All right,' she said. 'Thank you, we appreciate that. I'll get you home now and pick you up early tomorrow.'

Alice stared at the castle for a long moment, lost in her own thoughts, then she caught her breath and turned to Cate. 'All right.' Her voice was faint, as if exhaustion had caught up with her at last. 'Actually, no – there's no need to fetch me. I'll meet you there.'

'Oh? You sure?'

'It'll be easier for me to drive. I can head straight into Leeds afterwards, maybe make my late-morning tutorials.'

Cate stared at her. 'But you don't have a car.' Her tone was half surprised, half accusing, and she moderated it. 'Do you?'

Alice frowned, then smiled as if she were humouring a child. 'Of course I do,' she said. 'The train's usually easier, but – I don't live in the nineteenth century, you know, much as I might give that impression. I just don't park it at the house; it looks messy, and the road's pretty narrow. People complain.'

Cate drew a deep breath. 'Well, if you're sure.' Why should it be so surprising that Alice should have a car? It wasn't exactly unusual. Still, she couldn't put it out of her mind, though she realised it had simply never occurred to her. Did she think Alice had sprung out of her fairy tales – that she didn't really live in the real world? Of course she had a car, and it didn't matter anyway. Yes, it was likely these girls had all been lured into someone's vehicle, but *millions* of people had vehicles; the idea was ridiculous. If it wasn't for Cate Alice would be at home now, oblivious to events at the castle or in the wood or anywhere else. She'd never have been anywhere near this case if Cate hadn't dragged her into it, changed her from someone who turned white at a crime-scene photograph to someone who leaned over a dead body without blinking.

And she'd kept her off the list of visitors to the lake.

Watch her, Heath had said. Was that what he had been doing tonight, watching her? Was he watching Cate, too?

But Alice was turning, taking her arm. 'We should go,' she said, gesturing towards the car park. 'I don't think they need us any more, do you?'

CHAPTER TWENTY-SEVEN

When Cate arrived at the station Alice was already sitting in Heath's office, cradling a mug in her hands and breathing in the steam. Heath saw Cate in the doorway and gestured towards another chair. It wasn't until after she'd sat down that she realised she'd been seated with Alice, as if she were just another outsider, rather than with her senior officer.

Alice, though, looked up and smiled, and Cate smiled back. She reminded herself that if Heath recognised the need for Alice's input, it could only be a good thing for her. He might have felt some annoyance at the way she'd brought her along the night before, but that would surely pass; the important thing was the knowledge she could impart, that they did their best for the murdered girls. If Heath had ignored her at the crime scene it wouldn't be fair to blame her contact. And Alice *was* helping them: she had no need to do so if she had anything to hide.

'Ms Hyland was giving me her insights into the way the body was posed,' Heath said.

Alice nodded. 'I was just saying, I don't think there's all that much to tell from the body itself, or I don't think so. I went over some variants of "Sleeping Beauty" last night when I got in, and apart from the fact that she was in a gown and had obviously been attractive, I don't think there's anything I can tell from that.'

Had obviously been attractive. She was starting to talk like a policewoman, Cate thought.

'It's the other objects that had been left that give it away. To explain what I mean, I'll run through the story, if that's all right. Sleeping Beauty's mother – the queen – can't have children. One day she's walking by a lake, and a fish jumps out. It's going to die, but the queen takes pity on it and puts it back into the water. In return the fish says it'll grant her deepest wish – she will have a child. That child is Sleeping Beauty. Hence the contents of the bowl.' She paused. 'Fairy tales are often like that – random acts of kindness leading to a reward. It's often more integral than this, part of the moral of the story.'

'Wait,' said Cate. 'Fish?' She remembered the van that had gone around the houses when she was small, the fish-man selling his wares. Of course: that had been the smell coming from the golden bowl.

Heath waved Alice on, making a rolling motion with his hand.

'Anyway, the parents are proud, they have this big

christening and they decide to invite the fairies. The problem is that there are thirteen fairies and only twelve gold dishes for them to eat from. So they don't invite them all.'

'The dish was gold,' said Heath, and he clicked his fingers; Cate jumped in her seat. 'There was something else,' he said. 'We didn't see it at first because it was hidden underneath the dish. The SOCOs found a silver bracelet, a small one – too small to have fitted the victim. *Really* small, apparently – like something that might be given to a child.'

'Silver?' asked Cate. 'It sounds like a christening gift.'

'So that would fit the story too,' Alice said. 'Now, you probably remember this part: the fairies come along and bestow gifts. Beauty, musicianship, that sort of thing – oh, and they're all wearing their best red caps and shoes – but the thirteenth fairy, the bad fairy, she turns up wearing a *black* cap.

'So then she casts the spell – the one that says the girl will live to her fifteenth year, but then she'll prick her finger on a spindle and die.'

'The woman we found was older than fifteen,' interrupted Heath.

'She was. And there wasn't a spindle; it's odd, that, don't you think? You'd imagine that would have been the easiest thing to leave, to pinpoint the fairy tale. The last scene was obvious, Little Red. Maybe whoever this is got tired of making it easy for you.'

Heath frowned, waved at her to continue once more.

'Okay, so the other fairies do their best to commute the sentence, so to speak. Instead of dying, Sleeping Beauty – who is also called Aurora, or Briar Rose – will fall asleep for a hundred years. When she does, the whole castle falls asleep with her, and a forest of thorns grows up around it. There were thorns around the body, too, weren't there?'

'Something else is a bit odd,' said Cate. 'If she was supposed to be a princess, royalty – why dump her at the bottom of a ditch? What's he trying to say? It would have made more sense for her to be at the centre of the castle. Unless he's trying to make a point, to show contempt for the body.' It made her think of Stocky's words, what felt like a long time ago: *It's all about vanity.*

Heath cleared his throat. 'I'll tell you what it is, Corbin: it's a fuck-up. Excuse the language, Ms Hyland.'

Alice waved the apology away while Cate said, 'Sir?'

'Why would he leave half the clues way across the site? I think he messed up, that's why. He didn't mean to leave the girl in the ditch. I think he went to the platform first and set up the dish and the bracelet before going back for the body. Then either he got disturbed or he got spooked. He might have thought he'd been spotted – I've got people going door-to-door on Manygates, see if that turns anything up. Certainly he didn't count on how difficult it would be to get the girl up to the keep.' He looked at Cate. 'You saw those steps?'

Dumbly, she nodded. Why hadn't she seen it? The steps had been hard enough late at night when she wasn't carrying anything. And the killer had never split a scene before; he had created his tableaux in a single place.

Alice was nodding too, as if she had seen it all along.

Cate exclaimed, 'Her dress was dirty. I don't think that would have been deliberate – it did look as if there'd been some difficulty moving her.'

'All right, so he has a plan, to emulate the princess in the castle, only he can't carry it off, or something gets in the way. It begs the question: why he didn't dump her at night?'

They fell silent and again Cate mentally kicked herself. Heath had something – the others had all been posed at night, hadn't they? This was an important change – so why? The castle might have been an inescapable choice to meet the demands of the story, but with its elevation it was the most exposed scene yet. She remembered getting out of the car and turning to see the houses of Manygates Lane looking back at her. Maybe he had been disturbed; maybe he'd looked out at those same houses and panicked. Certainly it would have been easier in darkness.

'You know,' said Alice, 'there's another thing that's been troubling me. I can't seem to get my head around it.'

Heath waited. It was Cate who asked, 'What?'

'She was woken by the prince,' said Alice, 'in the story. It's the part everyone knows: Sleeping Beauty is woken with a kiss.'

'And?' Heath said.

'Well, the girl at the castle last night was – didn't you

say she was supposed to be alive when she was found? That someone tried to give her the kiss of life?'

Heath's cheek twitched. Cate straightened in her chair.

'But instead of waking, she died. It's like – the killer is saying something. Laughing at you, maybe; making some kind of point. Only I can't work out what, or how.'

Cate stared: there was something she was supposed to see. *Like the killer is saying something – laughing at you.* Yes, that was how it felt. She looked back at Heath.

He thought before he spoke. 'The killer couldn't have known the girl was going to die at that particular time. If he'd strangled her, she'd be dead already. If she was poisoned – he'd have to be some sort of poisons expert to get the dosage right, and even then, I doubt it could be made to work. And how would he even know when she'd be found?' He looked at Cate, then Alice. 'No, I don't think she was supposed to be left alive, not really. And I'm not sure she was; I think the witness got confused, scared maybe, thought he'd felt a pulse when there wasn't one. If she *was* alive, I don't think it was deliberate. I think whoever this is has started to slip, to make mistakes, and that's all the better for us. It could be the way we catch him.'

'Wait,' said Alice, 'that's it, isn't it? Or it could be.' Her eyes were shining. 'He didn't dump her at night. Why not? Anyone could have caught him. If he *did* use poison—'

Heath made a sound in the back of his throat. 'Bloody hell.'

'He *mistimed* it,' Alice said. There was a note of triumph in her voice. 'That's it! He *could* have planned to dump her at night, or at least when it was a bit darker; he still needed her to be found. But the poison worked quicker than he thought. If he wanted any chance of her death being witnessed, he had to rush it.'

'Hence the scrambled scene,' said Heath.

Cate swallowed. She opened her mouth to say, 'We don't *know*—' but Alice was speaking again.

'There is one other thing,' she said, and she pulled a face. 'I couldn't stop thinking about it when I got back last night. I don't know if it's relevant or not – I hope it's not. In some variants of the story, Sleeping Beauty wasn't woken by a kiss at all. That's just the popular version, the one that became acceptable, that got made into films and put into books, because the original story – it was much harsher, more violent.'

'What was it?' asked Heath.

'In early variants the girl sleeps on, even after the prince has arrived. He sees her and falls in love with her all right, but not in the way you'd think. He doesn't kiss her; at least, he doesn't *just* kiss her.'

They stared.

'It's another variant you could interpret as belonging to older stories yet – stories of myth and renewal of the earth. Sleeping Beauty – or Aurora, which means "the dawn" – gets pregnant by the prince while she's asleep. She gives birth to twins called Sun and Moon. And one of the babies sucks a splinter from her mother's finger, waking her at last. So the dawn returns, with the cycle of birth and life, and everything is renewed.'

'In which case the whole thing about the kiss doesn't make any sense at all. It's a coincidence.' Heath looked at Alice, but she had nothing else to tell.

Then a fist hammered on the door and Dan walked in. 'We know who she is,' he said. 'She was reported missing. Her husband is here. He's waiting outside.'

The man was called Ben Robertson, and Cate could see from the look on his face that he *knew*: he was trying to cling to what little hope he had, but he'd heard what they'd found at Sandal Castle, and that hope was fading. His wife was called Ellen, he said; they had been recently married and they were trying for a child. He glanced around when he said this, as though asking them if it was real, if it was still going to happen. No one answered.

He stared down at the floor between his feet and his eyes went distant. Cate knew he was looking at the future he had built in his mind, the one he could still almost see.

'I'm sorry,' he said as tears welled in his eyes.

He was a solicitor, and worked in one of the new high-rise offices on the outskirts of Leeds. He had left Ellen behind at the house that morning, and he hadn't said goodbye because he hadn't wanted to wake her.

'It has a burglar alarm,' he said, bewildered, as if that

should have taken care of everything. 'And the doors were locked, I locked up behind me when I left. I know I did.' His eyes hazed over as if doubt had entered for the first time. 'I *did*.'

The house hadn't been locked when he'd returned. The alarm hadn't been set. The house was empty.

'I got home and she wasn't there – but her car was there, her mobile phone. Her coat was there.' He went on recounting the things she'd left behind, as if they could coalesce around his wife and bring her back.

'She must have opened the door,' he said at last, and a note of something else entered his voice, annoyance maybe, an irritation both everyday and domestic, as if she'd left her dressing gown over a chair or forgotten to bring in the milk; as if everything was normal. Then it was gone and the tears fell, shining on his cheeks, making him look much younger.

When he found the empty house he'd waited for her to come home, and when she didn't, he'd started to make calls: her parents, her friends, but none of them had heard from her, and so he'd called the police. Early this morning, he'd heard it on the radio, what had been found just a few miles away from their home, and he'd come straight to the station.

Slowly, he pulled a photograph from his pocket. Instead of passing it to Heath, he gave it to Cate, looking at her as though she'd understand, as though she could fix this.

She saw a happy woman, her face framed by a wedding

veil, the white gauze setting off her smile. She recognised her at once – but perhaps she was wrong; she hadn't spent much time with the body. She passed the picture to Heath and he examined it. She saw the look in his eyes. Eventually, he met Robertson's gaze. 'I'm sorry,' he said.

CHAPTER TWENTY-EIGHT

Alice sat through the tutorials, her mind drifting. She couldn't concentrate. One of her students was going through her idea for her dissertation, reciting a textbook feminist theory of 'Cinderella'. For a moment she felt disorientated, as if she were back in Heath's office, trying to theorise about how someone had taken a young woman and killed her. She drew a deep sigh, then realised her student had paused, was waiting for a response.

'Good work,' she said automatically. 'You're on the right lines. Now I'd like you to take that theory and apply it to some different tales, put your own ideas and opinions into it. I don't want you to refer to a textbook for this one. Just have a good think about where the theory fits and where it doesn't.'

The girl nodded and gathered her papers. Alice pressed her lips together; she would probably be on the internet as soon as she left the room, scouring websites for other people's ideas and how she could use them.

She felt a sudden pain in her forehead and pinched the bridge of her nose between thumb and forefinger. She tried to remember a time when she *liked* this job, when she'd enjoyed sharing her knowledge of the tales she loved. And she *had* loved them, ever since she'd shared them with her mother. She frowned. That thought didn't help.

Was that why she clung to these stories so much? Because it was a way back to her childhood, the way they had both used to be? But the truth was, happy endings didn't happen. The more time passed, the easier it was for it all to slip away; that was what had happened to her mother, everything leaving her word by word, betrayed by her own mind. There had been no wicked witch, no wolf, no dragon. Not until now.

Alice roused herself. She couldn't dwell on this, not any longer. It was almost time for the next tutorial and she had to concentrate on her work, be a good teacher. She had to continue to encourage her students to discover these tales for themselves, to form their own theories; to make them *see*.

And then Alice thought of what she had said to her last student to make her do just that, and she started to remember, and to see how blind she had been.

CHAPTER TWENTY-NINE

The briefing was quieter than the last, the mood more sombre, as if everyone knew they were facing something larger than they had first thought, something that wasn't going to be wrapped up and delivered any time soon.

But it has to be, thought Cate. The look in Ben Robertson's eyes said that it had to be. They couldn't allow this to happen to anyone else.

'Quiet,' said Heath, although nobody had been talking, and everyone sat a little straighter in their seat. He was running through the initial reports, his voice as rough as it always had been, but lower. His manner was quiet too, and his movements slow, as if deliberating every motion.

'There was a cut on her finger,' he said. 'That was one of the first things they found. It's not a severe cut, but the girl in the story pricked her finger, so we suspect it was done purposefully to point up the "Sleeping Beauty" scenario.'

The name of the fairy tale seemed odd coming from

someone as bluff and matter-of-fact as Heath. Even the humour had gone. Perhaps it was a sign, thought Cate, of how seriously he had begun to take her theory, of how seriously he had begun to take Alice. He had called Cate into his office just before the briefing and asked her to take on the role of Alice's liaison officer. She had practically been doing the job anyway; now he obviously wanted to be able to call on the lecturer's expertise at any moment while making sure she wasn't overwhelmed by the things she saw. Unless he just wanted her to be in a better position to keep an eye on her, of course.

Cate felt a stab of guilt. Alice surely *did* need the extra support. She had sounded so sure of herself while talking Heath through her way of seeing, but she was a civilian, and she was probably putting a brave face on it. And now, because of Alice, she herself had been given an additional role to play; although of course that wasn't the important thing.

Heath continued, 'She'd also had a blow to the head, though that's not what killed her. It may have been a means of overpowering her, initially. And like Teresa King, there were ligature marks on her wrists.

'The full toxicology screen is still in progress, but there was partially digested plant material in her digestive tract that has been identified as poison hemlock, or *Conium maculatum*. It's fairly common, and contains extremely toxic alkaloids – apparently it's fairly widely known as being a poisonous plant. It is likely that this was the cause of death.

'Now, there's more. Poison hemlock causes what they call *ascending paralysis* – in other words, it freezes the victim from the lower limbs upwards: first her feet, then her legs . . . eventually it reaches the lungs and you get respiratory arrest. It's fast-acting and there are no side-effects like with many poisons – no vomiting, frothing at the mouth and so on. It would have been relatively clean, almost as if she was falling asleep from the feet upwards.'

Sleeping Beauty, thought Cate.

'There were other signs of force besides the bruising to her wrists. It wasn't obvious at first, but inspection under ultraviolet has shown up bruising around her mouth and abrasions on her gums, so it could be that she was forced to eat the hemlock.

'There are sheets coming round – more information about the plant. Apparently it's supposed to look a bit like parsley. I wouldn't know; I'm not a fucking chef. If you see anything suspicious, watch out for the purple blotches on the stems – they're known as Socrates' blood, since he died of hemlock poisoning. Read it, memorise it. Don't fucking eat any.'

Heath paused while the sheets were passed around. Then he began again: 'There was another poison there, too. They tested for the same stuff that was at the earlier scene and they found it; the fish left in the bowl was laced with pesticide, like the apple at the first scene and the bread at the second. That wasn't all.' He looked suddenly very tired.

'They also found the remains of a capsule in her mouth. She had swallowed most of the contents, but it contained more organic matter, traces of the same alkaloid as from the hemlock. He'd planted it there. They think it burst when her head was tilted back to give her mouth-to-mouth; it's lucky the guy doing it didn't end up in trouble himself. At any rate, we're unlikely to ever know whether it was the extra dose that finally killed her or if the time of death is a coincidence – or indeed if she wasn't dead already.'

Cate stared at him. The man who'd found the body – Gerry – he'd given Ellen Robertson the kiss of life. *But instead of waking, she died.*

Heath met her gaze and she knew what he was thinking. Unconsciously, she rubbed her cheek. The bastard set this up: Sleeping Beauty, condemned with the kiss that was meant to save her.

It's like the killer is laughing at you. Making some kind of point.

She had that odd feeling that she should be able to reach out and touch the answer, if she only knew the right way to see it.

But Heath had moved on. He cleared his throat, then said, 'Now, she's been poisoned, she's unconscious. According to our expert in folk tales this could have been the point where the killer raped her, like the prince in the story getting his bride pregnant. However, early indications show that isn't what happened. There are no signs of sexual assault.'

Heath paused.

Cate couldn't hear him draw a breath, but she saw it in the rise and fall of his shoulders. Whatever was coming next, he was finding it difficult.

'But she *was* pregnant,' he said.

There was a rush of exclamations, people shifting in their seats, and he held up a hand and quieted the room. 'I know what you're thinking: that the bastard knew her. That he picked her because she fitted the story he wanted to tell, as recounted to me yesterday by Ms Hyland, and as I told it to you. It isn't that simple.' He drew a breath. 'There is a strong possibility that Mrs Robertson didn't *know* she was pregnant. I spoke to her husband earlier and he said they'd been trying for months. He had no reason to believe his wife wouldn't have told him if she'd found out she was having a baby. Of course, she may have had reasons he knew nothing about, but there were no odd changes in her behaviour, nothing like that. He was quite sure she didn't know.' He looked at Cate. 'We need to speak to her friends and her family, but we have to proceed with the understanding that it could be a coincidence. It could be someone she knew, but it might also have been a complete stranger.'

CHAPTER THIRTY

Alice stood staring into space while the hold music played in her ear. She couldn't straighten her thoughts; she knew what she wanted to say but wasn't sure how she wanted to say it. The thought kept slipping away, as if still incomplete. She couldn't push an image out of her mind: Cate's expression when she'd seen her previously. There had been something wrong with it. What had they been talking about? She couldn't really remember. The policewoman hadn't liked the way Alice had spoken to Heath, and then there was that whole odd thing – *It'll be easier for me to drive*, Alice had said, that was it, and Cate had looked as if she'd taken a punch in the stomach.

Alice chewed her lip. She wasn't sure what it meant, only that there was a growing discomfort in her mind, a worm in the bud.

The hold music cut off and a steady, even voice answered: Cate. Alice took a deep breath and tried to remember what she had wanted to say. 'I had an idea about the case.'

'Wonderful.' Cate's tone was light, enthusiastic: that was better.

'I started to think, not about what these killings have in common with these tales, but what they don't.'

'Really? And what's that?' Now she sounded distracted.

'They're dead. All the girls are dead.'

There was silence, then: 'Is that it? That's kind of taken as read, isn't it?' Cate's tone was gentle, despite the words. 'I mean – no death, no killings, no case. Of course that would make our job a lot easier, but—'

'No – *listen*, all of the characters that have been chosen – Snow White, Little Red, Sleeping Beauty – are believed dead in the stories, or considered dead, or as close to death as makes no difference. And then they're brought back to life, but in these variants – these *murders* – of course, they're not.

'Snow White is believed dead to the extent that she's in her coffin, and yet she's revived when the poisoned apple is jolted from her throat. Little Red Riding Hood is cut from the wolf's stomach by the huntsman. Sleeping Beauty is woken with a kiss. It's like they *should* have the power of life, but that's the very thing he takes from them: in the moment of rejuvenation, of transformation, they're instead condemned to death. And the killer – maybe he sees himself as the prince somehow, or the huntsman, the one with the power to confer life on the heroine at the end of the tale, except he chooses not to.'

'Didn't you think the killer was a woman?'

'I – I did.' Alice paused. 'No, you're right, that does make sense too. There's always an evil stepmother or queen or something. Damn it. You can read this in so many ways.' She fell silent. 'It's just, I felt like I'd *seen* something, you know? And I started thinking about the way he's subverted the tales, and that was the thing I couldn't get out of my mind: their deaths. It's so final. In fairy tales there's always magic – the happy ending, a lot of the time, anyway. I think that's what I loved about them when I was little.'

'And yet they're red in tooth and claw.'

Slowly Alice said, 'Yes. Yes, they are.'

Cate didn't answer.

After a while, Alice spoke. 'I'm sorry. This made sense when I called you, or seemed to anyway. I think maybe I'm getting too involved with this. It's getting to me, that's all.'

'No, it's all right,' said Cate. 'Of course we appreciate your help. I want you to call me whenever you feel the need – even if you just want to talk. I know this has been difficult.' She paused. 'Actually, there's something else I wanted to ask you about. There was more poison found at this crime scene too, and not something that was in the variants of the stories you mentioned. Can you think of any reason why the fish should have been poisoned?'

Alice shook her head, then realised the other woman couldn't see her. 'Not one.'

'Are you sure? There's nothing you haven't mentioned – nothing you're keeping back?'

This time it was Alice who was silent.

'It's another departure, isn't it, from the stories? The poisoned bread at the second scene, and the poisoned apple at the first.'

'No,' Alice said faintly, 'there *was* a poisoned apple in Snow White.' She stirred, looked around at the papers strewn across her table. They didn't mean anything to her any more. She murmured something as Cate said goodbye, sounds that weren't quite words. She didn't know what to think. *Keeping something back?* Why would she? She'd helped with this case, given her time and her knowledge, and now – she remembered the vague thought she'd had during the conversation. Cate's tone had been kind, almost forcedly so. And then the policewoman had pushed her to speak with her silence, had played her own words back to her: *red in tooth and claw.* That was the way they worked, wasn't it? The police would try to trip people using their own words, probe their statements until something bled. When that person was being *interrogated*. When they were a *suspect*.

Alice replaced the phone into its cradle, turned her back on it. There were hot, angry tears in her eyes, and she wasn't sure how they had got there. She must be wrong – she was overwrought, that was all. She put her hand to her face. She had thought she had known where she was going, that she was the one with the expertise, in control. Now it felt as if she had left the path a long time before, had been wandering in the forest without even noticing.

That made her think of something, and she slipped her hand into her pocket. Waiting there was the gift the blue bird had given her. She didn't remove it, but in her mind's eye she could see its exact shade, and as she ran her fingertips across it she became calmer at once. It was as if the bird had become her guide, her anchor, a reminder of better times. She needed it; it made her feel better.

She took a deep breath. She should centre herself, go back to doing the things that made her truly her. She needed to forget this for a while, forget about death and ugliness. She would do her job, catch up with some reading. Maybe she'd even read the tale of the blue bird, relive its transformation into its true self, Prince Charming, bringing jewels, a marriage, a happily-ever-after.

She smiled and her eyes went distant. If only things in life were so easy. People in stories had adventures, they experienced life and death and everything in between, but it all turned out all right in the end. And they barely ever seemed to feel as alone as she did now.

CHAPTER THIRTY-ONE

Cate stared at the morning newspapers, flipping through the headlines: WOLF STRIKES AGAIN. BEWARE THE LONE WOLF. WOLF KILLER LEAVES THE WOODS. She had seen it coming, but it still didn't feel quite real. She threw them aside and rubbed the grime of newsprint from her fingers. She had to focus on the investigation, although it was a puzzle she couldn't solve: nothing connected.

She had checked with Dan and found that Heath had already had the team examine old cases going back for years. They had found nothing to fit, nothing that even remotely related to what was happening here. They'd also been trying to make connections between the dead girls: Chrissie Farrell, Teresa King and Ellen Robertson. What did a local teenager, a Leeds prostitute and a housewife have in common? Nothing that they could find.

The profiler was having difficulty piecing together anything meaningful too. Cate had seen the report, and it contained a lot of words but little to go on: he suggested the killer was likely to be male because of the physical strength required, but couldn't rule out a female because of the knowledge of fairy tales. They were likely to be from a dysfunctional family, with a domineering mother and a father who was either also domineering or ineffectual, possibly absent. He – or she – could have suffered some trauma at a young age, possibly involving being exposed to a dead body; that could have been a reason for them to find a refuge in fairy tales. It was also likely they had difficulties in forming relationships. In short, there was nothing at all that could help them identify a suspect. The profile would merely be something to compare them with, after they'd found them.

Chrissie, a young beauty in her first blossom. Teresa, embarked on the path of needles. Ellen, a young bride – that was like something in a fairy tale too, wasn't it? Didn't most of them end with a happy marriage? For Ellen, though, it had only been the beginning. She hadn't had a chance to make much out of it yet; there had been few new friends, few known acquaintances. Most of her connections lay miles away, in her past.

Cate sighed and tried to turn her thoughts in a more productive direction. She'd thought they'd catch the killer through their obsession with stories, but maybe that wasn't it; perhaps she needed to think more about the practicalities, things that were concrete. She half closed her eyes, picturing the beautiful Chrissie in her ball dress; Ellen Robertson, an attractive woman, well dressed and manicured; and Teresa King, a painted girl leaning against a wall. Is that how they'd appeared from the perspective of the killer, the wolf on the prowl? Maybe the way to catch them would be to understand how the victims had been chosen, what it was that connected them.

Cate frowned. The killer, whether male or female, had had to abscond with the victims somehow. Teresa King had quite possibly got into a car willingly, but with the others it would most likely have required strength. Had Chrissie Farrell gone with someone of her own volition? She'd been drunk when she'd left the dance, which would make it more likely. Ellen Robertson had apparently walked out of her house and vanished, at least until she was found dumped in the castle moat; the intervening time was a blank. There were signs of force, though – blows to Teresa's face and Ellen's head, and those ligature marks. The bodies must also have been moved some distance. He might have found it impossible to get Ellen up to the top of the motte, but the arboretum where Teresa had been found was still some way away from the nearest vehicular access; although that had been done at night and under cover. Chrissie, the first victim, had been left practically at the roadside. Had the killer been getting more ambitious each time, only to find his ideas had over-reached his capabilities at last?

She stared down at her hands. Oddly, she found words running through her mind, something that Alice had said:

My mother isn't well – she doesn't remember much. She's in a home now.

Why had that come to mind? She frowned. Hadn't Alice said she'd cared for her mother, before she had to send her away? But how much, and what kind of care? Perhaps she'd had to lift the old lady, so she knew the best techniques for doing so. No – what else had Alice said to her? *I couldn't really cope with her on my own.*

Of course she couldn't. No, the problem wasn't with Alice. Her current ambivalence towards her was surely more to do with the way she'd felt when Alice had mentioned her car – not so much irritated by the possibilities it raised as by the fact that she hadn't even considered it. She'd made an assumption. More than that, it was to do with the way Stocky had looked at her when she'd asked him to keep Alice's presence at the lake off the record. She couldn't blame Alice for that. Besides, she was her liaison now; she had a responsibility for her.

But the girls had been lured away, or snatched, or possibly some combination of both. The first two would have been straightforward – a helping hand offered to Chrissie, like a white knight offering rescue. For Teresa, just another job. And for Ellen – what? An unexpected caller, asking for help with some feigned crisis? There had been no sign of struggle, not at the house anyway; only those bruises left on her body, which suggested the battle had taken place elsewhere. The husband had got the same impression too, and he knew her best, after all. What had he said? *She must have opened the door*. The alarm hadn't been set, the house was empty.

The *alarm*. Cate frowned. The teacher, Matt Cosgrove, had been trying to set an alarm when he'd been held up at the dance, hadn't he? An alarm that wouldn't set properly, that kept going off. She shook her head. It was a spurious connection: as Heath said, she could find suspicion anywhere if she looked hard enough. And he was right, there was no real link: the Robertsons' alarm hadn't been set because Ellen had been at home, inside, supposedly safe. Cosgrove's hadn't set because – *why*, exactly? Had they ever even asked?

There could have been any number of reasons. He might have put the number in wrongly, or not hit the right buttons to activate it. Maybe something had been distracting him, making him clumsy. Or there might have been windows or doors left open; something to trigger any movement sensors dotted around the building.

Or maybe someone was still inside. That would have tripped the movement sensors too.

She rubbed her forehead. There couldn't have been anyone there, could there? The girl she'd questioned, Hayley Moorhouse, had said she was the last, that she was only still there because her boyfriend had been sick in the toilets. And she'd waved to Mr Cosgrove as she'd left; yes, that was it, because her father had been waiting outside in the car and he'd been angry. She could still see the way he'd fidgeted through the interview, picking at his fingernails.

He went ballistic about the time as it was.

No. There was something wrong with that picture. The man had been impatient, yes, but Hayley hadn't said that, had she? She'd said something else. She'd told Cate how he'd waited, and – she couldn't remember the words, but she could remember the look the girl had given her father. It had been too apologetic, too respectful to go with those words.

He went ballistic about the time as it was.

Then she remembered: it hadn't been Hayley Moorhouse who'd said that, it had been someone else, another girl, one who quite possibly harboured feelings of jealousy towards Chrissie Farrell. It had been Sarah: Sarah Brailsford.

Cate closed her eyes. She felt sick. She had spoken to the girl herself, and there was something there that she had missed. She could feel it: something she should have seen. *He went ballistic about the time as it was.* Why so? According to all accounts the dance had finished on time, and Hayley had corroborated that; she'd been held up, but everyone else had left. If Sarah left on time, why would her father have been so angry? Unless he'd set some early curfew on his child. But she had appeared to Cate to be an outgoing, confident young woman; someone who'd been hoping for a shot of the other girls' tequila, not wrapped in cotton wool. She'd struck her as someone her peers would be glad to gather into their clique – except Chrissie Farrell, maybe.

And why was that, exactly?

She remembered something else the girl had said when she had pushed her, applied a little pressure; and she remembered the way she'd looked away when she said it.

I thought he liked me too.

CHAPTER THIRTY-TWO

Alice picked out the *Green Fairy Book* from her shelf. Somewhere within its pages was the blue bird's tale. First, though, she reached for another book and leafed to an old poem by Charles Perrault, a collector of fairy tales born in seventeenth-century France. The lines were his own addition to 'Little Red Riding Hood', his variant of the story influenced by his own moralistic interpretation of the tale:

The Wolf, I say, for Wolves too sure there are
Of every sort, and every character.
Some of them mild and gentle-humour'd be,
Of noise and gall and rancour wholly free;
Who tame, familiar, full of complaisance
Ogle and leer, languish, cajole and glance;
With luring tongues, and language wond'rous sweet,
Follow young ladies as they walk the street,
Ev'n to their very houses, nay, bedside,

And, artful, tho' their true designs they hide,
Yet ah! These simpering Wolves! Who does not see
Most dangerous of Wolves indeed they be?

She stared at the page, not sure why she had thought of it. Then she leaned back in her chair and glanced out at the apple tree, as if by turning her thoughts to the blue bird she could conjure it from the air. And maybe she had: maybe she'd imagined the whole thing, its improbable brightness, its heartfelt song.

There are no rules when it comes to the blue bird.

Of course she hadn't imagined it. Birdwatchers were trawling the region for the creature, Bernard Levitt among them with his half-focused eyes, his vague smile; impossible to forget his name when he'd spelled it for her so carefully. Then there was the feather, so carefully placed in her pocket each time she changed her clothes, as if it were some kind of talisman. She didn't need to touch it to know it was there; she had run her fingers across its edge so many times she didn't like to look at it too closely; by now it was probably a sorry, bedraggled thing.

Alice smiled ruefully, opened the book and started to read. The words flowed like comfort from the page.

The story of the blue bird began, as many fairy tales do, in grief, with a king mourning for his dead queen. As many kings were, he was easily comforted in the form of a new wife. This one also brought with her a stepdaughter,

Turritella, who was far less lovely than Fiordelisa, the king's own child, reflecting her less-than-lovely personality.

Despite the queen's manoeuvring, Prince Charming fell madly in love with Fiordelisa – the more beautiful and deserving of the two. He would not accept the rich gifts sent in the name of the uglier daughter, and when he heard that Fiordelisa was to be locked away in a tower, out of sight, he begged to be allowed a few precious moments with her.

But Prince Charming was tricked. They met only in darkness, so he could not know that Turritella had been sent to him instead. Under the delusion of speaking to his love, he proposed marriage. When the day of the wedding came, though, he refused to honour the promise of his hand.

Unusually, in this story, it was the wicked sister who had a fairy godmother; in revenge for the prince's refusal, she cursed him. He was transformed into a blue bird, in which form he would have to live for seven years.

The bird hid away in a fir tree to escape the hungry eagles, but by night he emerged and searched the castle for Fiordelisa. At last, following the sound of her laments, he found her, and the prince sang so sweetly to his love that all who heard him thought the woodland inhabited by a spirit.

Unfortunately the queen discovered the princess and her avian suitor. She set a trap for him, surrounding his fir tree with sharp blades, so that when he emerged he was cut to ribbons. His life was saved only by an enchanter who persuaded the fairy godmother to change him back into a man; but unless he agreed to the unpleasant marriage, he would once again become a bird.

What happened next changed everything: the king died, and the people of the country demanded that Fiordelisa become queen. When the stepmother resisted, they killed her. Despite all Turritella's efforts the new queen found Prince Charming and they were at last united, though not before one final footnote: the ugly sister, Turritella, tried to interfere yet again, and to stop her once and for all, the happy couple had the enchanter transform her into a big brown owl, who flew away, hooting dismally.

Alice sat back and smiled over the twists and turns the story had taken, the description of Prince Charming under the fairy godmother's spell: *He had a slender body like a bird, covered with shining blue feathers, his beak was like ivory, his eyes were bright as stars, and a crown of white feathers adorned his head.*

She glanced towards the window. The blue bird she had seen had no white crown, but it had been beautiful. Poor Bernard Levitt in his flimsy hide: he had wanted to see it so badly. As in fairy tales, sometimes blessings fell to those who had never sought them. Take the unassuming Fiordelisa. She was so much more deserving than the nasty Turritella, who for all her scheming was turned into that big brown owl. And owls had their own share of stories;

they were often seen as a bad omen, or even thought to be spirits. Perhaps the story was really saying that the girl was killed. Worse things happened in many stories. And in fairy tales, birds were seldom what they seemed.

CHAPTER THIRTY-THREE

Sarah Brailsford sat at the kitchen table, her face contracted into a frown, wiping the condensation from a glass of juice with her fingers. Cate took a glass from her mother too and said thanks. 'I appreciate you arranging for us to see you,' she said, not to Sarah but to her mother. 'We don't want to interrupt Sarah's schoolwork.'

The woman almost managed a smile; she was distracted. 'I need to get her back soon,' she said. 'And I need to go into work myself.'

'Of course. This won't take long. As I told you on the phone, there were just a couple of things I'd been looking into around the dance, and I was hoping Sarah could help.' She turned towards the girl. Sarah glanced across the table towards her, but she stopped short of actually looking at Cate.

'Sarah, you mentioned to me before that you got in late, that your dad wasn't happy about it. Can you tell me what time that was?'

Sarah's mother shot her a hard look, which she ignored. 'Sarah?'

The girl looked up, away again. She bit her lip.

'How did you get home?'

'Why is this relevant?' asked Mrs Brailsford.

Cate turned on her best smile. 'I'm trying to work out which of the girls must have been there last, so I can piece together a timeline – who was still there, what they may have seen, and so on. It's quite routine.'

She turned back to Sarah, but it was her mother who spoke.

'She got a taxi. We've got a friend works for the cab firm, so we trust them. She has their number, and we gave her the fare. She was to call home though, if there were any problems – weren't you, Sarah?'

She gave her mother a slight nod.

'And so Sarah's father – your husband, Mrs Brailsford – he was waiting up, just in case he needed to bob out and fetch her?'

'That's right. Look, we always make sure she's safe—'

'Of course you do. That's not in question. So, just to check – what time did you get back, Sarah?'

This time the girl spoke, muttering the words, rubbing her hand across her mouth.

'*What* did you say?' her mother asked.

'About one,' Sarah repeated. 'Maybe a bit after. Dad went nuts. He'd have woke you if you hadn't had one o' them sleeping pills.'

'My pills are none of your business, young lady—'

'That's what Dad said, about what time I got in. Said it were best you didn't know.' Sarah sneered.

Mrs Brailsford took a deep breath and Cate held up a hand, stopping her. 'If you were that late, Sarah, you must have been one of the last there. So you must have seen Mr Cosgrove locking up – he had some trouble with the alarm, I believe.'

She didn't answer.

'We did speak to another girl who was there until around twelve, but – and this is the odd thing, Sarah – she didn't see you. She said no one else was there at all besides her, her boyfriend and Mr Cosgrove.'

'What is this?' said Mrs Brailsford.

Cate kept her focus on the daughter. 'So where were you, Sarah? If you were there, why didn't Hayley see you? What exactly were you doing?'

'Now wait a—'

Sarah pushed her glass away, slopping juice across the table, scraping back her chair. 'Shut up, Mum. Just shut up.'

'Don't you speak—'

But Sarah had turned to Cate, her face screwed up, in fury or misery, Cate wasn't sure which. The girl's voice came in dry gasps. 'I wanted to see him, all right? I just wanted to see him after, to *talk*. After what— I mean, I *knew* he liked me, he had to like me. I *knew* he did. That stupid cow, she didn't even *care* about him.'

Mrs Brailsford was listening open-mouthed. For a moment Cate couldn't think of what to say either; her heart raced. Her palms were slippery. 'Mr Cosgrove. You waited behind to see him?'

'That's what I said, isn't it?' Now Sarah looked sulky, but her cheeks flamed. There were tears in her eyes, though they didn't fall.

'So, what, you made yourself scarce until everyone else had gone? Somewhere Hayley didn't see you?' Cate paused. 'Mr Cosgrove – he was trying to set the alarm, but he couldn't. He couldn't because you were still inside.'

'I hid,' she said. 'I was behind the stage. There's a little room there, behind the curtains. I stopped in there. I wanted to see him, only that dimwit, Hayley – she was still there. I heard her go, though, saying bye like she didn't have a care in the world, all the time she was stuffing me up. And he said bye too, and so I looked out.'

Cate felt prickling down her back, the touch of light fingers. She took a breath. 'And what did you see?'

'What do you think I saw? I saw *him*. He had the keys in his hand, only he wasn't doing anything. He was just looking outside, staring for ages and ages, like he was watching something. Then he started fiddling with the alarm and it got kind of funny. I watched for a bit, thought it would make him laugh, you know, when he knew – but then—'

'Then?'

'He turned round and he saw me.' Her face screwed up

again, and this time the tears *did* fall. 'He saw me and he just looked like – like he—'

'Sarah.' Her mother stepped forward and put a hand on the girl's arm. 'Sarah, don't.'

'He looked like he fucking *hated* me.'

Cate absorbed the words, waiting. She knew there was more.

'He liked me before, I knew it,' Sarah wailed. 'I gave him a book, see. I gave it him and he took it, and it *meant* something, I knew it did. But this time it was like he didn't even *know* me. I tried to make him – I wanted to talk, but he—' Her words dissolved into a gulping sob. She rubbed at her face, and when she lowered her hands her cheeks were streaked, her eyelashes standing out from her skin in wet points.

'Did he touch you?' her mother said at last. 'If he touched you, I – I'll – Sarah, I'll *kill* him.'

The girl sniffed, wiping her nose on the back of her sleeve. She shook her head. 'He led me on. He took my present, didn't he? I thought he *liked* me.' She started to cry again, loud and gasping.

I thought he liked me. The same words she'd said before, right at the start of it all.

'So what did he do, Sarah? Did he ask you to leave?'

Slowly, the girl nodded.

Cate sighed. But he had been there, the teacher had been there and he had lied, had said nothing about seeing this girl after the dance, this *child*.

But then, wouldn't anybody have done the same?

'You were there,' she said under her breath, 'the two of you. And you didn't like Chrissie Farrell, did you, Sarah? Did you see anything of her? Did you—'

She didn't see the mother move, only heard the air hissing between her teeth; then she was standing in front of Cate, her face contorted. 'Enough,' she said. 'It's time you went, right now.'

'All right, Mrs Brailsford. I apologise. But a girl is dead, and I have to—'

'It's all *right*, Mum,' said Sarah. 'You have to stop being so— I can do this. Look, he didn't do anything. Is that what you want to know? And I went off on one. I said he shouldn't have taken my book. I said he shouldn't have led me on. And he kept saying he didn't mean to and he didn't know and he didn't want this, and that I should go home. And then after a bit I called the cab. I had to wait, and he waited too until it came. He didn't even speak to me, then – he just sat there staring into space. And then I went, and then, I suppose, so did he. That was it, all right? Is that it?' She looked from Cate to her mother. 'Can I go now?'

'There is just one more question,' said Cate, 'if it's all right with your mother. I just wanted to know – the gift you gave him. What was it about, Sarah? What was the name of the book?'

She sniffed, looked away.

'Were you studying folklore with him, Sarah? Was it something about that?'

She frowned, shook her head. 'Shakespeare,' she said. 'He was doing Shakespeare. I gave him a copy of *Romeo and Juliet*.' She glared at Cate. 'He shouldn't have taken it. He knew what it meant. He knew it as well as anybody.' She looked from Cate to her parent. 'He shouldn't have taken it if he didn't mean it, should he?'

CHAPTER THIRTY-FOUR

Cate frowned. A word was circling in her head, but it wasn't one she liked. *Vanity*, Len Stockdale had said. *Vanity*. And now they were on their way, the word wouldn't leave her. Was that what this had been about, all the time? A man so charming that a schoolgirl hadn't been able to keep her crush under control; one whom even Mrs Farrell, attending a dance for her child – her daughter's night – had become so distracted by she'd even uttered the same words.

I thought he liked me.

Now Cate was going to see him at last, along with Dan: they had permission to do so from Heath himself. And all she could think about was this – would she *know*, after all? Would she look into his eyes and be charmed as the others had been, or would she see a killer there, looking out at her from behind a lovely mask?

'Penny for them,' Dan said, glancing at her.

'I think he lied,' said Cate. 'I think maybe they both

did. Chrissie was there, she had to be. I don't think the girl was involved – I just can't see it – but I think maybe Chrissie saw them fighting, was jealous herself. Maybe she went to talk to Cosgrove afterwards; maybe he snapped, lashed out. The posing of the body – all that could just have been a blind. He wanted to make it look like a stranger killing, like some headcase . . .'

Dan gave a low whistle. 'I think you need to slow down.'

Cate subsided. She knew Stocky would have said the same thing.

'There isn't anything to show they even spoke that night. We need to work with the evidence, probe his relationship with Sarah, why he lied about seeing her. That's all we have, Cate, and let's face it: it's understandable under the circumstances, if you think about how it would have looked.'

She fell silent. Of course he was right. And there was nothing to connect the teacher with Teresa King or Ellen Robertson. But Chrissie had been the starting point, hadn't she? The beginning of it all.

Her eyes narrowed. Matt Cosgrove had been accused of having a relationship with Chrissie Farrell that went beyond school, and now there was this Sarah, with whom he might also have overstepped the boundaries by accepting her gift. Had he been doing other things too – out looking for casual sex, kerb-crawling even? If so he might have come across Teresa King. There had been nothing on his record to suggest he'd done such a thing, but that would only be the case if he'd been caught. Cate bit her lip. They should speak to his wife, see if she'd harboured any suspicions before any of this began.

But this latest victim – Ellen Robertson. She had moved to the area only a couple of months ago, hadn't yet had any children to connect her with the school, and she lived several miles away. It wasn't likely they would have met.

But had they?

She pinched the bridge of her nose. If it *had* been the teacher and he'd fought with Chrissie, he would have panicked afterwards. The first scene had been posed, but aspects of it weren't quite right, not in terms of the fairy story – the colour of her dress, even the choice of dump site. It hadn't been quite organised enough. Maybe he'd set it up in haste. And after that, when he became a suspect, he needed to take the heat off. Teresa King might have been unlucky, that was all; he'd needed to make it look like there was a pattern, a serial killer, and had picked her at random to use as a prop. He might even have used an accomplice to do it, made sure the police had eyes on him at the time.

But – *torture* her? Her fingernails had been pulled out. That was a sign of cruelty, not randomness. And someone had bled her before her death, taking the blood to send back to her mother. It was odd too that Teresa King's nearest relative had been a grandmother – almost as if someone had been watching her, making sure she fitted the story.

It was too late to wonder. Cate looked up to find Dan pulling in at the kerb on a long, ordinary street lined with boxy semi-detached properties. He let the car roll forward so that Cate could open her door without striking one of the trees planted along the pavement and pointed towards a plain house with blinds half drawn across every window.

'This is it,' he said.

Cate couldn't take her eyes from Matt Cosgrove's face. She knew she was staring from the way he kept glancing at her, shifting his feet as if he could evade her look.

'So tell us again what happened when you were locking up,' Dan said. 'We know that Sarah was there as well as Hayley. We want to hear your version of events.'

Cosgrove shifted his gaze to Dan. His eyes looked empty. When he spoke, his voice was distant. 'I shouldn't even be talking to you,' he said. He sounded tired; beyond tired. 'My solicitor would go mad.'

Cate could hear his wife pacing in the next room; she'd said she would put the kettle on but there was no hiss of boiling water, only the sound of her footsteps, back and forth.

'If you haven't done anything wrong, there isn't anything to worry about,' Dan said.

'That's what you folk keep saying.' Cosgrove pressed his mouth closed. There were flecks of dried spittle at the corner of his lips and it made him appear vulnerable. His cheeks were hollowed out, grey. He didn't look like a man who would inspire women to throw themselves at his feet. He didn't look like a man anyone would find attractive. His hair had been cut short; unevenly, as if he'd done it himself. There was a livid shaving cut on his neck, as if he'd been picking at it.

He didn't look how Cate had expected. He gave the impression of being hollowed out on the inside too, as if he had nothing left, as if there was nothing he even cared about any longer.

Prince Charming, she thought. Was that who she'd expected to find? If so, this wasn't it. This was no fairy-tale hero, not a teacher whose pupils would have admired and giggled and preened over him, tottering to see him on high-heeled shoes. She heard Stocky's voice somewhere in the back of her mind: *vanity*. She shook the thought away and forced herself to concentrate.

'I did see her,' he said. 'Hayley Moorhouse had gone, and I'd – I don't know, I was locking up, trying to set the alarm. It wouldn't work. That part was true.' His voice went distant. 'I – I remember standing there for a bit, at the door. It was a nice night. I was – I was distracted, I think. But then the alarm wouldn't work and I turned around and *she* was there.'

'Sarah?' asked Dan.

Cosgrove nodded. 'She was there, and I knew – I knew what she wanted.' He drew a deep sigh. 'Look, I didn't do anything wrong. I didn't touch the girl. I tried to get rid of her, but she wouldn't let it go. She thought I had a thing for her; I don't know why.'

His voice went quiet and Cate thought of his wife, in the next room. Her footsteps had fallen quiet too.

'I argued and then she called a taxi and she left, and I just sat there for a bit. Then I left too,' he said. 'Look, I didn't tell you: I admit that. But then what happened to Chrissie had happened, and people were saying things – I know what they said.' He looked up, and this time a light burned in his eyes. 'I didn't do anything,' he said. 'The girls – they used to talk about me, that's all. I used to think it was funny. Now I know it's not.' He put a hand to his head as if to run it through his hair and scraped at his scalp instead. Cate heard it rasping.

'And you didn't see Chrissie Farrell?'

'I didn't see Chrissie Farrell.'

'She gave you a gift,' Cate blurted. 'Sarah, I mean. She said she gave you something and you took it. Why did you accept it?'

He just looked at her, unblinking; then the door to the kitchen opened and his wife was there, her hair greasy as Cate had last seen it, but this time she wasn't avoiding anyone's gaze; her eyes were full of a cold anger. 'I'll show you,' she said. 'I'll *show* you.'

She stormed from the room and Cate heard her pounding up the stairs and crossing the landing. A short while later she was back. She carried a book and she thrust it towards Cate. It had a young girl on the front, a white, old-fashioned dress contrasting with her dark hair. Cate took it. She almost expected it to be a book of fairy tales after all, but no: it was *Romeo and Juliet*.

'Look at what she wrote,' Mrs Cosgrove said. 'Just look at it. He didn't even know. She said she found it, didn't she? She said it was so he could put it in the school library. He had no idea what she'd put.'

Cate flipped open the cover of the book. On the first page, in purple ink, someone had written *See you in class. xxx*. Next to it, in swirling lines, was drawn a heart.

'That's not all.' Mrs Cosgrove jabbed a finger towards the book. 'Show her, love.'

Mr Cosgrove slowly stirred himself, as if he had fallen into a torpor. He stepped forward, gently took the book from her. He flipped through it until, over his shoulder, she caught a flash of pink: he pressed down on the page and held it out.

There, on the thin paper, someone had struck through the lines with bright ink. No, not ink: with a highlighter. Cate read the words:

This bud of love, by summer's ripening breath
May prove a beauteous flower when next we meet.

'You see?' Mrs Cosgrove said. 'This is what you don't realise, what you've done to him: what *she* did to him. You made everybody think he's some kind of villain. You even made *me* doubt him.' She paused; her eyes filled with tears. 'This is the truth of it. Are you happy now? Can you see what you've done?' She paused. '*He's* the victim in this too.'

CHAPTER THIRTY-FIVE

There was birdsong somewhere outside. Alice could hear it through the window, although she couldn't see the blue bird anywhere. Still the singing went on, and she thought she recognised it. She couldn't seem to get the words from its tale out of her mind:

Blue Bird, blue as the sky,
Fly to me now, there's nobody by.

She grabbed her jacket, opened the door and headed outside.

The trees were wide-spaced and silent as Alice walked from the house, following the sound of birdsong. When she looked up she saw scraps of blue sky between the leaves; impossible to tell if the bird was flying among them. She knew it was there, though, from the shrill *chrr-chrr-chrr* it made. It felt so long ago that she'd first heard it; the sound that had heralded the springtime – and this whole chain of events. She could almost blame the bird for beginning it all, for changing her from a bystander to a witness to a suspect. *No, not that.* But wasn't that what she'd seen in Cate's eyes, heard in her voice? She pushed the thought away and then the blue bird was there, a flash of bright feathers in the highest branches.

Alice smiled and kept after it. It was as if she were a child again, following her instincts, believing in magic. Anything could happen; if the last days had showed her nothing else, they had taught her that. She put a hand to her pocket and found the feather. It was there, it had been given to *her*. It was real; the bird had come to her, and that had meant something.

She could see the bird clearly now, fluttering from branch to branch, and she followed.

The little creature led Alice through the bluebell glades and onwards into denser woodland. She didn't see the clearing with the white flowers and she didn't see anyone else. After a while she stopped trying to keep the bird in view; it was difficult to see, and anyway, she could hear its song.

She took the feather from her pocket, looked at it, replaced it again.

They went on, Alice uncertain now as to whether the bird was really leading her or merely fleeing her. Eventually they turned, skirting the bottom of the lake and passing into the woodland on the other side. This was drawing closer to where the girl had been found, and Alice peered into the trees. She hadn't realised she had come this far. What did she think she was doing? But somehow she couldn't just turn and leave the bird and go home again having understood nothing.

Anyway, the police still had a presence on this side of the lake; it would be safe – and surely no one involved would dare come back here. Alice breathed in and the air smelled fresh, redolent of new growth. It was all right, she *knew* this place. It was *her* place.

The bird began to sing again, high and insistent, and Alice ducked under a branch and headed up the slope once more.

CHAPTER THIRTY-SIX

'So what you're telling me,' Heath said, laying down his hand on top of a stack of files, 'is you've given the guy a new alibi. He was with this girl that night.'

'It looks that way, sir,' Dan said.

'And all we have is a jealous schoolkid; not even the same girl who ended up dead.'

'Sir.'

Heath drew a deep breath. 'All right. Well, at least we know for sure.' He shifted his gaze to look out of the window. 'So we've still got to find the bastard.'

Cate kept quiet. Heath was right: she'd gone chasing a lead and found only a broken man. But that was progress of a sort wasn't it? They'd closed off one line of enquiry. Now they had to find another way of catching the killer. She thought of Alice. What would she have said about this? Perhaps she too would have gone to the house expecting a villain: a wolf. But that wasn't Matt Cosgrove.

She bit her lip. It was easy, in fairy tales. Villains wore

their evil on the outside, didn't they? But before all this had happened, when Cosgrove still presumably had his looks – that's when she could have believed he might be a murderer. Now, with his pallor and his thinness – now he was vindicated, the innocent man – his looks had gone. And they, the police, had done this.

'So a schoolgirl's got a crush.' Heath spoke slowly, his gaze still miles away. Neither Dan nor Cate had moved; they both knew that Heath was thinking out loud. 'And you say it was his wife who found the book.'

'She did,' said Dan. 'She defended him to the hilt.'

'Did she now?'

Dan simply waited.

'She didn't at the time though, did she? When Cosgrove got back late, when she got wind of the rumours – she obviously thought there was more to it than that, or she wouldn't have come in to speak to us.' He paused. 'You don't think the other girl – Chrissie – might have been around that night too? That she threw herself at him after the other one had gone?'

Cate frowned.

'But we've been watching him,' Heath continued. 'We know *he* didn't snatch Ellen Robertson or Teresa King.'

'No.'

'But someone else did.'

She watched the words being batted from Heath to Dan and back again, realised she was witnessing an old routine: Heath bouncing thoughts off a member of the team. She wasn't sure he was even taking them seriously himself.

'The thing is,' he continued, 'while you were off talking to the guy, Intel turfed up another connection.' He let them take that in. 'It looks like Cosgrove and the third victim – Ellen Robertson – may have known each other. Both were members of the same gym, and according to what we know of the woman's schedule, they would have been there at roughly the same time of day, late afternoon.'

Cate stared.

'Odd, isn't it?'

Her thoughts raced. Ellen had only just been married. According to her acquaintances, she'd been happy. Maybe she'd met Cosgrove, said hello over the treadmill – but more than that? She surely wouldn't have had a relationship with him or anyone else.

But she'd left her friends behind, hadn't she? She'd moved here to be with her husband. How much time would she have spent alone? Could she really have become so bored she'd started to see someone else so quickly?

'Cate?' Heath raised his eyebrows at her. 'Thoughts?'

She sighed, shook her head. 'I don't know, sir,' she said. 'I suppose – it's *possible* they might have met, become involved somehow. But after – I mean, it doesn't really feel right. A quick fling, maybe: perhaps they just got carried away, made a mistake.'

'And she winds up pregnant.'

She stared at him.

Heath pushed himself up but made no move to leave. Dan stood too, and so did Cate. 'This is all supposition, Cate, you know that, don't you? We can hardly go back to him now unless we want to be up on harassment charges. It's all circumstantial. Anyway, what if it wasn't *him*?'

There was something about the way he emphasised the word, and suddenly Cate realised what he meant.

'We can still keep an eye on them.' Heath headed for the door and Dan followed, but Cate remained where she was, staring at the whiteboard in front of her. There were names, times, dates, with lines connecting them like some strange family tree. And Mrs Cosgrove was there, her name written with the rest, a straight clear arrow connecting it with her husband's.

Jealousy, Cate thought. *Jealousy, not vanity*.

She gave a spurt of laughter. Almost from the very beginning, Alice had seen it: she had always said, albeit for the wrong reasons, that the killer must have been a woman. And yet – all the talk about fairy tales, and now they might have discovered a real connection, Cate felt as if they were making up stories.

CHAPTER THIRTY-SEVEN

The final slope was steep, taking Alice upwards, away from the lake. From here it wasn't such a distance to the place Little Red had been found. The arboretum was away to her right, the collection of rare trees, each with an exotic name written at its foot, their novelty overshadowed now by bad memories. Ahead of her, if she kept going, she would reach open fields.

A sharp sound drew her head around; the blue bird was sitting in a low branch close by, and it was watching her. Black eyes, tightly curled claws. It turned and whirred away through the trees.

She slipped her hand into her pocket, took out the feather. It was crushed, and the curved edge was not so smooth any longer; there was nothing special about it now except its colour. But she had come this far. She replaced the feather and followed.

Now she couldn't see the bird at all. She ducked under the branches, feeling them claw at her hair, and pulled free. Her feet sank into the soft ground. When she listened, she could hear nothing; the bird had abandoned her. She probably couldn't even find it again, and there would be nothing to do but go home, her hair a mess, her feet dirty, feeling foolish. At least she wasn't the only one to be fascinated with the creature. The birdwatcher would have walked miles for a glimpse of what she'd seen. And yet it had felt as if there should be more.

She pressed on, battling the low, springy branches. She should get out of this thicket and go home. She was alone in the wood where a dead girl had been dumped, and the bird's spell was broken; she didn't feel safe any longer.

A dog barked somewhere up ahead and she jumped. There came a low whistle and the dog fell silent.

Alice looked behind her, in the direction of the lake. She couldn't see the water from here, only more trees. Her heart beat rapidly.

The undergrowth rustled and the animal she'd heard emerged in front of her. The dog was squat and powerfully built, its body black, its eyes an even rich brown. She could hear it scenting for her and she realised she had seen it before; she even knew where, though it had been only once. It had been the last time she had followed the blue bird; she had followed its owner to the police cordon by the road.

'He won't bite,' a voice called out, but it was not the voice Alice had expected to hear: it belonged to a woman, and it sounded friendly. She'd seen the dog with a man last time, hadn't she? The animal withdrew and Alice took a deep breath, pushed the undergrowth out of her way and stepped into a gap in the trees.

The woman standing there was older than Alice, and shorter, her hair dyed an improbable orange-brown. She sounded almost sheepish when she spoke again. 'I know I shouldn't be here,' she said, 'not really. I come for the berries, you know.' She held something out. It was an old margarine tub, with little pellet shapes rattling inside it. 'I come in from t'other road – from the south. There's a hole in the wall. Can't be bothered with the police an' all. What would they want with me?' She tilted back her head and let out a shrill laugh as if she'd said something funny.

Alice found the tension draining from her shoulders and she gave a small smile.

'Cat got your tongue, love?'

She smiled fully this time. 'Hello,' she said.

'Nice day for a walk, in't it?'

'It is.'

'Duke won't hurt you.'

'No.'

The woman thrust the tub towards Alice. 'Junipers,' she said in explanation, and she tipped back her head and shook with mirth.

Alice glanced at the dog. It was facing away from her, completely uninterested. It let out a low grunt, like an old man settling into a comfortable chair.

'I like my gin, me,' the woman said. 'I don't know about you, love, but a tipple sets me right up. Our Gary, he says it's bad for me, but I say with the juniper – *fresh* juniper, mind, not just what's in there already – it's like one of my five a day.'

'Is that your son?' asked Alice.

'Ay, love, he is. Interfering things, sons. Have you got any?'

'No.'

'Pity.' The woman's face re-formed into an expression of sympathy.

Alice stirred. 'So that's why you come here – for berries?' She glanced around and saw a tree that stood apart from the others. It looked different too, its foliage a deeper, richer green, and it was smaller, only a little taller than Alice herself. There was a sign at its foot, but not like the ones in the arboretum: this was older, darkened, and she couldn't read it. She remembered hearing somewhere that there was another arboretum, an older one, long since subsumed into the rest of the woods.

'I planted one in my garden,' said the woman, 'and it grew, but it's not nearly as fine as this. The berries wouldn't flavour a cup of tea, never mind my gin. I know it's not far from where— Well, it doesn't do to talk about that, does it?' She reached out, caught a berry between her thumb and forefinger and pulled. Her movements were awkward, her misshapen hands arthritic. The branch clung on then let go, springing away, and the woman tried to roll the fat purple berry between her fingers.

'It's a *juniper* tree,' Alice whispered under her breath.

'Are you all right, love? You seem a bit out of it.'

'Yes, I'm quite all right. Sorry. I'm a bit tired, that's all.'

'You should try gin – with juniper, of course. It'd set you right up.'

'Maybe I will.' Alice looked about as she spoke; she felt she had lost her bearings somehow, as if the woodland had changed around her.

'As long as you're not thinkin' o' gettin' preggers.'

'What? Oh – no, I'm not.'

'Good. It brings it off, see,' she said, 'although it's just an old wives' tale. 'Course, I should know, being an old wife.' She let out that laugh again, and Alice wished she would stop.

'Not much on talking, are you, love? They used to give it to women in labour. It loosened 'em up, see, made it easier. But if you're pregnant – same thing – not that you'd be drinking any gin, of course, if you was preggers, not these days.'

'No. No, I wouldn't.' Alice managed a smile.

'You should meet my Gary.'

'Should I?'

'He's single. Are you single? Looks like you could do with someone. Take you out of yourself a bit.'

'Oh.' Alice remembered the man she'd seen walking the dog after Little Red had been found. She tried to remember his face. Was he someone she'd want to see again? She didn't want to think about it, not out here. 'No,' she lied, 'no, I'm not single.'

'Pity.' The woman bent and picked up a plastic lid. She held the tub against her body while she pressed it down. The berries inside rolled back and forth. 'Well, love, I'm done.' She walked towards Alice and she felt the urge to back away, but resisted it; in a moment the stranger would be gone and she would be alone. She could look at the tree.

As she passed, though, the woman reached out and grasped Alice's arm, and she looked down and saw gold, the glint of too many rings on the clawed fingers. She forced an uncertain smile. She could smell the old pink fleece the woman was wearing under her coat, a scent of dog and unwashed clothes.

'You should get yourself a good man, love,' the woman said, and then she let go and bustled away, the branches rustling as they closed behind her.

Alice stood in the clearing alone. *Get yourself a good man*, the woman had said. Hadn't Alice told her she wasn't single? So why had she said that? Or was she just being talkative, trying to say she should get another, better man – one like her son?

It didn't matter; it was the tree that concerned Alice. Instead of going closer, though, she circled it, keeping her distance. There was something about it she didn't like. The juniper was a small, dense conifer with a twisting trunk. It wasn't like the specimens in the newer arboretum. It was older; this *place* was older. Alice glanced around, noticing for the first time that there was a ring of bare earth running all the way around the tree.

She scraped at it with her foot and dust rose from the ground. There were tufts of grass at its edges but they looked sick, attenuated and yellow. She crouched, glanced towards the tree as she touched her fingertips to the dry earth. Then she put her fingers to her lips: was that salt she could taste?

And yet the tree grew. Its berries were swollen, full and ripe.

I planted one in my garden, and it grew, but it's not nearly as fine as this.

Alice walked towards the tree. She took hold of some of its needles and they felt fat and a little waxy. There was nothing odd about it; it was she who was being caught up in strange ideas. She bent and peered under the lowest branches. Nothing was growing beneath them. There was only a patina of long-dead needles fallen around the trunk.

She touched her hand to the earth, not quite knowing why, and the dead needles slid under her fingers, at once smooth and sharp, and then she felt something else; it was a little stone, that was all, and yet when she withdrew she held it between her fingers.

When she lifted it up in front of her face, she almost dropped it.

She concentrated on catching her breath, put it on the palm of her hand and examined it. The thing was a tooth. It looked old, many years old, but perhaps that was because of the way the dirt had clung, accentuating each fissure on its surface. Alice didn't want to be holding it any more, didn't want to touch it, and yet she couldn't cast the thing away. The tooth was a molar, but it looked too small. She ran her tongue over her own teeth and they felt huge in her mouth. She thought this was a child's tooth. She couldn't leave it here in the woods. She had found it and she had to take it: it was hers now. She would have to give it to the police, try to explain how she had come to find it. She wasn't sure how she would do that.

She glanced around, turned and started to push her way back towards the lake, heading down the slope. After a moment, she started to run.

Alice was led into a tiny room and she waited, unable to keep still. The tooth was in her pocket. Her mind couldn't get away from the way it was nestling there against the fabric, dirt perhaps flaking from it and settling into the seams. Later she might put her hand in there, forgetting, and touch that same fabric. Then she remembered she had put it in the same pocket as the feather, her precious feather, and she grimaced. That was when the door opened.

It was Cate, as she had hoped. She could have spoken to someone else if she had to, but it was Cate she wanted to see, Cate who'd had that look in her eyes when they spoke in Heath's office, that odd note in her voice on the telephone. Now she would see that Alice was only trying to help.

However, as the time came for her to speak, Alice paled. How exactly was she supposed to explain this? How had she managed to find something the police had not? And what had she been doing in the woods at all? Cate was waiting for her to speak, but she couldn't put words together, couldn't concentrate. It wouldn't have to matter: it *couldn't*. It felt as if things were coming into the light; and the important thing was that the killer was stopped, the one who was sullying the things she loved. They would find him and stop him and Alice would have done her part. Cate would understand that she had helped.

Alice didn't say anything. She simply put her hand in her pocket and took hold of the tooth and held it out.

'Don't you see? I was right,' Alice said. She realised her eyes were stinging and was dismayed to find tears had sprung into them. 'There *was* an older case, more than one, even, but this one – there's a *body* buried under that tree. Don't you see that?'

Cate stared at the tooth that sat between them on the desk.

Alice went on, 'Someone, maybe way back when that tree was planted, buried someone under there, but this time it was different; I think it was a child. It might have been someone they knew, someone they were related to; maybe it was even *their* child. Whoever it was, they're buried under that tree. That's where they got the teeth.'

'You mean you think someone has been digging there?' Cate asked doubtfully.

Alice faltered.

'You think the killer dug up this first body and took the teeth so that he could put them in Little Red's mouth?'

'Yes – no. I don't know. The ground didn't look disturbed. I never thought of that. I just—'

'So how did you find the tooth?'

'It was just lying there, on the ground. Under the tree.' Alice blinked at Cate, her eyes unfocused.

Cate looked puzzled. She sighed, and started again: 'So there's nothing to say there's a body under there at all. You found something on the ground, something the killer might have left there, or dropped accidentally.'

'No – I mean yes, I found it, that's what happened. But I think I was *meant* to find it.'

Cate didn't have to reply: Alice could see the expression in her eyes. She took a deep breath and went on anyway, 'There *is* a body under the tree, I feel sure of it. You can see it in the way the berries are – it's – the tree's *feeding*. It's hard to explain, but you can feel it when you're there. It's like life feeding on death. And the ground around the tree, it's been salted. Someone did that, like a ritual or something.'

Cate shook her head and put a hand on Alice's arm.

'Alice, you should try to keep calm. Just listen to what you're saying. I think maybe this has all been a little too much for you. I should never have brought you into it, but I did, and it's too late now. The things you're saying—' She glanced towards the door.

'But the tooth is enough, isn't it? You have to look under there. Aren't you at least going to do that?'

Cate paused. 'We'll look around,' she said.

'No, you have to look *under*. There's something there, I know there is.'

'Alice, you have to see how this appears. There's no real connection, no story here, no Sleeping Beauty or Snow White. There's nothing posed or deliberate. Its not like the other murder scenes, and there's no body as far as we know. The killer could have kept those teeth for years, made use of them with Little Red and dropped one under the tree as he passed. It might help us find out where he went, how he got in and out of the woods, but nothing else.'

Alice drew back her arm. 'But there *is* a story here,' she said, barely holding in the anger. 'You don't see anything at all, you never have. You always needed *me*.' Her voice faltered and she took deep breaths, got control of herself. 'There *is* a story, possibly the most important one of all.'

'Which is?'

'The juniper tree. "The Juniper Tree" *is* a story, one that almost holds the other stories within it. Don't you see? The answer's here somewhere, the answer to it all.'

*

'"The Juniper Tree" begins with a rich man and his wife who can't have children,' Alice said. 'One winter's day, the wife is peeling an apple under the juniper tree in their garden and she cuts her finger. She wishes for a child as white as the snow and as red as the blood.'

Cate's eyes narrowed. 'That's like "Snow White".'

'Exactly. And yet, it goes on to be a different story entirely. When the child – a boy – is born, the mother dies of happiness and the husband buries her under the juniper tree.'

'But the teeth we have are a child's—'

'Wait! The man marries again. This time the wife is wicked, but she gives birth to a girl, Little Marlene. Over time she starts to wish that their fortune would be inherited only by her own child, and so she begins to hate her stepson.

'One day, her daughter asks her for an apple. The mother, feeling perverse, tells her to wait until her brother gets home from school. When he does, she offers *him* an apple, and when he reaches into the trunk where the apples are kept she slams down the lid and cuts off his head.'

'Nice.'

'Red in tooth and claw, remember?' Alice felt calmer now that she was relating the story.

'Then Mum gets scared. She props the boy up, balances his head back on his shoulders and wraps a handkerchief around his throat. When Marlene pesters her for an apple again, she tells her to ask her brother. The girl does, and when he doesn't answer she slaps him and his head falls off. She runs to her mother, terrified.'

'Jesus. Nice story.'

'Oh, it gets better. The mother pretends that it's Little Marlene who's killed her brother, but she says she'll help cover it up, like the good kind mother she is. So she cuts him into pieces and makes him into a stew. Then she feeds him to his father, all the while pretending the son has gone off on a visit to some uncle.'

'The teeth in the mouth?'

'Well, maybe – it's not mentioned specifically. In fact, in this story, the grieving sister gathers up his bones, wraps them in silk and places them at the foot of the juniper tree, where they vanish into the ground.'

'Ah.'

'That's it, you see? After that, the tree bursts open, there's mist and flame, and out of it all pops a fabulously coloured bird. It's red and green and gold.' Alice's voice went far away. 'I think that's why I didn't think of it before.'

'What?'

Alice stirred in her seat. 'Nothing. The bird is obviously the dead child returned, transformed into something else. It goes off on its travels, singing a beautiful song. It's so lovely that people pay to hear it. The bird gathers their payments – a gold chain, a pair of red shoes and a mill-stone.'

'A millstone?'

'Yes. A millstone.'

'And red shoes. Isn't that another fairy tale?'

'It is indeed. See how the same motifs crop up? But this isn't about the shoes. The bird goes back to the family home and sings its heart out in the garden. When they hear it, the husband feels happy and Little Marlene feels sorrowful, but the wife is afraid; she feels as if the world is about to end. The husband goes outside to investigate and the bird drops the gold chain around his neck.'

'Oh. I see what's coming.'

'The bird has gifts for everyone. The girl gets the red shoes. When the wife goes outside she gets the millstone dropped on her head and she's crushed to death.'

'So how did the bird carry the millstone?'

Alice shrugged. 'It's a fairy story, remember? It's magical. The whole thing's magical: the millstone . . . the bird.' Her voice faded before continuing, 'Anyway, there's a thunderclap, smoke, flames, things like that, and when it clears, the boy is standing there, restored, as right as rain. They greet each other and then go in for tea.'

'They what?'

'They all go in for tea. I suppose it's as good an ending as any.' Alice half smiled. 'Anyway, what I'm saying is, the juniper tree – it's a part of it. The tooth wasn't dropped there accidentally. The tree is a rare thing; it doesn't grow naturally in those woods. It was planted years ago in the arboretum, the *older* arboretum, and that's where the killer chose to leave the tooth.' She met Cate's gaze. 'That's why it's so important that you take a look at what's under there. There's another body, I know it.'

Cate stirred. 'But it doesn't *fit*.'

'*Fit?* Of course it does.'

Cate met her eye with a steady gaze. 'Look, I'll see what I can do. You'll need to show us where it is. And you might need to speak to Heath.'

Alice didn't seem to hear her. When she spoke again her voice was distant. 'I always felt there was more to this,' she said. 'It was only when I saw what kind of tree it was that I was sure.'

'The tree?'

'Yes.' Alice closed her eyes.

'How did you find this tree, anyway?'

She didn't answer.

'Alice?'

'You wouldn't believe it.'

'Well, maybe not.' Cate paused. 'But give me a go.'

Alice sighed. 'I've been seeing a bird in the woods: a blue bird. I followed it, and it led me to the juniper tree.'

'Alice – are you all right? Are you even remotely aware of how that sounds?'

'I know. But it's true.'

'Then it's just a coincidence.'

'Possibly – yes, it could be. But you know, it always struck me as strange.' Alice looked up, her voice dreamy. 'I always thought it was an odd story, and not only because of the way little pieces of other stories seem to appear within it. It was always just – weird, you know, because of the name: "The Juniper Tree". I mean it wasn't about the tree at all, was it, really? It has its role to play, but it always seemed to me that the story was about something else.'

'What, Alice?'

Alice turned. She could feel the way her eyes were glowing; she knew the policewoman would think she was crazy, but it was too late. 'It was about the bird,' she said. 'It was *always* about the bird, don't you see?'

Cate didn't say anything; she just stared at Alice.

After a long moment, Alice changed the subject. 'There was someone else there,' she said, and she told Cate about the woman who had been picking berries in the wood. 'Her son's name is Gary. I don't know the surname, but he's on your register of people who were near the lake when the girl was found. I saw him giving his details to the police, if you want to track them down.

'You know, I'm not mad. I know the bird probably just went to the tree because it liked the berries. Of course it's a coincidence. But I'm not the only person who's interested in it. There's someone else in the woods, trying to find it.' She told Cate about how she'd met Bernard Levitt, waiting in his hide. It felt good, handing it all over to the police, everything she had seen and felt. 'I don't think he saw anything, but you never know. He might have seen something that day and assumed it wasn't important. Something besides the bird, I mean.'

CHAPTER THIRTY-EIGHT

Cate looked aside, peering into the car park at Newmillerdam as she went past. She wasn't going there, not today; she wasn't heading towards something but away from it, diverted from the main event. Alice would already have been collected and taken to the scene, leading police officers to where she'd found the juniper tree. Not Cate, though, not this time: no sooner had she been made the woman's liaison officer than she had been sidelined. Perhaps Heath didn't think she had the skills to manage the situation; he hadn't said the words, but his actions couldn't have made it clearer. Unless of course he just wanted to take things over himself.

She frowned, lost in her own thoughts as she took a turn that led away from the woodland. Behind her, others would be on their way to investigate the lead she'd found; but then, if she had been the one listening to her own stammered explanation, she wasn't sure she wouldn't have turned her away too.

At least they *were* going to investigate.

Now she followed a winding road that led towards Crigglestone and the address she'd been given, passing a bus stop with a wide turning-circle and descending into a dip in the road before coming out the other side. The address was just off the High Street and as she took each turn she glanced at road signs, remembering her training: *Always know where you are*. She shrugged inwardly even as she did so. Would Stocky have been pleased to think his training had stuck? But he'd lost faith in her in other ways, more important ones, and that felt like such a long time ago.

What she thought of now was Alice, wending her way through the woods, just following a bird, probably not paying any attention to where she was or where she went. She shook the thought away. Alice *had* to be right, didn't she? If Cate had been misled, Heath would never give her another chance – if it wasn't already too late.

Of course, Cate hadn't told him about how Alice thought she'd found the tree. She had only told him about the tooth and the fairy tale, though from the expression on his face, that had been more than enough. She hadn't wanted to see that look in his eyes; even as she spoke she realised that it was the second time she'd found herself covering for Alice. And of course she was supposed to be offering her support to her contact – but was that really the reason she'd done it?

Heath's steely eyes, Alice's dreamy expression: she felt

caught between the two of them. For now though, it was only her, and a job to be done. She turned onto a side road, slowed and started looking at the house numbers. She heard a dog barking even before she saw the right one.

The animal was as Alice had described, short and squat and deep in the chest, its fur entirely black. It probably had some pitbull somewhere in its lineage. It was an unlikely pet for an older woman – perhaps her son, Gary Wilson, had made the choice. It strained on its chain as Cate stepped out and opened the gate. It wasn't barking now, nor snarling; its tongue lolled against the black frills of its lips.

'Not so fierce,' she said to it, and it wagged its tail.

The woman who answered the door didn't say anything when she saw Cate; she just stood in the doorway, waiting.

'It's the police, Mrs Wilson,' Cate said, and showed her badge. 'I wondered if I might have a word?'

The woman squinted. 'Police, is it? Eh?'

'Could I come in?'

The woman pushed the door wider and Cate stepped inside, seeing gaudily flowered wallpaper and a carpet with a faded strip pointing the way to the lounge. She smelled something sharp and herbal, and beneath that, a slight mustiness.

'I understand you were walking in the woods,' Cate said. 'Could you tell me something about what you were doing there?'

The woman pulled a face. 'Why wouldn't I be in the woods, love? I always go to the woods. That's where I take my walk. I like a gin, see, it's medicinal an' all, and I need the juniper berries to go in it. It's how my mother took it, and her mother before that.' She held out her hands. 'It's for the arthritis, see.' Her hands were loosely curled into fists, her knuckles lumpen. 'No one'll tell you, but gin's good for arthritis. Me mother swore by it.'

'Not the juniper berries?' Cate asked mildly. She wasn't looking at the woman's hands, though; she was staring into the corner of the room where a birdcage stood on a high stand, covered by a faded tea-towel.

'Eh?'

'It's not the juniper berries that are good for arthritis?'

'Oh – aye, love, maybe them too, eh?'

Cate smiled. 'I wondered if you saw anything while you were out walking?'

'Oh no, love, not me. Terrible thing though. No, I mind my own business. I just get my berries, that's all. Maybe you should ask our Gary.' She peered more closely at Cate. 'You single?' she asked suddenly.

Cate waved the question away.

'No, no one is these days, are they? That reminds me; I did see someone. Nice girl, she was. In her own world, like.'

Cate covered her smile. 'All right, Mrs Wilson. Do you ever gather anything else in the woods, by the way – herbs, medicinal plants, anything like that?'

'Not me, love, I wouldn't know what to do with 'em. Probably poison myself. No, it's just for me gin. I try sloe sometimes, but it's not the same. My arthritis, see.'

Cate nodded, then gestured towards the corner. 'What's in the cage, Mrs Wilson?'

'Oh, that, love, them's me budgies. I always cover 'em up while I have me cup of tea, or they make a hell of a racket. They know I'm not paying 'em attention, see. They like attention, they do.' She didn't stop talking as she approached the cage. 'You can have a look, but they're not right friendly with strangers.'

She whisked the tea-towel off the cage as if performing a magic trick. There was a pair of budgies in the cage, as she had said. They were green. They turned their faces towards Cate, their eyes bright but devoid of understanding. One ruffled its wings as if in a shrug, stretched out one claw.

'Thank you, Mrs Wilson. You've been extremely helpful.' Cate led the way down the hall, said goodbye. Once standing alone in the garden she cast her eyes around, this time looking for any trace of the plant that Heath had mentioned in his briefing: *Conium maculatum*, poison hemlock. There was no sign of anything like it, only a stunted tree reaching out its limp branches over the grass.

Bernard Levitt had a bungalow on one of the housing estates at the other side of Sandal. The estate was neither old nor new, and full of other bungalows that looked more or less like it; some had dormer windows that spoke of loft conversions, while others had porches or extensions bolted onto the front or side. All were well kept, the lawns carefully mowed, the paint more or less fresh. It was commuter belt incarnate, the sort of place where the sight of a police car would set curtains twitching and tongues a-wagging.

Cate took care to close the car door softly, smiling around as she walked up the path. It wasn't likely but she glanced around the garden anyway; there was no *Conium* there either, only tired hydrangeas and a rockery studded with alpines. She knocked loudly, realising as she did how quiet the estate was. It was so quiet she jumped when a voice spoke, not far away: 'Please, come around the back. I was just clearing up.'

She looked at the corner of the house but couldn't see to whom the voice belonged, so she followed the path around and stepped on to the driveway. A clean, dark blue saloon was parked there, and behind it stood the regulation three wheelie bins. She squeezed through the gap between them and the side wall of the house before rounding the corner to see a broad garden.

'Back here.' The voice was thin and a little high. Levitt was stocky, wore thick glasses and the kind of haircut his mother might have done for him, and his face was shining with sweat.

Cate saw what he carried in his hands and she started.

It was a dead bird, a wood pigeon, pale wings hanging

limply from its body. It hung loose in his hands. Levitt saw her looking, took hold of one wing between his thumb and fingertip and stretched it out. '*Columba palumbus*,' he said. 'Beautiful things. Quite beautiful.'

He gestured towards the end of his garden. There was a wooden strut running from a small shed to the fence and from it hung bird feeders, all shapes and sizes, strings of nuts and transparent globes containing grain and other substances Cate didn't recognise. There was a birdhouse too, large and intricate, with multiple holes and arches carved into it; and a birdbath set into the ground. The largest structure was an aviary, which had been built onto the side of the shed.

Levitt coughed and stepped towards her, then bent and picked up a hessian sack that had been lying on the ground. He put the bird into it, gently easing it into the opening. As he did so, his mouth twisted, in distaste or sorrow, Cate wasn't sure which.

'It's the cats, you know.' Now he looked disgusted. 'Do you like cats?'

'Not especially.'

He nodded, as if she'd given a satisfactory answer. 'They kill hundreds of birds each year. Hundreds, possibly even thousands – you wouldn't believe how many cats there are on this estate.'

Cate thought of the closed doors, the apparently empty streets. She doubted she'd be surprised at all.

'I'm sorry. I'm being rude.' Levitt turned towards her

and held out his hand to shake. 'Ah – wait.' He wiped it on the back of his trousers, half-heartedly held it out again before letting it fall. 'Well – no. Can I help you with something?'

'I'm a police officer, Mr Levitt. I'm investigating the body that was found at Newmillerdam. I heard you liked to spend time in the woods there and wondered if you might have seen anything.'

'Oh. Well, I have been spoken to before, you know. I walk there quite often; someone already asked. Still, since you're here – can I offer you a drink? Lemonade, perhaps?'

It was so like something a child's mother might ask that Cate had to bite back a laugh. 'That would be lovely,' she said.

Levitt kept speaking to her from the kitchen, his voice accompanied by the sound of cupboards opening and closing, the chink of glasses and the pouring of liquid. He came in at last, one glass in each hand, and set them on the table. Cate took hers and sipped. It was Bernard Levitt who started talking again. 'You know, they say cats are the only creatures that torture their prey,' he said. 'They'll play with a bird for hours before they kill it. Pin it down, claw at it, watch it trying to get away. It's a terrible thing.' He sat down.

'Besides humans,' said Cate.

'What?' He turned to her, took hold of the frame of his glasses, as if that would help him see what she meant.

'The only creatures that torture their prey, besides humans.'

'Oh. Oh dear, I see what you mean. Well, I suppose you would know.' He shot her a sidelong glance. 'The things you must see. I mean, to say something like that, you must have— Terrible. Terrible.'

'You say you're a bird lover,' Cate said. 'So, you've been watching them down in the wood?'

'That's right. I take my hide down there. I suppose you've heard about the blue bird? It's quite the sensation. I'm sure you watch the news.'

'I wondered if you'd seen anything else, Mr Levitt, while you were there. You'll have heard about the murder case. I know you've been asked already, but I'm here to check if you'd seen anything unusual, anything that might give you concern. Anything at all might turn out to be important, you know, even if it doesn't seem so at the time.'

'Well now, let's see. No, I don't think I have. No, I'm pretty sure – but I'm very focused, you know. I tend to go off the beaten track, so to speak, where I know it'll be quiet. That's when the birds come to me.' His face fell. 'I never have seen it yet, though. I'm hoping it'll still be around. There's no reason it shouldn't survive this long, not in springtime. It might even be nesting somewhere.'

'So you haven't seen anything – any*one* else out there?'

'Well, no, I'm afraid I haven't really seen anybody. Oh wait. No, there was someone: a young lady, pleasant, blonde. She was walking in the woods on her own. Other than that, no, I haven't seen anyone at all.'

Cate got back into the car and sat there for a moment, lost in thought. Just when she had the interviews wrapped up, there Alice was again, in the middle of everything. She was already wondering whether to mention it to Heath. What on earth had Alice been doing when Levitt saw her – was she too looking for her blue bird? It was as if she was retreating into her fantasy world. Hopefully that wasn't because of the things she'd seen.

She frowned, thinking of Alice chasing after the blue bird, Mrs Farrell sweeping the cloth from her budgie's cage; Levitt turning towards her, the limp wood pigeon in his hands. There seemed to be birds everywhere she went today.

But lots of people kept birds; it didn't mean anything. Now, if ever, was the time to prove to Heath she had a sensible head on her shoulders.

And then something else came back to her, another voice: at first she thought it was Alice's, then she knew it wasn't.

I shouldn't mention it really, only there was this bird.

It had been a young girl's voice.

It was sitting on the wall, an' it were bright blue.

It was the girl she'd spoken to after the school dance, when she was trying to find out what had happened to Chrissie Farrell.

Just sitting there. Pretty, though. It was really pretty.

And then she remembered Matt Cosgrove; the teacher's blank, empty eyes. *I remember standing there for a bit, at the door,* he'd said. *It was a nice night. I was – I was distracted, I think.*

Had he too been watching the bird?

A sound made her jump. She reached for her radio, then realised it was her mobile. She fumbled for it, answered the call: it was Dan.

'You need to get down to Newmillerdam,' he said. 'They've found something.' He paused. 'Heath wants you at the scene. Apparently it was you who came up with the lead.'

CHAPTER THIRTY-NINE

The police officers were back, along with the photographers and the SOCOs and the police tape, the whole sorry parade. They bustled amid the once-peaceful wood, the locus of their activity a single dark green tree.

The juniper stood roughly the height of a man, dwarfed by the surrounding giants of beech and ash. Its fat purple berries were held out in clusters like small fists, some kind of benediction perhaps, or an apology. Its branches stirred in the late-spring breeze, and when they did, the whole tree swayed.

The tree was swaying because there was a gaping hole at its foot where the ground had been excavated. Fresh earth was piled to one side, alive with the movement of insects and worms emerging from the dark.

It was only when Cate stood on the very edge of the hole that she could see the thing that had become entwined in the roots, so darkened by time that it looked like a natural outgrowth of the tree. It silenced her.

The thing was a child. Tree roots had meandered between its ribs, sending tendrils into the space where its heart had been. Everything was the same colour, as if the child had become tree, and tree, child. Its face was turned away from her sight, as if it had been burrowing into the ground like some woodland animal. The skull had cracked, half hidden by the soil that clung to the bone. It was not clear if the damage had been inflicted deliberately or by the pressures of the earth.

There was nothing else, nothing to suggest it had been posed, nothing at all except the ragged strips of cloth in which it had been wrapped.

Cate heard someone approach and stand at her side. They didn't speak, and for a moment she didn't look at them. She imagined it would be Dan, but when she turned, it was Heath.

He met her eye, gave a slight nod. Then he put a hand on her shoulder.

The touch surprised her and she drew away. His hand fell to his side; she couldn't tell if he was irritated. His expression didn't change.

'So. We found something.'

She nodded.

'Your friend – Hyland – was right. There *is* more going on here. The body in that hole – it didn't land there yesterday. How old is that tree, do you think? We're going to have to cut it off her.'

'Her?'

'The pathologist thinks it's female, but we can't be sure yet. We can't even turn the head to see if the teeth are missing. But it is possible that this is where they came from, even if they were removed before it was buried. The ground hadn't been disturbed when we got here; no one's been digging here recently.' He paused. 'She had an alibi, you know.'

At first, she wasn't sure who she meant; it was Alice who'd sprung into her mind. Then she realised. 'Mrs Cosgrove?'

'She was at work all day when the Robertson woman was taken. Her colleagues vouched for her. She went out for lunch and, lucky her, met a friend; she paid her share on credit card. It looks tight. And this body—'

He didn't need to explain the rest. The child's body looked as if it had been there for years; it could be at least as old as Mrs Cosgrove or her husband. And the police had no one else. This find – *Alice's* find – had blown everything wide open.

Alice. Again, she was in the middle of everything. How had she known about the tree, really? Her story of following the bird was ridiculous. But then, how could the girl be connected to this body, other than by her knowledge of the fairy story? Alice was younger than either of the Cosgroves. It didn't make sense.

She looked up to find Heath watching her. This time she noticed the lines around his eyes, the strain about his lips.

'Ms Hyland told me the story of the juniper tree,' he said, echoing Cate's thoughts. 'Strange, isn't it? This body is obviously earlier than the others. If it *is* connected to a story, like them, this could be our killer's first victim. And if it is – it seems his reasoning must have been different. If we can find how or why the child was killed . . .' His voice sounded weary, but it had an edge to it.

'It was lucky Alice Hyland found the tooth,' he said, 'hmm? Anyone else might have assumed it was nothing but a coincidence.'

Cate left Heath and went to catch up with Dan. He wasn't waiting by the perimeter, though four white-hooded SOCOs were gathered nearby. She approached, searched each of their faces and frowned. He wasn't among them.

She found the register of attendees to the scene and scanned the list, saw that she was right: he had already gone. There was nothing left for her to do here, and she felt hollowed out, exhausted.

She signed herself out, but instead of heading straight for the car park, she found herself veering towards the place where Little Red had been discovered. Two bodies found in the same stretch of woodland – that wasn't what they'd come to expect. She wondered if there might be some similarity in the scenes that they'd missed. Had a particular type of tree once stood where Little Red had been dumped? She didn't think so.

Cate reached the edge of the arboretum. It was quiet

here, and still. It looked as if more of the fallen trees had been cleared away, but she couldn't be certain; perhaps the wardens had abandoned their work here for a while.

She walked across the space. At first she couldn't see any sign that the girl had been there. There was nothing to see, but how many people would come and stand here anyway, telling her story once again? It was like Alice had said: *It wouldn't have happened if it wasn't for the stories, would it? Without that she'd be nothing but a dead girl dumped in the woods. At least this way someone cares.*

Yes, they cared. Had been made to care.

Alice had been made to care.

She frowned. Yes, Alice had been made to care, had been made to share her expertise, to get involved.

What else had she said?

You need to look at old cases. This might have been happening for years.

And lo and behold, they *had* found another body, the proof that Alice was right once again, proving her the expert. They had found the body because Alice had led them to it. She hadn't even done it through deduction or clues; no, she'd gone straight there, inventing that wild story about the bird, as if it would explain everything.

Cate frowned. That dreamy look on the girl's face – making her seem dazed, overwhelmed by everything – was that for real? Did she really live so deeply in her fantasies, or was she just making herself appear stupid when she was in fact very clever?

She shook her head. She knew some murderers would try to insinuate themselves into an investigation, follow everything that happened, but Alice hadn't done that: it was she who'd dragged Alice into it. When Alice had first seen a crime-scene photograph, the shock had been genuine. It certainly wasn't something she'd wanted to look at. Was it?

Cate took a deep breath. She had to get herself together. She opened her eyes, let them slip out of focus and saw the hazy memory of a dead girl lying on the ground: Teresa King. She remembered the photograph sitting in pride of place next to the television, a mother and her daughter wearing the same dress and almost the same smile. A husband crying for his wife, for a child who would never be born. She owed it to all of them to *think*.

And then she saw something else lying on the ground, something that might have been waiting for her to find it. She stepped forward, crossing the imagined line where the crime scene had begun.

There was a dead bird lying in front of her. It was large and black, its feathers still shining. It was a crow or a rook, Cate wasn't sure which. It looked intact. There was no spray of feathers to show where a predator had caught it, no injuries that she could see. There was a low buzzing though, and a fly rose from the body before settling again, crawling in amid the gloss-dark feathers. The bird had huge claws, the skin dry and wrinkled, closed on nothing.

It was always *about the bird.*

She stared at it; then she roused herself, rubbed her eyes and turned in a slow circle, looking at the trees that stood around her. It felt as if there was something else she should see, something she should understand, but there was nothing. She turned and began to walk away, towards the car park and normality and traffic and houses and paperwork, things that made sense.

She stopped. There was another dead bird in her path. This one was a robin, its claws tight and delicate as a dead spider. Like the crow, there was nothing to show how it had died. Ignoring her distaste, she took out an evidence bag and slid the creature into it. It must have been dead for a while, was cold in her hands, its body a small centre of firmness beneath soft feathers.

Cate pulled out of the Newmillerdam car park and on to the road, where she quickly picked up speed. She turned left, in the opposite direction to the police station; they wouldn't miss her for a while yet.

Soon she was on an open road with woodland on one side and fields spreading away on the other. She opened the window, gasping in the scent of wheat, the harsher tang of oilseed rape. The route to Ryhill felt familiar, as if it was somewhere she was supposed to be. It wasn't long before she saw the row of red-brick houses at the edge of the village and slowed for the turning that led in the direction of the Heronry. It was both a lifetime and no time at all since she'd been there last.

The road dipped and she glanced into the trees, shadows flickering across her vision. The clearing came up on her left. There were no other cars, no one here that she could see. The area had been cleared since the body was taken, and not only of Chrissie's remains; there was no sign even to show it had been used for fly-tipping except a well-trodden area scabbed with bare earth.

She got out of the car. This wasn't like the woods, a place where she could almost sense the life running through the trees. Here they looked more like survivors, clinging to their sorry bit of ground.

She stepped off the path and onto the hard soil. She felt a little like Alice. The girl had been caught up in a fantasy, half lost in the stories she told, and now Cate was doing it too: she hadn't even let anyone know where she was going. She reached for her mobile, brushed the smooth surface with her fingertips and let her hand fall. What on earth would she say, that she had come here following – what? A bird? She bit back a laugh.

The branches were still, the air calm, as if nature was holding its breath. There was nothing here except brambles spreading their tendrils across the spaces, their thin fingers meeting and clasping.

It was only when Cate turned back towards the car that she saw the flowers.

She couldn't think how she'd failed to notice them before. They were massed together in a line, still wrapped in plastic, the contents damp and browned with recent rain or dew. Some specks of colour held on, splashes of pink or blue or yellow amid the petals that had been washed colourless. There was a single bunch that were fresh, little yellow roses, and Cate thought of the photograph she'd seen, the girl in a yellow dress, her mother in white.

That couldn't be all. There had to be something else.

She started to search, walking in as straight a line as she could to the far end of the clearing and into the trees, where undergrowth made progress impossible, and back again, a little to the side of her previous route. When she reached the car she repeated her actions, covering the whole area as best she could. There was nothing. Once she found a few feathers, fluffy and grey, but there was no bird; perhaps they had fallen from some nest, or been carried here on the wind.

There was no other place to look, except one. She went to the flowers, wrinkling her nose at the sour scent. She didn't want to touch them, though another part of her wanted them gone, all signs removed, leaving this place to forget what could be forgotten and letting Chrissie be what she now was – a smiling girl in a picture. She picked up the first, the plastic crackling under her fingers, and replaced it a short distance away. Then the next. When she'd moved them all she crouched down and looked at the space she'd created. The flowers had been hiding nothing; there was no dead bird, nothing there at all. What had she expected? This area had been searched and searched again, SOCOs crawling all over it. Of course they would have found a bird, if there was anything to be found.

But birds fly.

Cate pushed herself up and went back towards the car, but instead of getting inside she went past it and into the lane. She started to walk the narrow, rutted path with trees growing along its edge. She caught glimpses of water between the trunks, a stretch of lakeside. The fishermen who had found the body might be there now, hunched over the water, staring into it and trying not to think of what they'd seen.

Down this lane and the next, if she kept going long enough, was the Heronry. How far *would* she go? How far before anything she discovered became meaningless? She sighed. She should go back. This was useless, and there was paperwork to be done; she could be helping Dan, learning from the team. She put a hand to her face and found it sheened with sweat, not from exertion but the frustration radiating from inside her. She turned into the cool air that was blowing off the water, and that was when she heard a low buzzing.

She stepped off the tarmac and onto uneven tussocks of grass and listened. Now she couldn't hear it at all, but she thought she knew where it had come from. She went further in among the trees, stepping from hollow to hollow between their roots.

The bird was lying at the base of a large birch that was greened with moss. It was small, some kind of finch, she guessed. Its feathers were damp and clinging to its body, its beak closed in a neat isosceles triangle. She took a bag from her pocket, and when she headed back to the car, she carried it with her.

The hill where Sandal Castle stood was brighter, but markedly cooler than the woods had been. Cate felt a sharp breeze on her arms, watched as it ruffled the field below and skimmed the lake with shades of dull zinc. She stood on the cropped grass at the far edge of the ruin. The castle was behind her, its withered fingers accusing the sky.

She had seen flowers here too, as soon as she stepped out of the car. They lay along the banking, a mass of plastic and dying leaves. She had walked past them and around the path that skirted the castle, glancing at the plaque that told of the adjacent battlefield and the death of Richard of York; she had wondered how long the memory of this girl's death might last.

She could see the rest of the path from here, and it was empty. She retraced her route and turned, went deeper into the ruin itself, until she stood at the bottom of the steps leading up to the motte. Even in daylight they looked steep, hard-going; in its day, with a stone keep rising from the top, this place must have been impossible to breach. There was little wonder Ellen Robertson hadn't been carried to the summit. She had been slightly built, as had all the victims, but trying to get up there with her dead weight ... even if she'd still been alive, her body would have been paralysed by the hemlock. She started up the steps, looking back over her shoulder at the line of houses along Manygates Lane. Dumping a body at the castle was a huge risk to take, even without coming up here. Someone had been dogged, persistent: driven.

The platform at the top of the motte was empty, nothing there but the bare wooden planking. Spreading away below were fields, clusters of houses, the flat grey shine of the boating lake. There was a windsurfing lesson in progress down there, and she saw a brightly striped triangle flop into the water, heard a distant wordless cry. White specks rose and passed above the water: gulls, circling. Up here, at the castle, there were none.

Cate scanned the rest of the site; she couldn't see any irregularities, not so much as a stray crisp packet among the grass and stone. She went back down the steps and walked around the remains of the barbican, peering across the inner moat to the rough pile of rocks in its centre; into the moat itself. Then she checked around what remained of the curtain wall. There was nothing, no birds, living or dead.

She turned and headed towards the entrance.

The visitors' centre was open, yellow light spilling from its windows. Cate pushed open the door and saw ranks of books, gift-wrapped soaps, jars of jam. There were displays that echoed the things she'd seen outside – aerial views of the site and battlefield, reconstructions of what life in the castle would have been like. There were no visitors, not today.

The woman behind the counter greeted Cate and she smiled back. She ran her hand over a display of souvenirs meant for children, pencils, notepads, erasers, all with the familiar outline of the castle printed on them. She roused herself and went to the counter, identified herself, and asked her question.

'Yes,' the woman replied, 'it's all looked after quite regularly, since they built the centre, anyway, and decided to put a bit more into the place. There's the grass to look after, and litter, all sorts of things. 'Course, he had to break off, after they found that girl: how awful. I can't bear to look out of the window any more.'

'Has he been back since then?' Cate asked. 'I wondered if he'd found anything unusual.'

'Oh, I don't think so, love. He didn't like to come back at all after what happened, but of course he'd have reported it if he found anything. He knew the situation. We had the police come and talk to us, you know.'

'We appreciate your help.'

'Of course, love. Anything we can do. That poor thing. I'll tell Martin you were asking. We hope you catch them. Martin was ever so upset. He hasn't seen anything, though, like I said. Well, not apart from the birds.'

Cate had been edging towards the door. She stopped and looked round. 'Birds?'

'Yes, he found some dead, you know, around the castle.

That upset him, too; he said to me he almost packed it in after all that, except he needs the job, you know. Three children, he's got.'

'You said he didn't find anything unusual – but there were birds? Dead birds, on this site? When was this?'

She looked worried. 'I haven't said anything wrong, have I? It wasn't anything to do with that girl. It was afterwards that he noticed them. And it wasn't anything out of the ordinary, really, just some dead birds.'

'Could he see what had killed them?'

'I don't think so, love,' she said uncertainly. 'He didn't say so. He took them off to the incinerator – I hope that was all right. And it's all been fine since— Miss?'

But Cate didn't look back. She was already heading towards the door.

Cate retraced her journey to the main road, but again she found herself turning away from the police station and back in the direction of Sandal. She still didn't quite know what she was doing, only that she could feel something happening, cogs slipping into place and beginning to turn.

After a time she turned off the road and on to a housing estate, driving alongside a row of bungalows, each appearing much the same as the last. She found the one she was looking for and scanned the frontage. Nothing appeared to have changed that she could see, but it felt empty: there was something about the way the curtains were half closed, half open, and anyway, the car was missing from the drive.

She went up to the front door and knocked, unsurprised when there was no answer.

She turned away from the door and walked down the drive. After a moment's hesitation, she eased around the corner, squeezing past the bins and into the back garden. She was effectively trespassing, but she could say she was only looking for Levitt where she'd found him before, couldn't she?

There was the aviary clinging to the side of the shed, the bird feeders strung in rows along a line like lumpen washing. Beneath them, on the neatly mowed lawn, lay a dead magpie.

Cate walked towards it, feeling as if she were dreaming. Its black feathers flashed green and blue; its breast was a slab of pure white. She could not see what had killed it.

One for sorrow, she thought.

'Oh, hello. Are you all right there? I thought I heard something.'

Cate jumped. She turned to see a head balanced on the fence, surrounded by a cloud of curly grey hair. It nodded at her.

'I'm quite all right, thank you. I was just – looking for Mr Levitt. I'm a police officer. I have a couple of questions he might be able to help us with.'

'Oh.' The woman's eyes grew round. 'Goodness.' She seemed impressed.

Cate straightened, stood tall. She thought of adding, *It's fine, there's nothing to worry about*, but decided not to. Anyway, the woman wasn't looking at her any longer. Her eyes were fixed on the dead bird at Cate's feet.

'Oh, shame,' she said, 'another one. Why is it always his garden? He blames my cat, you know, but it's not her. I got a collar with a little bell. It's always his place, though – and him so keen on birds. Sod's law, I suppose.'

'Really? Does it happen a lot?'

'I'm afraid it does. Not everyone is as fond of birds as Bernard. Or me, of course. Not everyone's cat has a collar like my Pippin.'

Cate looked down. The bird didn't appear to have been mauled by a cat. She poked at it with her toe.

'It's a pity you won't catch him, love.'

'Sorry?'

'Bernard. He won't be around for a while, I don't imagine. He went out earlier; I happened to hear the gate. He had an awful lot of things with him. That great big tent of his, I think.'

'Did he say where he was going?'

'Oh no, not to me. I didn't see him to talk to. Anyway, I'd better be getting on. The washing won't do itself.' She gave a sudden smile and her head disappeared over the fence.

Cate left the magpie where it was and went to examine the aviary. The structure had a double layer of fine mesh, so that her vision blurred when she looked inside it. There was one large cage and a smaller one, just big enough for a person to stand inside. Of course, that's what it was: one cage for the birds, another for the man. He would open the first door and secure it behind him before opening the second, to prevent the birds inside from flying away. For now, though, there were no birds.

Cate looked around once more, ran her hand over the metal frame.

'Clever, isn't he?' Grey Curls was back in her place at the fence. 'He makes it all himself. Has a workshop, you know. I asked him to fix my grandson's bike, and he did ever such a good job. Such a nice man.'

'A workshop, you say? That's here, is it, in his garage?'

She shook her head. 'Ooh, no, he's very considerate. He doesn't like to hammer away near people's houses. No, it's' – she scrunched up her face until her eyes were almost lost to view – 'it's out near the woods somewhere, I think. Some place it doesn't bother anyone at all.'

Cate burst out of the lift and into the offices. Several people looked up, but when they saw her they looked away again, down at their desks or into their computer screens. Was there something studied about the way they refused to catch her eye? She didn't have time to think about that. She crossed the room, knocked hard on Heath's office door. Then she saw Stocky sitting at his usual desk, a cup of coffee raised to his lips. He shook his head – just slightly – as the door opened.

'Cate.' Heath did not look pleased, but she didn't care. She slipped past him into the room, relieved to see it empty. She set the things she was carrying down on his desk.

He closed the door behind her, each movement deliberate, as if carefully considered, or as if he were trying to remain calm. He returned to his desk and stared down in distaste at the things she had brought.

'What the hell is this?' His voice was low. Somehow that was worse than if he'd shouted.

'Sir, I found this in Newmillerdam Woods, near the Little Red site.' She indicated the robin, curled and dead and out of place on his desk. 'It was near there, anyway. It didn't die at once, though, or the SOCOs would have found it. We have to get it tested. I think it's been poisoned.' Her words spilled out in a rush. She felt suddenly breathless, as if she'd been running. 'We have to hurry.'

He opened his mouth, licked his bloodless lips. 'I repeat,' he said, 'what the hell *is* this?'

'I found it,' she repeated, 'I *found* it, sir. The other was from the original site, near the Heronry. The magpie's from Bernard Levitt's garden. I didn't find one at the castle, but the groundsman apparently has. I think they're a part of it.' She drew a deep breath.

'Tell me.'

'It was Alice who made me think of it.' At this Heath shot her a hard look, but she pressed on, 'We were talking about the things that didn't fit, anything about the scenes that *didn't* work in terms of the fairy tales they were supposed to represent. The first one was that the girls were dead.'

Heath raised his hands; let them fall again.

'The second was the poison. Chrissie Farrell had a poisoned apple. Now that does fit the fairy tale, but the next scene had poisoned bread, and that *didn't* fit. Little Red was supposed to be taking the bread to her grandmother, so why would it be poisoned? And the third – that one had a bowl of poisoned fish. The fish were part of the story, but the poison was not.'

'Except that the *girl* was poisoned.'

'Yes, but why leave poison at the scene? And it was a different type to the one found in her body. It wasn't done by accident. I don't think anything was. It was a deliberate choice, and that should mean something.'

'And?' He made a rolling gesture with his hand. *Get on with it.*

'I believe he was trying to poison the birds, sir.'

Heath stared.

'It was done on purpose. Poisoned food at every scene. And later we find—'

'Dead birds. Right, I got it.'

Cate knew from his face that he had not. 'Sir, there were dead birds in Bernard Levitt's garden. At least two of them. He's a birdwatcher, he's been seen in the woods a couple of times. We had him on the register of visitors to Newmillerdam after the body was discovered. I went to talk to him and I found him scooping a dead pigeon off his lawn. The neighbour says it happens all the time.'

'And?'

'I know it sounds odd, sir, but I feel sure there's a connection. I think we should get a search warrant, have a poke around, see what we can find; we should take some of the nuts from Levitt's bird feeder. I think they might be poisoned too. I want to get them tested, along with the magpie and the birds from the murder scenes. If the poison is the same—'

'Why the hell would he do that? It would mean he doesn't like birds.'

'It could mean a lot more than that, sir.' Cate paused. 'And I found out he has a workshop, somewhere remote, where he wouldn't disturb anyone. He could have taken the girls there, did what he wanted to do before dumping the bodies. His neighbour said he'd gone off somewhere earlier. He could be headed there now.'

Heath lowered himself into his chair. He touched the plastic in which the dead robin was wrapped, then rubbed his finger and thumb together in distaste.

'I want you to get out, Corbin,' he said.

'Sir?'

'I said get out. I don't want you anywhere near this, you hear? It was clearly a mistake, bringing you into it. You're not ready.'

'But Detective Superintendent—'

'You've lost sight of this. You've lost all judgement.'

Cate gawped.

'PC Stockdale told me how you kept Alice Hyland off the register,' he said. His voice was quiet, but his eyes said everything.

'Sir, I—'

'This isn't the time for you to speak. You can explain yourself later. Needless to say, I warned you. I said you should keep your distance from that woman. I told you to watch her.'

'You made me her liaison—'

'Yes, I did, and that should have been the perfect opportunity to keep an eye on her. Well, you failed, Corbin; and now it falls to me to do what needs to be done. You're off the team, with a recommendation for further disciplinary action. You've interfered with the records in an important case. Enough.' He nodded towards the door. 'Now get out.'

'But—'

'You're done talking. You had your chance and you've told me nothing concrete. Poison is left at the scenes: we knew that. And some birds died, boo-hoo. It's pure bloody coincidence.' His voice dropped lower. 'You've been reading too many fucking fairy stories, Corbin. You know, my first instinct about you was right.' He walked to the door, held it open. 'I should never have taken you seriously.'

Cate glanced back at the dead birds she'd placed in the centre of her superior's desk. They lay there, pathetic, sorry things. She should never have brought them. She tried to look at Heath as she walked out, to hold up her head, and found she couldn't; her cheeks were flaming. Other people were looking at her, though, as she left; she could feel it. She couldn't meet their eyes either; she edged around the room without seeing any of it and found someone standing in front of her, blocking her way. It was Len Stockdale.

He took her arm, gripping it tightly. 'It's okay, love,' he said in a low voice. 'Come with me.'

He led her into a side office, gestured to a chair. She didn't sit, didn't want to. He pulled another chair across anyway and sat facing her. He reached out but didn't seem to know what to do with his hand; he let it fall. 'I tried to stop you,' he said.

She shook her head, confused.

'I wanted to catch you before you went in to see Heath. The word was out before you got here; I'm really sorry, lass.'

'So you knew I was off the team, before—' She remembered the way Heath had looked at her when she walked into his office. Had he even listened to a word she'd said?

'It's not the end, lass. You'll be back on the beat again soon, eh? Back with the rest of us.'

It didn't matter about her, what her position was or what Heath thought of her; it only mattered that they stopped the killer. She had thought what she'd told Heath would change everything – but was she being stupid after all, caught up in the odd way Alice saw everything? Heath was right; poison was left at the scenes and birds ate it and died. There was nothing strange about it. And Levitt loved birds, didn't he? What had she been thinking?

'I mean it, love. I wasn't gloating or anything.' Stocky sounded contrite. He stood, took one of her hands and squeezed it. Cate looked at him blankly and he looked away. 'I was going to try and warn you about how things stood. He's bringing her in.'

'Who? Mrs Cosgrove?' Cate frowned. Had they managed to connect the teacher's wife with the child's body after all?

'No, Cate, not Mrs Cosgrove.' Len paused. 'I think this is why he's chucked – I mean, dropped you from the team. It's that contact of yours – Alice. He told you not to trust her, didn't he?'

Cate caught her breath. 'You *told* him,' she said, her voice wavering. 'You told Heath I asked you to keep her off the register.'

'I *had* to, Cate, don't you see? When I heard she'd led us to another body – it could have been important.'

'But it wasn't,' she snapped. 'If it was I'd never have done it. What the hell have you got against her? Alice has nothing whatsoever to do with this, except for the way she's helped us. Helped *me*.'

He took a deep breath. 'You still don't see it, do you, Cate? Think about it: how *did* she find the body? And the thing about fairy tales – it's *her*. Heath spoke to her about finding the kid and he wasn't happy at all – he thinks she imagines she's *in* a fairy tale half the time. Plus, she knows the area. She had the opportunity and she had the knowledge. Even if you look at the profile – it said it would be someone who has difficulty forming relationships. She lives alone, doesn't she? Then there's the way she hung around the scene of the crime, then went off into the woods without a fear in the world. The only thing that gives any doubt is whether she'd have the strength – but she's fit, healthy. The victims were small, light. And she even said herself the killer was a woman, didn't she? It's like she wanted to be caught, or was so arrogant she thought she never would be. It was her – *vanity*, Cate. You see, it always was about vanity, in a sense.'

Cate looked away.

Stocky spluttered with impatience, 'Don't tell me you don't see it. It's *her*, Cate, everything points to it. If you hadn't been— I mean, it's easy to get caught up in things. If you hadn't been so close, you would have seen it for yourself. The way she's injected herself into the investigation. The way she just happened to "find" the child's body.'

Cate shook her head. 'But it's about the *birds*. She said so. We have to test them, find out—'

He sighed, turned towards the door. 'It's too late, lass, and it doesn't matter anyway. Heath must be pretty confident: it's Alice they're bringing in. They're heading to her house now.'

CHAPTER FORTY

Alice paced up and down her bedroom, darting looks at the window. She couldn't settle anywhere. She had found the key for them, she was sure of it, with the finding of the juniper tree; but that was where the story appeared to have ended, at least for her. She had been involved as long as it took to lead them to it, to put a hand on its trunk like some Judas condemning it to death. Now they hadn't even told her what they'd found there, but surely, whatever it was, she was the only one who could *read* it, at least in the way it had been intended.

She shuddered. Perhaps they hadn't found anything at all and she really was going mad; or maybe they weren't telling her for some other reason. The way Cate had looked at her when she'd told her how she found the tree had spoken volumes, far more than Alice had wished to know. She turned towards the window once more. *It was the bird.* The bird had been the start of everything, summoning her with its insistent singing, leading her to places she didn't want to go. Why had it chosen Alice – because it knew, somehow, that she was the only one who could understand? She scowled. That probably wasn't what her students would say. She had been distracted of late, not doing her best, giving vague responses to their questions. She should forget all this, reclaim those things that had been hers: a job she loved, peace of mind.

A sound broke into her thoughts, sharp and loud, something tapping against glass. She stood still and listened: it wasn't coming from the back of the house, where the apple tree grew. It was coming from the other side, and there was another noise beneath it, a car approaching in the lane, groaning over the uneven surface as it dipped in and out of potholes.

Her gaze went to the feather the bird had given her. She had placed it on her dressing table, though it was so ragged now that if she had seen it in that state on the ground she would never have picked it up. The once beautifully aligned filaments had distorted and twisted and could never be put back together again. Still, its colour hadn't faded; it was like a fragment of sky brought into her room. She took it, rubbed it against her cheek, slipped it into her pocket.

There was a dull thud, followed by more sharp taps.

Alice followed the sound, going to the window that overlooked the front of the house. As soon as she drew near, she started back: something had passed across the window, a whirl of wings and air gone again so quickly she couldn't be sure she'd really seen it. When she hurried to the glass, though, she did see it; and she heard the dull thud of its body striking the window, its wings battering furiously. The blue bird landed on the sill and turned towards her, its beak sharp-looking, and it pecked: *tap-tap-tap-tap-tap*, an imperative sound. Alice clutched her chest, felt her heart beating in a staccato rhythm that matched the bird's ferocity. Her focus shifted and she looked past the creature into the lane.

A car was coming towards the cottage. There was nothing odd about it, not on the surface; but Alice knew there was *something*. Behind the first car, following close, was another. Both were nondescript, silver: anonymous. She looked closer, peering through the windscreen between flashes of reflected hedgerow and sky, and she caught her breath. She recognised the man who was driving. He had stared at her just the way he was staring now, concentrating as he eased down the narrow lane. He hadn't been wearing ordinary clothes, though, not then; he had been dressed all in white, the clothing of the police when they entered a crime scene; the same clothing she herself had had to wear. He was with CID.

She drew back inside and ducked out of sight.

Even while she stood against the wall, she couldn't work out why she had done so. She was *helping* the police, wasn't she? But then, why had they come to her like this? This was no smiling Cate, no quiet knock on the door, but instead, a procession of cars so that everyone could see. Her cheeks burned.

She twisted and glanced out once more. As she did the bird exploded into view, blocking out the cars and the police, splaying its feathers.

She had to get out. She didn't know how she knew that, or why the police had come, or why the bird was here; but somehow it had warned her. She took one more look out of the window. She had parked her own car further down the lane, narrowing it, and the police had slowed to ease past. She didn't have long.

She ran out of the room, swinging around the doorframe and pounding down the stairs, almost falling in her haste, then ran for the back door. She wasn't thinking, didn't know where she was going or what she would do when she got there. Her mind was empty; panic came to fill it, pushing away rational thought.

She went out of the door, pulling it hard after her, but didn't stop to check if it had closed properly. She ducked low as she ran across the garden. She knew the gate would rattle and so instead she threw herself at the wall and slithered across it on her belly, her top riding up and her skin scraping against the stone. She didn't stop to look at that either; she ran on, still bent low as she headed into the woods.

When she had gone some distance, the soft dark of the trees began to calm her. She slowed, then stopped, leaned against a tree trunk and rested her face against it, just letting her breathing steady itself. The bark was rough against her skin. What on earth was she doing? What if they'd *seen* her? They'd probably only come to let her know what was happening, or maybe to ask more questions, and she had run away like a criminal. She should go back. But what if they *had* seen her? She could already imagine the looks she would receive. If they hadn't turned against her already, they certainly would now. No. If she didn't go back, she could always say she had just been heading out for a walk, nothing more; that she hadn't seen them. She let out a long breath, glanced up into the branches of the tree. There, above her, the blue bird looked back.

She started away from the trunk and regarded the creature. For a while it didn't move, didn't show any sign of noticing her at all. Then it gathered itself and fluttered onwards, on to another branch in another tree a short distance away.

Everything was silent; she didn't even breathe. The bird tilted its head, fixed its black eyes on her and opened its beak. For a second she imagined it was about to speak, actually found herself waiting for it. She even felt she knew what its voice would sound like: high and silvery and laced with mockery.

She glanced towards her home. She had to go back or go on. The bird left its perch once more, flew deeper into the woods. After a moment, she followed.

As she walked away from her cottage she tried to tell herself that she *was* simply going for a walk, that was all;

she had every right to do so. This was her home, and she had done nothing wrong. She could walk here anytime she chose. If she happened to step out as the police arrived, it was not her fault. And the bird had just happened to be there too, swooping low into the path before angling upwards once more. But she knew she was only trying to convince herself; the bird's bright feathers were an undeniable reminder of what she was doing. As if to reinforce her awareness of its presence it began to sing as it flew – high, fluting notes. To her ear it sounded different now. It was like the song of the bird in the tale of the juniper tree:

Kywitt, kywitt, what a beautiful bird am I!

And it *was* beautiful. Alice kept watching it as she walked, stepping over gnarled tree roots.

There were things in these woods, she decided. It kept its secrets hidden from her even while she was inside it; it was a place where anything could happen, wherein lay madness and death, where girls – girls like her – should stick to the path.

She paused, looking down. The tree roots were thick and sinuous, winding across the ground. It was not the path. She realised she hadn't been on a path for a while. The bird was leading her deeper into the trees. All the same, she thought she knew where they were going.

After a while she saw that she was right. There was the

gleam of anemones pale against the grass, and an open space; she stepped into it, a clearing she recognised. She had no need to look about her; she knew exactly where she was supposed to go. The bird was waiting there now, though the structure didn't look like the one in her dream; instead, it was an odd assortment of canvas and branches leaning against a tree.

She waited. Nothing happened and nothing moved. There was nothing to be done but walk towards it. The flowers brushed against her feet. She stopped when she was a short distance away from the hut.

The structure had been built around a broad oak. Branches as thick as Alice's arm were lashed around its trunk. She could smell the sharp fresh sap where they had been cut. Smaller branches wove between them, filling the spaces. Another structure had been built onto the first, a kind of rough porch providing an entrance. That was draped in canvas painted with the green and brown patches of camouflage, and over the door, something was written in dripping white letters:

BE BOLD, BE BOLD – BUT NOT TOO BOLD

Alice finished the verse under her breath: '*Lest that your heart's blood should run cold.*'

CHAPTER FORTY-ONE

It was nothing but a small smudge on the screen, a cluster of pixels Cate couldn't make out. She enlarged the image and it resolved into a white square with a black line around it, clinical and clear and simple. She frowned at it. The document had come from the Land Registry, and it said the white square was owned by one Bernard Levitt. It lay at the end of a turn-off from the road that skirted Newmillerdam. The road was two narrow lines that led nowhere, the white square the only building on it. All around it was a swathe of green. Bernard Levitt must really value the peace and quiet of his neighbours.

Cate closed the file and pushed herself up from her seat. She didn't need to make a note of the address; the place was engraved in her mind, that simple white square. As she left the building she saw Stocky doing his endless paperwork; he saw her and tossed his head, but he didn't stop her and she didn't wait for him to do so. She wasn't sure if his gesture had been meant as an apology or a greeting or something else, but she didn't look back as she slipped out of the door.

Her mind raced as she pulled out of the car park and headed for Newmillerdam, forcing herself to drive at a steady pace. There were too many things she didn't want to think about: she knew Stocky would think she was mad going off like this, but then, he already did. Heath would put it down to insubordination, have her disciplined. She didn't think she could handle that, the smear on her record; it would be as if her ambitions – her dreams – were already finished. She had heard of it happening to other people, cautionary tales; she had never thought she might one day be counted among them. When she'd heard the stories, she'd thought they'd been stupid. Was she being stupid, now? Probably.

She gripped the wheel tighter. She had seen the dead birds, held them in her hands. It had to mean something.

She kept on down the road, passing cars travelling in the other direction – familiar makes and models that spoke of a world that still knew normalcy, domestic ordinariness.

What are you doing?

The road came up on the left, unseen until the last second; she slammed on the brakes, hauled the wheel around. She squeezed her eyes shut involuntarily as the tyres dry-slid across the earth before gripping, then looked up to see dust settling on the windscreen. This could hardly be called a road at all; it was simply an opening in the fence and a gap between the trees with a track worn into it, narrower than she'd expected, and darker too.

So much for the two neat lines she'd seen on the plan. The rutted earth appeared to head directly into a broad oak that stood in its path. She stared at it a moment longer, narrowing her eyes, dimly realising that she could hear something through the glass: birdsong.

There was a faint double pathway, about the width of car tyres, leading around the oak and into the wood.

Cate pressed down on the accelerator and the car rocked into motion, jouncing over the uneven ground. There was a dip where the track skirted the tree, and she caught her breath; she could too easily imagine the vehicle getting stuck here and having to call for someone to tow it out. The long grass was full of hidden twigs which tapped and pinged against the undercarriage. This wasn't a lane anyone would venture down accidentally. It looked like part of the wood; it was hard to see how a vehicle could get through at all. She accelerated harder as she turned the wheel, anxious to keep up the momentum, and the car headed upwards once more and she glimpsed a structure ahead of her through the trees.

There was a shed at the end of the track. It was hard to make out, but the shade of green it had been painted was just a little too bright, too strident against the woodland. As she approached she saw there was older paint showing through in patches, green and brown and the nondescript grey of old wood, edged by a metal frame-work that was blotched with rust.

She pulled up at the side of it. The shed was large and long, big enough to keep a car inside, easily big enough for a workshop. Ahead of it, under the first of the trees, another car was parked. Cate thought she had seen it before.

She stayed sitting behind the wheel for a long moment. There was no movement, no one there that she could see. She turned to look at the shed. It was a patchwork thing, the boarding irregular, although it had been maintained after a fashion. The roof was reinforced by corrugated-metal panels, some long since rusted, some still streaked with silver. A fresh coat of bitumen ran in a low strip around the bottom. There was a large window set into the side, the glass intact but coated in a fine net of cobwebs.

Cate opened the door and stepped out.

At once birdsong swelled around her, underlined by the constant susurration of branches shifting in the breeze. She smelled the woodland air, an accumulation of growth and decay and fresh sap; beneath it something else, at once sweet and bitter. She could almost taste it: rotting vegetation, maybe, or a dead animal lying in a ditch, being steadily dismantled by maggots or beetles.

She went to the parked car first. It was empty. The colour of the aged Volvo was almost masked by a fine layer of dust. She knew she *had* seen it before, an ordinary car on an ordinary drive on an ordinary street. She could picture it there, imagined the way he would carefully wash off each speck of grime after visiting this place. Would he have to wash it inside too? She peered into the passenger window, checking for traces of anything that looked like blood or hair, but she couldn't see anything. The back of her neck prickled and she glanced around, but there was nothing, no sign of the driver or anyone else.

She turned to the outbuilding. The window was dark, reflecting the sky, a lacing of light and fine leaves that was surprising, for a moment, in its beauty. From here she had a better view of the front and she noticed for the first time the roll of barbed wire that was blocking the door.

She stared at it. So the shed was secure, no one there; but then, it could be some kind of trick. Maybe he was inside it after all, had somehow pulled the wire up to the door after he'd gone in, making it look like the place was empty. But if he was in there, wouldn't she have seen a light as she pulled up? Or had the sound of her engine warned him of her approach?

Of course, he might be watching her now, not from inside the shed but out there, in the woods. She looked around at the trees and saw only a silent circle. All she would hear was the movement of air in the branches, the ever-present birdsong and her own breathing. She had to take a look; she couldn't keep standing here, just waiting for something to happen.

She went to the side of the shed, keeping an eye on the

door as she passed it. Before she reached the window she listened again, trying to hear any movement from inside. Then she stepped in front of the glass, cupped her hands around her face and peered in.

The shed was empty. There was only the low hulked shape of a table, its outline softened by fabric that had been draped over it. There were objects under the covering, bulking it out in shapes she couldn't recognise. Behind that were shelves filled with everyday workshop detritus: tins of paint with bent and spattered lids, slivers of cut-off wood, hand-tools – a hammer, an assortment of screwdrivers, pliers. The cloth covering the table was blotched with what was probably old paint.

She stretched, tried to see further inside. There wasn't much else that she could make out. A pile of twisted and broken metal leaned against one wall and she thought at once of birdcages, an empty aviary. Next to that, half lost in shadow, was what appeared to be a welder's mask. The visor was mottled, as though splashed with something that had stuck and smeared and not been cleaned away. Cate squinted. If she could see it more closely – but she couldn't, could she?

She took a half-step back, took a deep breath. She tried to decide if that smell – the unpleasant smell – was stronger here. Now she wasn't even sure she could smell it at all, or if the taint in the air merely came from the sour taste at the back of her throat.

She walked around the shed slowly, still listening for

any sounds, walking through tufts of grass, loose stones and pieces of old wood, fragments of concrete. There were no other windows. She finished at the front of the structure and looked at the door, which was made of wood and set flush into its frame in a neat finish. The barbed wire kept her from going too close, but now she could see the padlock that fastened it; it looked large and strong and new.

She examined the wire, a wide roll; it too appeared to be new. The wire had been fastened to a long plank of wood at its base with large staples. She bent and grabbed the end of the wood, shifting it outwards. The wire came with it, roiling with the motion, and she jerked her head away from the sharp points.

Now she could edge between the wire and the door, but she saw at once that wasn't any use: she would never break that padlock, not without the right equipment. She took hold of it, feeling the metal cold and heavy in her hands. It was a combination lock, and grime clung to the crevices, but it hadn't rusted, and didn't look brittle. The door had a small rusted keyhole set into it. She pulled back on the padlock. The door didn't even rattle in its frame: it was obviously mortice-locked too.

She let the padlock fall back and it clanged against the wood, an incongruous sound. She looked about her, sure the noise would have brought someone, caused something to change, but it had not.

That was it, as far as she could come. She had no way

inside, no search warrant and no back-up. There was nobody in danger to justify her breaking in, nobody here at all that she could see. She flicked another brief glance over her shoulder.

She went back around to the window and scanned the interior once more, the tools and the old metal and the stains on the table. Then she focused on an object sitting towards the end of one of the shelves. It was shiny, new-minted; that was the reason she'd noticed it. She couldn't make out what it was, not from this angle, but it chimed with something in the back of her mind. She leaned against the wall, momentarily closing her eyes. Whatever it was, it wouldn't come to the surface; it was just another dead-end she could connect with nothing.

She took a deep breath. Then she walked away from the hut and into the trees. She scanned the ground until she found what she wanted.

The sound of the window shattering was an insult that rang into the clear air. It resolved into the sprinkling of fragments of glass before fading into silence. The smell assaulted her at once, much more strongly: old blood and heat and darkness, and Cate's throat convulsed, rejecting it. She staggered back, spun around. No one had come; no one had seen.

She was still holding the rock and she used it to break away the glass teeth jutting from the wooden frame. She would just take a look; it wouldn't take long. Then she would know. If there was nothing here she needn't even report back. No one need know what she had done – breaking procedure, ignoring orders. This would be dismissed as nothing more than mindless vandalism, an anonymous prank.

She took off her jacket and spread it across the window frame, covering the sharp edges, then she gripped its edge and pulled herself up. She got her waist across it, the wood digging into her ribcage. She moved quickly, swinging her leg around; once she'd got her knee onto the sill it was easy to edge across and into the drop. She fell hard on to the floor, landing in a crouch.

She stayed there, one hand braced against the cold concrete, while her breathing slowed. She shifted her fingers against the floor. It was damp, clammy, and a little sticky. She drew back her hand.

She straightened, breathed in. For a second the stench was too much: too thick and too real in her mouth; then, almost at once, it became easier. When it had been mingled with the sweet air of outside, the scent of other places and other possibilities, she had recoiled; now it was all there was. It coated the back of her throat.

Despite the light from the window, Cate still couldn't make out what the shapes on the table were. The cloth covering them was made of canvas that was spattered and grimy. She didn't want to touch it. She was no longer sure the stains it bore were paint.

She edged along the wall to her left, not wanting to touch anything. Other scents were coming through beneath the meat stink: paint thinner and woodstain, the earthy scent of plant pots, the sharper note of sweat, and something chemical: bleach. She reached the shelves on the opposite wall and saw there was a large container of the stuff, much bigger than the one she used at home. Why so much? She became conscious of her own breathing, coming short and fast; her rapid heartbeat.

The next item on the shelf was a battered cardboard box with a picture of a bird on it. Cate leaned in, caught the dusty scent of seed. Further along was a glass bottle, an old one with a myriad tiny bubbles caught in it. It was half full of some kind of liquid. There was nothing to identify its contents.

She edged between the shelves and the table until she reached the object she'd glimpsed through the window. It looked quite ordinary at first. It had a short wooden handle into which shining metal had been set, like a small garden fork, but there the resemblance ended. The prongs had been hammered and filed out of recognition so that they were shaped into short, close-set spikes. They looked sharp. Cate reached out a finger to test them, pulled back before she touched it. She knew at once what it was and what it had been used to do. She turned, slowly, looked at the table, imagined a girl lying there. The object was a claw – he had made a claw, and used it to tear open the flesh of Teresa King's belly. She squinted at it: she thought she could see something dark caught in the indentations where the metal was set into its wooden handle.

Cate spun back, fixing her eyes on the cloth covering the table. It had moved, she was sure of it. Her breath became ragged and she forced herself to be silent. She took a step, the canvas twitched again and she choked back a spurt of laughter; she looked down and saw where the cloth hung to the floor, where her foot had caught it. There was nothing there, no one inside the shed but her, and she should get out, now, call for back-up. She glanced at the window, narrowing her eyes against the glare. If someone came, she'd be trapped in here – but there was something else she wanted to see.

On the side wall, almost lost in shadow, she could see patches, too regular and too ordered to have been formed by stains or damp. She moved closer. She thought she knew what they were, but it wasn't until she was up close that she could see the photographs pinned to a notice-board. There were people in them, women she recognised: Chrissie Farrell, her beauty framed by that black hair and a golden crown, her skin paled by a too-bright camera flash. Teresa King, her crumpled form covered by a virulent red hood. Ellen Robertson, lying on the ground, though no flash had been used and the picture was grainy, the girl almost lost in shadow.

The next picture was different. It didn't show a dead girl. It showed someone alive, her bearing serene, walking across a clearing sprinkled with white flowers. It was Alice Hyland. Fingers of cold reached down Cate's back. She had seen Alice walking in just such a way, wearing just such an expression: she could almost have taken the picture herself.

Thank God, she thought.

She strode to the window, reached for her jacket, felt for her mobile. Then she paused; she had to catch her breath, think about what she was going to say. And more than anything else, she wanted to be outside when she did it, away from this place, clean air on her skin and in her lungs.

She braced herself against the edge of the table and climbed out of the window, almost spilling to the ground in her haste. It didn't matter; she was in the wood again, and everything was as quiet as before. She grabbed her jacket from the ledge and took a few steps until she stood under the edge of the trees. She could hear the soft whisper of leaves, the piercing notes of birds. She took a few deep breaths and started to feel better. She would call Heath, get some help, have him bring the team.

As she began to do so, she stared at the ground. There were flowers growing there; she recognised ragged robin, celandines. Her eyes widened. Another plant was growing among them, taller than the rest, a froth of small white flowers standing proud above its leafy stems. It looked a little like parsley, but its stems were blotched with purple.

Alice gathered herself. She made the call and prepared herself to wait.

Heath was short with her on the phone, but he listened, and now he was on his way. At least they had time. Levitt might have been watching Alice Hyland, but they had snatched her out of his reach; she knew the police had gone to fetch her, albeit for all the wrong reasons. And whatever the girl had been put through, at least that meant she was safe.

CHAPTER FORTY-TWO

Alice stood in front of the lean-to. She felt a long way from the police, from her own home, and yet she had a sense that she was supposed to be here. The structure in front of her was nothing like the one in her dream but somehow it *felt* the same. She couldn't see inside it, but she could picture the book as clearly as if it were in front of her, its wooden pages like something that had grown. There was something she was supposed to find there, something she was supposed to understand; still, she didn't want to go inside.

She looked around and saw only the trees, silent now. Even the constant noise of birdsong had ceased. There was no one there, and after all, she would only be a moment. Still, she couldn't bring herself to move. The thought flashed into her mind that she should go back, find the police, bring them here. Then a small bright shape flew down and perched over the doorway and looked at her. That decided it: if the blue bird was unafraid, she must be alone. It surely wouldn't have come here for anyone else.

She went to the doorway and looked in. The walls were neatly woven of branches and sunlight filtered through them in a soft glow. It was soothing. The latticework curved around so that it felt natural, more like a cave than a room, and it charmed her. It was as if part of her was still in that other place, the one she'd seen in her dream; the place that belonged only to stories. She took a step forward, breathing in the fragrant scent of cut wood, relishing the cool shade. There was nothing inside but a couple of chairs; it was as she had thought: the place was empty. She walked in, looking more closely at the way it had been made. Someone had cut thick supports which arched over her head, bound together where they met the trunk and the lowest branches of the oak tree. Between them smaller twigs had been woven or tied, and there were flashes of colour among them: the wilting heads of wild flowers, just beginning to droop. The floor rustled, shifting under her feet. It was made of bulrushes, which must have been gathered by the lake. It smelled like springtime.

Now that she was closer, she could see the chairs properly. There weren't two, as she had thought: there was a large plain wooden chair, a folding chair with a faded fabric seat, and another, so small she hadn't noticed it; this last was a stool, so tiny it could only have been meant for a child. Each had a bowl set upon it.

Alice couldn't take her eyes from them. She couldn't move. She knew what they meant, what it all meant. What *had* she been thinking? The chairs must have been placed here for her. She should get out, get as far away from here as she could. She whirled and stepped towards the entrance, distantly noticing as she did so a narrow slot that was cut into the canvas. She knew what it was, remembered seeing it from the outside, only now it was light instead of dark; perfect for watching without being seen.

There was a small sound and the light from the doorway dimmed. Someone had stepped in front of it and was silhouetted, their eyes nothing but pale ovals. Whoever it was shifted, took a step forward. The pale shapes resolved into a pair of glasses on a smiling face.

Alice stared. Then she swallowed, and forced herself to smile back. The expression felt strange on her face.

He took another step forward. He was still blocking the entrance; it was too narrow for her to slip past him. He was still smiling, and now she could see it was not a good smile.

She tried to take steady breaths. It was a coincidence, that was all. It was only the birdwatcher, he had built a new hide and she had stumbled over it. If he'd meant to hurt her he could have done so before.

Be bold, she thought, but she found herself taking a step back anyway, away from him.

Bernard Levitt nodded, a genial expression, a friendly greeting, as if finding her there was the most natural thing in the world. He gestured with his arms and she realised he was carrying something that was folded and draped across them. She stared at it.

He smiled again more broadly, freed one of his hands. He picked up the bowl from the middle chair and put it on the floor, then carefully placed the thing he carried upon it.

'There,' he said. 'Everything just right.'

She didn't reply.

Levitt turned to her and stretched out his hand; he couldn't quite reach her, but he motioned anyway, as if he were stroking her hair. He was wearing leather gloves. 'Just right,' he said again. He went to the wooden chair, moved the bowl and set it on the floor beneath, and did the same with the stool. Each bowl had a dried, viscous mess inside, like the residue of porridge.

Alice edged away and felt the wall pressing at her back. 'This is not a story,' she said. 'I'm not Goldilocks; it's not a fairy tale.'

He looked at her with surprise. 'But of course it is.' He threw his head back and grinned, revealing yellowed teeth.

'If it is, you have to let me go. Nothing happened to Goldilocks; it wasn't like that. She didn't— She ran away, and the bears let her go.'

'She was a nasty little thief,' said Levitt. 'Are you a nasty little thief, or just a nasty little liar?'

'A liar?'

'I know you saw it.'

Alice didn't know what he meant, couldn't think; she was looking at Levitt, his solid build, wondering if she could push him out of the way and run all the way back to the house. It struck her that the police might already be coming after her, that they might have seen her heading into the woods. They could be following her now, bringing help with them.

Levitt looked amused, as if he knew what she was thinking. He tilted his head and sing-songed: 'I hope it comes to you, Mr Levitt.'

Alice realised he was impersonating her, though she hadn't actually spoken those words.

'Oh yes, I hope so, Mr Levitt. Because I haven't seen it, no, I never saw it, not at all.' He paused. 'Now you stand here and tell me you're not a liar. That's funny. That's very funny.' Levitt abruptly sat down in the largest chair, reached over and grabbed the stool. He placed it in front of his own seat, slapped his hand down on top of it. He eyed her, waiting.

Alice's gaze went to the entrance. He wasn't blocking it any longer; she could run, get past him. Then he moved, faster than she expected, and drew his chair back so that it barred the way. 'Sit down,' he snapped. 'You can stay or go later, as I choose. For now, I have a story to tell. So sit down.'

She sat. The stool was meant for a child and it was unsteady under her, rocking on the uneven ground. She had to spread her feet to brace herself; now she couldn't move quickly at all.

'I'm going to kill you,' Levitt said confidentially. He leaned in towards her so she could feel his breath stir the air, smell the slow rot in his mouth. 'But first you can listen. You like stories, don't you, Alice? Well I'm going to tell you the story that is me. Would you like to hear it?'

Slowly, she nodded.

Levitt straightened in his chair, delighted, patting both knees with the flat of his hands. He looked for a moment like a delighted grandpa. 'That's lovely. Well, my dear, then I'll begin.

'Once upon a time, I had a sister. She died when I was young. My sister, little Marlene.'

Alice opened her mouth to say that wasn't her name, couldn't have been her name, that he'd only stolen it from another story; but his gaze had lost focus, as if looking at something far away, and she knew she didn't want to call him back.

'My mother loved little Marlene. It was just like in the stories. The younger sister is always the most loved, don't you find? The youngest and the most beautiful. Age, growing up – they're nothing in fairy tales. My sister knew this because my mother told her so every day in her tales, and oh, how they loved them. They had row upon row of books with pink covers and blue covers and green covers, and they read them over and over, always together.'

Suddenly Alice thought of her own mother. She wished she could see her, now, just for a moment. Why hadn't she seen her in so long? Her mother had once read her stories too, and Alice had told her stories in return, though not so magical, not invented: everyday stories of their lives together. Now she would forget, everything would fade, if Alice wasn't there to tell them.

Levitt grimaced. 'Little Marlene would sit on my mother's lap and my mother would hold the book in front of her so that she could see and I couldn't. It was like the book and her arms and my sister and my mother – they were a little circle and I couldn't get in. I tried, more than once, but they said it wasn't for me: I was too old and too male, and they had all the power, you see, because they owned all the stories, the good ones and the bad, the ones about the princesses and towers and birds and the kingdom.

'It was always the younger sister who gained a kingdom.' Levitt sighed, lowered his gaze. His expression was resigned. 'Who has the kingdom now, do you think? Now she's in her grave, now there's nothing left of her but her teeth?'

Alice caught her breath and Levitt smiled as if she'd applauded. 'Quite,' he said. 'Yes, quite!' And he leaned in. 'Did you know cats are the only creatures that torture their prey before killing them – except one?'

Alice couldn't answer, but he continued as if he'd never asked the question, 'Ah, the youngest. Always the youngest. Not surprising perhaps, when the oldest is the book of all the mistakes you made, too late to put them right. She could have tried, you know? But she wasn't interested in boys, not really. She always wanted a girl, and when little Marlene came along – well, you know the line, don't you, dear? So refreshing to talk to someone who *knows*. "The devil got into her so that she began to hate the little boy."'

Levitt looked up, waiting, and after a moment she nodded.

'All right, so picture the scene: younger sister adored; father left, long before anyone could remember – God knows what she did to him. It could have been so different, don't you think? But it wouldn't be a good story if there were no loss, no death. No devil.' He paused. 'I didn't push her.'

His mouth worked; his lips were damp. 'I didn't push her and I didn't tell her what to do. I only suggested, you know. Anyone can *suggest*. And she didn't do anything, not really, she never did. I'd always be the one doing everything, and she'd just sit there singing her little songs, or pretending to be a princess, preening and spreading her pretend skirts out on the ground.'

He was breathing heavily. 'I was supposed to look after her, and I did. I *did*. We went into the woods. Mother had one of her headaches, and I hadn't helped, she said, what with my building blocks and my cars and my games. They weren't things she liked, and by then, I don't think I was something she liked either. But this time she didn't like little Marlene, so she told us to go out and play.

'There was a place we went, where *I* went. Marlene just followed me – she didn't *do* anything, you know? It was always for me to decide. And I liked this place. There was a rope hanging from a tree, a faded old blue rope. It hung out over a long drop and you could swing high, way out, and see it beneath you, everything solid and not, at the same time. It was something magic, like in their stories, not that I thought about that at the time. No, I was a boy, and all I wanted to do was swing. But even that grew dull after a while, and so I decided I wanted to see *her* swing.

'So I told her,' he said. 'I told her she should swing high, and that she would be like a bird, a silly bird from one of her tales. Just like that. And she believed me.' The light faded from his eyes and he looked away, so that Alice thought he had finished, that he wasn't *going* to finish.

He drew a long breath and went on, 'I didn't want her to fall. I only wanted to see her fly, see the feathers.' He fell silent, barely conscious of Alice's presence. Then he spoke again, chanting the words so that they sounded like a song or a rhyme he'd once heard: 'She fell and broke her pretty neck. Tore and soiled her pretty dress. Snapped her bones. Then she was all, all gone, and Mummy was so sad. So very, very sad.' He looked up, but his gaze was somewhere far distant. 'Her scream was the cry of a bird. I heard it, after. Her voice, crying in the night. In the dark.'

Alice's mouth was dry. 'It wasn't your fault,' she tried.

He whipped his head around. 'That's not what my mother said. She made me know it, my mother dear. She blamed me every day. She made me *feel* it, too. She made me bury her with my own hands, just where she said little Marlene would have wanted to be: under the juniper tree in the wood. It was a young thing then, nothing to it at all.

'We went away after that, for a long time; they said she was ill, but it took a long time for her to die. After she did I couldn't bear it any longer. I had to come back here, where I knew I belonged. And Marlene – oh, she was just the same, don't you see? She'd always be young, always be beautiful. Like Snow White in her glass coffin – frozen in time, always lovely and admired, never to grow old and become the crone or the witch or the wicked stepmother, never to disappoint—

'*Was* she beautiful, do you think? In her grave, with worms threading through her skin? Do you think the maggots ate her eyes?'

Alice didn't answer.

'And my mother had always told me that one day my sister would come back. She would come back for revenge.' Levitt looked at Alice. 'All the stories that were my sister's became mine. My mother read them to me, but oh, how she read them: they became terrible things: fierce and terrible.

'Most of all, though, she read the story of the juniper tree. And she told me my sister was coming, just like in the story, creeping up through the ground, clawing her way out to take her revenge on her worthless brother. And I learned to be afraid.

'But I learned something else too. All the time she grieved – all the time she cried – she was a false mother, an unnatural thing; because she wasn't sorry, not underneath. Not in her heart. No. I don't believe she was.

'I think it was her, all the time. She must have hated my sister. She saw how she was growing more lovely and further away from her every day, and she wanted to keep her the way she was for ever. That's why she sent us to the woods: she *wanted* us to leave the path. She was tired of us. She wanted me to make little Marlene go on the rope, she wanted it all.'

He looked up and his voice grew faint. 'It wasn't my fault,' he said. 'Not my fault.'

Alice's eyes widened.

'You know this, Alice, you *understand*. You know the stories say they're stepmothers, the wicked ones, but they're not; they never were. The true stories, the old stories, they *knew*: it was the real mothers who grew bad, who had the canker inside them. It's the thing they tried to hide, isn't it? The story they don't like to tell.

'I was just the one she wanted to blame, that was all. All those tears – I shouldn't have cried them. I was innocent. It wasn't my wrong, it was hers.' Levitt parted his lips in the semblance of a smile. 'Innocent,' he said. 'I did what I was supposed to do, what she'd planned for me to do. That's all I'm doing now.

'And all the time, the stories went on. Oh, how she loved those stories. She made me suffer. She said they always have their revenge, that good little girls never really go away. Sometimes I'd wet the bed, she was so— But inside I knew what I knew: and it was the story of the juniper tree, most of all, which taught me. Two children, one the mother hates, one she loves. She kills the one she hates – cuts his head off with the lid of the trunk, you know this, Alice – and then lets the other child think *she* killed her brother. That's what my sister's death was. My mother was the playwright; I was merely the player.

'After that it was better. I learned from the stories, grew to know more and more of them. She didn't like it. She started to mock me for it, laughed at me, but I didn't care; I knew it was only because she was afraid. There was magic in the stories, I had seen that. All I had to do was bide my time, to learn from them, until I found a way to take it – to *use* it.'

His eyes flashed. 'And then I saw the bird and I knew I was right. I knew my sister at once, I would have known her anywhere. She had come back, just as my mother said.'

'What do you mean? You can't think your sister became the blue bird – and anyway, you never saw it.'

'Ah, but I *did* see her – of course I did, you silly girl. I saw her long before any of you, before anyone else. When I saw those feathers – she was always something special, my sister.' He looked around as if the bird would be there, inside the hut. 'You know from the tales that birds are never what they seem. The blue bird is a glamour, a trickster;

birds in the stories – they could be anything, anyone. And I have to *know*.'

'You have to know what?'

He grimaced. 'I have to know if she blames me.' His eyes were weak now, watery. 'I have to know if she listened to my mother's stories too, if she was twisted by them, tainted. I sometimes think, perhaps she came for revenge after all. But I don't think so.' He shook himself. 'The youngest,' he said, 'the most beautiful – it's always about them, isn't it? I hear her song, you know; day and night, ever and ever in my head.' He batted his hands at his ears.

'But it's not your sister,' Alice said. 'It's only a *bird*, don't you see?' And as she spoke she remembered the way she'd followed it. Why had she done that? Her hand went to her pocket, to the feather she kept there.

Levitt followed her movement with his eyes. He smiled. 'I know you carry it with you,' he said. 'I saw you, walking through the wood. The way you took it out and looked at it. You knew. You *knew*.'

Alice shook her head. 'It's not real, any of it. You're crazy. You need help: none of this is real. It's just – it's stories, nothing but fairy tales.'

'Oh, but it *is* real, little Alice.' He smiled. 'The stories *are* real. I *made* them real, don't you see?'

Alice remembered a princess, thrown into a ditch. A dead girl's face hidden by a crimson hood. A beauty in a photograph, lying dead under the trees, her eyes open. And she found she could not answer.

'Their lives were forfeit,' Levitt said, 'to something greater than themselves.' His voice grew soft. 'It was always going to happen, don't you see? This way, it *meant* something. They never had to grow old, never had to lose their beauty. They'll always be that way now. They became part of something bigger, something more important. They became part of the *story*.

'That was why I gave them my sister's gifts: the looking-glass, the christening bracelet, even her milk teeth. My mother used to say she was the tooth fairy, back then; she kept them in a jar for years and years, until she forgot them – but I remembered.'

He sighed. 'I needed their power, Alice. Little Red, Sleeping Beauty, Snow White. And I need *yours*.' He paused. 'I think she knew,' he whispered. 'The first one, she'd been drinking, but I think she knew anyway, don't you? Later she said she didn't, but by then it was too late. The second went with me as if it was what she'd been waiting for all her life. And the third: so *potent* – I could feel the life in her, you know. The *lives*.'

'You knew she was pregnant.' Alice stumbled over the words.

'Not me, not then. But I knew where to find her. I knew what story she would fit.'

Alice shook her head. 'How? How did you know?'

He smiled. 'She showed me,' he whispered.

'What do you mean? Who showed you?'

'The bird, of course – my sister. She showed me who to take. She sang their songs in my ear.'

'The bird?'

'She came to you, didn't she, Alice? She led me to you. She *delivered* you here.'

'But—'

'The bird is my *sister*, Alice. Did you think it your friend? Well, it is not. *She* is not. She wants me to come to her, Alice, and I am.' He picked up the thing he had placed on the chair, ran his fingers over it. It was covered in feathers, and some of them fell from it and drifted to the ground. He unfolded it and spread it in front of him: it was a cloak.

'I studied them,' he said. 'I know the *Streptopelia turtur* and the *Cygnus columbianus*. I know the *Asio flammeus*, and I know its true nature, and I know its forms. The *Luscinia megarhynchos* has no secrets, the *Cuculus canorus* no tricks, not for me, because I understand them all.' He tapped his finger on the side of his nose, as if letting Alice into a secret. 'I fed them, you know. I gave them seed soaked in pesticide. I put it in their water. I gave them poisoned bread and poisoned fish – because I need their power too, Alice. I need it if I'm going to follow her, if I'm going to *know*.'

Alice stared at the cloak. It was covered in feathers of all kinds, feathers meant for flight and warmth and display, feathers of every colour, grey feathers, brown feathers, red and pink and every shade between; the sharp blades of wing feathers, the rounder form of contour feathers, bursts of soft down. It gave off a musty, unclean scent.

'Crow and sparrow and robin and finch,' he said, 'raven and owl and wren. They all came to my garden, Alice. See what they gave me.' He ran his fingers over them, at once loving and gloating.

'I don't understand.'

'No,' he smiled, 'you don't. But you will. I see it in you, Alice. You have the same power in your veins as the others, except it's better this time, stronger; because you believe, because you *know*. I need you to *believe*.

'They were all supposed to live. Did you see that? Princesses all, and they should have lived happily ever after, but I stopped them at their moment of transform-ation. I took their power into myself. And the blue bird chose you, just like them. She picked you out.'

He paused, running one finger over the feathers, then he stood taller. 'The bird is calling to me, do you hear her? I took their magic, Alice; I stopped their stories and I began another.' He held up the cloak. 'I'm drawing closer to her, to my sister. I shall see her once again, in a form she knows; and I'll talk to her, and I will understand what she wants from me at last.'

He swung his arms around and placed the cloak around his shoulders. 'That was what I learned,' he said. 'People are always transformed in tales, are they not? A girl becomes a bird. Brothers become swans, and are only changed back when dressed in magical shirts, made with their sister's love and her blood.' He was breathing heavily and Alice could hear it, a sound that was almost intimate.

'Now I'm going to change too – but it isn't *finished* yet. There's one feather missing, Alice: one transformation left.' He set down the cloak and put his hand behind his ear. 'Don't you hear it? She's waiting.'

Alice *did* hear it then, a pure, high fluting note from the woods: a bird, filling the air with its song.

'I need more magic,' he said. 'You'll give it to me.'

Alice pushed herself up and stumbled away from him, found herself pressing against the wall of the hut. She edged around it but he was too quick; he stepped in front of her. She looked into his eyes and saw the madness in them. He was going to kill her, and he would lay her out like the others, a dead girl with a story to tell.

She leaned forward, grabbed the stool she had been sitting on and held it out in front of her.

'Now, Alice – I only want the feather. That's all.'

She shook her head.

'Just the feather – she gave it to you, I know: I saw it from the hide, saw the way you looked at it. She never once gave me a feather. I *need* it.'

Alice shook her head. 'No – you're wrong. I *did* have a feather, but I don't have it with me. It's at home.' She paused. 'I'll fetch it for you. We can go together.' *Home*, she thought. Would the police still be there, waiting for her? She glanced towards the entrance as if she could see them marching through the woods.

'Such a liar.' Levitt smirked. 'Hear it squeal. There's no one coming, Alice. And I saw you, remember? I know you keep it in your pocket. You have it now, you *must* have it. How could you give it up? You wouldn't. I know you wouldn't, because you *feel* it, don't you? You feel its magic, its strength. *Her* magic.'

Alice went cold. It was true, wasn't it? She tried to remember a time she had been parted from the feather since the blue bird came, and could not think of one. It was in her pocket now, the same as it always was.

'Give it to me.' Levitt held out a shaking hand.

'No,' she said. 'Only if you get out of my way. I'll go outside and leave it for you on the ground.' By then she could be running back through the woods, far away from him.

He smiled, his eyes shining as if she'd made a fine joke. 'You don't need to do that, Alice. Don't worry. I'll come and take it.' He stepped forward, but as he did so he twisted to the side and grabbed something that had been leaning against the side of the hut.

'I made this for you,' he said.

CHAPTER FORTY-THREE

The police were on their way, striding across the woodland floor with Heath at the head of the line. Cate waited for them by the broken window; she glanced at it, reminded herself there was no need for them to know she had been the one to break it. She'd taken the rock she'd used and thrown it back into the woods. Now she had misgivings – what if Heath knew? – but she would do it again if she had to. The important thing was that they had found the killing place; now they would go after Levitt, and they would stop him.

'Well?'

'This is it, sir. This is where he did it.' She pointed. 'If you look through the window you can see the tool he made to kill Teresa King. And I think there might be blood on the table.' She hesitated. 'I leaned in, took a look around. He must have been watching them, sir, before he snatched the girls. There are photographs of them inside. It's hard to see, but I believe there are pictures of Alice Hyland too.'

Heath didn't speak. Instead he went to the shed and peered in; glanced back at Cate and boosted himself halfway onto the sill.

'It's dark,' he said. 'I can't see a damned thing. You sure this window was broken when you got here, Corbin?'

Her mouth had gone dry. She was about to answer when he let himself drop to the ground and turned away. 'Get a torch,' he said to one of the officers, and the man headed away towards the cars.

Heath met her eye. 'Very good, Corbin,' he said. 'Looks like you found it.' He grimaced. 'I can smell it.'

'Me too. But I don't know where he is. At least you brought Alice Hyland in, though – she'll be safe. He must have been watching her. The picture—'

He drew a breath. 'I don't know how you figure that, Corbin. Either your eyesight's better than mine or someone's been trespassing, because all I can see is the edge of a noticeboard.' He held up a hand to stop her. 'Ignore that for now. Look, we don't have her. We went to her place and she wasn't there.'

'But – they are fetching her, aren't they?'

His voice was terse. 'When you called this in, I told them to stop looking, got them back to base. There was no reason to believe Hyland was involved any longer.'

Cate stared at him; then she turned towards the woods. Below the canopy, everything was dark.

'We need to set a perimeter here,' he said. 'I'll get a

description out on Hyland, get a search warrant for this place. Then we can go inside, hmm, Cate?'

She had stopped listening to his words. She turned; her face was stricken. 'I have to try and find her.'

'No,' Heath said decisively, 'I'll have the team go back to her house. We'll track her down.' He reached for his phone.

Cate stared into the trees once more. She knew that what Heath had said was the right thing, but she also knew it wasn't any use: Levitt's car was here and Levitt was gone. He was already after Alice, she felt sure of it. Whatever was going to happen, it would be in the woods; the place Alice talked about, that drew her as if it was part of the fairy tales she saw in her mind. *Don't leave the path*, she thought, but it was too late for that: Alice was already in there somewhere, and Levitt was with her.

She turned further to the north; she thought that was the direction in which Alice's house lay. In the next moment, she was moving. She heard Heath's voice behind her, a sound without words, but she didn't look back as she rushed into the dark.

CHAPTER FORTY-FOUR

The thing Bernard Levitt was holding out towards Alice had a short wooden handle and sharp, curved metal spikes. They gleamed in the dim light that leaked through the walls. He smiled, made slashing motions with it, clawing at the air, demonstrating. 'A bear,' he said, 'do you see? The other was a wolf. This one's a bear, and it's for you. But if you're good ... if you're very, very good, I'll give you a chance to take the poison first. Then it won't hurt so much.' He passed the claw from hand to hand as he stripped off his gloves and let them fall. 'I don't need these any more. We're almost done, aren't we? Now, Alice.' He gestured towards the bowls on the floor, lined with scraps of food.

Alice stared. It wasn't dried porridge after all; it was a thick paste, some sort of organic matter.

She clung on to the stool she held in her hands. Her palms were sweating and it was slippery and heavy.

'Three ways to die,' he said, 'and all of them just right. And then do you know what's going to happen?'

Alice knew it wasn't any good, that it had never been any good. She wouldn't be able to fight him. This was the way it was, how it was supposed to be: she had loved fairy tales from being a small child, all their rawness and beauty and yes, their magic. She had wished so hard and so often to live among their people and their ways and their deep, dark woods, and now they had come to claim her. There was only this.

'You're going to burn,' he said.

Her whole body twitched.

'You'll blacken and you'll crackle,' he said. 'You might still be alive, when it starts. You'll smell your own flesh as it roasts. You'll feel your face as it stiffens and your lungs as they sear. And I'll be watching, Alice. I'm always watching. I'll see everything.' He set the claw down, leaning it against his leg, and took a small bunch of twigs and a cigarette lighter from his pocket. He tried several times to ignite it, and finally sent a tiny flame – so small a thing – sparking upwards. He held it to the end of the bundle and it started to smoulder, sending acrid white smoke into the air. It was herbal and sharp and she immediately wanted to cough.

'It's the smoke of the juniper tree,' he said. 'That should complete the spell, don't you think?' He pointed at the walls and Alice saw that he had woven juniper branches into the structure too, some with berries still clinging to them. 'The Celts believed that juniper smoke aided contact with the dead.' He wafted the smoke around in little jerks.

'It will create the perfect conditions. Of course, juniper has other properties, too; other stories. Some say that anyone who digs up a juniper tree will be dead within the year. Do you think that's true, Alice? You had my sister's tree dug up, didn't you?'

Alice moved – she had to do something so she struck out, thrusting the stool forward. His eyes opened wide with astonishment as it punched into his stomach, as if he hadn't seen her holding it, hadn't expected she could touch him. 'You—' he said, and the words failed, but he didn't fall; he didn't even stagger. He threw the burning bundle aside and moving, quickly, grabbed the stool by two of its legs. The awkwardness had left him; even his face looked smoothed-over, making him younger, leaner. He was smiling again, but Alice didn't want to look at that smile any longer or his yellow teeth. He dragged at the stool and she held on, caught for a moment in some child's half-hearted tug of war; then he yanked it hard, out of her hands, and swung it, smashing it into her shoulder.

Everything went blank, but only for a second. Alice was on the ground and she was clawing at it, but it wasn't right; the ground was coming away in her fingers and she realised it was because the floor was made of rushes, of course it was, because she was in the hut: Levitt's hut. She couldn't hear him, couldn't tell where he was; there was only a sound in her ears: a high buzzing that went on and on. Then there was a face, up close to hers, and

Alice remembered that she should be in pain because he had hit her, and she was down; but it didn't hurt, not yet. She tried to cry out, but there was only a dry gagging, and when she heard that sound, she knew she was finished.

'Oh, Alice,' he said. 'Oh, my pretty little Alice. Where's my feather? Give it to me.' Levitt started pulling at her clothes, trying to get into her pockets. 'Where is it?'

She tried to push herself up. The pocket holding the feather was beneath her, she knew. She had carried it everywhere, had thought the blue bird her friend, and all the time it had meant her for this: for *him*. She tried to reach it herself but he pulled at her, rolling her over on the floor. The buzzing in her ears had changed note, becoming higher and sharper. Her face was wet, but not with tears. She wasn't crying; her eyes were *hurting*, stinging, because somewhere there was a flame. She craned her head back, looking for the fire, and instead she saw the claw he had fashioned, its sharp points: *I made this for you.*

She stopped trying to reach into her pocket and felt Levitt's prying hand enter it, his fingers grasping against her thigh. She let him, stretched out her arm, ignoring the shriek of pain it caused her shoulder, and her fingers rasped against the handle. Then the thing he'd made was in her hand and she swung it towards him.

The claw met something at once solid and yielding, landing there with a dull sound. She pulled on it, trying to drag it loose, but it had gripped and it held; she had to let go. It was his now, it would stay with him, and she would die here, lying in a fairy-tale hut in a fairy-tale wood, and she would be alone.

Levitt screamed.

His cry went on and on, turning into a loud keening that didn't sound like him, didn't sound like a man at all. Alice rolled away, her shoulder flaring white-hot, onto her side. His chair was there and she put out one hand and tried to pull herself up. Instead something slid down on top of her, something old and musty and unpleasantly soft, like a solid layer of dust. As she pawed at it, trying to push it away from her, she realised it was feathers, masses of them, feathers of all colours save one.

The smell of smoke was strong in her nostrils. The hut was burning; the wood was starting to crackle and spit. She opened her mouth and drew in a deeper breath, and it was dense and choking at the back of her throat; she started to cough. She curled up, felt the cloak of feathers against her face; then it was lifted away and she gasped for air.

Levitt was standing over her. There was blood smeared across his face and he wasn't smiling any longer. He clutched the cloak tight, pressing it against his chest. It wasn't until he stepped towards Alice, standing over her legs, that she saw the claw was still embedded in his back, its handle jutting upwards.

'You'll burn,' he said. His voice was low and hoarse, but she heard it quite clearly. She blinked; her vision was clearing but everything was growing faint anyway. Smoke was spreading from the walls, and light was dancing amid the branches. It was whispering to her, the voice of the flame punctuated by sharp imprecations of splitting wood. Levitt was standing above her. She would never get out; she could see that he knew this. He had only been waiting for her to understand, to enjoy the look in her eyes when she did.

'You'll burn.' This time it was a whisper, and Alice didn't so much hear the words as see them on his lips.

She forced herself to move, though not towards Levitt; it was too late for that. Even wounded, he was too strong for her. She couldn't fight him. Instead, she shuffled away, half rose to her feet, put her hands against a part of the wall that wasn't burning and pushed. If she couldn't get past Levitt she would force her way through to get away from the smoke. The wall was pliant and it bulged under her hands, but there was something wrong with it. The branches didn't snap or break apart; instead she found something smooth there, at once giving and unyielding. It sprang back, pushing her with it, and her fingers hooked into it and then she understood: wire. He had lined the walls with wire. This thing he had built was not a hut; it was a cage.

She turned to face Levitt. He was laughing at her, and she could see the madness in his eyes, but there was triumph there too. He had been right: soon she would burn. At least then she wouldn't have to look into his face.

Alice closed her eyes. They felt hot and angry, as if they were already burning. She stepped forward, her legs gave way and she fell, landing on her knees. She couldn't catch her breath. She stared down and saw pale smoke rising from the rushes lining the floor. She let out a strange sound and didn't recognise her own voice; it turned into another choking cough.

There was a flash of colour amid the rushes and she realised what it was at once. He had forgotten it in the pain and the heat. It was the one thing she had held on to amid everything that had happened and she reached for it now. The feather was ragged and spoiled, but she didn't care; it was hers.

She heard Levitt cry out as her hand closed over it.

'I need that.' His voice was the voice of a child. 'I *need* that.'

She looked up at him, held it out, her hand flat, the feather balanced upon it. It wavered in the simmering air. He came for it, letting the cloak slip from his hands, and as he reached out she closed her hand into a fist, crushing it, and she threw what remained as hard as she could towards the burning wall.

Levitt howled his anger and strode after it as she scrambled away, stumbling over the fallen stool. She picked it up and hurled it after Levitt, but it was no use; he batted it away as if he hadn't even felt it. One of his fists closed over something; his eyes gleamed.

Alice stepped back. The doorway was behind her now,

but if he came after her . . . she knew it was too late; she had nothing else, no fight left in her. She wouldn't be able to run. She moved towards the entrance anyway, sensing clearer air; it was blessedly cool against her skin. The smoke inside the hut had thickened; it was twisting and writhing. She heard laughter within it. 'Did you know?' His words came low and rough between dry, sputtering coughs. 'Did you know juniper smoke aids contact with the dead?'

She couldn't see him clearly any longer, only a darker shape within the grey; moving awkwardly like some lumbering beast. It barely looked like a man any more. It let out a guttural cry and something swiped the air. It was reaching for her, welcoming her in; it sounded like death.

There was an answering sound behind her and as she turned, something brushed by her face, something blue as the sky in springtime, its voice clean and pure as sunlight. It was the blue bird, come for her at last; then it was gone, flown by her and into the choking air. She caught a glimpse of outspread feathers, grasping claws; she heard Levitt's cry of anger, saw one hand pawing the air.

She didn't see him fall, only heard it. There was a thud, and another sound, the meaty crunch of metal claws punching deeper into flesh and bone. Levitt let out a single brief howl; then he was silent. Smoke took him, wrapping itself around him, smothering his body.

Alice could smell scorched feathers. It was a choking stench, bitter and impossible to breathe. She staggered towards the clean air, blinded by smoke, her eyes pouring, and felt something wrap itself around her feet: the cloak. Its touch was soft and insidious and she tried to pull away, almost fell. She couldn't get out; even now, it wouldn't let her. She bent and thrust her hands into it, pulled it clear. Then she threw it behind her, into the burning hut.

There was a burst of orange flame and for a moment she thought she saw something else: a bright splash of colour hanging in the air. Then she was outside, there was cool air on her face, the soft air of a springtime evening, and Cate was there, supporting her arm, keeping her from falling. Her lips moved, but Alice couldn't hear the words. She could only draw deep, blessed breaths of air, and then it all came back; there was a loud *whoomph* as the structure Levitt had made collapsed inwards. For a second it was lost in billowing smoke, then a bitter burst of sparks rose and Alice could see a pile of branches, canvas, wire. It was a bonfire, nothing more, consuming what lay beneath, sending flames up into the oak tree, whipped into greed by the clean air.

'Christ,' said Cate, 'is he in there?' She took a step towards it, put up a hand to cover her face.

Alice knew it was too late; she'd never get close.

Cate whirled to her as if she'd heard her thoughts. 'I have to call Fire,' she said, 'before this spreads. I followed the smoke here; I should have called them sooner.' She moved away, started barking instructions into a mobile.

Alice did not go with her. The heat was strong on her face but the cooling breeze lifted the hair from her neck. She knew what she thought she'd seen, but couldn't be sure she'd seen it. The thing in the heart of the fire had been a many-coloured bird. She remembered Levitt's words: *I'm going to follow her*. And then, *the stories are real. I made them real, don't you see?*

She rasped the line from the story: 'How splendid it was with its red and green feathers, and its neck like burnished gold, and eyes like two bright stars in its head.' The bird in 'The Juniper Tree', the bird of all colours; the bird that made everything happen.

She shook her head. It was the effect of the smoke, that was all; it had made her see things, *feel* things that weren't there. Things that couldn't have been.

There's one feather missing, he'd said. *One transformation left.*

Now he had joined his sister at last, though not in the way he had intended. It was all gone, the place he'd created, the dreams he had spun; even, in the end, the blue bird itself, and Alice felt inexplicably sad. Her hand went to her pocket, but of course the feather was not there; Levitt had taken it, had clutched it to himself as he had fallen.

One feather missing. And he'd found it, if only in death.

Alice turned her back on the fire and saw the trees standing around her. They shifted in the wind, sighing their secrets to each other across the clearing. She couldn't gather her thoughts, didn't know what had happened; she only knew that something magical had gone, passed from this place and into another, some place she couldn't follow.

She heard Cate's voice. 'They're coming,' she said. 'They're bringing help. You're safe now.'

Alice did not answer. She tilted her head and looked at the sky. The blue was fading from it too; night was drawing in. The air was growing colder and she shivered despite the heat from the fire. The woods had fallen quiet. There was no fluting from the trees, no squabbling of rooks or sweet trilling of a blackbird. There was no sound except the crackling of the flames; there was not a trace of bird-song in the air.

CHAPTER FORTY-FIVE

Outside Alice's window, it appeared to be snowing. Large flakes billowed and dashed themselves against the glass. They gathered on the sill and did not melt. She crossed the room to look at them.

The apple tree was losing its blossom. The grass below was speckled with white, the petals dampening in the dew. The tree's branches were dark against the distant woodland, where an early mist hung in the air, draining it of colour. Already she could sense the sun's heat, waiting. Soon it would burn through the shroud hanging over the wood and summer would begin.

In her garden, purple irises and bright larkspur were replacing springtime greens and yellows. Soon the woodland would be full of people once again, walking and laughing, their shouts filling the air; it would no longer be a place for the dead but for the living. Only the stories would remain, stories of Chrissie Farrell, Teresa King, Ellen Robertson, and a long-forgotten child. Alice allowed herself a moment to think of them. Bernard Levitt had sacrificed them all to some story he had carried inside himself, tales of his past that had never been told, and instead, had festered. She closed her eyes, leaning against the glass. When she opened them again she saw that there was something lying on her windowsill.

Slowly, she opened the window.

There was a feather on the ledge, half hidden by fallen apple blossom. She reached out, then drew back her hand without touching it. The feather was impossible: it had two colours she had never seen together on any bird: a pale, clear blue and a deep, bloody crimson.

She drew a breath, reached out again and picked it up. It had been left for her, a gift. She placed it in the palm of her hand and saw what it truly was: not one feather, but two.

She looked out again over the woodland. She half expected to see two bright shapes flying above it, forming new shapes in the air, weaving new songs between them, but there was nothing.

One feather missing, he'd said. *One transformation left.* And at the end he had grasped it, the feather from the blue bird; he had held it in his hand. She closed her eyes and remembered how she'd staggered from the hut, the cloak that had wrapped itself about her feet. Had that been with him too, in the end? Had she thrown it within his reach? She tried to remember and found she could not. When she closed her eyes, though, she could see the hut, and it was burning: livid flames, white smoke, and a many-coloured shape hovering within it. A bird, its feathers of crimson and green and gold, its eyes like stars.

She shook her head. It had been an image from a story, nothing more; she knew her mind had tricked her into seeing it, just for an instant. He'd said he needed her power; he'd said he needed her to believe. What made her sad now was this: she had not believed, not really. All the years she had loved the old stories, and in that moment when she'd staggered from the hut they had failed her, and she had failed them. Levitt had killed them for her. When she'd looked back into the fire, she had known: there was only smoke and blood and violence. Levitt had been deluded, and he had died. The thing she had seen was nothing but a mirage.

And then Cate had said something to her, as she'd helped her from the fire. She hadn't been able to hear properly, but she'd seen it on her lips: *Did you see that?* the policewoman had mouthed, and hadn't there been something in her tone? Wonder, perhaps? Had it been Alice's belief he had needed in the end, after all?

She closed her hand over the feathers. She didn't need to look at them again. She could picture the bird she had seen in her hallucination, its vivid colours, the bright band of gold about its neck. It was the bird from 'The Juniper Tree', the story taken life. Perhaps Levitt had followed his sister after all, in one way or another. She doubted it would make him happy. Whatever happened, he would take his own darkness with him. He could never escape from that.

I have to know if she blames me.

Maybe now he knew.

Alice picked up her coat, hanging over the chair, and slipped the feathers into her pocket. Levitt had died believing the blue bird had picked Alice out for death, but perhaps he had been wrong after all; at the end, the bird had helped her. Maybe, if she tried, she might be able to find a way of believing it had meant to do it.

She slipped on her coat and thought of the way the blue feather had been a comfort to her, the way her hand would travel to her pocket to feel its smoothness. She didn't need it any longer. She was no longer Alice who was lost, who wandered through a story of someone else's making. She would create her own story now.

No, she didn't need the feathers, but she would take them for Cate. The last time she'd seen her Cate had been passing, visiting a house nearby, and she had sounded happy.

'I decided to stay,' she said, as if this would come as a surprise to Alice, who had never known she'd thought of leaving. 'I've found a house, not too far from here. I'm going to do it up: it's going to take ages.' She had said this last with glee, as if it were something to be treasured. And then: 'I suppose I just decided that something can happen anywhere. Sometimes you have to decide that *this* is where your life begins.'

She'd had no idea what Cate had been talking about, but she had caught the girl's enthusiasm and found herself smiling back; and then they'd been laughing together, helplessly. Yes, she would give the feathers to Cate. Perhaps she would need a little magic for the path ahead. It felt right somehow. Something that was bound up with the dead girls – Chrissie, Teresa, Ellen – and their ending, moving on with Cate. It seemed to fit. And everything would move on, at one with the fading of springtime and the coming of the summer: not a happily-ever-after, but a new beginning, the year renewing itself, leaving events behind as if they had never been.

AUTHOR'S NOTE

The settings I have used in *Path of Needles* are half real, half invention. The lane at the edge of Newmillerdam exists, but there is no house positioned quite like Alice's – I rather liked the idea of her living somewhere in the land between reality and fantasy. Where places are real I have used them fictitiously, and I can only apologise for turning some beautiful locations into the scene for horrors . . . the Heronry, Newmillerdam and Sandal Castle are all lovely places to visit. The old arboretum with its juniper tree is pure invention, but the new one, along with the lakeside path, make for a pleasant walk and are much more peaceful than Alice finds them.

Path of Needles was born of my love of fairy tales, and there are many books I have found invaluable on the subject. I spent many an hour as a child buried in Hans Christian Andersen's stories, and still have my copy of that book, so beautifully illustrated by Michael Foreman. That has since been supplemented by various collections by the brothers Grimm, Italian folk tales gathered by Italo Calvino and Angela Carter's *Book of Fairy Tales*, among others. The blue bird's tale, as mentioned in the text, can be found in the *Green Fairy Book* edited by Andrew Lang. The 'Be bold' inscription is taken from 'Mr Fox', a delightfully grisly story in Joseph Jacobs' *English Fairy Tales*. 'The Juniper Tree' was collected by the Grimms, while Perrault's 'gentle wolves' verse comes via a translation by Robert Samber from 1729.

The Classic Fairy Tales edited by Maria Tatar gives an interesting taste of how some of the stories have evolved over time and geographical distance, and some of the interpretations that have been placed upon them. Other interpretations can be found in *Fairy Tales, Their Origin and Meaning* by John Thackray Bunce. *The Trials and Tribulations of Little Red Riding Hood* by Jack Zipes contains many varied versions of the story and there are some fascinating articles on fairy tales and their meanings, including *The Path of Needles or Pins: Little Red Riding Hood*, by Terri Windling at her Endicott Studio website.

ACKNOWLEDGEMENTS

As ever, heartfelt thanks to everyone at Jo Fletcher Books for helping to turn my dreams into actual pages, including Nicola Budd, Ron Beard, Lucy Ramsey, Steve Cox, Mark Thwaite and Caroline Butler – and particularly, of course, Jo Fletcher.

Path of Needles has led me into new territory as a writer, and I owe a huge debt of gratitude to those who have provided signposts along the way. Particular thanks to Des Booth for advice on various points of police procedure, and to Paul Finch for bearing with the questions – any errors remain entirely my own. Thanks too to Astero Booth.

I've also been given invaluable guidance in more technical lands . . . Wayne McManus, you are, as ever, a web genius; and thank you to Mark West for the wonderful videos.

For friendship, laughs, advice and from time to time a supporting shoulder, I'd like to thank members of the

British Fantasy Society and the gang at FantasyCon. Thanks too to Roy Gray, Andy Cox and Peter Tennant.

My appreciation also goes to everyone at the Richard and Judy Book Club, and to everyone who lent their support to A Cold Season in their websites, blogs and publications, or by simply sending kind words – thank you so much. For the beautiful hardback edition, thanks to Pete and Nicky Crowther.

Last but not least, love always to Fergus, my parents Ann and Trevor Littlewood, Ian, Amanda and Callum, and to Liz and the Beadle clan.